CALL OF DESTINY

CALL OF DESTINY

Being the first part of

ONE SMALL STEP OUT OF THE GARDEN OF EDEN

Robert Wagoner

Beechstreet Publishing
Vermont

CALL OF DESTINY

A Beechstreet Publishing Publication

ISBN: 978-0-9826285-0-8

Printed in the United States of America

First edition printed April, 2009

To my wife and children.

CHAPTER ONE

Senior Year

*S*MACK!

The small diner was brimming with the typical Friday afternoon crowd of energetic teenagers looking to put the long week of school behind them. Contemporary music blared throughout the room, cowed only by the roar of young men and women engaging in various frivolities. Yet the unexpected cracking sound brought the bustling establishment to a complete standstill, and all eyes fixed themselves on the corner booth from where the noise had originated.

An irate, young female shot up from one side of the table and quickly gathered her things, while the male senior sitting on the opposite side—displaying a rather painful-looking handprint on the side of his face—watched in embarrassment as she fixed herself to leave.

"Drop dead, Mike!" she huffed, looking him in the eye reproachfully.

"But Jennifer—"

Michael's pleadings came too late, for Jennifer stormed out of the diner. He sighed, relieved that he had accomplished his objective;

his noticeable concern for the young woman's feelings was simply a courtesy. Nevertheless, he suffered under a round of *ooohs* and judging gazes by gawking onlookers, particularly from three all too familiar seniors watching from a nearby table.

"It didn't take her too long to come to her senses," the largest of the three fellows cynically exclaimed as the room returned to its normal chaos.

Michael feigned another courteous return expression, futilely attempting to hide his disdain for his classmate. "I'm okay with that, Fellinger." Hoping to avoid a confrontation, he stood up from the table and casually walked out of the diner.

The warm, afternoon sun accosted him from the side as he headed down the sidewalk toward where he would catch transportation home. However, the sound of the diner's door opening again broke the air, followed by footsteps ominously moving in his direction. Michael cringed, knowing the senior had waited for the opportunity all afternoon.

"Hey, Gillen!" an irritated Danny Fellinger called from behind him. "You know she's my cousin, right? You shouldn't treat her like that."

Michael, his face still throbbing from where Jennifer had slapped him, rolled his eyes and kept pace in the direction of his destination.

Much to his relief, Michael soon turned the corner, taking the opportunity to walk a little faster. The transport that would take him home lay directly ahead, though it was still too far away for a quick escape. And Danny Fellinger and company were rounding the corner too.

Continuing toward the transport, young Gillen could hear the trio quickly closing the gap. Just as his antagonists came within an arm's reach of him from behind, Michael felt one of them wrench the small book he was carrying from his back pocket. Indignant over the trespass, Michael stopped and turned around defiantly.

Fellinger, his cohorts standing supportively behind him sneering, held the book in one hand and surveyed the cover. The thug, whose stature matched that of a sequoia, towered over Michael, casting an intimidating shadow over him. Despite being a little taller and more athletically endowed than most of his classmates, Michael was no match for the sizeable Danny Fellinger.

However, Michael remained undaunted. Fellinger's size, though very much a concern, was never the problem in all their confrontations over the years. No, it was always about the same old, tired subject. Michael loathed the thought of another altercation. However, he would have no choice in the matter, for Fellinger looked quite perturbed. Michael knew the senior was unsettled over being the victim of Michael's stellar performance on the physics test earlier that day. Breaking the grading curve had made Michael the target of the lesser inclined Fellinger. Though Michael was bound to pay for such an infraction, he resolved to remain calm.

"'*Neil Armstrong: A Look at the Man Who Helped Shape the Twenty-Fifth Century*,'" Fellinger cynically read aloud the cover. Then he tossed the book back at Michael. "Get your head out of the stars. The last thing this solar system needs is another Gillen making trouble."

"At least I'll have that option," Michael countered reproachfully, making a not-so-veiled reference to his antagonist's physics test score. However, he couldn't believe that he had let such a comment slip.

Fellinger's face became like flint and he leaned in toward Michael threateningly. Briefly looking at the fading, red handprint on the side of Michael's face, Fellinger pushed an index finger hard against his chest. "Your family's garbage, Gillen.... That's why your mom and dad are here on Earth. They're hiding out in the middle of nowhere because no other place in Terrae Solaris will have them, not after all the trouble Jonathan Gillen created. He was *garbage*, Gillen ... just like *you* are garbage. Isn't that what *Gillen* means?"

Michael fumed, keeping eye to eye with his nemesis. He could hear Fellinger's friends standing behind him, laughing at the remarks the senior had made. Common sense told Michael to let it go, to walk away. However, his anger boiled within him, bringing to mind all the other times Danny Fellinger had insulted his family—and all those others who had done the same thing over the years too. The conversation wasn't over either. No, Fellinger would continue his rant until he had accomplished his objective.

Michael knew that he would eventually haul off and punch the gargantuan.

Michael Gillen sat surrounded by the familiar wilderness valley that was his family homestead. From the clearing next to the lake, he could see his house—or at least what was visible of the underground structure—located at the base of the distant hillside on the same side of the water. Between the clearing and the home lay a thick canopy of trees that made the clearing his favorite sanctuary, though a small access path cut through the thicket.

The dour seventeen-year-old reclined against a large rock, facing the water and deep in thought. Occasionally bored and continually frustrated, he would sometimes skip a stone across the water, morbidly fascinated with watching it plunge to its demise—how fittingly ironic. However, those times were rare, for he mostly kept to himself.

To call him a boy would have been unfair, for his long, masculine frame demanded recognition. Yet to call him a man would have been presumptive. For in the deep pools of his blue eyes burned the brashness, high-spiritedness, vacuousness, and naïveté that is youth. No, the lad found himself precariously caught between worlds. To him, growing up had become a cruel rite of passage, and this day was no exception. So overwhelmed by the tragic circumstances that had played out earlier with Danny Fellinger, young Gillen had escaped to his favorite place of refuge.

Michael remained pensive, but mostly just pouting. With his head hanging low so that his long, brown hair draped conspicuously in front of his eyes, the teen nervously played with the torn fabric exposing his bloody knee. Mindlessly, he kept inserting a finger into the hole— burning pain abruptly shot through the leg upon accidental contact with the fresh wound. His other hand cathartically stroked the stubble covering his face, keeping well clear of the gash at the corner of his mouth and the badly bruised cheek above it. Nevertheless, the whole side of his face throbbed in great pain. Out of the corner of his eye, he could see the rip in his favorite shirt, also spotting the prominent stain where blood had dripped from his mouth.

Yet whatever troubled him physically paled against his personal demons. He was tired of it all: tired of the humiliation, tired of the embarrassment, tired of having to defend himself, and tired of getting no support. *No one understood him.* Life had become completely unfair, providing no means of escape either. Therefore, he would sit there sulking until the intense emotions passed.

"Hi, Mike," a familiar voice echoed from the canopy of trees.

Michael looked up and saw his older brother appear from the thicket, coming toward him on the path. Finishing his senior year of college, David had been away since Christmas.

David was the typical twenty-two-year-old of the day and very much the polar opposite of Michael. The sibling had neatly cropped, ash-blond hair and a clean-shaven face, while conservative clothing covered his filled-out, columnar frame.

At the same time, David possessed other qualities that set him apart from his contemporaries. Though having a swagger about him—especially around his younger brother—David nevertheless remained more than personable. He also lived by strong convictions. Of course, Michael found all those redeeming qualities to be quite irksome.

Though he would never say as much, the lad was happy to see him again. Missing having an older brother around, Michael was more than excited that David had come to visit on spring break. However, this wasn't the time for reunions. No, the crisis of the day consumed the teen. And more than likely, David had come on the behalf of less than sympathetic parties—*Mom*. Therefore, Michael resolved to give David no quarter.

"When did you get here?" Michael asked, trying to sound uninterested. Playing to his demeanor, he looked away toward the water once more.

"About twenty minutes ago," David replied as he sat down, keeping a respectful distance. He tried not to make noticing Michael's injuries too obvious. "I thought you'd be here. You always are." He looked skyward as if taking it all in. "Though it's a little early. I can't see one star yet." Then he laughed.

"Give it time."

"Why don't you come back to the house?"

"And get yelled at *again*?" Michael scowled. "No thanks."

David nodded supportively. "Don't worry. I smoothed things out with Mom. She's not mad anymore about you coming home all bloody."

Michael went slack-jawed and shook his head. Then he huffed, "Why can't she just *talk* to me—like she does with you?"

Shaking his head once more, he turned his gaze out onto the lake and sulked.

"You know how moms worry," David tried to console. "Come back to the house. Dad's almost home. He's gonna start grilling soon. It'll be fun."

"I'm not in the mood," Michael replied, looking down.

"Bad day?" David asked sympathetically. "What'd you do, break up with Sasha?"

"*Jennifer*. Sasha was three girlfriends ago."

David picked up a stone and tossed it into the water. Unfortunately, the stone didn't skip as he had intended. "Hey, I can't keep track of your girlfriends, especially from college. When I met Sasha at Christmas, I should have figured you'd break up with her." He smiled as if to provoke him. "She was too nice."

Michael didn't take the bait. "How did you know I broke up with someone today?"

"It's a Friday," David replied smugly. "You always break up with your girlfriends on a Friday."

Michael just nodded his head.

After a long pause, David shook his head incredulously. "I don't get it, Mike. Why do you keep dating all those bubbleheaded girls? That's got to be six this year alone."

"Why not?" Michael smiled at him, puffing out his chest a little. After all, chasing girls was one pursuit in which David could never adequately compete. "Senior year's coming to an end ... *so many girls and so little time....*" But upon seeing his older brother less than impressed, he added dismissively, "I like their company—for a while, at least. Besides, it's just casual dating ... something to do."

"I don't know how you do it, looking like you do," David replied, giving him the once-over. "You need a good haircut and shave, and you could stand to dress a little more respectably—maybe even tuck in your shirt once in a while."

"Did *Mom* send you out here to lecture me?"

David's gaze turned indifferent, perhaps a little too intentionally. "No, I just wanted to see my little brother." He paused, gazing out onto the lake for a long moment before turning back again. "If it's just casual, then why do you have to break up with them? All this dating might be fun, but it's not proper. You know I'm not in the minority on that view."

He paused for effect, his concern mounting. "Mike, you're not doing anything that Mom and Dad wouldn't approve of, are you?"

"What's that supposed to mean?" Michael shot back, offended and embarrassed at the implication. Watching David continue the inquisition by expression, Michael exclaimed, "*No!* Give me some credit."

David relented, making a stopping gesture with his hands to surrender the point. "Just makin' sure."

The two brothers went silent for a while, letting the beautiful view of the lake become a diversion from the discussion. David took into his hand a long blade of grass directly in front of him. The plant was off to itself, growing out of the stony soil beneath him. Focusing his gaze upon the blade for a long moment as if examining it carefully, David said, "So it looks like Jennifer didn't take it too well." At this, he smiled coyly.

"Very funny."

"So who beat you senseless?"

"Danny Fellinger … and he didn't beat me senseless. I got a lot of good shots in myself."

"Incredible," David remarked, upon which Michael nodded as if appreciating the esteeming sentiment. Then David added, "Butthead."

"What?"

"I meant *you're an incredible Butthead!*" David declared, causing Michael to withdraw and lean away in a huff. "Danny Fellinger is twice your size. How many times are you going to give him an excuse to beat on you?"

"When that blowhard finally shuts up. I'm not going to let him talk about Great Grandpa like that."

"That's not going to stop," David countered. "And Danny Fellinger isn't alone. You can't fight all of Terrae Solaris by yourself. As long as your last name is *Gillen*, you're going to have to put up with what people say about *Jonathan Gillen*."

The words infuriated Michael. "How long are we going to put up with this? They can't blame Great Grandpa for everything that happened … and they certainly can't blame us either! It was too long ago." Michael bowed his head sullenly. "You don't know how hard it is to stand there and just take it."

"Yeah, I do," David replied, somewhat indignant with his brother. "I got into some scraps early on myself. You just don't remember." After a long and formidable gaze, David sighed as the emotion drained from his face. Once again, he became warm and empathetic, though completely serious. "Mike, maybe you should realize that *some* of what they're saying is true."

Michael tilted his head curiously, while an incredulous expression came over him. "*What* are you talking about?"

David looked around quickly, ensuring they were alone before turning back to Michael. "Promise me you won't tell Mom and Dad what you're about to hear."

"I promise."

"You were too young to remember," David began, "but I was there right before Great Grandma passed away. I remember her telling Dad how Great Grandpa regretted some of the things he had done ... and how he tried unsuccessfully to make amends."

"So Great Grandpa regretted inventing the gravitational field generator?"

"No," David replied. "But at that time, deciding how to proceed with developing the solar system was an emotionally charged issue. Putting gravitational fields into settlements like Mid-Earth Station immediately displaced *Weightless* neighborhoods. Tensions between the *Weightless* and normal humans skyrocketed. Despite the warnings about how divisive his invention would be, Great Grandpa went ahead with his experiments anyway. In the end, those warnings were right."

"That's impossible," Michael remarked as he shook his head back and forth. "Solaris wouldn't be the same without artificial gravity. Things would be much worse."

"Maybe," David conceded. "But Great Grandpa bribed Mid-Earth Station's governor for the right to implement his generators, reasoning that success at Mid-Earth would be more prestigious than some new, obscure settlement in the Outer Rim." He picked up another stone and tossed it into the water. This time, the stone slipped gracefully across the surface several times until going under. "Not that Great Grandpa making a better choice would have prevented everything that has happened to the *Weightless*, but you're going to have to accept that some of what people say is true. Otherwise, your own denial will take you to a very dark place. So just learn to let it go. Let Danny Fellinger say whatever he wants."

Michael returned his big brother's imploring gaze, deep in thought. Eventually, he turned dour. "I can't. I'm just not forgiving like you—and I'm not in the mood to hear about your faith again."

"I understand," David replied. "Just stop fighting. You're worrying Mom and Dad."

Michael shook his head defiantly. "It's none of their business."

David became visibly irritated with his rebellious, younger brother. "Okay, let's talk about something that *is* their business: What are you going to do after graduation?"

"I don't know," Michael offered hesitantly. Trepidation crept out from behind his flint-like expression. "Something…. I'll figure it out." He looked intently into David's disapproving eyes. "But one thing's for sure: I'm not going to fall into that *'we're Gillens and we change the world'* propaganda. I'm not going to become some overachiever just because Mom and Dad think it's our legacy."

"You're a butthead."

"What kind of *Christian* talk is that?"

David remained unwavering. "It's the truth. Sorry, but sometimes that hurts too. Mom and Dad just want you to do something with your life. You're incredibly smart, talented, and able to accomplish anything you put your mind to. Dad told me you would be valedictorian if you had just stayed out of trouble.

"But you let your pride and this *lone wolf* thing get in the way: You don't get along with anyone, and you don't have *any* close friends. You dress slovenly, let your hair grow long, and don't shave—making yourself a target for guys like Danny Fellinger…. With just a little prodding from them, you fall right into their trap and give them an excuse to beat on you. You bring it on yourself. *Your impulsiveness is always getting you in trouble….* You're hurting Mom. That's not fair to her … not after everything she's done for you."

Young Michael sat there for a long moment, fuming. David said nothing. Rather, he somewhat enjoyed watching Michael pout while at the same time trying not to prove him right.

After a long pause, Michael eventually said, "Don't worry: Once I graduate, I'll be out of their hair. I promise."

"I doubt that," David replied, frustrating Michael even more. After pausing to let the tension subside, he fixed his gazed on him. "You know, Mike, you come out here almost every night and stare up at the stars for hours…. You want to be an explorer, but you've never been off Earth even *once*." After a long, intentional pause, he added, "But I brought you something that just might help you."

David pulled a small reader from his back pocket and activated the device. Coming to life, the device projected a holographic image, about a third of a meter square, into the air just above the unit. David fumbled through the controls while quickly navigating the device's file system."I saw this in a magazine and just knew you'd be interested," David confidently exclaimed while handing the reader to his younger brother. At that same time, an article appeared in the display.

Michael briefly read the headline and the first part of the article before grimacing cynically at his brother. "*Earth States Military Academy*? You want me to go all gung-ho military?"

"Just keep reading."

Reluctantly, Michael complied. Soon into the article, the young man perked up and looked at his brother in surprise. His demeanor softened noticeably.

"If this is something you want to do," David began, relishing his brother's change of heart, "I suggest you apply quickly. It's already late in the process, and I'm sure open placement slots are going fast. I'll even write a recommendation, if you want me to. But one thing is for sure, with this new era of space exploration upon us and NSEA recruiting out of the academy, Earth State Military Academy is where you'll want to go after graduation."

Michael nodded appreciatively at him before returning to his reading.

Patting his younger brother encouragingly on the back, David stood up and began toward the path to the thicket.

Michael continued poring through the article, pausing only long enough to call out to David. "Hey, bro … thanks! I really mean that…. And tell Mom that I'm sorry."

David, already halfway to the trees, paused and nodded his head sheepishly. Going a few more steps, David abruptly turned around and smiled coyly at Michael. "And don't worry: I have it on good authority that the academy *does* take buttheads…. See you at dinner."

Celeste DeCarreau relaxed quietly in her favorite antique chair, having one hand folded over the other and elbows resting comfortably on the thick arm cushions.

The living room in which she sat remained hushed, save the low hum emanating from the medical console sitting on the adjacent end table. Occasionally, the frail, old woman would check the tubes running from the device to the treatment wrap concealed beneath her dress. The inspections were purely ceremonial, for the machine was entirely adept at completing its intended function. So she instead passed the time by enjoying the beautiful, grassy landscape just outside the living room window.

However, the beautiful summer day outside was simply an illusion, a diversion for the mind. In fact, the window wasn't really a window. Rather, the feature was a complex projection system built into the wall—a virtual window of sorts. In fact, every window in the house was virtual.

Neither was the modest dwelling really a house. Rather, the home was part of a multi-thousand family residence complex. The complex, like the rest of Fra Mauro City, lay buried deep beneath the surface of the Moon in the Fra Mauro Highlands.

Nonetheless, the place was her home: a place Celeste owned outright—her reward for years of hard work and dedication.

The old woman nervously fiddled with her fingers to pass the time. Abruptly, a smile came to her face when the sound of the front door opening broke the silence. Appearing from the corridor outside was a comely, young woman.

The teenager's face, already aglow with youthful effervescence and striking beauty, lit up even more brightly upon catching sight of the old woman. Immediately, she made a beeline to the chair, bent down, and kissed her on the cheek. "Hi, Grandma! How was your day?"

"Welcome home, Katherine," Celeste smiled again. "Today was *just* wonderful!"

"Really?" Kate DeCarreau asked quizzically, quickly checking the dosage settings on the medical console. She could see a grimace from the old woman out of the corner of her eye. Having satisfied herself that everything was okay, Kate evaded her grandmother's disapproving gaze by ducking into the kitchen for a snack.

"I'm surprised to see you home so soon," Celeste called out.

Kate came as far as the kitchen doorway, holding a small pastry in her hand. "Where else would I be? School's out, I don't have to work, and it's a Friday. What should I be doing?"

"Having some fun for once."

"Grandma, you don't think I enjoy spending time with you?"

"You flatter me," Celeste exclaimed, her thin, blue eyes brightening as she smiled again. "And you're a terrible liar." Then her face became more serious and concerned. "You need to get out with other seniors, go out with your friends to the shops, or do something to unwind—you're always here."

"I'm fine," Kate assured, leaning her shapely frame against the doorway. Curling a single finger and putting it to her forehead, she combed a long strand of brown hair from her eyes. "Don't worry about me." Then she went back to settling herself in for the day, energetically preoccupied with a handful of trivial tasks. The first task was turning on music so that it played softy in the background. She smiled as the soothing tones washed over the quiet room, and she proceeded to go about her business.

"How come you're not out with a certain, young, soccer captain?" Celeste asked probingly, becoming almost dizzy from watching her granddaughter bebop around the house. "I haven't seen him lately."

"We decided not to hang around each other anymore." Kate said dismissively, keeping on the go as if unfazed. "But that was weeks ago." Of course, she could see out of the corner of her eye that her grandmother wasn't buying the explanation.

"*Katherine*."

Kate stopped in mid-stride, letting her shoulders sink while sighing deeply. She had been caught. Turning around, Kate admitted, "Okay, *I* decided that we shouldn't hang out." As if the wind had gone out of her sails, Kate sat down in the empty chair next to the old woman. With head hanging low, the young woman became pensive. "It was for the best. He wanted to be more than just friends."

"*Katherine*," Celeste sighed supportively. "Not *again*."

Kate looked up defensively. "Aren't you the one who always told me to be aloof?"

"Aloof—not absent."

Celeste stretched out her frail arm, putting her bony hand on Kate's knee. "Did you really *not* have any feelings for him? Because you looked like you did."

"I don't know," Kate eventually and very hesitantly replied. She remained pensive for a long moment before asking, "Can we not talk about this right now?"

Celeste smiled back at her, even patting Kate's knee enthusiastically. "You're right! It's too good of a day for downers." Then she pointed to the table sitting in the foyer. "Go get the reader. We got something very special today in the mail."

Curiously, Kate retrieved the reader from the table and returned, holding out the device for her grandmother to take.

"It's not for me," Celeste exclaimed with a smile. "It's for you. Open the mail, dear."

More curious than ever, Kate activated the reader and began accessing the mail. First up was a rather official-looking correspondence, and so she opened the letter and began reading. Coming to the end of the first sentence, Kate looked at her grandmother, completely stunned and perplexed. With eyes wide open, she exclaimed in disbelief, "It says I've been accepted … *to Earth States Military Academy?*"

"I put your application into the academy," Celeste announced, beaming with pride. "Other places too…. But this is by far the best!"

"But how?"

"Oh … it wasn't hard. A little bit of personal data from here … a swiped granddaughter's essay added from there … some personal insight … and poof!" Celeste paused proudly. "You really need to watch what I ask you to sign. Sorry, dear, but I knew you wouldn't apply voluntarily. Are you mad at me?"

"No," Kate replied, still stunned and growing concerned about getting her hopes up. She left the chair and knelt down in front her aged grandmother attentively. "I'm very happy. I didn't think I could ever get in—at least I know. But what's this about?"

Celeste struggled to lean forward in the plush chair, the excitement getting the best of her. Looking intently into Kate's deep brown eyes, she said, "It's about your big chance, Katherine, a chance for you to get out of this town—finally make a life for yourself."

Kate began to well up a bit while reading the rest of the letter. "I don't know what to say." Then she looked back up at the old woman once more. "But Grandma, we can't afford this."

"I already made arrangements to sell my equity in the house. You can use the money now, and I can still live here for as long as I need to."

"Grandma, no," Kate pleaded, realizing for the first time all the dreaded implications of her newfound opportunity. With eyes welling up even more, the young woman shook her head. "Please don't. This is *your* house. You worked so hard. I'll just stay here with you."

The frail woman looked intently into her granddaughter's face, smiling empathetically. A sense of contentment came over her. "Katherine, this is hard enough…. The doctors may be good, but they're not miracle workers. We have to face the inevitable…. You need to move on."

"I can't leave you," Kate pleaded, looking down self-consciously. By then, the first tears began making their way down her cheeks. "Please let me stay and take care of you."

Celeste, fighting back her own tears, delicately took Kate's face in her hands, gazing at her beautiful features and childlike innocence. Kate's tears came even harder, and Celeste couldn't help but join her.

"You have a heart of gold, child," the old woman spoke through her own sobbing. "I can't tell you how proud of you I am, and I love you *so much*…."

"*Please, Grandma, no.*"

"But I won't let you refuse," she said while Kate continued to cry. "I know what's going on with all those boys…. You've had such a hard life, and you deserve better…. I'm sorry that I'm the only family you have, and I'm sorry that I'm leaving you so soon…. But you've made too many sacrifices already. If you stay here after graduation and take care of me, you'll just waste away *with* me…. You'll never leave…. No, make me proud…. Go make a *life* for yourself…. And at the right time, find *someone* you can share it with."

Kate sobbed incredibly, at a loss for any appeals. "I don't care about finding someone … but I *will* make you proud. I promise."

"Is that what you want, child?" Celeste asked, sadness draping itself over her. "A life that you don't share with anyone?"

"Yes."

The thin, diminutive man stood in front of the large picture window, taking in the grand city of Tyre stretched out before him. Being the capitol city of Europa, Tyre was a huge and bustling metropolis. The dense city stretched all the way to the horizon, completely covering and concealing the icy surface of the Jovian moon, Europa. Tyre remained unmatched in its splendor and majesty among other Europan cities, eclipsed only by the familiar sight of Jupiter itself. The gas giant leviathan, colored as if a brownish red-and-white marble, hung forebodingly in the blackened sky above.

From his vantage point in the Prime Minister's Residence, the middle-aged man with graying black hair could make out Parliament in the distance. The opulent structure stood out majestically against the backdrop of the larger city, conveying its special purpose. Other government structures and landmarks appeared in the same fashion, purposefully constructed to convey the grandeur of what had been the heart of Europan democracy.

Yet the elaborately hewn Parliament building now stood as a relic. Empty and lifeless, the structure had become a sad memorial to a time long gone. No, the ideals of democracy, having run their course, had been found wanting.

That was simply the *official* story. No, the thin, somewhat gangly man standing before the picture window had systematically laid siege to those ideals. Having been completely underestimated by his opponents, the tiny, balding man had eliminated everything standing between him and the power he so desperately sought.

The day had been a monumental day, the day he had delivered the final, crushing blow to the old government. With the consent of the Europan people, Aurelian Galerius now ruled all of Europa. Being just shy of his forty-eighth birthday, the man was determined not to let Europa slip from his hands—as his predecessors had.

No, he would rule Europa with an iron fist.

While the powerful leader surveyed his kingdom, two lower-ranking soldiers appeared from the entryway. They proceeded affixing to the wall two large, ominous-looking emblems of the new order; one would go on each side of the large window. Galerius relished the moment.

Another man, similarly dressed and being about the same age as the leader, entered the room. Carrying a wine decanter and two glasses, the slightly taller man set the glasses on a small table to the side, filling each glass about halfway and handing one of them to Galerius.

"Carus," Galerius began, lifting his glass and prompting his close friend to do the same, "Here's to a *very* successful day."

"Yes, *my Lord*," Carus replied with a smile.

Galerius mused for a long moment. "I really like the sound of that."

Then Carus lifted his glass a little higher. "To Aurelian Galerius, sovereign ruler of the Europan people…. Long live Aurelian Galerius!"

At that, the two clanged their glasses together ceremonially and drank.

"If only my dissenters had reconsidered," Galerius mused, quickly glancing over to where his pistol sat. "Perhaps it would have gone better for them. But *that* is the business of leadership."

"Should I schedule a public celebration tomorrow?"

"No," the powerful leader replied. "Just make sure that the regional governors publicly endorse my appointment. If they have any hesitation, just remind them that my dissenters had the same concerns. We'll be more than happy to get them together." He took another sip of wine and then smiled grimly. "But now that we have control of the military and police forces, I'm sure we'll have no problems."

"Everything is going as you outlined in *The Europan Experiment*, my Lord," Carus added. "I look forward to the day we can celebrate the annexation of Ganymede, Callisto, Titania, and Triton. Someday, you'll rule all of Solaris. You should be very proud."

The statement caused the plotting ruler's face to churn uneasily. "Don't be so presumptive. We have years of work ahead of us." He paused, deep in thought. "And there's one element we haven't yet considered: the Terrans."

"I doubt they'll get involved," Carus replied, looking at the massive, red planet hanging low in the sky and filling most of it. "Earth is so far away. They think these tiny Jupiter moons are too far removed to be a threat." He paused for effect. "By the time those isolationists finally decide to get involved, we'll have control of the rest of Solaris. Their own apathy will be their downfall."

"I'm not so certain," Galerius shook his head. "Their fleet bases along the asteroid belt give them a reason to be concerned. Ceres, in particular, is a most formidable stronghold, loaded with Terran warships. As long as they have ships so close to the Outer Rim, they will care—and they'll be a threat. No, we need to drive them back to their territory, decimating their forces in the process. Once we gain control of the Outer Rim, we can work our way toward Earth. We'll be unstoppable."

"Taun can handle their military," Carus added, "once we have the combined resources of the other Jupiter moons, that is."

"True, but we don't know the Terrans well enough to know what they know, to know what they'll do. We need to infiltrate their command structure."

"What do you have in mind?"

Galerius' eyes gleamed once again, and Carus was more than familiar with the look. The expression was the same one the diminutive leader had worn when first planning his reign of terror. "My plan to infiltrate the Terrans is already in progress. Before they know it, Earth States will find themselves at our mercy, just like the rest of Solaris."

CHAPTER TWO

Michael the Rook

Young Michael Gillen sat among the crowd of incoming freshmen, nervously waiting for orientation to begin. Just like all the other new cadets, he wore his mandatory rook arrival uniform: unflattering pale beige slacks, clean white dress shirt uncomfortably tucked in, and black tie hanging off his neck. He held a maroon ball cap clearly labeled *rook* in his hand, resting it on the orientation package sitting on his lap. The uniform was certainly hideous. The free-spirited lad knew the outfit was a harbinger of the structured military life he would inhabit for the next four years.

Despite having a gut full of butterflies, young Gillen was actually eager to start school. Matriculation into Earth States Military Academy offered the opportunity of a lifetime: a chance to shed his past—Danny Fellinger and all—and start anew. Attending the university meant a chance to grow, a chance to find himself. His mind was aflutter with all the exciting possibilities his education could bring him. Perhaps one day, he might even realize his ultimate dream of becoming a deep space explorer.

He struggled to shake from his mind the many cobwebs, his only souvenir from the long, lazy days of summer. Oh, he had accomplished a *little* that past summer, such as taking his brother's advice by getting off world for a while. Availing himself of programs set up by the university, Michael even toured Mid-Earth Station, the largest freestanding military and commercial space station in Terrae Solaris. However, he had spent most of his summer idling away. Part of him longed to return to those vapid days, where concerns of the oncoming and sometimes demeaning challenges awaiting him were still far off.

However, adulthood beckoned, so Michael commended himself to the rite of passage set before him.

The ear-curdling roar filling the large auditorium hushed when the first speaker came to the podium. An older woman named Harriet Benchley quickly went through the session's agenda, making sure to stress the importance of paying attention. After reviewing the orientation package materials, she yielded the floor to the orientation's keynote speaker.

The older man appeared from the side of the stage, dressed in a rear admirals' uniform. His slender frame easily disappeared behind the podium as he stepped to the microphone.

"Good morning everyone," the man called out with a smile that demanded recognition and respect. "I'm Doctor Abner Caffry, President of Earth States Military Academy. I'm also a retired rear admiral with over thirty years of military experience. I would like to welcome all of you, the incoming class of 2503."

His expression became very determined. "You've taken your first step today into an exciting future. You follow in the footsteps of many *great* and accomplished leaders, who all started in the exact same manner as you have done." He gestured to the main entrance at the rear of the stately old auditorium. "By coming through those doors.

"Earth States Military Academy is a *proud* establishment with a proven track record of equipping its students with the discipline, integrity, confidence, critical thinking, adaptability, loyalty, and honor *necessary* to fill the challenging leadership roles so vital to Earth States in the twenty-sixth century. We will empower you to succeed far beyond anything you dare imagine."

At this point in the forward address, Michael felt called by the man's words.

Caffry continued, "Today, you step into this university as mere rooks, having no privileges or status—the lowest of the low! You will soon learn how easy you've had it until now. For a while, you will long for those easier days. *That* is a guarantee!

"But our intention is honorable. The first step in becoming a leader is to learn how to follow. As rooks, you will learn this vital skill step by step. Everything you accomplish will be earned, whether it is rank or academic success—nothing will be handed to you." He paused, briefly glancing down at his notes. "As you progress, you will be given training and opportunities to demonstrate leadership, allowing you to aspire to the highest levels of achievement in this institution. When you leave here, you will find yourself prepared to handle any challenge, whether in military or civilian pursuits.

"Rest assured that we will not let you fail. As I said before, this institution has a proven record of accomplishment and excellence. That is why just this spring, the National Space Exploration Administration—a civilian organization—entered into partnership with us to train the next generation of deep space explorers, a program head and shoulders above anything found within the borders of Earth States. NSEA did this because they recognize our unique abilities to produce excellent contributors"—looking around the room as if eyeing up every new cadet in the auditorium—"*you* in just four short years!"

He paused, taking in the enthusiasm that radiated throughout the young audience. However, his face suddenly turned grave. "Now before you go letting your head get filled with all kinds of wild ideas, I want to give you a *sober* warning. I implore you to examine your motives today.

"As future leaders, you aren't being called to fulfill a destiny of adventure and glory. No, you are being called to fulfill a destiny of *service*.

"For whatever reason, trouble is always lurking in the shadows, just waiting for an opportunity; crisis is no more than a day away. Moreover, it's not just military risks. No, circumstances and events are always pulling at the fabric of our society, weakening that fabric. Social issues threaten the very core values that have made us who we are."

He paused, waiting for the right moment. "Why am I telling you all this? Because rising to meet these challenges is hard. Success in the face of great adversity demands great sacrifice. So put your ideas of glory behind you. Pick up instead the mantle of duty to which you are being called;

put your shoulder to the wheel; be willing to give yourself—your very life if necessary—to the service of something greater than yourself; to something that is enduring and honorable. Only in that will you find glory and honor." He surveyed the audience beseechingly for a long moment. "Thank you, and good luck!"

After a thoughtful pause, Caffry yielded the podium to the orientation administrators.

The muffled sounds echoed subtly into the small, adjoining room just off the main auditorium. With the freshman orientation program still in full swing, the cadets gathered in the smaller room could hear tidbits of class registration instructions being given outside.

The small group of upperclassmen cadets, donning various rank insignias, stood in a semicircle around one ranking cadet officer. They faced away from the auditorium, listening as the leader systematically delivered his last minute instructions. While speaking, Gabriel Burke, the ranking cadet, paced before his subordinates commandingly. Occasionally, the young man would hand out one of the assignment packets tucked securely under his left arm.

These junior cadets were about to embark on their next, exciting assignment. Having completed two years of rigorous leadership training, the new team of freshman advisors was about to be turned loose.

One of the female cadets standing near the center of the group listened carefully, keeping her blue eyes trained squarely on the leader pacing before her. The attentiveness was not due to nervousness. Rather, the lively, twenty-one-year-old brimmed with anticipation. Had she radiated any more energy, her long, auburn hair tucked neatly beneath her military cap might have unfurled. She seemed to catch the leader's attention sporadically while he continued his discourse.

"…So you've got about forty-five minutes to look over your group's roster and bios before this auditorium turns into complete chaos," Gabriel Burke exclaimed. He handed a single packet to one of the subordinates. "Read them carefully and be familiar with the names and faces of your rooks."

"Sir," one of the male juniors in the back row called out, "Are the recruits being given instructions to meet us somewhere?"

"No, they'll be busy trying to figure out how to register for classes," Burke replied, pausing to let the seasoned juniors have a laugh at the freshmen's expense. "This is an informal introduction. However, you should arrange a group session sometime before the rest of the upperclassmen arrive on campus."

The young officer passed out a couple more packets. "Now remember, this is a new program. Since all of you are supplementary to your rooks' commanding superiors, your job is simply to make them feel welcome now. As you get to know them, you should fully expect to transform into a mentor. Don't take your assignment lightly, because you are responsible for each cadet's success."

Still pacing, Burke looked down at the last packet in his hand, pausing as if deep in thought. Then coming to stand directly in front of the female cadet with auburn hair, he held out the packet for her to take, abruptly withdrawing it before she could take hold—not in jest, but rather in concern.

"Cadet Ricci," he began in hushed tones so that only she could hear, "You've got quite the balancing act this year, given your dual medical and exploration majors. You sure you want to do this?"

Kara Ricci blushed at being singled out, and some of her uncontainable energy faded as self-consciousness crept into her expression. So in the same subdued tone, Kara replied, "Off course, Sir. I can handle it."

"*Kara,*" Burke replied in a whisper, bringing his face as close to hers as was respectfully possible, "*Most of these exploration cadets aren't coming here for the corp. You're bound to have problems, and you're already loaded up. Why don't you take the medical group?*"

"*No, Burke,*" she sharply retorted in a whisper, her blue eyes clearly conveying her frustration. "*I'll take the exploration cadets, just like I requested.*"

After eyeing her up for a long moment, Burke begrudgingly handed her the packet. Shooting one last look her way, he resumed his pacing and continued giving final instructions to the group.

With her roster and bios securely in hand, Kara Ricci quickly surveyed the data. She pored over the packet's contents, slowly losing attention to Burke's ongoing instructions.

Coming upon a particular bio, the young female cadet lingered on it. She gazed at the picture for quite a long time, glancing only occasionally at the bio data to the left. She could tell just from the picture that the young man, crowned with a mop of longer, brown hair, had a rebellious streak. He would certainly be trouble. Yet, she couldn't move to the next bio either.

"He's a little scruffy, but he's cute," Kara heard herself say loud enough that most of the group heard her too. Immediately, she cupped her hand over her mouth as if to force the words back down her throat, and her eyes grew wide in embarrassment over the blunder. However, discretion came too late; her peers had a good laugh at her expense while watching her blush.

Gabriel Burke looked less than pleased at the interruption. "Cadet Ricci, work on your *MRS* degree on your own time."

Once again, the group had a good laugh at Kara's expense.

Another wave of fellow freshman cadets buffeted Michael Gillen, who desperately tried to stand his ground against the swell.

Having heard all orientation speeches and instructions, the rooks went about completing various assigned objectives: registering for classes, completing a myriad of personal and medical forms, fulfilling financial aid obligations, and getting squad assignments and itineraries for the upcoming drill camp. The frenzy of activity in the crowded auditorium created a churning and chaotic storm within the structure. The swell threatened the many support booths and tables lining the hall's perimeter, as the tide of rooks began shifting toward them. Michael found himself in the center of that storm.

Young Gillen had no time for the confusion transpiring around him. Having fruitlessly gone from one table to the next and always finding he was in the wrong place, Michael wanted to surrender—not an option. Not to give up, the aspiring rook stared down at the orientation instructions, though feeling as if a thick, impenetrable fog covered his mind.

His trepidation mounted with each passing minute. Though the objectives were clear and the instructions seemingly simple, he had made no progress. However, the young man took comfort that the crowd of rooks around him emanated a similar discontent. Eventually determining to find someone more informed, Michael decided to look for such an astute person among the crowd.

As he lifted his head to begin his search, the swarm of cadets encompassing him slowly parted. The task immediately became irrelevant, for across the hall, about twenty meters away, stood a fetching, young female cadet.

Michael Gillen was completely mesmerized.

She didn't notice him gazing at her from across the room, nor did she notice anything else. No, the vixen was similarly distraught and confused, desperately studying her orientation materials. Michael was more than content with her preoccupation, for he could scarcely avert his eyes.

Even from a distance, the young woman was strikingly beautiful. Her face was that of a goddess, radiating an uncommon allure even among her youthful peers. Long, brown hair flowed down elegantly over sculpted shoulders. The rook arrival uniform she wore, unflattering and drab on everyone else, draped itself adoringly over her slender but feminine form. More than anything, the nubile young woman had an elegance and grace about her that Michael found intoxicating.

After quite the long gaze upon the damsel in distress, young Gillen could help himself no more. He began toward her, determined to put her mind at ease.

Her eyes remained trained on the orientation materials in hand. However, upon coming within a few steps, Michael caught her pouty expression changing ever so slightly. She was aware of his presence, and her shields were up!

"I see you're just as confused as I am," Michael exclaimed confidently, brushing off the cold shoulder she was giving him. When she continued studying the packet in her hand, he added, "It's so confusing. You think they could have made this easier."

"I'll get by," the young woman replied matter-of-factly, glancing at him just briefly.

Michael Gillen found himself caught completely off guard, almost stumbling over himself. Her striking deep brown eyes, trained on him for the briefest moment, took him captive. He didn't know why, for the glance was almost reproachful. Nevertheless, his thoughts jumbled in her presence—an unprecedented response. Even when she looked away, Michael remained captive. He struggled to recover. "I—I can help you if you want."

"Thanks, but I'm fine."

Not to be cowed, Michael became more determined than ever. "Can you believe these clothes they gave us? I look completely ridiculous. The uniform seems to work for you, though."—upon realizing what he had just said—"I'm sorry. I didn't mean anything by that."

However, the fetching, young female continued ignoring him, becoming somewhat irritated at Michael's obvious intentions.

"I'm not looking forward to getting my hair cut," he commented, not to give up. "I kind of like it long. How 'bout you? It would be a shame if you had to cut your hair short."

She looked up briefly, watching him run a hand through his mop of long, brown hair. "Actually, all I have to do is wear it up when I'm out." She paused, particularly noting the attention the lad paid to his locks. Her eyes narrowed mockingly. "But good luck with the haircut. I hope it isn't too traumatic." Then she abruptly added, "Hey, I'd like to continue this ... but I've gotta go."

Eager to leave, the young woman turned and began walking away.

"I'll walk with you," Michael implored, turning and matching her gate. "I'm Michael, Michael Gillen. But you can call me Mike."

"I don't think so," she replied dismissively, crinkling her nose and turning her head side to side.

"So can I have *your* name?" Michael asked.

"Why? Don't you like yours, *Mike?*" she said and then laughed cynically.

She has spunk! Michael thought, not used to such an unwavering rebuff. Sparring was normally just part of the game, and Michael could play it better than anyone could. Ironically, the more aloof she became, the more enchanting she became too. So he stared her down, just as determined to get an answer.

The female cadet kept walking, trying to ignore her adversary. However, when Michael remained unrelenting, she paused in mid-stride. Sighing in frustration and turning toward him, she put her hand on her hip disapprovingly. "It's Kate … DeCarreau."

"See, that wasn't so bad, Kate DeCarreau," Michael smiled, reaching out and shaking her hand. "Nice to meet you, Kate." He smiled again; surprisingly, she reciprocated. Finally having her attention, the young man briefly indulged himself in just admiring her gaze. "So, maybe we can get together sometime. How 'bout after drill camp?"

"Sorry, but I don't think so. I'm going to be pretty busy."

"I can work around your schedule, and it'll be my treat."

DeCarreau sighed once more. "Look, you seem like a nice guy … but—"

"I think you're only saying that to get rid of me," Michael filibustered.

"True," DeCarreau replied, irritated that Gillen was ignoring her obvious desire to be left alone. "So why don't you do me a favor and just walk away?"

"What's your problem?" Michael sharply asked, attempting a new tactic. "I just came over because you looked like you needed help. That's all."

"I doubt that," Kate replied, staring him down. "But just so I'm not guilty of jumping to conclusions"—holding up her orientation packet—"What part of this orientation do you consider yourself an expert in?"

Michael thought for a moment, trying not to get lost in her gaze. Even irritated, Kate remained completely alluring. Her curtness with him, though formidable, seemed less mean-spirited—more desperate than anything. Nevertheless, she still waited for an answer.

Eventually, he shrugged his shoulders. "Well, none…. We're both new here. I just thought we could help each other out. You know, *esprit de corps?*"

"I don't think so," Kate cynically laughed, her eyes turning sharp. "Please go away. I don't need this now—or ever."

Michael smiled and looked her square in the eye, meeting her frosty stare. He watched her gaze abruptly turn hollow, as if she had flinched. "I don't believe that."

"*Go away!*" Kate pleaded, unnerved at his penetrating and unrelenting gaze. Her heart leapt into her throat, and the breath in her chest went strangely cold. Realizing that one moment longer might become unbearable, she let out the most indignant huff she could muster. "Fine!" With one last cold stare, the young woman turned and walked away.

Michael Gillen stood alone in the middle of the auditorium, shot down and embarrassed. A few onlookers who had heard the end of the exchange snickered as they passed. Michael paid the mocking no mind. All he could think about was the beautiful, young siren he had just met.

Watching his future love interest—at least that's what he considered her—fume away, the enamored, young man felt a tap on his right shoulder. Another female cadet appeared from around the same side, smiling warmly and intently at him.

Had he been in any other circumstance, Michael would have reveled in his turn of fortune. *One rejection, another opportunity,* he would have thought. Yet he didn't. Not that the female upperclassman cadet standing before him wasn't attractive. In fact, she was quite attractive: auburn hair, bright blue eyes, a great figure, and a high-spiritedness that just wouldn't quit—everything.

Instead, Michael remained more than preoccupied and smitten by his rejecter.

"Michael Gillen?" the female cadet asked, still smiling.

"Yes?" he replied while turning toward her, though glancing occasionally in the direction Kate DeCarreau was heading.

"Hi, Michael, I'm Kara Ricci," Kara said, extending a warm hand to him. The two began to shake hands. "I'm a third-year student. Welcome to Earth States Military Academy."

However, Michael's attention had trailed off while Kara spoke. Ricci uncomfortably took note of this, bringing him back with an abrupt, vice-like grip on his fingers—for just a second. Michael quickly withdrew his fingers like a hurt puppy.

"*Ahhh* ... thanks. Call me Mike."

"Today is your lucky day, Mike!" Kara smiled with uncontainable energy. "You've been given the *rare* opportunity to be assigned to me. I'll be your cadet advisor for the next two years."

Once again, Michael's attention turned elsewhere.

This irritated the young woman, who began to smart at gushing over his picture earlier. Determined not to give up, she gently turned his chin in her direction with her fingers, smiling at him. "Hey, Ace, I'm over here."

"Sorry. What were you saying?"

Kara began to repeat herself, explaining the mentor program. Michael, in turn, made a fair effort to listen. Yet the attempt was to no avail. Eventually, he was gazing in the same direction once more.

Seeing his preoccupation, Kara laughed. "Forget about it, Sport. You're wasting your time with her."

"What?"

"Sorry, but I was ... *kind of* ... standing behind you at the end of your conversation. She shot you down, Ace; you're swimmin' in the drink. She's *clearly* not interested."

Michael paused thoughtfully for a long moment. "Do you really think she wasn't interested? Because I didn't get that impression."

"Great!" Kara laughed as her eyes lit up. "An idealist! I love that. It's going to be a great year."

Michael took in the cadet's overwhelming personality, not sure how to react. Though making fun of him, her intention didn't seam cruel. Kara Ricci just seemed to embody a unique liveliness, a trait he found quite endearing.

Just then, Kara reached out, abruptly grabbing a rather disoriented rook walking by. Obviously, she was looking for him too. "Tom Andrews?"

"Yes?" the startled rook answered, readjusting his gangly frame to face her.

"Hi, I'm Kara Ricci," she smiled. "I'm your cadet advisor for the next two years." Then she gestured toward Michael and partially laughed. "This is Mike Gillen. He just came back from his first combat mission." When Andrews obviously didn't understand the inside joke, she added in a more serious tone, "You two are in the Deep Space Exploration Prep Concentration together."

"Mike, nice to meet you," Tom Andrews warmly exclaimed as the two shook hands.

"You two should get acquainted," Ricci suggested. "You'll be spending a lot of time together." Then she looked around the auditorium. "Hey, I need to go find the other cadets in my group, but I'll be in contact with you. I want to get our group together in the next several days."

In a flash, Ricci left the two rooks—gone like some sort of super hero.

Michael Gillen sat at his desk in his *Solar History and Politics* classroom, fighting the urge to slump in his chair. Today was the first official day of classes for the fall term, and yet he already felt exhausted.

The weeklong freshmen drill camp, having started the day after orientation, was finally behind him. He had survived long days of five-thirty AM wake-up calls, grueling physical training, squad drills, uniform care instructions, inspections, and academic placement tests. However, the start of classes heaped even more requirements onto an already-loaded schedule. Moreover, five-thirty in the morning was just too early to get up.

The young cadet felt completely uncomfortable too, finding the required Class-B uniform far more restricting than the rook arrival uniform. Worse, having too many buttons, epaulets, and the like—all of which required exact placement, the uniform required continual pressing and polishing! The stubble on his chin was sadly gone, as he was required to maintain a clean-shaven face. And *his hair*—cut off as if having been some sort of nuisance; he couldn't even see it without looking in the mirror! Everything was just unbearable.

Nevertheless, Michael realized a wonderful opportunity lay before him. Graduating from the academy afforded him limitless opportunities, including his lifelong dream of exploring the stars. So he put aside his consternation—and the temptations of the beautiful, late-summer day just outside the classroom windows—and hunkered down.

Michael looked around the classroom, sizing up his competition. The students were a mix of freshmen rooks and upperclassman, which the young cadet found quite odd. He would come to learn that the university tended to mix classes, as part of its leadership development program. This ensured that seasoned upperclassmen interacted with less-experienced cadets.

The long-faced professor, an older man with grey hair and an unkempt beard, stood pacing in front of the class of thirty cadets. He was the only one in the room not garbed in military dress, choosing instead a mismatched combination of slacks and shirt with an overly large sweater. His hands went nervously in and out of the sweater pockets while he reviewed the course syllabus and objectives. At this point, the man transitioned into discussing the course material.

"This class is designed to not only teach you history," Professor Rhydderch began, "but to help you see how *current* events are being shaped by historic events. We want to empower you with the ability to dissect both components into their critical elements, thereby understanding how to address the problems fueling current dilemmas." Then he paused, looking around. "So for the remainder of the class, let's experiment with this objective. Here's the question: What do you consider to be *the* historic event having the greatest impact on the twenty-fifth century?"

The old man waited, surveying the class for the first participant. After enduring several long moments of silence, he exclaimed with a smile, "Do we have any future leaders here?"

"Space travel," one of the male cadets near the back offered.

"A little bit of an obvious answer," Rhydderch replied, scratching his beard. Then he smiled. "I see a future for you in politics." The professor paused as a low chuckle rippled through the classroom. "True, you wouldn't have people living throughout the solar system without space travel. Can you please elaborate on your point, *Mister...*?"

The cadet nervously cleared his throat. "*Bowen.* The twenty-first and twenty-second centuries continued experiencing a rise in socialism, as people demanded higher standards of living as a right. This caused economic stagnation as the policies normalized individual achievement. However, when space travel by individuals and private organizations became possible, the achievers eventually left Earth, hoping to make a life not constrained by these economic policies. Yet they also found life off world very difficult. The need to survive forced them to become even more resilient, even causing them to return to conservative social values. As a result, those developing nations thrived and prospered— thus, Terrae Solaris."

Almost immediately, another male cadet raised his hand. "But didn't the reemergence of western religions like Christianity also have a significant impact on these new nations?"

"Yes, they did," the professor replied. "And all these factors dynamically changed the solar system forever." He paused, extending his hands out reflectively. "So here we are, the descendents of those *slackers* who never left or feared venturing beyond the Moon. We readopted those conservative morals, making them part of our culture for over two centuries. So how did that happen?"

"It was forced upon us," a female cadet near the front replied.

"How so?"

"While conducting business with the developing Inner Rim— Mars and Mercury—we found ourselves unable to compete economically, despite having fewer basic survival problems than non-Terran settlements. The gap between our standard of living and the non-Terrans' increased. We saw ourselves dying out. So by complete necessity, we readopted those values."

"Right!" Rhydderch exclaimed, looking around the class. "And that is significant. Purely voluntarily, we turned back the clock. Not just in our governments, but in our families as well: divorce rates plummeted; sexual promiscuity became frowned upon rather than celebrated; out-of-wedlock childbirth became almost unheard of; social decorum became the norm. Once we saw the benefits and realized that personal conduct was the key to success, we continued to reinforce those values in the public forum."

Rhydderch, who was pacing back and forth while talking, stopped and turned toward the whole class, smiling. "A planet of hedonists transformed itself into a nation of prudes." The old man laughed as he surveyed the class. "And because of that, an entire class of young, brazen future leaders blushes at the slightest mention of sexual issues and events."

"But Sir," one of the cadets interjected again. "Can't we also attribute much of this to the reemergence of religion? Historic data suggests that these old-world values emerged first among families identifying themselves with Christianity. In addition, the regions first readopting those values were highly correlated with where missionaries from other planets and moons settled. Perhaps this change occurred because people began believing in those values."

Michael recognized the male cadet as the one having given the *religion* answer earlier. *Oh good,* Michael thought cynically. *Another David.*

"But we've recently experienced declines in '*good*' behavior," Rhydderch countered, "even though the population remains fairly religious."

"That's because the culture is abandoning the acceptance of those views as supreme," the male cadet replied. "Recent data suggests that belief in those religious tenets, especially Christianity, have softened over the last generation."

"We're not here to argue the truth of those beliefs—just their impact on society," the old man politely exclaimed. "Save that for Professor Beitel's philosophy class." He paused for a moment. "You seem to have a flair for religion. Perhaps your calling is to a chaplain post."

Another, stronger wave of laughter rippled through the classroom.

"That wasn't a dig," Rhydderch warned the entire class. "I was *very* serious. We need men and women brave enough to examine the integrity of our social norms—to challenge us."

The aging educator began pacing the front of the room again. "For on this very campus, we have found that the number of cadets engaging in sexual activity outside of marriage has risen to nine percent, fifty percent higher than ten years ago! Out of wedlock births, though rare, have doubled. No, it's a very serious problem." He looked around the class and smiled. "And I see that all of you are blushing again. So I will drop this topic for now—but be prepared to revisit it in the future."

"Okay," Rhydderch continued. "We've proven that events can have very positive impacts. Let's examine some key *problems* we can solve. Keeping on point, what were the most significant downsides to space travel?"

"It's like we're living in the old world again," another female cadet said. "Maybe worse...."—the professor prompted her to continue— "With millions of kilometers between the planets and moons, the amount of effort and time required to traverse the distance has caused a schism. All of these places have their own cultures. We find ourselves very different from those other cultures, and we don't trust them. They don't trust us either. The Ceres Skirmishes was the best example of that."

Rhydderch's face lit up. "Correct. Even after thirty years, the Pallas Treaty has yet to resolve the many problems on those small Jupiter moons. That is a *big* discussion that we will get into next week." He looked at his watch. "We've got limited time, so let's continue on. Who can articulate a current problem for us to solve?"

The upperclassman directly to Michael's right raised his hand. The male cadet, donning a majors' rank insignia, wore such a serious expression. "Artificial gravity generators and its impact on the *Weightless*—and us too."

Michael cringed.

The most peculiar grin came over the professor's face, causing several cadets to chuckle while the man comically stared down the cadet. "Mr. Burke, as an upper classman, you should know better." Then he smiled. "Didn't I ask for a problem we could *solve*?"

The whole class erupted into laughter. Michael, however, more than wanted to crawl under his desk. Burke also remained straight-faced and determined, his brown eyes radiating an unchanneled indignation.

"At least we can pinpoint the exact problem," Cadet Burke countered. "Jonathan Gillen. He *rashly* introduced the device into the Mid-Earth settlement, despite being warned of its consequences."

Michael took a long, hard look at the Cadet. Burke was clearly someone not to take for granted. His strong chin and cut frame gave him a natural confidence and arrogance that seemed insuppressible. His majors' rank screamed success. Worse, he wore an additional insignia indicating he was part of the DSEP program.

Burke was also one of those people who despised him. Burke just didn't know it yet.

"It's interesting that you should bring that up, Mr. Burke," Professor Rhydderch mused. "We are *privileged* to have someone in class who can shed some light on this issue. I think he has a much different opinion. Right, *Mr. Gillen*?"

Michael cringed once again; his worst nightmare was coming true. Crawling under his desk was no longer enough. Perhaps a premature death might provide an escape from Burke's cold stare.

"My great grandfather's invention is why Solaris is successful," Michael exclaimed, feigning confidence before a dubious audience. "Its benefits were desperately needed, because not everyone wanted to be a *Weightless*. The invention merely let people decide freely whether to accept genetic alteration. All those other problems you allude to would have happened anyway."

Burke remained dissatisfied. "My great grandmother and great grandfather were *Weightless*! That's not—"

"So was Jonathan Gillen at first. People forget that."

"My great grandmother wanted her family to undergo genetic re-alteration," Gabriel Burke retorted. "My great grandfather refused. So they split up."

"Would you have rather been a *Weightless*?" Michael countered, suppressing his nervousness.

"No."

"Then I don't understand your problem," Michael exclaimed. "The gravitational fields let your family revert back to being completely human."

Burke didn't back down. "The time wasn't right for such decisions. My great grandmother struggled her whole life because her husband left her, and my family never rebounded from it. Jonathan Gillen could have started his project somewhere in the Outer Rim—that's where he was advised to go. He should have left Mid-Earth Station alone."

"There were a lot of families impacted," Professor Rhydderch softly interjected, putting his hand up to stave off the increasing tension. "Let's face it: Preferences over genetic make-up were a heated debate at many family dinner tables at that time…. Some *Weightless* wanted to return to an unaltered state while others wanted to remain as they were. Even many unaltered families living in space argued over becoming *Weightless*—before everything worked out as it did…. So we've all been affected by this." He looked around the room. "In fact, how many of you have a *Weightless* ancestor or relative somewhere in your family tree?"

A few hands raised, one after the other and very hesitantly. So Rhydderch added, "Okay, how many aren't afraid to admit they have a *Weightless* ancestor?"

Over a very long moment, about two-thirds of the hands eventually raised.

"See, this is a widespread issue," Rhydderch offered, looking at his watch. "And it's clear that we won't solve it today. We'll discuss it more in the future. I guarantee it."

35

At this, the hour bell rang outside in the hall, indicating the end of the class. At once, the cadets sprang from their chairs and headed toward the door.

"By Wednesday," the old man exclaimed over the din of rushing cadets while holding up his reader, "Make sure you read Aurelian Galerius' *The Europan Experiment*"—but when no one acknowledged him—"Anyone know who Aurelian Galerius is?"

Within the herd of rushing cadets, Michael Gillen made a beeline to the door, hoping to find a nice rock outside under which to hide himself. He remembered David's warnings, realizing he was in for a *very* long year—no, four years!

Chapter Three

Freshman Cadet

"Tell me again," one of the female rooks began, a touch of cynicism resounding in her voice. "Why are we here? We're not supposed to be off campus."

Kara Ricci sat on the opposite side of the large, corner table in the bar, her shoulders falling in frustration. Having heard the same question twice, she wished the pizza she had ordered earlier would arrive. Perhaps that would distract the table of ravenous freshman and rescue her from the awkward predicament.

"Don't worry about it," Kara exclaimed with as much confidence as she could muster. "No one from the academy ever comes this far across town." When the ten cadets continued their skeptical gaze, she added, "There *is* a purpose to being here. Who knows what it is?"

Michael Gillen sat at one corner of the table, watching Kara labor over her first session with her group of freshman rooks. Garbed in their physical training clothes—PTs—and concerned over the consequences of violating academy rules, the rooks weren't about to give the aspiring advisor any quarter.

"Good pizza is worth the price of getting expelled?" Tom Andrews replied comically, attempting to ease the tension. He was successful, for a light round of cynical laughter rose up from the table.

It was the evening of the third day of classes. Michael was enjoying his time away from campus and the humiliations of rookdom, a grueling phase the young cadet couldn't wait to finish. Kara's insistence that they all wear their PTs, though odd, gave him a chance to get away from his constricting uniform too.

"We won't get expelled," the female rook exclaimed, clearly not impressed with Tom's joke. "But they'll extend our time as rooks."

"Yeah," another added. "Let's catch a transport back before we get caught."

"Everyone will be fine," Kara replied. "Besides, we're already off campus, so let's enjoy ourselves." She paused. "So can anyone tell me the purpose for being here?"

No one answered.

Okay, enough of the mentoring, she thought.

"All of you have expressed interest in the Deep Space Exploration Program," Kara began, a little frustrated. "The partnership with NSEA puts the academy at the forefront of the biggest undertaking in Earth States' history. Because of the length of such long-range missions, NSEA needs young candidates who can perform right out of the box: hence, the partnership with the academy's DSEP program." She looked around the table intentionally. "Ladies and gentleman, this is your once-in-a-lifetime chance for immortality."

"What does this have to do with us being off campus?" the same female rook retorted.

"It's about out-of-the-box thinking."

The rook remained unrelenting. "So you consider breaking the rules to be thinking outside the box? That doesn't inspire confidence."

Kara's natural confidence and energy return with a vengeance.

"Then think about it this way," she began, her blue eyes becoming steely. "No one is guaranteed an official slot until their junior year. The academy has only twenty slots per class, with forty cadets in your class already signed up—more are expected too." She pressed her index finger firmly onto the table. "That means *tough* competition. Parochial thinking won't get you a slot. So start thinking out of the box."

Michael sat back, enjoying Kara's unmitigated spunk before her now-cowing detractors. Though he had only known her eleven days, Kara was quickly growing on him. Her dynamic personality was infectious, and she had a tremendous sense of humor too. Sharing an intense interest in space travel with her, Michael already considered Kara a good friend.

The server arrived, swinging two large metal pizza pans over and onto the table. No sooner had the pans hit the table's surface than the young rooks set into the food voraciously.

"So what kind of narrow thinking doesn't get us a slot?" Michael asked before taking a bite of his pizza.

"NSEA came to this school because of our tradition of developing good leaders," Kara replied between bites. "But the school is entrenched in military-style leadership."

"What's wrong with that?" another male rook asked.

"Nothing when you're tasked with keeping the peace *here*," Kara replied. "But send a small group of explorers away in a tiny ship for decades where they are completely dependent on one another"—pausing for effect—"that's different. Rules and regulations don't work. The people NSEA chooses will be eclectic: people who know how to think outside the box, who know how to bend the rules without breaking them. That's why NSEA is working with the university to tailor the leadership development program for their needs."

"So how's the DSEP program working for you?" another cadet asked.

At this, the junior thought for a moment. "It's hard to say, since I'm only in my first official week of DSEP. However, I already have one advantage: my dual concentration. I'm also a medical student. It's hard to juggle both, but the benefits are great."

"What do you mean?"

"NSEA needs young people, who can survive the rigors of extended space travel," Ricci replied. "But each exploration team needs experienced medical people too. So they accelerate my training, putting me right into very practical learning experiences right away. I'm even interning part-time at a local hospital.... All of you will get those same types of unique opportunities."

The ten cadets listened intently as Kara explained the program. However, during the long conversation, the rooks caught sight of the junior looking oddly toward the door. Her face immediately went pale, and she bowed her head self-consciously. All of them followed suit as President Caffry came to stand over them.

"Good evening, cadets," Caffry greeted them soberly before looking at Kara. "Good evening, Cadet Ricci."

Ricci lifted her head warily. "President Caffry, this is a surprise."

"This is my wife's favorite pizza place," the old man said, gesturing to the woman taking her seat at the far table. "Looks like you cadets must like it too."

Kara nervously started gathering her things. "…We were just about to leave."

At that cue, the anxious-looking cadets began to get up and head for the door.

"I'll bet," Caffry smiled, looking at the scrambling cadets. "I haven't gotten to know everyone on campus, but I'm guessing this is a table of rooks." Everyone stopped apprehensively. "Cadet Ricci, I'm a little surprised. Don't you know better than to allow rooks off campus?"

Kara remained uneasily silent.

"Sir, Kara had us out on a cross-country run," Michael offered hesitantly. "We saw the place and came in, despite Cadet Ricci's warning otherwise."

Michael stood his ground as convincingly as possible. The old man stared him down, studying his face. At that moment, the young rook realized he might have made a grave error.

"*A cross-country run?*" Caffry mused sardonically. "That's very creative, cadet. I see everyone wearing PTs, yet no one seems tired. Anyone want to fess up?"

Though Caffry waited for a response, none of the other rooks confessed.

"Yes, Sir, we were on PT," Kara added.

"It's getting late," Caffry replied, his look turning dour. "You'd better start running now in order to make it back to the campus before dark. I just hope all that pizza doesn't make anyone sick. *Let's go….* You've got ten kilometers of road ahead of you."

The rooks huffed, shooting Ricci disapproving glances before making their way out of the bar.

As they started to leave, the older man called out, "And on my return trip, anyone I see not running will be in my office tomorrow on disciplinary charges!"

Upon moving out of the old man's earshot, one of the cadets flashed Michael a disapproving look. "What kind of stupid answer was that?"

Michael, receiving the evil eye from the whole group, replied, "The answer that keeps you out of the president's office tomorrow.... Come on, let's get running."

Kara had gone to the counter to settle the bill. Anxiously waiting for the cashier to complete the transaction, she cringed when Caffry came up beside her.

"Kara, what were you thinking?" he asked.

Ricci looked down at the floor, once more dumbfounded. "I don't know, Sir. I guess I *wasn't* thinking."

"This isn't the type of behavior I'd expect from a cadet advisor," the old man warned, "especially one holding a DSEP training slot." He gazed at her tersely. "I hope we haven't wasted one of our very precious slots on you."

This mirror must not be working, a distraught Michael Gillen thought. He turned to the side, carefully examining his uniform in the reflection before turning to the other side. Something just wasn't right. So the young rook continued to fiddle with the outfit, desperately desiring to avoid getting another demerit.

The uniform problems were fittingly symbolic of the cadet's mounting frustration: Michael was having difficulties fitting in. Not that the first two months of the fall term didn't yield many successes. In fact, the cadet was excelling in his studies and had aced several DSEP evaluations.

But one thing Michael had learned: Military life just wasn't for him. The cadet, realizing just how much of a free spirit he was, found the rigorous code of conduct too cumbersome. Demerits were many;

the discipline, overwhelming. Worse, upperclassmen would badger incoming rooks, him especially. The proud, young man found the assaults unbearable. To him, rook status was a systematic hazing sanctioned by the university.

Moreover, Michael might as well have worn his last name like a scarlet letter. The campus was peppered with upperclassmen and freshman alike, all having disdain for the Gillen name. Once word spread of his arrival on campus, detractors came out of the woodwork. Cadets like Gabriel Burke, availing themselves of their rank, made his rookdom a complete nightmare. His brother, David, had been right so long ago: Michael would always have someone to contend with, no matter where he went.

However, all these thoughts were far from Michael, for he was late getting over to Kara's dorm. He hadn't planned anything special for the day, just the typical leisure activities the two friends normally engaged in during the weekend. In fact, he spent most of his free time with Kara. Knowing Kara did not like to be kept waiting, the rook feverishly adjusted his uniform, trying to figure out what was wrong.

Just then, something caught his eye. Crowds of cadets had streamed by his ground-level window all morning. With his dorm room located in the basement, Michael received the unappealing privilege of watching anonymous feet scurry by all day. However, the sleek, attractive set of legs just passing by, framed between a grey skirt draping the knees and feet clad in a low heel, was surprisingly familiar.

He rushed to the window, straining to see in the direction the legs had disappeared. His face lit up; cares for his uniform evaporated. Kara would have to wait.

In a complete frenzy, the rook quickly grabbed his cap and rushed out of the room, barely accommodating his roommates' desperate pleas to shut the door. Like a shot, he was up and out of the dormitory. The morning sun warmed his face the moment he stepped outside, though a slight chill hung in the fall air.

The chase was on.

Having made it outside, Michael forced himself to subdue all visible traces of his determined pursuit. Instead, the rook complied with the protocol of rookdom and *walked the gutter*: eyes forward, no talking, making steady and deliberate steps, and keeping at all times on the very edge of the sidewalk. All rooks were required to traverse the campus this way

Speeding along as fast as protocol would allow, the young rook kept his prize squarely in his peripheral vision. She was fifty meters directly ahead of him on the same crowded path.

Each step became increasingly risky as Michael closed the gap. Perhaps his hurried pace would catch an upperclassman's attention; perhaps his subtle uniform problems would give him away. Perhaps Kate DeCarreau would disappear into one of the restricted brownstones lining the busy walkway.

If only fortune would smile on him.

Michael was in luck. DeCarreau, still a short distance ahead of him, turned off the main walkway and onto an obscure path leading away from the main quad. Quickening his pace, Michael made his way onto the path: a narrow, gravel walkway snaking behind one of the brownstones. Thick evergreen trees lined the side opposite the building, hiding the path from most of the campus. Only he and DeCarreau traversed the secluded trail.

Once out of sight, Michael immediately broke formation.

"Hey, how ya doin'?" Michael warmly greeted her, quickly coming up along side and matching the female cadet's gate. Obviously, any concerns for demerits had fled from the enamored rook's mind.

DeCarreau—still a rook too—said nothing, did not return his gaze, or interrupt her stride one iota. She just kept *walking the gutter*, carrying a pack slung over her right shoulder.

"Don't worry: It's okay."

"*Go away*," the young woman whispered. "*You're going to get us in trouble!*"

Michael desperately but politely stepped in her way, breaking her stride. He rebuffed her expression of annoyance, though clearly captivated by her gaze. "No one's even around."

DeCarreau stole a glance in both directions, realizing he was right. Nonetheless, Gillen remained her biggest problem. After shooting him another impatient look, she stepped around him and continued on her way. However, upon noticing the determined, young man keeping pace with her, she chided, "What's your problem? This is against regulations."

"But I haven't seen you since orientation."

"Good," the fetching, young female unexpectedly smiled while keeping her pace. "My plan's working ... *until now*...." Her expression turned dour. "Please don't talk with me. I don't want to risk losing any time accrued as a rook."

"If you don't talk to me," Michael mused, strolling along as if he were on a Sunday jaunt, "I'll just follow you wherever you go. I'll keep right by your side the whole way."

Kate smiled once more while still looking ahead and continuing to walk. "I don't think so."

"Do you doubt my persistence?"

"Not that it's any of your business," DeCarreau began while repositioning the pack on her shoulder, "but I just *happen* to be going to the pool facilities. My first stop is the women's locker room to change. So no, I don't think you have the guts to follow me. And if you actually follow me into the locker room ... then I don't want to have anything to do with you."

"Maybe I *would* follow you anywhere," Michael countered, not to be cowed, "at least into the water. You see, I don't like swimming that much. Though I grew up by a lake, I rarely ever used it. But if it meant we could get to know each other better, I'd be more than happy to jump in the pool—uniform and all."

"We didn't have any lakes where I grew up," Kate exclaimed as she stopped, looking him directly in the eye. "I would have given anything for such an opportunity." Her gaze went razor-sharp. "So, I'm not interested in getting to know some spoiled rich kid who didn't have the sense to take advantage of something so rare."

DeCarreau began walking away.

"I'm not spoiled!" Michael replied as if astonished, letting her continue ahead of him. Deep down, he loved the banter, finding himself captivated by her scorn. Moreover, he *just knew* the beautiful, young female was masking her true feelings. So he put his hands to his chest as if to plead. "And I've got other qualities and interests too. You just need to get to know me."

Kate stopped dead in her tracks. Huffing, she turned around and returned to where he stood, and her face turned as biting as ever. Jamming an index finger forcibly into Michael's chest, she exclaimed,

"Haven't you gotten the hint!?"—glaring at him—"I'm not interested. And don't go showing up at the pool trying to impress me, 'cause it won't work!"

While enjoying her reproachful gaze for the long moment, Michael heard the most unpleasant echo from far above. "*Rooookkks!*"

Immediately, the two cadets looked up in the direction of the noise; their faces turned grave. Much to their dismay, a couple of upperclassmen were hanging out one of the third floor windows at the back of the brownstone, displaying the most condescending gaze.

"Stay right there!" one of them shouted from the window. Then they quickly disappeared into the structure, most likely to intercept Gillen and DeCarreau.

Kate bowed her head in frustration, close her eyes, and put her hand over her eyes while shaking her head in disbelief. After a long moment, she looked back up at him in a none-too-pleasing fashion. "If I have to do *one* pushup or *one* extra minute as a rook ... *you're* dead!"

However, by the time the terrible incident would play itself out, the two rooks would end up doing one hundred pushups—right on the spot—and two extra weeks as rooks.

The incident also went on their permanent records.

The weather at Earth States Military Academy was cold and blustery: a typical mid-January day. The winter of 2500A.D. had arrived with a fury, as if attempting to leave its mark on the fading century. The old buildings and grounds lay blanketed in white, having a good six inches of snow covering everything but the shoveled walkways. Cadets and professors alike went about the institution, shrouded in heavy winter garb. Yet the icy walkways remained sparsely inhabited, as most had retreated to the comforts found indoors.

Such was not the case at the university's outdoor athletic facilities. Being fully equipped with powerful environmental generator units, the playing fields remained balmy and clear up to fifty meters above the ground.

Michael Gillen suddenly fell facedown into the mud near the center of one of the practice fields, forced into the ground by his opponent. The cadet wore his PTs, a red pullover indicating his team designation, and a lot of mud. The play was over. So he stood up, shook the mud from his clothes, and watched Gabriel Burke smugly celebrate his reception all the way back to the Blue team's huddle. All Michael could think was *where's the penalty flag?*

About twenty other students were on the field, participating in a game of flag football. The instructor had divided the mix of male and female cadets into two groups: the Red team, on which Michael was playing, and the Blue team, on which Burke was playing. The game had been going on for the past forty-five minutes, and time was running out. The losing team would get the pleasure of running penalty laps around the field's perimeter: something neither team relished.

The score was tied.

Michael ran up to the instructor, who was playing referee. Though young Gillen strongly pleaded his case, the instructor insisted that he had made the right call. After a bit of jawing back and forth, the cadet set off to where his team had huddled.

Despite the botched call, Michael found the co-ed class quite enjoyable, considering it a refreshing change of pace and a good start to the new spring term. The class also allowed him to work out his consternation over how bad things had gone. After all, the young cadet had lived under a curse of bad luck since the start of the fall term the previous year.

Making his way back to the Red team huddle, Michael spied Kate DeCarreau jogging back to the huddle too. She also wore a red pullover marker over her PTs, though he thought the marker looked much better on her. With Kate in the class, he only had his mind half on the game at hand. However, this game was an opportunity to impress her, for he was quite the football player—the previous play notwithstanding.

"Okay guys," Lazon Emery, ranking senior and captain of the Red team, called out. "Let's bring it in." As the last Red team member came into the huddle, Emery began barking out orders. "Gillen, I want you to switch with Cuddy. Burke is getting the best of you."

While Cuddy nodded, Michael shot a look at his captain. "No, he isn't. He went out of bounds—wasn't even eligible to catch the football."

"No one saw it, so it doesn't count. Let's—"

"I can do this," Michael pleaded. "I promise."

Emery paused for a short moment, intently eyeing up the freshman. Finally, he huffed, "Okay, don't blow it!" Having resolved the matter, the senior continued barking out orders to his team, which was on defense.

Quickly, the two teams made their way to the line of scrimmage. Michael stood opposite Burke, waiting for the snap. Burke's expression betrayed him as the intended receiver. Out of the corner of his eye, Gillen could also see Kate standing just to his left. This was his chance to make up for the last play, maybe even impress her.

The ball snapped, and both teams immediately set in motion. Burke shot across the line as if on fire. Michael, an adept safety in his own right, kept pace and prevented the junior from breaking away. The two jostled each other roughly while Burke attempted his pattern. Michael kept close on his heels, refusing to give his rival any quarter. Then the junior abruptly shifted directions, forcefully shoving Michael in the process.

In a stroke of bad luck, Michael was off-balance at the time. He stumbled backward uncontrollably, landing hard on his backside. Lying on the ground, the shaken freshman helplessly watched Burke, now unimpeded, catch the pass and waltz the ball straight into the end zone.

The sound of the instructor's whistle broke the air. "Touchdown for Blue! Okay, folks, Blue is up by one touchdown, and time's running out. Remember: Laps are for losers!"

Michael Gillen sat dejectedly in the mud, while his teammates walked by and gave him disapproving stares. When Kate DeCarreau came by, she flashed him a sarcastic look. "Nice job, *Romeo*. You should have listened to our captain."

He cringed in embarrassment. The universe was conspiring against him!

The two teams set themselves in formation on opposing ends of the field. Blue kicked the ball to Red, who desperately needed another touchdown. However, the kick return was paltry, putting Red deep in their own territory.

Time was running out quickly.

Michael went through his play assignments, merely going through the motions. Because of his foible, Emery had relegated him to running decoy pass patterns—a sort of banishment for letting Burke score at such a critical time.

As the clock wound down, young Gillen fumed over his treatment. After all, he had performed well the entire game, even scoring once. Worse, that no-good Burke had gotten the best of him once more—in front of Kate DeCarreau nonetheless! Having borne up under Burke's relentless assaults for five months—undue humiliation during his rookdom, defamation of the Gillen name in *Solar History and Politics* debates, and the insults in front of other cadets outside of class— Michael resolved not to let the person he hated the most get the best of him.

Red advanced the ball up the field, though moving too slowly to score in time. Michael, now playing like a man possessed, continued beating his nemesis on every play. If only someone would give him the ball!

So beginning a campaign to win back his status, Michael pleaded with Emery to pass him the ball. The senior captain predictably resisted. Gillen appealed, begging Emery to watch him outfox Burke on the next play. Despite seeing Michael deliver on that promise, the senior ignored his insistence for two more plays.

"Okay folks!" the instructor hollered from his place on the field. "Two minutes until the losers run laps."

Presiding over the Red team huddle, Lazon Emery looked out across the field toward the elusive goal line. With time quickly dwindling away, the senior realized the circumstances called for drastic action.

"Okay, Gillen, you've made your point," Emery announced. "Do you're thing: Stay shallow and come to the center as if to decoy, otherwise you'll attract too much attention. When you reach center and see my arm going back, break to the post. Look sharp, because the ball will already be in the air when you turn."

"Got it!" Michael replied enthusiastically, noting some displeasure among his teammates.

Cuddy, one of the more utilized receivers, protested. "Hey, don't do this. I can get open."

"They're expecting you to get the ball," Emery replied. "No one's expecting Gillen anymore."

After shutting down the protests, Lazon Emery brought his team to the line of scrimmage. Michael set himself up far to the right, met once again by Gabriel Burke on the opposing side. Burke had that same smug grin on his face.

At the snap, Michael fired off the line and plowed into his adversary. The clash was an attempt to lure Burke to ease up, as if Michael were still the decoy. Then Gillen bounced off him quickly, turning predictably to run to center field. Burke followed closely, though pulling off a little upon seeing Emery looking to Cuddy as if to throw.

Reaching center field, Michael spotted Emery pulling the ball back to pass. Gillen immediately broke toward the end zone, catching the dumbfounded look on Burke's face as inertia carried the junior out of the play. In just a few steps, Michael would be completely passed him.

That is when Michael felt Burke's foot tangle itself perilously between his steps, intentionally knocking him off-balance. The two abruptly heaped into a pile and fell hard onto the ground. As the back of Michael's head hit the muddy surface, he could see the ball flying well over him on its futile path.

Burke had humiliated him once again!

"*Is that how you win?*" Michael fumed, shoving Burke after making it to his feet. "*By cheating!?*" Out of the corner of his eye, the freshman could see the instructor running on an intercept path toward them.

Burke shoved back hard. "You ran into *me!*"

"Gillen, break it up!" Emery yelled from a distance. "We still need to run a play!"

"*You tripped me, you SOB!*" Michael exclaimed, getting up in Burke's face and grabbing the junior's shirt. He could hear his teammates in the background pleading for him to stop, but Burke's treachery had undone him.

Burke pushed hard against the enraged freshman. "That's just like a Gillen, trying to rewrite history!"

The tiff erupted into a full-blown brawl when Michael struck Burke square in the face. Burke reciprocated, and the two went at each other furiously. Upon arriving at the scene, the instructor labored to pull the two apart.

"Both you two!" the instructor yelled, wedging himself between them. "Straight to my office!" Upon seeing them continue facing off at each other, he yelled, "Now! And if I see anything more, you'll fail the class!"

The two adversaries grudgingly relented and took off jogging toward the athletic office. Looking at his watch, the instructor turned to the cadets. "Sorry Red team, but your classmates used up the remaining time fighting. Blue team wins. Red team, you owe me laps."

The cadets dispersed. The Blue team set off for the locker rooms, while the members of the Red team reluctantly headed to the track. Kate DeCarreau stood in place for a long moment, watching Michael Gillen jog to the instructor's office. All she could do was shake her head in disbelief—and run her laps.

Michael Gillen stood uneasily in the office of the venerable President Abner Caffry, waiting for the discipline hearing to begin. His face touted several notable bruises and cuts. Having been given time to clean himself up from the fight, he stood garbed in his normal Class-B uniform. However, the young cadet would have worn his dress blues if it would help his case. A similarly bruised Gabriel Burke stood beside him, also awaiting his fate and similarly dressed. With the conflict fresh in their minds, neither said a word to the other. Kara, having been called because she was Michael's cadet advisor, stood off to the side near Michael.

The appearance of Caffry coming through the doorway interrupted the awkward silence, the tall man's head coming just inches from the top of the old wooden doorframe. All three cadets snapped to attention. Caffry shut the door behind him, looking at them disparagingly while negotiating himself around his desk.

"Fighting in gym class?" he said curtly while sinking deep into his chair. "How grade school!" Looking squarely at Burke, the old man continued, "Normally, I would expect the discipline for such an altercation to be handled by the cadet advisor commander ... but isn't that you, Mr. Burke?"

"Yes, Sir."

"I'm quite disappointed, Mr. Burke," Caffry exclaimed. "But since you're more than willing to scrap, I guess I'm more than willing to handle this myself." Then he looked at all three. "I spoke to the instructor, who filled me in on the details. All I can say is that it doesn't bode well for either of you." Once again, he turned to Burke. "Mr. Burke, why are we here?"

The junior stood up straight and with his eyes forward. "Cadet Gillen was frustrated that I was outperforming him, so he took a swing at me. I just defended myself."

"That's a lie!" the younger cadet retorted, holding the same protocol. "He tripped me."

The old man appeared unconvinced. "No one saw Mr. Burke trip you, Mr. Gillen. Not even your own teammates." He paused for a moment as if studying Michael. Then his eyes narrowed and his index finger came up. "When I caught you off-campus last fall against regs, you told me you were on a PT run. You can be incredibly creative when you want to be, Mr. Gillen. Are you sure you don't want to change your story—*or* your plea?"

"No, Sir." Michael replied, visibly disturbed by the accusation.

"Cadet Ricci," Caffry turned toward her, "You're Cadet Gillen's advisor. Can you think of anything to help this first-year out of his predicament?"

"No, sir," Kara replied. "But if Cadet Gillen claims Mr. Burke tripped him, then that's what happened."

"That's pretty bold, considering Mr. Burke's excellent reputation."

The old man looked at Kara inquisitively before turning back to the other two. "Both of you will serve time on guard duty for the next two weeks—right in the main quad where everyone can see you." The old man paused and his face steeled. "But I'm unsettled that two cadets, one in our DSEP program and the other desiring entry, could act this way. Rest assured that this incident will go on both of your records."

Then he dismissed Burke, who left promptly.

Caffry leaned back in his chair, gesturing for Michael to stand at ease. "Mr. Gillen, I'm concerned about you." He opened the folder on his desk. "Despite flawless academic work and excellent preliminary

DSEP testing, you have *issues*: anger problems ... conduct violations ... you name it! Moreover, you were almost the *last* freshman to shed your rook status." Then he closed the folder once more. "Not a very convincing record so far for someone wanting to join the most prestigious program at our academy.... So what's going on?"

Michael hesitated, unsure how to answer. "Nothing, Sir. Just adapting to life here."

"You call this adapting?" Caffry probed. But then he shrugged apologetically, putting his hands out. "If you came from a broken family or had some other similar challenge ... I could understand. We can deal with those types of problems." He paused sympathetically. "But you come from a fairly normal—albeit infamous—family. It looks like the only problem you've ever had is *you*."

Michael stood in place, watching Caffry waiting for a reaction from him. Yet the young cadet remained uneasily silent.

Of course, silence didn't please the aging administrator. "If you don't turn around soon, we're going to have to deal with your application to the DSEP program more severely.... *Got it?*"

"Yes, Sir!"

"Good," Caffry replied. "Dismissed." When Ricci began following Michael out the door, he called out, "Kara, can you stay for a second?"

While the young woman paused at the door, Caffry stood up and shut the door behind Michael. Looking down at her quizzically and with much concern, he asked, "Kara, what's going on here? How can you so easily dismiss Burke's claims? He's our top NSEA candidate right now." He pointed his thumb toward the door. "This other guy is a troublemaker. Yet when I read your reports, you give him nothing but glowing recommendations."

"I know Cadet Gillen, Sir," Kara replied. "Though he's rough around the edges, he has a lot of qualities NSEA is looking for. He just needs polished a bit."

"A lot of polishing, I would contend," Caffry retorted, though quickly relenting. He gazed down at her thoughtfully. "Kara, I'm old, and I've seen a lot in my day. My gut tells me there is more to this that what you're letting on.... Are you sure your feelings for this young man aren't clouding your judgment?"

Kara looked up at him, embarrassed. "Sir, Cadet Gillen and I are friends—*that's it*." She gazed up at him indignantly. "I stand behind my reports."

"Okay, I surrender," Caffry smiled accommodatingly before turning serious again. "Watch out Kara. Don't let this cadet ruin your future."

CHAPTER FOUR

Epaulet Stripe Number Two

NEWSFLASH: Achelous, Ganymede (Aug 6, 2500A.D.) – In a move having significant solar system-wide implications, the people of Ganymede voted overwhelmingly in favor of Europan annexation. Although some rioting against such a move quickly erupted in Achelous, the capitol city of Ganymede, police and military forces controlled by Aurelian Galerius of Europa quickly swept into power, disbursing and putting down the disturbances.

The Western Republic of Mars immediately condemned both the election results and the move by the Europan government, calling for Europa to return immediately to the terms of state outlined in the Pallas Treaty, which requires Europan non-aggression and a stand-down of all military build-up.

Some have accused Aurelian Galerius of interfering in the Ganymede election process. However, historians and political analyst alike consider the alliance just one more predictable event in the struggle to resolve the terrible economic problems of the Jupiter moons, caused by the Pallas Treaty.

Pundits predict that unless the Mars Federation, executor of the treaty, progress in achieving significant amendments to the agreement or stop Europan military expansion soon, the Outer Rim is bound to return to a state of conditions that preceded the Ceres Skirmishes.

Senior cadet Kara Ricci navigated the hallway as if running the campus' obstacle course. Today being move-in day for the new fall semester, the dormitory hallway teemed with families settling in their daughters. Junk lay everywhere, and the noise level had become most unpleasant.

Carrying two small bags suspended from her hand, the twenty-two-year-old gracefully dodged and pirouetted her slender frame through the confusing maze, working her way upstream to the other end of the hall. Continuing her crusade, she made it almost to the door to her dorm; only an abandoned box and an oncoming family stood in her way.

Upon executing another flawless half-pirouette around the obstacles, Kara felt herself backing clumsily into someone. The sound of something hitting the ground immediately followed. She turned around to apologize, only to see Kate DeCarreau kneeling down and fumbling with her things. The sophomore had been carrying two large boxes, one of which had spilled onto the floor.

"I'm *so* sorry," Kara exclaimed while kneeling down to help DeCarreau. "I didn't see you."

"That's okay," Kate replied, trying to pick up the items before the horde around her broke something. "This is the second time someone has run into me. Don't worry: I've got it."

Nevertheless, Kara continued helping Kate pick up the items from the floor. "You're ... *Kate* ... Kate *DeCarreau*, right?"

"Yes."

"I *know* you," the senior cadet added with a spark in her eye, remembering how much Michael had pined over the young woman the previous year—deep down, Kara found this completely irritating! However, Kate would not have known any of this; hence, her quizzical expression. "I mean, *we never met....* But I saw you around campus last year."

"Yes ... I remember seeing you too."

The two young women went silent for an awkward moment, until Kara smiled and said, "*So* ... welcome to the upperclassmen dorms. I guess we're going to be floor mates this year.... You, me, and a hundred other girls, that is." Then she half-laughed.

"Thanks," Kate replied. Having retaken control of her cargo, the sophomore turned to make her way down the hallway.

"Hey, Kate," Kara called out, pointing to her door. "The cafeteria is closed now"—lifting up the bags in her hand—"and I brought back take-out. Do you want to come in and have lunch? I have more than enough."

Kate smiled while straining with the boxes. "Thanks, but I've still got some unpacking to do."

"What was I thinking?" Kara exclaimed, gesturing as if hitting herself in the head. "I can be so obtuse sometimes.... *Here*, let me help you carry those."

Kara took the top box from Kate, putting her take-out bags on top before grabbing it. Then the two girls proceeded down the hall, continuing to chat as they walked.

Nineteen-year-old sophomore Michael Gillen sat at the head of the picnic-style table, mediating his small team of recruits for the *Applied Sciences* project. The eager, young project leader, feeling the rush of executing his first leadership assignment, barely noticed the stream of students passing by on the adjoining walkway. He also didn't notice the alluring serenity of the warm September afternoon, or the coolness of the shade cast over the table by a towering oak sitting at the edge of the grassy quad. No, he focused all his attention on the intense discussion at hand.

Each team in the *Applied Sciences* class, five in total, needed to submit a project proposal to the professor. Once approved, the groups would then craft their idea into reality over the next month, finally demonstrating the projects in a science fair-type competition. The proposal was what fueled the consternation among the lively group; no one could agree on an idea. However, Michael, brimming with confidence, sat back and waited for the right moment.

"Who else thinks we should just surrender to the other teams?" Tom Andrews quipped in comical tones. "I've got a white hanky. Who has a stick?"

A quick round of laughter rose up from the table. Michael, though giving a respectful smile to Tom, remained determined. Fate had dealt him another cruel challenge—and a chance to avenge himself for the previous year's mistakes too. So he thumped the table with his index finger for effect. "We're not surrendering, especially to Gabriel Burke and his team. I'll submit burning ants with a magnifying glass before I let that guy get the best of me."

"You could just fight him like you did in *Physical Fitness* last year," Kate DeCarreau sardonically replied, "and leave the rest of us out of it."

A round of *ooohs* went up from the young group of cadets. Andrews smiled at Michael and said, "Well, *Mr. Team Lead*, I think that was a dig."

"I guess I deserve that," Michael replied, clearly not fazed at the chiding.

No, Michael wasn't daunted. In contrast to a year ago, the young man was strangely comfortable with the strict military atmosphere—uniform and all. Furthermore, having another stripe on his epaulets gave him a much-needed sense of accomplishment. His role as *Applied Sciences* project leader, secured by his academic performance the previous year, would finally give him the chance to prove himself. Best of all, his project leader status had allowed him to draft Kate DeCarreau onto his team, thus giving her no choice but to interact with him.

So finding himself at the start of a brand new term, the sophomore brimmed with anticipation. After all, a new year meant a chance to start over.

"Okay, does anyone have an idea?" Michael asked once more.

"A *good* idea," junior Zack Cuddy added, tired of hearing too many bad ones. "After all, this is twenty percent of our grade."

"How 'bout a demonstration of terraforming techniques on Venus?" Danilo Caceras offered hesitantly, shrugging his shoulders.

Marta Janssens shook her head. "No, that's been done to death. No one would consider it practical anyway." She paused in thought. "Why don't we do some simulations of the erosion of Saturn's rings? Demonstrate the gravitational forces over time—make it a dynamic model."

"I don't think that's cutting-edge enough," Kate replied.

"But we could introduce things like manmade satellites and comets on that erosion."

"I agree with Kate," Tom Andrews exclaimed. "That's a science fair project for highschoolers. Let's face it: With every team's submission confidential, we don't know what kind of competition we'll be up against. No, we need something spectacular."

Upon much debate and discussion, the frustrated group came back to where they had started: nowhere. Therefore, Michael decided to make his move.

"I was waiting to see if anyone had a better idea," he began, lifting his cap and running his hand through his cropped, brown hair, "but I've got the perfect project: We're going to build a prototype of a navigational field generator, one that enhances the current design already used in spaceflight."

"That's impossible!" DeCarreau shot back. "—and beyond us."

The young man smiled. "Not necessarily." He looked around the table confidently. "Navigational field generators are very similar to gravitational field generators. If there's one thing my family knows, its field generators. I've been tinkering with improvements using my great grandfather's original specs—just modified them a bit."

He paused, surveying the reactions. For once, his heritage appeared to give him some credibility, for everyone at the table was listening intently. "The original designs were forgotten when technology evolved, but the old specs offer certain advantages recent designs have overlooked—like they forgot the original intent. We can finalize the work I've already done, create a prototype, and demonstrate it."

Marta Janssens shook her head, gesturing to the rest of the group. "The work still sounds way beyond *us*."

"No, I already have a smaller prototype working—I've had it since high school. I just need some help calibrating the design. That's where you guys can help. And you'll get to learn something that you won't find in textbooks; that's my contribution."

The group appeared to warm to the idea, even expressing some enthusiasm. However, Tom Andrews looked at him quizzically. "Why didn't you just propose the idea up front?"

"I was trying to foster teamwork and collaboration."

With a long pause and a gathering of approving glances, Danilo Caceras finally spoke up, "Okay let's do it. Go ahead and submit the idea to the professor."

Michael hesitated uneasily. "Actually, I already submitted an idea. I told her we were working on a spaceflight navigation demonstration."

"*What?*" Kate asked, stunned at the revelation. She was not alone in her angst, for the others stared at him with the same disapproving look.

"Let me get this straight," Tom laughed cynically. "You let us sit out here all this time debating a project choice, when you've already submitted an idea that *isn't* the one we're actually going to work on—that you already decided in advance we were go to do—*to foster teamwork and collaboration?*"

The incredulous gazes continued.

"Sorry," he recoiled apologetically yet stalwart in his posture. "But everyone admits this is the best project—and this *is* a *type* of spaceflight navigation demonstration. By giving professor Fierro a more generic description, we can have a fallback if our navigational field generator doesn't work."

He looked around the group imperatively, searching their expressions and begging for consideration. Eventually—and very reluctantly—the group came around. Finally having their seal of approval, Michael added, "Trust me.... It will be a slam dunk."

The group continued discussing the project for a long time, formulating a strategy, dividing the work among the team, and figuring out how to finish the generator in secret.

Sitting on the opposite side of the massive oak tree beside the table was Gabriel Burke. The senior reclined against the tree, holding an open *Applied Sciences* textbook while pondering various project ideas for his team. He had merely chosen the spot for its shade. However, upon hearing the entire conversation taking place on the other side of the tree—with no one from Michael Gillen's team aware of his presence—the young man realized that fortune had smiled on him.

Shortly after the project team had dispersed from the picnic table, Michael pursued Kate DeCarreau through the quad.

"Kate," he eagerly smiled, coming up along side the attractive cadet and matching her gate.

Kate glanced at him briefly and asked, "Which project are you here to talk about?"

"What do you mean?"

"Well," she began, continuing to walk, "Is it the *Applied Sciences* project?—or the one where you try to get me to go out with you?"

"Why can't it be both?" Michael shrugged, enjoying the opportunity to gaze upon her.

"Because only one will get you a favorable response. I'll let you figure out which."

"I can't understand it," the young man replied. "It's been a year since we first met, and you know me well enough by now. Why won't you go out with me on a harmless date?"

"Maybe it has nothing to do with you," Kate mused, looking ahead and walking. "Maybe I'm too busy with school and work study programs. Maybe I'm not interested in seeing anyone right now. It could be so many things that have *nothing* to do with you."

"Is that what it is?"

Kate stopped abruptly, turning toward him. Putting one hand on her hip and staring him down sharply, she replied, "Maybe it has *everything* to do with you." Huffing, the young woman pointed back to the picnic table in the distance. "You know, that stunt you pulled back there was pretty stupid! You shouldn't have submitted our project idea before getting our input. What's worse, you're taking a big risk giving the professor a red-herring idea." She paused, bobbing her head condescendingly. "I just hope you know what you're doing, because I need the grade."

Bearing up under her reproachful gaze, Michael's confidence evaporated. His shoulders sank and his head dropped in defeat.

Upon realizing how easily she had cowed him, Kate relented. Her stance relaxed, and she looked down at the ground uneasily before gazing back up at him again. "Let's just get through this project— through the term. Let's not complicate it, okay?"

Kara Ricci, garbed in a very casual slacks and tank top combination, went about in her socks, tidying up the living room area of her dorm room. As a cadet advisor, the twenty-two-year-old female enjoyed the privilege of rooming alone, which also meant that the mess she was cleaning up was all hers too. Having made much progress, the senior began putting out snacks for the evening: one oversized bowl of popcorn, among other things.

Upon hearing a knock at the door, the young woman's blue eyes lit up. She went for the door but then veered off to first primp herself in the mirror. Staring at the reflection, she straightened her outfit nervously, wondering if the tank top she wore was too revealing. Coming to the inescapable conclusion, Kara pulled on a light, terry roundneck jacket hanging from a wall hook, fussing to get it just right. Finally combing her long, auburn hair through her fingers one last time, she sighed, gathering herself, and reached for the doorknob.

"You're late, Mike!" Kara called enthusiastically while opening the door—

Her eager expression evaporated. Standing before her was not only Michael Gillen, but also his newfound shadow, Tom Andrews.

"...and Tom," she smiled awkwardly, attempting a recovery. Andrews appeared a little uncomfortable at her reaction, though Michael remained completely oblivious.

"Do you mind?" Michael asked, making his way into the room while adjusting his uniform for comfort. "Tom and I were working on our *Applied Science* project. I asked him to tag along."

"*Ahhh* ... not at all...," Kara replied while waving politely for Tom to enter. Following behind him, she pulled the terry jacket closely around her and added, "Not a very exciting night. We were just going to watch the presidential debates."

The two young men settled themselves into the living room in front of the television; Tom took the chair in the corner while Michael sat on the couch. Continuing to play the host, Kara watched from the kitchen area as they conversed. She was happy to see the two becoming friends; Tom was a nice enough person—just a very unexpected guest.

After getting everyone drinks, Kara sat down on the couch. She wrapped her legs underneath her, leaning in toward the popcorn bowl separating her and Michael.

The televised debates were already in progress.

"I can't believe it," Kara laughed, taking a handful of popcorn while handing the bowl to Tom. "Ten minutes into the debate, and Senator Mitchell is already ranting about the Europan threat."

"He's going to lose," Tom replied. "People in Earth States don't care about Europa. It's just an obscure place in the Outer Rim."

Michael looked over at Andrews, taking in the comment. Tom rarely offered an opinion not laced with humor. The somewhat gangly framed cadet with brownish-black hair chose a more casual personality, which Michael found refreshing. So many cadets on campus were unnaturally driven to succeed. Tom, on the other hand, went about every day as if it were the weekend yet still managed to keep up.

"I don't know about that," Michael countered. "Since Aurelian Galerius came to power just over a year ago, the Europans have already annexed Ganymede—like the Pallas Treaty was never signed."

"Blame that on the Mars Republics," Kara added. "Those Martians have spines like noodles. It doesn't matter, though. Earth States will never get involved in the squabbles in the Outer Rim. Let's face it: We may be all gung-ho military here on campus, but most of the country is small town and civilian. No one will support sending our troops so far away."

The three continued watching the debates, though mostly just enjoying a leisurely evening. Kara, eventually becoming bored, began provoking Michael on various and trivial matters, seeking a laugh at his expense. Michael retaliated. Soon, flying popcorn frequently volleyed back at forth between them. Kara became almost giddy.

From his chair, Tom attempted to ignore the ruckus—to no avail. He squirmed uncomfortably while keeping his eyes trained on the television. However, it soon became clear to him that the two were deeply preoccupied with each other; he was a fifth wheel that evening.

At one point upon which the two were almost wrestling (because Kara had become pejorative about Michael's fixation with his hair), Tom finally asked, "So how long have you two been dating?"

The ruckus abruptly stopped. Kara and Michael sat in silence for an awkward moment.

"What do you mean?" Michael asked quizzically.

"You two seem really close, and you know a lot about each other. I just *figured*"—his head bobbed about beseechingly.

"We're just friends," Michael replied dismissively, not even noticing Kara's perturbed grimace. "Kara knows a lot about me because she stayed at my family's lake house this summer."

Kara laughed awkwardly, trying to recover. "I had to, Mike. Out of all the cadets in my advisory group, you're my biggest problem child. I had to keep an eye on you." Then she turned toward Tom. "No, we're *definitely* not dating." A smug look came over her face. "Michael's already spoken for."

Michael squirmed uncomfortably, the reaction easily noticed by his antagonist.

"I forgot to tell you, Mike," Kara sarcastically began, reaching into the popcorn bowl. "She lives on this floor now. If you want, I can take you to her room so she can shoot you down again." Giggling, she turned toward Andrews. "Tom, have you ever seen Mike get shot down? It's rather funny."

"That's okay," Michael huffed, eager to get off the subject.

Kara became relentless, more serious too. "You know, Mike, I can't understand why you're wasting your time on her. She obviously doesn't like you."

Michael rolled his eyes in response.

"I'm *serious*.... It's been a year, and—nothing!" Then she turned to Tom, who was obviously and uncomfortably out of the loop on the subject. "His brother told me how he used to date one bubblehead after the other back in high school. Now, he worships this *one* girl from afar." She gazed back at Michael chidingly. "It's not healthy."

"This one's special," Michael retorted uncomfortably, completely missing Kara's disapproving and somewhat frustrated gaze. "I can wait. Besides, I'm making progress."

"Do you mean like the progress you're making on securing your slot in DSEP?" Kara laughed. "After what happened last year, they're just looking for you to screw up."

"As a matter of fact, that's going well too," Michael countered, finding himself at a loss over her disapproving expression. Despite all attempts to convey a light sense of humor, Kara was visibly annoyed at him. Somehow, he had touched a nerve. "Tom and I are working on a dynamite project for *Applied Sciences* class. It's going to be an easy *A* and a notch on my belt for the leadership program."

"Yeah, I already heard about it the first time you told me," Kara exclaimed dryly. "But you didn't tell me you're up against Gabriel Burke. I had to find that out on my own." She took another handful of popcorn. "Don't underestimate him, Mike. He's not just looking to graduate top in his class: He's trying to secure a spot on the NSEA team.... Gabriel Burke *always* manages to pull out a win."

"*Gabriel Burke!*" Michael mocked. "I hate that guy.... *Gabriel*.... What kind of name is *Gabriel?*"

"It just so happens to be the name of an archangel," Tom replied, though quickly realizing Michael wasn't looking for an answer.

"That's stupid," Michael declared.

Kara looked at him squarely, astonished at his ignorance. "...Just like *Michael* is the name of an archangel." She laughed again, smirking. "You're such a butthead."

Kara Ricci and Kate DeCarreau sat in the crowded bleachers, watching the two football teams square off against each other. With the game between downs, each team huddled on their side of the line of scrimmage.

The university marching band played an upbeat pep song from the bleachers, while cheerleaders on both sides of the field led the crowd in a traditional cheer. Though Earth States found themselves down by a field goal, the lively crowd remained upbeat. After all, the early October game was only in its second quarter.

"This is great," Kate exclaimed just as the two teams lined up. "I wish I had come to one of these games sooner."

"I'm glad I invited you," Kara replied. Earth States snapped the ball, rushing only two yards. "But what did you do with all your spare time last year?"

"I didn't have any spare time last year—too much time in work-study."

Kara smiled and shook her head. "I understand that. I lucked out: My work-study is part of my normal degree. I work twenty hours a week at the local hospital as a medical intern—an advanced co-op that DSEP sponsors. I get paid while working my way to becoming a doctor." She paused, watching the action on the field. "So how are you getting along this year?"

"Not as bad as last year, but it's still been tough," Kate sighed and leaned in toward Kara. "I get so envious of students whose parents are paying their way. My grandmother donated her whole estate to my education, but I still have to put in a lot of hours of work-study just to stay afloat."

"Your social life must be dismal."

At that point, Earth States offense passed the ball for fifteen yards, gaining the first down and moving into the visitor's territory. The stands erupted into loud cheering, while the band did their thing.

"That's the way I want it," Kate sighed again. "Men are always trouble anyway." She paused, discreetly gesturing for Kara to look in the direction where Michael Gillen sat. He was far down on the opposite side of the bleachers with Tom Andrews, completely preoccupied with the game. "Especially him...." Another pause. "I know you two are friends. I'm sure you were wondering." Upon watching Kara nod, she asked, "Did you invite me here because of him?"

Kara shook her head back and forth considerately. "No." She smiled coyly. "I just figured that anyone having the sense to turn him down must be someone worth getting to know." The cadet laughed.

However, DeCarreau's attention lingered in Michael's direction. Kara, realizing she had seen the preoccupied gaze many times during the game already, smiled. Her eyes brightened too. "You *like* him, don't you?"

Though Kate's return expression was as good as a confession, the cadet shook her head dismissively. "That's not good enough…. He's too much trouble. And I need to keep focused on my education—make sure my grandmother would have been proud."

"That's noble," Kara smiled. "Most cadets are here for their own self-interest."

"She died last year—the only family I had." Upon seeing Ricci gesture for her to continue, Kate added, "When I was eight, my mother became terminally ill. I guess the illness was too much for my father, because he abandoned us." The young woman turned pensive, and the brightness faded from her eyes. "I never saw him again…. We lost everything, so my grandmother took us in. Soon after, my mother died…. My grandmother always felt bad that her son had abandoned me, so she did everything she could to give me a normal life…. That's why I'm here."

"Wow," Kara remarked sympathetically while bowing her head. "I guess we have something in common. I'm on my own, too—a foster child my whole life. My mother abandoned me when I was little…. I moved from family to family but never found anyone who wanted to adopt me."

Once again, Earth States' offense made a first down.

After the noise died down, Kara continued, "When I was a senior in high school, I was taken in by this really old, rich woman. She wasn't the parenting type—I think it was her idea of charity. She saw my grades and decided to pay for my tuition…. She died too, but we were never close." Then she smiled. "But her money came in handy."

A little overwhelmed by the exchange, the two female cadets turned their attention back to the game. Earth States' offense continued to drive down the field. Finally, Kara turned once more to Kate. "Kate, are you sure this is all about your grandmother? Maybe you're afraid of getting hurt."

Kate paused reflectively, looking down to the far side of the bleachers once more. "I don't know…. But he's trouble, and I don't need that. Besides, can you really say that this is the right place to get involved with someone? I mean … what about you? Have you met anyone here that's really worth the risk?"

"Well," Kara began, looking down and nervously playing with her fingers. "There's this *one* guy I kind of like." She shook her head side to side. "But I don't think he's interested—has too many other things on his mind." She looked back up at Kate. "I don't know…. It's just so difficult being attracted to someone and waiting for him to make the first move. I hate being proper." She paused. "But maybe we have the same problem…. Maybe both of us need to learn to take some risks."

Suddenly, the crowd came to their feet! Gambling everything on a long forth down, the Earth States' quarterback rocketed the ball deep as the receiver raced toward the end zone. With coverage nipping at his heels, the receiver went up and snatched the ball from the air. Unfortunately, the oblong ball bobbled in his hands until finally spilling out. The defensive safety, being in the right place at the right time, neatly tucked the falling ball to his chest and came down with an interception.

———————————————————————

The *Applied Sciences* classroom was brimming with anticipation. With the project competition demonstrations upon them, the five teams of cadets huddled in various parts of the classroom, eagerly and nervously awaiting their appointed times. Draped demonstration materials sat in the center of each group, and the cadets exchanged curious glances at each other's hidden projects.

The Gillen team relaxed in their chairs near the center of the room, eagerly waiting to demonstrate the navigational field generator prototype sitting covered before them. Being so confident in the prototype's success, Michael had actually asked the professor to go last.

Professor Elizabeth Fierro walked into the room, followed by the five senior science faculty leaders invited to witness the demonstrations. The thirty-something, *Applied Sciences* instructor carried herself with the unwavering confidence typical of any senior-level professor.

"Good morning everyone," Fierro greeted the class. "I can't wait to see your demonstrations today." Fierro gestured toward a very smug-looking Gabriel Burke. "Mr. Burke has requested that his team go first. If there aren't any objections … Mr. Burke, please have your team take the floor."

Michael, feeling rather smug himself, watched Burke's team carry a sizeable, draped object to the oversized desk at the front of the class. With his team standing ready to the side, Burke addressed the class.

"Despite tremendous improvements in technology," the senior cadet began, "Interplanetary travel still poses significant risks." He paused for effect. "With this in mind, we propose enhancements to a very standard piece of interplanetary travel equipment…."

A round of impressed gasps went up across the room—students and faculty alike—as Burke's team unveiled their demonstration. However, Michael sat in his chair, horrified and dumbfounded—all the while watching his team glare vehemently back at him!

Burke gestured toward the device and announced, "The standard navigational field generator."

"But our generator is better!" a fuming Michael Gillen protested, his blue eyes sharp with indignation. "Burke's is a cheap knock-off. He obviously cheated."

Gabriel Burke stood his ground before Professor Fierro. "My team *delivered* the project idea that we *submitted*. Gillen didn't. Those were the rules."

Once again, the room exploded into confusion as both teams pleaded their case.

Kate DeCarreau stood nervously among her fellow team members in Fierro's office, watching Michael appeal the failing grade she and the rest of his team had received.

She was furious with him. Certainly, Burke had somehow stolen Michael's idea, for Burke's prototype *was* a cheap knockoff in comparison to Michael's brilliant masterpiece. That was clear just by looking at the two devices sitting on the professor's desk. Nevertheless, Michael had acted rashly and impertinently by not submitting his intended idea in the first place. His stupid plan to surprise everyone, even the professor, had bombed—just as she and the others had warned him over a month earlier.

"Enough!" Fierro shouted above the din, felling the room silent. She looked at Gillen and Burke standing front and center. "Now as I see it, this issue can be broken down into two components: The first component is whether Mr. Burke and/or his team cheated—or whether *you* stole the idea, Mr. Gillen." She paused. "But from each team's explanation and the final results, all I can see is a similarity of idea; the two devices are actually very different." Fierro surveyed both teams. "So unless someone wants to confess, I can't conclude that *any* cheating occurred."

The room remained silent.

"Okay," Fierro began. "At this point, the Burke team is excused."

Michael sighed heavily as the six opposing cadets depart victoriously: the turn of events didn't bode well for his team.

Then Fierro continued, "The second component of the issue is the original idea submitted by your team, Mr. Gillen. You submitted a different project proposal: a demonstration of different methods of spaceflight navigation."

"But this *does* have to do with spaceflight navigation," Michael countered.

"That's *not* how you explained it to me, and you know it. I was also more than clear that you needed to submit to me the *specific* idea for approval *prior* to beginning the work…. I'm sorry, but I have no choice but to give everyone on the Gillen team a failing grade. The work is more than excellent, so I'll give everyone fifty percent credit."

Michael could feel the frustration and anger rising up from his teammates behind him. Unable to bear their contemptuous stares, he remained facing the professor. "You can't do that."

"Yes, I can. That's the consequences of not following the rules."

"No," Michael countered apologetically, his head dropping and eyes closing briefly. He ran a hand over his face despairingly before looking up at Fierro. "*I mean* … my team didn't know I had submitted a different idea. I purposely misled everyone, including you, to create a bigger impression when we revealed our project. This is all my fault."

Fierro looked at him disapprovingly for a long moment. Then she pointed her index finger at him accusingly. "*That's* what you should have told me when you first came in here."

Michael remained silent under the condemnation.

The professor leaned back in her chair. "Okay, Mr. Gillen, I'll give your teammates seventy percent of the points. That's still the lowest project grade. However, they'll have *you* to thank for dropping them half a letter grade below their potential…. You will receive a zero, and your failure as team leader will go on your permanent record…. Everyone's dismissed."

The cadets began dispersing from the room, while Michael shrank under his peers' condemning stares. He turned to the professor and asked, "Can I take my project now?"

"No," Fierro stated, her tone deadpan. "It's *very* good work. I'm going to submit it on your behalf to some research groups I know; they'll be very interested. I just wish I could give you the academic credit you deserve."

Out in the hallway, Kate—still fuming over what had transpired—met Kara Ricci, who had just arrived.

"I just heard about what happened in *Applied Sciences*," Kara exclaimed with eyes wide. "How'd everything go?"

At this point, Michael squeezed by the two female cadets, saying not a word—not even making eye contact. So they stood in place and watched him walk away.

"Just as I feared," Kate began, still watching Michael in the distance. "I just lost half a letter grade because of him!" Then she turned back to Ricci. "See what I mean, Kara…. He's too reckless."

CHAPTER FIVE

Visitations

NEWSFLASH: Asgard, Callisto (Oct 15, 2500A.D.) –
In less than a single standard day, Callisto has fallen to
invading EuroGan forces. Spurred on by overwhelming
success, Europan and Ganymede forces quickly took
control of the capitol city of Asgard and all military and
industrial activities on the Galilean moon orbiting Jupiter.

Aurelian Galerius, the enigmatic leader of Europa,
immediately welcomed the Callistan people into what
he called the "Family of Europan Excellence."

Once again, the Western Republic of Mars
immediately condemned the invasion, calling on the
Europan forces to halt all further expansionist aggression.
Officials from the Mars Federation, who oversee enforcing
the Pallas Treaty, refused to indicate if they would take
military action against the EuroGans.

Though never considered a significant military
power, Callisto nonetheless is the largest industrial state
in the Jupiter system. Economic experts predict that

the addition of the industrial power into the Europan sphere will enable Galerius to seize control and influence over the entire Jupiter system.

Already, *Weightless* representatives from Elara, including Mos Thieren, are calling on the rest of Solaris to come to their aid, noting Aurelian Galerius' complete contempt for the *Weightless* people.

Michael Gillen made his way down the narrow walkway, not really concerned where he was heading. The early afternoon sun barely peaked through the leafy branches above, the shade made possible by a very late, quickly fading fall foliage season. Already, yellow, red, and brown leaves littered the grounds. Before long, winter would descend mercilessly on the university.

Deep down, the young cadet was already travailing under a *different* kind of winter. The three weeks since his *Applied Sciences* project debacle had gone slowly and torturously. His former teammates, save Tom Andrews, had all but abandoned him. Once word had spread about his failure, no one—*in any of his classes*—would work with him on team projects. The nineteen-year-old lived in an odd sort of exile, isolated in a sea of his own peers.

That's what made campus life so unbearable. Alone with his thoughts, his conscience sought out every opportunity to remind him of his shame. He blamed himself for his impertinence, for letting his team down, letting Burke steal the glory, disappointing Kate, and the like. If he could somehow escape himself, Michael would do it in a heartbeat.

Following the curving path around one of the brownstones, the young cadet spotted Kara in the distance. She was coming toward him, neatly dressed in her Class-B uniform and walking arm in arm with her gentlemanly escort—*David*. The two were engrossed in some light-hearted conversation, and Kara was her typical, bubbly self.

Actually, Kara appeared even more effervescent than normal. Though glad to see his brother, Michael bristled at the sight. During her visit to the Gillen lake house the previous summer, Kara always lit up a little more in David's presence. Michael didn't like the changes in her demeanor—the nineteen-year-old just didn't know why.

"Look who I found wandering around," Kara said to Michael when the three met.

"What are you doing here?" Michael asked, looking at David.

"Can't I see my little brother?"

Kara smiled at David. "Maybe you should stay with me. I'm better company … at least *lately*." After sending a coy look in Michael's direction, Kara exclaimed, "I'm sure you two have some catching up to do." She kissed David on the cheek warmly, lingering there longer than Michael thought proper. "It was nice to see you again, David. Keep in touch." After shooting Michael one last coy look, Kara walked off.

"This is a very nice campus," David remarked as the two began down the path together. He put his hands in his pockets, for the older Gillen was a little underdressed for the weather.

"I'm Glad to see you, but what are you doing here?"

David turned a blunt shoulder toward the direction in which Kara had left. "Kara called me. She was worried about you … told me what happened and insisted that I come."

"That sounds like Kara," Michael chuckled, watching the leaves gently blow over the path in front of him.

"You're lucky to have her for a friend," David exclaimed. "Or is it something more than that?"

"*You two* seemed pretty chummy," Michael countered, his voice a little sharp.

The older Gillen shook his head. "That's what's so interesting: She only gets that way around you. I sense something going on between you two—and not only from her."

"No," Michael grimaced as he walked, looking at his brother as if he had three heads. "We're just good friends."

"I'm not so sure," David replied. "Just make sure you know what you're doing. I don't want to see her get hurt." After suffering under another incredulous gaze, David decided to change the subject. "So what's going on?"

"Nothing … just watching my future career aspirations crumble into pieces."

"Is it just the project?"

"That's a big part of it," Michael sighed, looking to his brother for compassion. "Everyone treats me like a leper now. But worse, last week I had my interim review with the DSEP Placement Committee for next year's slots." He shook his head in disbelief. "They're not sure what to do with me. Academically, it's a slam-dunk. But they also claim I'm undisciplined—not sure I measure up to the high standards of the program. Everything came up: the fights, the arguments in class over the *Weightless*, the project...." After walking a few more steps in silence, he added, "I'm tired of always feeling like I need to prove myself."

"Maybe you need something enduring that defines who you are."

"Is this going to be another religious lecture?" Michael asked, cautioning. "Because I've told you before ... that Jesus stuff's not for me."

"I wish you would listen," David smiled. "You've seen what becoming a Christian has done for me." The two walked a few more steps in silence, the conversation having become awkward. "But I didn't come here to lecture you. Actually, I came to say goodbye."

"What?"

"I finally got the go-ahead from my church: I'm moving to the Outer Rim next week. I'll be living on Elara for two years, helping the disadvantaged *Weightless* there—it's a missionary trip too."

Michael was aghast. Though David had planned such a trip for years, the younger Gillen never thought his older brother was crazy enough to go through with it. After all, Elara was a tiny asteroid moon circling Jupiter—a prominent *Weightless* settlement. "How can you help those mutants?"

David remained unfazed. "Hey, the *Weightless* are human too, no matter what they look like. They need to hear about Jesus Christ just as much as *you*." He smiled coyly. "Maybe they'll even listen."

"Then let Mos Thieren help them," Michael shot back. "That chief mutant is always railing on Great Grandpa—blaming our family for everything that's happened to them. For once, let him do something other than just talk."

He paused, letting his anger subside. Yet the images on the news from the Jupiter system hung uneasily in his mind. Elara lived in the shadows of the rising Europan Empire. With Aurelian Galerius spewing forth hate speech against them, never were the *Weightless* more wary of outsiders—especially a Gillen. "Besides, you could get hurt ... *or killed*."

"I know," David replied soberly—uneasily. "But it's something I have to do."

The answer did not satisfy the younger Gillen's concerns. In fact, David's gaze betrayed his anxiousness over leaving. Michael's face filled with consternation. The cadet huffed, shrugged his shoulders in disbelief, and asked, "David, this is absurd. *What* am I missing here?"

"Mike," David began, stopping and looking him in the eye. "I've already told you a billion times—and you've seen the changes in me to know it's real.... You just don't want to accept it." He paused for a long moment. "No, I'm doing this; I'm going to Elara. I'm willing to give up my whole life to serve Jesus Christ, the One who died for my sins so that I could be forgiven. He's my Lord, and I can be at peace wherever he sends me.... *He's* what *you're* missing."

Michael just shook his head cynically and sighed.

Senior Kara Ricci sat across the small table from Michael Gillen, listening to him spill his guts. The half-eaten pizza in front of them continued getting cold, and her adult beverage was almost empty again. She had barely consumed any of the drinks herself. No, Michael, still just a sophomore, had stolen sips the whole night.

She began worrying about him. Michael wasn't a drinker, even avoiding such frivolities during the New Years celebration, more than four months earlier. Yet the glass was to his mouth again. Looking at him taking another generous sip, she thought his behavior was setting a bad precedent for the twenty-sixth century.

The young female cadet happily engaged her companion in conversation, though looking up nervously every time the bar's door opened. Michael, never recovering from his *Applied Sciences* debacle five month earlier, had become rather aloof—even toward her. So forgoing an opportunity to get away on spring break, Kara spent the time attempting to bring Michael out of the gutter. This night was part of that mission. In addition, the evening was a chance to get away from the military rigor of the university; it was simply a leisurely night across town in street clothes and without a care in the world. Kara could let her hair down—*literally.*

There were other things to accomplish this evening too.

However, tiring of Michael's wallowing and hoping to lighten up the conversation, Kara interjected, "Remember the first time we came here?" she laughed. "Almost two years ago for that stupid mixer." She shook her head. "I don't know what I was thinking."

"Do you know that came up with the DSEP Placement Committee?" Michael asked, his tone more serious than what Kara had intended. "Caffry actually took the time back then to record the incident in my records, noting how he thought I was lying."

"You were," Kara laughed, still trying to keep things light. "A 'PT run', I think you told him." She laughed again. "You did it for me...." She smiled endearingly. "Michael the archangel, always coming to my rescue—always acting like a butthead!" Then Kara laughed hard.

"That's me," Michael sighed, staring down at his glass of soda. "I'm screwing up everything. I still can't find cadets willing to work with me—other than Tom—so half the team assignments I end up doing by myself. That makes it really hard to keep up."

"At least you've kept out of trouble since then—no new discipline problems or demerits."

Michael stole another generous sip of her beverage and laid his chin on his hands, sulking. "I don't think it's enough. My grades are the only thing keeping me competitive in the DSEP selection process.... I don't think I'm going to make the cut." After a long, thoughtful pause, Michael added, "I wish David were here."

Kara placed her hand over Michael's wrist compassionately, realizing just how much her friend was despairing. She said nothing. In fact, his despair became hers too, remembering how Michael's romantic notions of deep space exploration had sparked her own love of the idea. Yes, Michael had turned her simple career choice into a glorious calling! The thought that he might not qualify for the program, though unthinkable in her mind, filled her with sadness.

However, the longer she consoled him, the more she pondered his despair—and all the alcohol he had imbibed—the more the twenty-two-year-old waxed anxious. Abruptly, she exclaimed, "Mike, let's get out of here."

"But Tom's supposed to show up any—"

"Don't worry about that," Kara replied, nervously gathering her things—

The sound of the bar door opening struck the air, causing the female cadet's head to fall in frustration. In response, Michael turned, catching Tom Andrews swagger through the door and toward the table. That's when Michael's face went pale: following right behind Tom was Kate DeCarreau—arm in arm with Gabriel Burke!

Burke escorted the very alluring DeCarreau to the far side of the bar, followed by a couple of his close friends. Michael fumed the whole time, finding no words to express his angst. No, he was completely beside himself, and Kara's guilty expression only made things worse.

Though Tom sat down, Kara motioned to leave. However, Michael remained firmly planted in his chair, resentfully looking across the room where Burke and DeCarreau sat. Reluctantly, Kara sat back down.

Though first oblivious to the tension, Tom soon noticed Michael's indignant preoccupation and the pseudo-silent treatment his friend imposed on Kara. *Why do I even get together with these two?* Tom asked himself.

The evening proceeded tenuously.

A short time later, Kate DeCarreau came to stand in front of the bar's jukebox, carefully selecting music for the evening while Burke ordered food and drinks at the counter.

"I didn't think you had time to date," she heard Michael say from behind her. He sidled up next to her and surveyed the music selection too, appearing intentionally indifferent at her presence.

"Maybe I found the time," Kate replied dryly, still looking at the selection display.

"But *Burke?*"

"He's a real gentleman," Kate said as if still trying to ignore him, "and he has a lot going for him too…. I remember him submitting a dynamite project in *Applied Sciences*—got the highest grade. For some reason, I didn't do quite as well."

Michael fumed, gently pulling her around by the forearm so that she looked him in the eye. "If you're trying to set me off, it's working! Did you arrange this with Kara?"

"I'm just trying to move on," Kate exclaimed curtly. However, standing so close to him, the touch of his hand upon her arm and his eyes searching her out, the young female couldn't feel more self-conscious. Yet mustering a terse stare, she added, "I told you from the beginning to leave me alone … *please*.…"

As she stared him down reproachfully, Michael found her gaze hollow, put on. Eventually, the veneered expression cracked altogether, and the young woman became more vulnerable than ever. With the utmost confidence, he exclaimed, "I still don't believe it."

Kate fell silent, anxiously returning his penetrating gaze.

"I guess they'll let anyone in here nowadays," a familiar voice came from behind Michael.

Michael turned to face Gabriel Burke and his smug expression. Kara, having not noticed Burke approaching Michael until too late, was already making a beeline toward the standoff.

"Burke, go away," Kara exclaimed, putting herself between the two male cadets.

"Lighten up, Kara," Burke replied with a foreboding sharpness in his voice. "We're just celebrating. I met with some people at NSEA today. I've been accepted into their program."

"I guess they'll let anyone in NSEA nowadays," Michael postured.

"Not everyone, especially not you. I made sure of that."

"What do you mean?" Michael demanded, his eyes glaring at the senior while moving threateningly closer. Burke's friends, having spotted the discord from their table, moved into the periphery of the discussion, causing Tom Andrews to sidle up nervously behind Michael.

Kara caught Michael's weight against her, stopping the young cadet's forward progress. "He's just goading you, Mike. Let's get out of here."

"They wanted to know if I had any suggestions about their program," the senior sneered. "So we had a nice, long talk … about *you*…. Let's just say you should find another career." He glared at Michael resolutely. "Of course, I had no trouble convincing them. All I had to do was mention the name *Gillen* … that about says—"

Michael waylaid him hard! Burke took the blow, falling back violently into his companions. Steadied by his friends, Burke immediately charged Michael. With Tom Andrews jumping to Michael's defense, Kate and Kara found themselves swallowed up in the brawl. The whole bar erupted into chaos!

"*Under age drinking and disorderly conduct*!?" President Caffry shouted, standing almost nose to nose in his office with a very rigid

Michael Gillen. The aging man's eyes were narrow and his face like flint. "What were you thinking?"

Michael kept silently at attention for a long moment. Though his face flaunted a sizeable bruise to one cheek and a nasty cut to his lip, the cadet was actually in a fair amount of pain all over. Eventually, he eked out, "I wasn't, Sir. I'm sorry."

"I should throw you out of the university right now!" Caffry exclaimed, turning and throwing the police report on his desk. "You've taken your axe-grinding off campus and completely embarrassed the academy—an entire bar in ruins! Do you know how much time and money it takes to pacify a disgruntled local businessman?"

"No, Sir. But I'll make amends. The university shouldn't have to pay for my mistake."

"That's what Mr. Burke said too," the old man replied. He sighed, letting his body relax while easing into his chair. "At ease...." Another long pause. "Gillen, I'm not your enemy.... I find no *joy* in bringing you in here like this. In fact, we've invested a lot of time in you with the preliminary DSEP evaluations. We want you to succeed because your actual work is exemplary."

After another pause, Caffry continued, "But you seem bent on self-destructing, and you want to take Burke with you—I'm not excusing his behavior either, rest assured.... I know you've had some problems to deal with lately.... We've talked about them...." He paused tellingly. "But the time for talking is over. I can't kick you out of here for a single, off-campus offense—though you will have to deal with the authorities on your own."

The old man picked up another folder. "I also can't speak for the entire DSEP Placement Committee, although they take stock in my opinions.... As far as I'm concerned, it will take a miracle for you to get a slot in next year's program." Caffry looked him straight in the eye. "Start choosing another career, because the deep space program won't be an option."

A lazy Saturday night, Michael Gillen cynically thought. Having just come from the showers up the hall, the young man stood dressed in nothing but a large, blue towel wrapped around his waist. His dorm mates had just left for the remainder of the weekend, allowing him to do whatever he pleased. So he opened the refrigerator, grabbed a beverage, and began drinking it.

He could be completely relaxed, much to his chagrin. Unlike the other DSEP candidates pining over their applications for the next week, *Michael could be completely relaxed*: no more worrying about making the cut, no more counting off the days until the slot assignments were announced—not for him! No, Caffry had given him special insight over two weeks earlier, the day of the bar brawl. Though not being an official response, the message was clear: *Don't count on it!*

Instead, the almost twenty-year-old cadet was more than free to spend another night wallowing in his own misfortune. *Why even get dressed?* he thought.

A knock at the door broke the silence, and Michael sighed heavily. Surely, his absentminded roommate had forgotten something for his trip.

"*Cuddy*," Michael called out, beginning to open the door, "Don't you ever remember your keys?"

Much to the cadet's surprise, standing in the doorway were President Caffry and Kara Ricci. Both were dressed casually. Neither said a word at first, being a little taken back by Michael's lack of clothing.

"I guess I'm out of uniform," Michael remarked in a dry, sardonic fashion.

Caffry remained stoic. Worse, Kara remained deadpan as well, unsettling the young cadet. Kara, in particular, gazed at him with sad empathy, her expression almost painful. *Maybe Caffry's decided he'll kick me out after all*, Michael thought.

"Cadet Gillen," the old man greeted him. "Can we come in?"

"Sure," Michael gestured. "Have a seat in the living room. I'll be back."

After quickly dressing, Michael sat on the couch facing Caffry. Though Michael had preferred to stand, the old man had insisted that he sit. Kara sat next to him on the couch, remaining unnervingly quiet and still wearing a grave expression.

Looking at Michael, the old man folded his hands and leaned toward him.

"Cadet Gillen—*Michael*," Caffry offered soberly, "I spoke to your father a little while ago. Though he will contact you personally, he also wanted you to hear this directly—not through a communication. As well, I asked Cadet Ricci to accompany me here since she's still your cadet advisor."

While the old man paused, Michael swallowed hard. His father, displeased with the bar fight, had threatened to revoke his status at the university. Watching Kara begin to well up, he realized Caffry had come to notify him of his father's decision. *This is it*, he thought.

Caffry continued, "Your brother David has been killed.... I'm sorry."

Michael went strangely cold, and he soon felt Kara's hand sympathetically alight upon his shoulder.

"That can't be," Michael shook his head in disbelief, having David's visit six months earlier still fresh in his mind.

"It's true, Mike," Kara reluctantly added, unsuccessfully fighting back a few tears. "I saw the report myself.... *I'm so sorry*."

A dreadful darkness seemed to fall over the young man. "*How?*"

"No one knows for sure," Caffry gently began. "The official report from Elara says David's death was an accident." He paused cautiously. "But the authorities have found evidence that some *Weightless* sympathizers were involved. Evidence is sketchy—always is in these cases. David had used an assumed named to protect himself, but they think some locals had recently discovered his real identity. Our government is sure it was an assassination, though they won't call it out publicly.... I'm very sorry, son."

"I'm sorry too," Kara once again added.

Caffry continued, "The incident took place a couple of days ago. Your brother's body is already being transported to Earth for the funeral. It should arrive in about ten days. When you're ready, come to the administration building. We'll hook you up with a transport immediately." Then he paused. "Don't worry about your studies. Since it's already May, there's too little time left in the semester anyway. Just go home and be with your family. I'll make sure your grades get prorated, if that's what you desire."

"Thank you, Sir."

Caffry stood up, adding, "If you need anything, you know where to find me." Then the old man headed toward the door. With Kara accompanying him, the two whispered with each other at the door. All the while, Michael sat on the couch, leaning forward with his hands folded and staring blankly ahead.

When Caffry had gone, Kara reluctantly sat down once again next to Michael. At a loss for words, she instead stroked his back sympathetically, fighting back her own tears.

With each passing moment, Michael spiraled down into his own despair. *His brother was gone.* The young man became almost comatose, while a thousand grim thoughts raced through his mind. The air in his chest went cold. As if losing his breath, his chest heaved twice before he could catch himself, and his face filled with angst. "I can't believe he's gone.... I told him to stay home."

"He was really a good guy," Kara said, watching her friend begin falling apart. She anxiously brought her hand up over her mouth as she felt herself being drawn into his despair. Her eyes welled up even more.

Michael's face twisted painfully. He rocked back and forth, unsure of himself. Sadness swelled within him mercilessly—as if tearing him to pieces—and his chest heaved uncontrollably. "I told ... *I told him not to go!*" Then Michael abruptly collapsed onto Kara's lap, weeping uncontrollably.

Kara finally broke down completely, her own sense of loss imposing itself on her. Days at the Gillen lake house the previous summer filled her thoughts, making her realize just how fond of David she had become.

But worse than anything, Michael lay collapsed before her in despair. Wrapping his arms tightly around her legs as he wept, the young man held on to her for dear life and would not let go.

The bright morning sun coming in through the window reflected off the white ceiling, accosting sleeping eyes rudely. Kara Ricci, a thick fog covering her mind, stared up at the brilliant surface while coming to life. She reckoned she must have slipped into bed quickly the previous night and had forgotten to close the blinds.

But as the cobwebs began to clear, the young woman realized that the ceiling was particularly unfamiliar, as was also the steep wall just at her head. For that matter, so was the pillow and mattress beneath her—*and where were her clothes?* The bed covers draped over her were the only things she was wearing.

Suddenly, everything came back to her.

Kara shot straight up, keeping a sheet over herself with one hand. Nervously, she called out, "Mike?"

No answer came back. The room and adjoining rooms remained completely still. Michael was gone, and her clothes lay heaped in a pile near the bed. Kara sighed, nervously wondering where he had gone. *How did this happen?* she thought.

But she knew full well.

Memories of the previous night flooded her thoughts. Somehow and very much unexplainably—deep in the despair and travail of mourning over David's death—she had kissed Michael, kissed him long and hard. The impulse was unintentional, certainly brought on by the intense moments they had shared. Nevertheless, the kiss felt good—it felt great! Having longed for the moment, her embarrassment before him would be a worthy price to pay for the fleeting pleasure.

But then, Michael looked at her with a gaze she had never beheld from him. That's when he unexpectedly reciprocated, kissing her again, just as long and just as hard. Her heart melted under his embrace, and every pining desire for him—suppressed far too long—came upon her as a flood. All reason and caution fled at the taste of his lips and the euphoria of being held in his arms.

Somewhere in those first few, powerful moments, they found themselves swept away by a glorious and newfound passion: a desire expressed, a willingness conveyed, a mutual consenting; all without words. So with reckless abandon, she gave herself to him.

But where was he *now?*

Sitting on the bed and waiting for Michael to appear, Kara wrestled with all the mixed emotions the night had engendered. For certain, there was the shame of what she had done, and she smarted at the thought of becoming one of *those*. After all, the rigid and moral society she found herself a part of looked down on such imprudence. Her chance to remain chaste until marriage had sadly vanished, and the thought of anyone finding out about her indiscretion filled her with dread.

Yet at the same time, Michael had *finally* realized his true feelings for her. After years of pining for him secretly and hoping he would come around, she had finally spent hours in his arms, swooning under his doting affection; wonderful days of being in love together awaited them.

Michael was finally hers, making the impulsiveness worth the price.

Continuing to bask in the memories of the previous night, Kara remained propped up by her arm. When she adjusted herself on the bed, her hand inadvertently slid under the sheet. That's when she felt a sharp, unexpected stabbing at one of the fingers. Quickly bringing the injured hand to her mouth to console, dislodging the sheet from its place—she saw a small note pinned to the mattress cover. Written in Michael's familiar handwriting were the words, *I'm Sorry*.

Her shoulders sank and the sparkle in her blue eyes faded.

Kara stared at the note vacantly, reading it repeatedly while her eyes welled up. Suddenly overwhelmed by a thousand dreadful feelings, the young woman let her head fall into her hands.

Chapter Six

Unfortunate Reunion

NEWSFLASH: Phrynia, Titania (May 10, 2501A.D.) – In a stunning turn of events, the socialist government of Titania has pledged allegiance and support to the Europan empire, forming an alliance of trade and mutual protection with the Jovian power. Leaders from both sovereigns announced the alliance to their peoples in a joint news conference held in the capitol city of Phrynia today.

Neither of the two Mars republics offered an opinion or statement on the alliance, though officials in charge of overseeing the Pallas Treaty charged that Europa and Ganymede are still in violation of the terms of that treaty.

In the boldest move yet of any nation in the Outer Rim, Titanian socialist party leaders cited interference of trade by the Mars Federation as the key reason for entering into the alliance. They also charged the two republics with engaging in covert support of antisocialist factions, in an attempt to seat a pro-Mars government on the Uranus moon. The Mars Federation offered no response.

The Europan Empire pledged all necessary resources to expel Inner Rim interests from Titania.

Michael Gillen quietly walked arm in arm with his mother, escorting his parents into the funeral home. The three Gillens, dressed in their best clothes, kept close to one another while moving toward the door in deliberate fashion. The small family—now that much smaller—had remained uneasily silent since leaving the house, and hollow expressions covered their faces.

Michael could sense the reassuring presence of Tom Andrews following closely behind him. Tom, having arrived the previous day as promised, had become a loyal friend of late, always there when Michael needed him. This day was no exception.

The funeral home door swung open, and the director met them at the door.

"Hello, everyone," he greeted in a respectful tone, holding the door until everyone had made it into the foyer. Gesturing for them to follow, the well-dressed man went on ahead. "You'll have an hour before we open our doors for visitors, but let us know if you need more time." Having led the family down the long hall, he stopped at the entrance to the large viewing room. A casket sat at the far end of the room among an array of flowers and ornaments.

Of course, the sight completely unnerved Michael.

At the director's cue, the Gillens reluctantly entered the viewing room. Michael found each step more unbearable than the one before, fighting the urge to turn and leave. He had dreaded this moment since learning of David's death, eleven long days before. The long wait for David's body to return had only compounded his dread.

The open casket grew larger until the four came to stand before the morbid display. No one said a word. Marge Gillen, beginning to weep, received comforting embraces from husband and son.

Michael gazed down at David's lifeless body. David wore his best suit, having his arms folded over his chest and looking as if he were sleeping. But he wasn't sleeping. In fact, with the life gone out of him, David wasn't David. No, whatever lay before him was just some morbid facsimile of his brother. Michael welled up, fighting the urge to break down completely. His thoughts filled with dread over his loss, and the grief consumed him bitterly. All other troubles faded into the ether, and this one thought made him completely inconsolable.

David was gone.

Kara Ricci sat alone at her desk in the quiet dorm room, garbed in sweat pants and socks with a long, unbuttoned sweater draped over her white tee shirt. Her attire was the only thing casual about her, for the twenty-two-year-old cadet was hard at work. With only a few days left until setting off to NSEA for her new career in the astronaut corps, the graduating senior busily finished long-overdue reports required by her position as cadet advisor. Once done, the young woman could then begin the long process of saying goodbye to Earth States Military Academy, the place the former foster child had called home for the last four years.

She was more than happy to be busy, having filled the last twelve long days with whatever preoccupation she could find. The hard work kept the painful thoughts at bay—kept her eyes dry.

Her reader projected a half-meter square display into the air above the desk. The file on the screen was one of the cadets in her advisory group. The picture of the young female underclassman, smartly clad in her dress blues, displayed on the right while the bio data hovered in the top left. Kara's final evaluation floated just below it.

Kara scrolled through the entire evaluation, quickly editing it. Once satisfied that her evaluation was thorough, she hit the submit button. *On to the next candidate*, she thought, bringing up the next file. While the file loaded, she crossed her left leg up onto the chair underneath her right, effectively letting her left foot hang off the side of the chair.

Looking up at the new data, Kara's eager expression fell. Her blue eyes, now devoid of their natural glimmer, remained helplessly fixed on the screen. As she gazed desperately at the image, her left foot began to quiver nervously; the fingers of one hand commenced furrowing her thick, auburn hair awkwardly.

The picture hovering to the right was Michael's.

She gazed at his beautiful face for a long time, just as she had done so many times over the last two years. She even touched the projection with her finger as if caressing his cheek, causing the pixels to scatter momentarily.

Michael might have recoiled at her calling him *beautiful*—he would have much preferred the word *handsome*. But to her, he *was* beautiful; he was a beautiful person. Michael had given meaning to her disappointing life; he had become her purpose. Even with everything that had happened between them, he was still beautiful. She still longed for him.

But that's all the young female could do: long for him. He hadn't called—not once since leaving twelve days earlier. Her phone remained hauntingly silent and her message box empty. Not that she didn't understand Michael's situation—certainly, she did. But after their last night together ... what they had shared ... *nothing*?

Kara hated him—hated herself too!

Shame overwhelmed her for what she had let happen—but indignation over what Michael had taken from her. She felt less of a woman now, scarred by his fickleness. The sweetness of his embrace and the exotic fare of his touch had soured in her stomach. For in her haste to secure his affections, she had instead given herself over to his despairing cravings. She had gambled and lost.

Michael didn't desire her, at least not in the way she needed him to desire her.

As if to add to her own despair, Kara worked the reader, frantically searching until Kate DeCarreau's picture hovered in the air to the left of Michael's.

Kara stared at the striking, young female's picture for just as long, self-doubt filling her the whole time. Kate had become a close and loyal friend, something of a luxury for Kara. Yet Michael's desire for Kate was a constant reminder of her own inadequacy, and she envied Kate deeply.

But more than anything, Kara despaired over what she had become. She despaired over all her plotting, keeping Kate just out of Michael's reach. Not that DeCarreau didn't have her own misgivings about Michael—certainly, she did. Yet Kara had availed herself of all opportunities at hand, keeping Michael away while fueling Kate's doubts—all for an opportunity that wasn't meant to be. The unfortunate night at the bar over three weeks earlier, when Michael had fought Burke—losing his slot in the deep space program too—had been her *coup d'état*, regrettably.

Kara stared at the two pictures for quite a long time. Her eyes welled up, and her expression twisted. She hated herself for what she had done, for the jealousy and manipulation.

And what she desired with Michael ... that was just an illusion, created by her own desperate desire to be loved. She knew about illusions; Kara had chased them her whole life, from one foster family to the next. She was chasing meaninglessness; *Michael didn't love her*. She could either continue chasing the illusion or move on. But did she love Michael *enough* to move on?

After pausing for a long moment, Kara wiped the tears from her eyes and cleaned herself up. Soon, the female cadet found herself standing uneasily at the other end of dorm hall, knocking on the door in front of her.

"Kara?" Kate greeted her upon opening the door. "What's up?"

"Can I come in?"

"Sure," Kate smiled, gesturing for Kara to enter. The two made their way into the living room, which was awash in the soft tones of music playing in the background. Kara looked around before sitting down—oddly enough—on the floor in front of the couch. No one else appeared to be around.

Kate closed the reader sitting on the couch, causing the schoolwork hovering in the air to dissipate. She joined her friend on the floor, noticing Kara's drawn face and puffy eyes. "You look terrible. Is something wrong?"

"Well...," Kara began hesitantly, wishing Kate would not have asked. "Remember that guy I told you about a long time ago? The one I was *sort of* seeing?"

"Still too many other things on his mind?" Kate sympathetically asked, recounting their conversations. Of course, Kara had never revealed the person's name, so the guy was barely a shadow in Kate's mind.

Kara partially welled up, letting her chin drop while shaking her head sullenly. "No...." she laughed awkwardly, still averting her eyes. "He finally gave me his full attention."

"Let me guess, you found out he's a real jerk, right?"

"No," Kara sighed. "—well, he *is* a jerk!" She paused for a long moment, becoming pensive and shaking her head again. "But it's just not going to work out. We're both going in two different directions." Another pause. "It's probably for the best. I'm going to NSEA soon anyway. That's my goal."

"I'm still sorry," Kate exclaimed, as sweet as butter.

The senior cadet smiled back appreciatively. "Thanks, but that's not what I came to talk with you about. Actually ... I want to ask you a question."

Michael Gillen stood arm in arm with his mother once more, dressed once again in his best suit and still completely mortified. His father stood close on her other side, allowing the grieving couple to share the tremendous loss while comforting each other.

Michael, however, refused to be comforted. Instead, the young man stood there crushed, as if a mountain had fallen on him.

He took comfort that the gathering was the last step to ending three long days of unbearable ritual. After suffering through the condolences offered by the many visitors to the funeral home, most of whom he had never seen, Michael was relieved that the funeral service was ending. Gathering at the cemetery on a gorgeous spring day, everyone had come to say goodbye to David.

But it wasn't a beautiful day.

David's polished mahogany casket lay tellingly closed in front of the Gillens, resting over top of the open grave on its lowering device. Grass matting surrounded all sides of the casket, and various flowers and ornaments decorated it nicely. David's pastor stood facing them on the opposite side of the casket, holding a Bible in the air and eloquently addressing the small crowd.

However, Michael didn't hear a word the man spoke.

The grieving brother couldn't listen anymore. The man sounded so much like David, making the words too painful to bear. Oh, the pastor *had* talked about David's life as a child and teenager, bringing to mind fond memories that still played warmly in Michael's head.

Nevertheless, young Michael couldn't listen to how much the disadvantaged *Weightless* had benefited from David's sacrifice. The *Weightless* had killed him. It didn't matter that the ones responsible weren't the ones David had helped. No, they were all responsible. He hated the *Weightless*! Hated all of them bitterly! He hated Mos Thieren, their enigmatic leader—the man who unfairly blamed the Gillen family for their problems—that much more!

And he hated the pastor, the man who had sent David to Elara in the first place.

Michael refused to listen to the man bloviate over the greatness of God. He didn't care that God loved the *Weightless* too; he didn't care about some guy dying on a cross so long ago it didn't matter; he didn't care about sin—what was it anyway? He cared not a wit about God's providence—whatever that was—or some silly notion of heaven and some intangible reward. David was dead; that's all he knew. He was gone forever. *His brother was gone!*

No, all this was preventable! If God is so great, why did he let it happen!? If God is so good, why didn't he save David!? No, this was all *His* fault. God was responsible, and Michael hated Him for it. No, for now on, any notions of God were banished from his thoughts. That would teach Him!

Kara Ricci anxiously sat in the center of the small room in front of three long tables laid out in the shape of a U. Ten DSEP Placement Committee members, comprised of university administrators and NSEA directors, had taken up position on the outside of the tables, facing her.

Though having already received admission into the prestigious NSEA astronaut corps, the graduating cadet felt as nervous as ever.

After initial pleasantries, such as congratulating her on her program appointment and trading quips about no more final exams, the committee dove right into their intended purpose.

"Kara, we're deciding which sophomores to place into next year's program slots," Cyril Davidson, NSEA's executive director, began. "We want to ask you a couple of questions to make sure we clearly understand your recommendations, so don't be nervous."

"Yes, Sir," Kara replied. However, the assurance provided the young woman no comfort. Fatefully aware of the true intent of the unexpected meeting, Kara was scared to death.

"We were impressed with your thoroughness," Davidson continued, "and agree with most of your recommendations, including your supplemental recommendation—the one cadet who wasn't in your advisory group."

"Thank you, Sir."

Davidson glanced at the other committee members before fixing his gaze on Kara once again. "But we're at a loss to know why you gave Cadet Michael Gillen such a glowing recommendation."

Kara swallowed hard as ill feelings and self-consciousness washed over her. She didn't know anymore. She didn't even want to think about Michael, the memories of what had happened being too painful to bear. Writing his recommendation, Kara had become detached from herself, for her own feelings about him had become hollow and empty. That was the only way she could keep going. Moreover, the last thing she wanted to do was explain herself to this austere committee.

"Kara, this is a completely confidential discussion," President Caffry interjected. "We just want to understand."

"To be honest, this committee is divided over Cadet Gillen," Davidson smiled, looking around the table. "This is a very eclectic group, with a lot of different views on what comprises the ideal candidate. We aren't sure if he's destined for greatness—or destined for great failure."

Kara leaned forward, somewhat surprised. "So Cadet Gillen hasn't been excluded out of hand?"

"No," Davidson replied, looking at Caffry. "But he's certainly no shoe-in, either. This cadet has many problems.... I guess you could say we're looking for a reason *not* to reject him." He paused thoughtfully. "But more than that, we're a little concerned with your recommendation. Despite being one of our top recruits into NSEA this year, you barely even noted his faults. We want to understand your thinking—not question your judgment."

But to Kara, that was exactly what they were doing: questioning her judgment. And she couldn't help but agree with them, for she had acted foolishly with Michael. However, they were on the other side of the tables; she was out front, subdued under their judging gazes.

"It is true that Cadet Gillen has a history of impulsiveness," Kara offered cautiously, trying to expel the emotional onrush of her own personal experiences—a futile effort. Her left foot began to quiver nervously. Though the young woman was oblivious to it, the committee noticed immediately. "Of course, how many twenty-year-old males are emotionally mature? Just give him time."

Caffry became visibly unsettled. "But this is an issue of trust, Kara. Exploration teams have to gel; they have to rely on each other implicitly with their lives. Can you honestly say that you could entrust yourself to this man?"

Kara paused nervously. "Yes."

"You sounded more convincing in your report," Cyril Davidson remarked sympathetically. "Are you sure?"

Kara remained silent.

"I took a look at your advisor report logs," an older female sitting near the center of the tables remarked, holding the folder up as if to examine. "You spent more than twice the time with him as any of the other cadets in your group. Is your relationship with this cadet more *personal* than your recommendation indicates?"

"Kara, this is confidential," Caffry interjected, noting Kara's mounting nervousness. "I promise: Not a word of this leaves this room."

"Yes," she confessed reluctantly, her eyes betraying her too.

"How personal?"

Kara Ricci, fearfully spellbound by the inquisitive gaze of the committee, watched her worst moment coming upon her. Unable to lie to protect herself, she was about to be humiliated in front of the prestigious board.

"Kara, we have to ask," Davidson assured. "But none of this will impact your placement at NSEA."

The young woman didn't care. The only thing she cared about was leaving with her dignity intact; opening her mouth would not let that happen. Yet they waited patiently, too patiently. Each moment of hesitation became worse than the previous.

"*Very personal,*" Kara finally blurted out, her eyes welling up and her face twisting slightly. Her chin dropped too. "More personal than I would ever want to admit—even in a completely confidential discussion." Helplessly fighting a swell of emotions, Kara searched desperately for some sort of justification, some sort of absolution. However, it was too late, for the committee members looked at each other tellingly. She had been humiliated. "But it isn't personal anymore."

The room went silent while the committee allowed Kara a moment to gather herself.

"From everything I see here," Davidson began, leaning toward her compassionately. "Even *you* aren't convinced that Michael Gillen can overcome his impulsiveness. I know you think we should admit him into the program, but I see no evidence that persuades me to do such a thing…. I'm sorry…. Thank you for your time."

Kara remained seated and silent for a long moment, contemplating Michael Gillen. He *was* impulsive—*reckless*, as Kate DeCarreau would have said. With Michael to blame for everything that had just happened, the embittered, young woman *so* wanted to hurt him, let him pine away at an unrealized dream—just as she would pine for him. Perhaps that would ease her own angst.

"Kara, you can go now," Caffry called, for she was staring at the floor.

That when Kara looked up at them.

"You say you see no evidence to persuade you," she began, mustering her courage. "But it's sitting right here: *me*. You selected me for the astronaut corps *because* of Michael Gillen. The rest of us are just trying to find a career, but Cadet Gillen was born for this. His love of space travel is what made me love it too—made me excel in my work because of how much he excelled in his work. Talk to anyone close to him in the program … they'll tell you the same thing."

She paused self-consciously. "His personal life is a complete mess…. I learned that the hard way…. But in taking the bad with the good, I am who I am today because of Michael Gillen."

She looked around the tables, eyeing up the committee as if looking at all of them at once. "And if I found myself stranded ten light-years from home, the only person I would trust with my life is Michael Gillen.... If the program can't see that, then I don't want to be in the program."

Michael Gillen reluctantly made his way down the dorm hallway, coming to stand in front of an all too familiar door. After hesitating for a long moment, the young cadet took a deep breath before knocking. Too soon for his liking, the sound of the doorknob turning broke the quiet.

"Michael?" Kara exclaimed with surprise, guardedly opening the door just far enough to fit in the gap. She wore her typical around-the-dorm casuals: sweat pants, tee shirt, and a long, draping sweater. Her expression was polite but aloof, even somewhat self-conscious. "I thought you were done for the rest of the year."

Michael, clearly taken back by her wariness, let his eyes avert from her gaze. "No, my parents thought I should come back ... get my mind off of things...."

"Yeah...," Kara smiled sympathetically, averting her own eyes while somewhat nodding her head. "I'm really sorry about what happened to David.... He was a really great guy...."

The two went awkwardly silent for what seemed like an eternity. Finally, Kara piped up apologetically, "Hey, I'd invite you in, but I've got a lot of packing to do. I leave tomorrow for NSEA."

"I *heard* you got in.... Congratulations."

"Thanks...," the young female cadet sheepishly replied with a slight smile and awkward pause. "Burke got in too—I'm sure you hate that." She smiled again.

Once again, they suffered under a long pause.

"I got into next year's DSEP program," Michael exclaimed, trying to fill the silence.

"That's what I hear.... Congratulations."

The young cadet nervously strained at his neck. "I think I got lucky.... They must have felt sorry for me for losing my brother—or something like that.... Decided to give me a second chance, I guess."

"Well, you deserve it," Kara smiled warmly, gazing at him endearingly for the first time. "I know how long you've waited.... I guess anything worth having is worth the wait." She continued smiling at him. When the air went silent once more, Kara took a step back. "I have to pack ... but it's been great seeing you again.... Good luck with DSEP."

Michael reluctantly stepped back as the door began to close. Abruptly, he brought his hand up, stopping the door before it had even closed halfway.

"Kara ... I'm sorry for what happened the night before I left.... I shouldn't—"

"No ... no ... don't apologize," she politely rebuffed. Once again keeping the door close, Kara averted her eyes from him. "It was my fault. I should have never kissed you ... opened Pandora's Box, I guess."

"But I shouldn't have—"

"It was a mistake...," Kara cut him off. "...something stupid." She shrugged, letting her eyelids float. "We were distraught by the bad news—*David was your brother*. You were a wreck, and I should have known better.... I just got caught up in the moment." She looked down at the floor sullenly before gazing back at him. "But I know how you feel about Kate."

Michael let his head fall in defeat, and the two went awkwardly silent once more.

Upon seeing Michael remorseful, Kara put her hand on his shoulder. "And *hey* ... don't worry.... I think Kate's going to come around.... I've got a good feeling about it...." At this, she welled up ever so slightly. That's when she hastily stepped back again. "So just hang in there...."—taking a deep breath—"...I've got to pack."

Once more, the door began to shut, this time quicker and more forcibly. Even more forcibly, Michael jammed it with his foot.

"*Kara....*"

The young woman became mortified, looking down and not saying a word.

"Kara, I'm trying to apologize."

At this, Kara could take no more. Letting the door swing open, she looked at Michael crossly. Putting one hand on her hip, she reached into her sweater pocket with the other and pulled out a tattered slip of paper. Holding it up, Kara chided through tear-filled eyes, "Yeah, I got your note already…. See … '*I'mmm Sorrrry*'!"

Michael stood there, dumbfounded and guilty. Kara walked away in disgust, disappearing into the dorm room but leaving the door open. So he followed, making sure to shut the door behind him.

"You know," Kara began, pointing an index finger at him accusingly while tears floated in her eyes, "I defended you for the past two years! Everyone said you were trouble…. But *I* stuck up for you…. Caffry warned me, but *I* didn't listen…." She paused. "But you know what, Michael? He was right…. You're reckless…. You only think about *yourself*…. You hurt people—you hurt *me*!" After pausing awkwardly, she huffed, "When are you going to grow up and take responsibility for yourself?"

Michael was clearly back on his heels. "I—I never meant to hurt you."

"You did more than that, Michael," Kara exclaimed, coming almost nose to nose and looking him in the eye. "You made me out to be a fool. You took something from me that didn't belong to you."

At this, Kara turned away indignantly. She brought her hands up as if pleading, and her chin quivered. "*I mean* … I know what I did was wrong. I should have never kissed you … and I certainly shouldn't have let things go as far as they did." She paused, shaking her head. "But at least I had sincere feelings for you…. *At least I thought I—*" She stopped herself unexpectedly and paused with such angst. Finally, she composed herself and said, "My feelings *were* sincere."

After a long moment of wallowing, Kara abruptly turned and looked him in the eye—and with such scorn. "But you kissed me back too. You looked back at me … *and the look in your eyes*…." She shook her head in disbelief, yet seeming to savor the bitter memory. Then her face twisted. "You deceived me!"

"I didn't deceive you," Michael pleaded, unable to return her piercing gaze. "I was confused."

"The note says otherwise, Michael. You pretended to have feelings for me."

Michael stood in place, taken back and very hesitant. "I wasn't pretending."

"You were *insincere* … just looking for comfort from your grief. *You used me!*"

"You're wrong!" Michael shouted.

"*Why!?*" Kara probed contemptuously. "*Why am I wrong!?*"

"*Because!*" Michael shouted again, his face twisting! His open hands shot up in front of him pleadingly, fingers grasping desperately at the air while his whole torso shuddered in angst! "*Because I do have feelings for you!*" He paused self-consciously, hoping to let the intensity pass. "I know that now."

However, the intensity didn't pass. The two stared at each other silently for quite a long time, exchanging awkward expressions. Though seeing his embarrassment, the young woman gave him no quarter. Instead, her face churned even more—increasingly so with each passing moment. Finally, Kara held up the tattered apology, her eyes pleading. "Then what's this about, Michael?"

Michael hesitated.

Finally, he sighed and looked away. "I should have listened to David…. He saw it and warned me not to hurt you. When you kissed me—*I don't know*—I finally realized what David was talking about…. I thought that maybe I was kidding myself all this time about Kate…. I got carried away too…. I don't know why. It seemed so right at the time…. But now I know it was a mistake—not just the indiscretion, but everything…. I'm sorry."

Kara watched him through a long silence.

"I don't think you know *what* you want," Kara offered sympathetically, turning his face toward her with her fingers. "And that's your biggest problem." She moved close, gazing deep into his eyes. "You're chasing a dream, Michael…. Kate's an illusion…. How long are your going to chase her before you realize that?" Kara came even closer, tellingly close. "But I'm *here* … *right now*…."

Her eyes pleaded with him desperately, beckoning his affection. Yet the more Kara searched him out, the more downcast her face became.

"That's what I thought," Kara said remorsefully, bowing her head in defeat while pursing her lips. Feeling a newfound hole forming within her, Kara remained close while wrapping her arms protectively around herself: desperately desiring the comfort of her best friend, yet knowing such comfort would only make the gaping wound worse.

That's when Michael brought Kara into a consoling embrace. "I wish I could…."

"I know," she somewhat laughed, a few tears floating in her eyes. "I knew it was useless…. I guess I had to try one last time."

"Kara, please forgive me," Michael pleaded. When she remained silent, he gently took the thick of her arms in hand and looked her in the eye. "You *are* special to me."

Kara looked down, averting her eyes. "Don't worry: I *will* get over it…. It's just going to take some time…." Then she looked up at him, kind of laughing. "But don't be surprised if one day I show up and kick your butt." She laughed again, wiping the tears from her eyes. Smiling warmly, endearingly, she whispered, "You're special to me too, Michael … *forever*…. I mean that."

Kara hugged him warmly, proceeding to kiss him on the cheek platonically before letting go. "Goodbye, Michael."

"Bye," Michael replied sheepishly, moving toward the door and opening it. He looked back again. "I'm sorry…. I really mean it."

"I know," Kara replied, smiling as Michael began through the doorway. "And hey, Kate's a nice girl … *really*…. I hope she comes around…. I *know* she'll come around…. Just—just try to be her friend first. Let her see the person *I* know."

Michael nodded and left. Starting down the hall, he heard the ominous sound of the door shutting behind him. He continued on, his shoulders hanging low and his head down. Though having gained Kara's forgiveness, Michael felt worse than before.

Making his way out of the dormitory and into the warm, spring sunlight, Michael continued the long, painful walk back to his dormitory.

Kara's words still echoed in his mind, and her expressions of disapproval and hurt weighed heavily on him. They cut him deep, for he knew she was right. He was reckless and impulsive. He had hurt not only her, but so many other people too—and those memories accosted him. His long gone brother, David, lay in his grave, his words of warning to Michael having gone unheeded.

But more than anything that had transpired in Kara's dorm, one thought stood out above them all: Kara kept calling him *Michael*—not *Mike*. Kara had never used his formal name, except in jest.

Something between them had changed.

Pondering all these thoughts, Michael looked up and saw Kate DeCarreau passing by and heading in the opposite direction. She gave him a quick smile and continued walking.

Had it been any other day, young Gillen would have certainly reversed directions and pursued DeCarreau. But wallowing in his own despair, he instead gave her a rather indifferent nod and continued on his way, not looking back even once.

The distance between them increased as they headed away from each other.

From where she kept to herself while going in the opposite direction, Kate pondered Michael's gesture. She waited for the familiar sound of hurried footsteps coming up from behind her, arming herself with snappy banter. Yet the pavement behind her remained disturbingly quiet. After walking a short distance, Kate stopped and turned around. Much to her surprise, Michael Gillen was far down the walkway, continuing away from her.

She stood watching him depart, not sure what to make of the incident.

CHAPTER SEVEN

Meeting in the Sky

Twenty-two-year-old Michael Gillen relaxed in his seat aboard the NSEA transport, enjoying his flight from Earth States Military Academy. His eyes remained fixed on the spectacular view out the window to his left. Earth, far smaller than before and panning to the edge of the window, hung in space like a precious jewel. The planet's striking blue marble-like appearance mesmerized the young graduate. However, the transport executed one last course adjustment, and the sphere fell completely out of view. Soon, the transport would arrive at is destination: Mid-Earth Station.

Michael looked around the small transport, amazed to be counted among the exclusive group of twelve new NSEA recruits. Tom Andrews sat in the first seat just across the aisle. Michael was pleased to have his best friend entering the deep space program with him. Even better, the empty seat just to Michael's right belonged to the *third musketeer*.

Michael sank deep in his chair, relishing the transformation of events that had taken place over the previous two years. Having seen only disaster in his freshman and sophomore years of college, the former cadet could now boast of graduating top in his class *and* the DSEP program.

The sound of a door opening broke the silence. That was his cue. Cyril Davidson, the NSEA executive director, was holding closed-door interviews in the small office at the rear of the transport, and Michael had the unfortunate pleasure of going last. Therefore, he got up from his passenger seat and made his way down the short aisle. A little more than halfway to the back, he met a very pleasing-looking Kate DeCarreau returning to her seat next to his. *She* was the third musketeer.

"Your turn," she declared with quirky smile while squeezing passed him on the narrow aisle. "Have fun."

The still-enamored graduate received her gaze happily.

Michael found Kate to be the best surprise of all the past two years. Upon arriving at the DSEP orientation his junior year with Tom Andrews, Michael found her there too. *What a windfall!* he thought. Kate having an interest in space exploration only made her that much more attractive. With only twenty cadets in the exclusive program and the luck of the draw on several team projects, Kate, Michael, and Tom became fast friends.

The young man had heeded Kara's advice to befriend Kate first, rather than simply chasing the young woman all over campus. Moreover, still smarting from his indiscretion with Kara, Michael determined *never* to make the same mistake again. Therefore, Michael took to heart the *friendship thing*. Through their two years as friends, he had grown close to her *as a friend* and truly enjoyed her company. He just didn't know how to pursue a relationship with her beyond mere friendship anymore. Nevertheless, he was more than willing to be patient.

"Sit down, Michael—or do you prefer Mike?" Cyril Davidson gestured as Michael entered the room, closing the door. The middle-aged man, having hints of grey peppering his thinning, brown hair, also motioned to the tray of refreshments sitting in the corner of the room.

"You can call me either," Michael replied. "But most people call me Mike." Upon sinking into the exquisite leather chair, the young recruit caught sight of the overly large observation window before him. The brilliant star field in the window captured his gaze—and imagination too.

However, the nervous twenty-two-year-old guarded his thoughts. After all, he was new to the program, having years of challenges ahead of him before actually getting the chance to explore the stars.

"So how does it feel to be a graduate?" Davidson smiled before taking a sip of his tea.

"Wonderful, I just wish my first two years had gone as well as my last two."

"Yes, quite an impressive turnaround you made," the older man smiled again with a most intriguing look in his eye. "You almost didn't make the program—good thing you had a very influential advocate." Pausing, his face sobered. "But the entire selection committee was awed by your last two years of stellar work. That's why you're here…. So tell me, how did you turn it around?"

Michael hesitated, leaning forward and folding his hands thoughtfully in front of him. After gazing at the floor for a quick moment, he looked back up at his inquiring superior. "Well, around the time my brother died, I ended up hurting someone very close to me. That entire summer, it was all I could think about." He waxed pensive. "It made me realize just how much I was letting everyone down. So that next fall, I decided I wasn't going to let that happen anymore. The rest is history." His eyebrow came up as he sighed. "I just wish I'd learned it sooner."

The two remained silent for a long moment, and the older man seemed to take in the explanation encouragingly.

"That's just part of growing up. Sometimes, the only way to learn is to make those mistakes. But the point is that you *did* learn."

Just then, the vessel turned, and Mid-Earth Station came into the star field. Still quite a distance away, the behemoth satellite merely appeared as an oversized star, though quickly growing in prominence. The irregular cuboid-shaped station, over five hundred cubic kilometers in size, was the largest freestanding satellite in Terrae Solaris.

Davidson continued, "That's why I'm offering you an esteemed position." He paused, gathering himself. "We're launching a fifty-year round-trip mission to Alpha Centauri—the first deep space mission ever. We've got two teams of six designated for the launch: a primary team and a secondary team—the backup team in case the primary team can't go." The older man leaned in toward his younger protégé. "I want *you* to take command of the Secondaries."

Michael sat there dumbfounded, staring at his superior and waiting for the punch line to drop. None came. "You're kidding, right?"

"I never kid about such things. We want Tom Andrews and Kate DeCarreau too; you three make a great team, and we want great teams."

"But I didn't think NSEA was anywhere near launching a ship?"

The older man set his teacup on the table beside him and folded his hands. "You'll find we move fast. We still have over two years until launch, but there are a lot of changes taking place." Then Davidson repositioned himself in his chair. "Originally, we had five missions in the works long-term, but we're scaling back to two missions and accelerating them—this business with the Europans made us think twice. And let's face it: President Turner is a one-term president. In eighteen months, Senator Mitchell will most likely win the office, already having enough power to shift funds to support the Mars Federation's efforts against Aurelian Galerius. We want to make sure we're in a position to achieve at least two launches by the time he reduces our funds."

By then, the odd shape of Mid-Earth Station became clearly visible through the observation window, though the transport was still too far away for Michael to make out any of the details.

"Do you think the Europans will drag us into the conflict?" Michael asked.

"No," Davidson replied. "But those goons already own all of Jupiter and are well on their way to annexing all of Saturn. The Titanians have already pledged Uranus' allegiance to the EuroGans, and Neptune and Pluto are just a matter of time. *That's* the entire Outer Rim.

"The Mars republics are going to have their hands full keeping the Europans out of the Asteroid Belt. As long as Earth States maintains fleet bases there, Mitchell will be more than happy to help them—behind the scenes that is. You know how much he hates the Europans, so that means less money for us."

"Wow," Michael exclaimed, reeling at the analysis. He paused in thought and then said, "I guess *somehow* this all works out for me. I'm just surprised you don't have a better backup commander candidate already on your staff."

Davidson looked at him intently. "We don't make these decisions lightly. You do great work. After all, our exploration ship designs have navigational field generators in them that are based on your improvement ideas—the military is looking at them too. How many ESMA graduates right out of the chute can say that?"

Young Gillen humbly nodded in acknowledgement.

"And if you play your cards right," Davidson added. "You'll be up for primary team commander the next mission."

"That's excellent," Michael shrugged, taken back by the once-in-a-lifetime opportunity.

"But there are concerns," the older man added hesitantly, carefully crafting his words. "Today we are going to announce the primary and secondary teams—not to the press, just internally. Gabriel Burke will be announced as commander of the primary team."

"Okay?" Michael asked, carefully managing his expression. After all, Davidson appeared to be making a full scan of Michael's reaction. Regardless of how much progress he had made over the previous two years, the young recruit still held much disdain for Gabriel Burke.

Davidson continued cautiously, "Your biggest responsibility as backup commander is to support Burke. Many of your disciplinary actions from the university involved conflicts with him, and your two best years occurred when he wasn't there. So,"—looking Michael squarely in the eye—"Do you think you can work that close to Mr. Burke without having problems? He can be quite demanding."

Michael Gillen had come to a crossroad. No, working with Burke was the last thing he wanted. Moreover, Burke would not go easy on him. Yet the opportunity was greater than both him and his nemesis.

"A lot's happened since then—I've changed," Michael replied, keeping eye to eye with his superior. "This is something I've dreamed about for a long time. I'm not about to let a personal conflict get in the way. If Burke is comfortable with me being his backup, I'll make sure I don't let him down."

The older man gazed upon the new recruit, sizing him up. After a long moment, Davidson slapped him on the knee. "Good, I'll hold you to it…. And Burke has already agreed too." Just as Michael was about to sigh in relief, Davidson added, "There are other concerns too."

"Like what?"

"What can you tell me about your relationship with Kate DeCarreau?"

Young Gillen remained outwardly calm and collect. Inwardly, he was leery—and very surprised. "We're good friends. Tom, Kate, and I spent a lot of time over the past two years working together. We were in the same DSEP isolation team during our senior year—we're all good friends."

"Yes, I know," Davidson replied. "But haven't you held an attraction for Kate the entire time you were a cadet? And you still have this attraction, right?"

"Yes."

"Have you ever acted on this attraction—in any way?"

The probing questions caught Michael off guard. *How does he know all this stuff?* Michael thought, being more than aware of where Davidson was going. "No, Sir. Kate and I are not dating or pursuing any type of relationship other than just being good friends. Is this a problem?"

Davidson readjusted himself uncomfortably in his chair, even doing a wide, sweeping survey of the cabin with his eyes. "God has blessed me with a great sense of pragmatism. We let young people step into some very critical roles, ask them to risk everything for an impossible dream, and then shoot them off in a tiny ship." He curled the fingers of one hand to his chest. "I personally don't care about what happens between crewmembers once a group of astronauts set out into the great unknown."

The older man became very sober. "But let's face it, we live in very idealistic and traditional times. Earth States is a very parochial place, and many of the mission directors hold fast to the moral expectations of the day. Many of them expect young men and women to work closely together, yet avoid acting on the impulses such an environment engenders. They demand a high level of propriety and look down on those who stray from it. Therefore, the overriding rule at NSEA is that exploration team members don't date. Violating that rule can quickly turn into a public scandal—at least within NSEA.

"And it's not just the morals.... It's also a matter of team dynamics. Keep in mind the types of people attracted to fifty or one hundred-year deep space exploration missions: They are people with no ties to Terrae

Solaris. Though very talented, many come from broken homes and bad circumstances. You might not be able to relate, since you're one of the few exceptions. Trust me: They can be very codependent. They bring a lot of baggage with them. Even the hint of favoritism among members can ruin a team.

"That's why dating between team members is strictly forbidden. So let's keep all this between you and me, and make sure you show some discretion. I don't want to have to disqualify you or Kate."

Young Gillen looked at his superior, a little embarrassed but also very disappointed. After all, things between him and Kate were going so well. "Okay. I promise."

By then, a very up-close view of Mid-Earth Station filled the observation window. In fact, the transport was traveling close to the station, making its way down a landing channel.

"Good," Davidson exclaimed, slapping Michael's knee once again. "We'll be arriving shortly. As soon as we get in, I'm going to call the two teams together and make the announcement."

Within an hour, Michael Gillen sat in a large conference room, somewhere within the very large NSEA complex on Mid-Earth Station. Though being just one of forty or fifty people, his place among the crowd watching Davidson at the podium was anything but obscure.

After having given a long-winded speech about opportunity and destiny, Davidson announced the formation of the two teams. The Primaries consisted of Gabriel Burke as commander, Shay Taggart as Environmental and Stores Engineer, Maura Enzler as Systems Engineer, Ben Morris at Propulsion, Phil Marcotte as Navigations Engineer, and Kara Ricci on Medical.

The secondary team—Backups, as they were referred to quaintly— was headed by Michael Gillen, with Tom Andrews on Environment and Stores, Kate DeCarreau on Systems, David Tashjian on Propulsion, Colleen Abello on Navigation, and Ale Mertens on Medical.

Despite the astronaut's assignment titles, NSEA required all explorers to support two or three other positions, thus ensuring complete redundancy of expertise.

Davidson began wrapping up his speech, "…So congratulations and good luck to all those I just announced. This is a very historic day, but we have much work ahead of us." He gestured toward where

Michael and most of the new recruits from the transport sat, smiling. "The first order of business is to get all these *newbies* settled in and through orientation and preliminaries. Since half of the Secondaries are newbies, we will begin training the Primaries alone for the first ninety days. After that, training with both teams will commence. Until then, we have a very important job for our newbies."

A bit of laughter rose up among the more senior members of the audience.

"Newbies, we need your help giving our primary medical officer experience running cryogenic calibrations. We also need calibration specs for anyone on the exploration crews, just as we obtained from the primary team when they arrived. So after orientation and preliminaries, every newbie will report to Kara Ricci to be turned into a Popsicle. Standard medical protocol calls for three five-day suspension sessions, at least a month apart, for each crewmember. So good luck!"

With a hearty round of laughter—but not from the newbies—the meeting adjourned.

A very nervous Michael Gillen lay in his open cryogenics chamber in the NSEA Cryogenics lab on Mid-Earth Station, wearing nothing but a single, white hospital sheet. The top of the sarcophagus-like chamber hung suspended from the ceiling above him, its robotic surgical arms, IV tubes, and sensors dangling menacingly toward him. They seemed to reach out to him impatiently, as if relishing the beginning of the gruesome cryogenics procedure.

Once more, the NSEA recruit surveyed the immediate area, searching for any sign that the procedure was about to begin. The effort was pointless, for the privacy barrier around his chamber blocked his view. Nevertheless, the entire lab containing thirty or so other suspension chambers remained quiet, so he laid his head back down and stared up warily at the medical devices above him.

Michael tried convincing himself he had nothing to fear. After all, NSEA was conducting widespread cryogenics experiments and testing. Numbers of similar labs existed throughout the facilities, with over a thousand volunteers having successfully undergone both short and long-term sessions. Of course, perhaps the thought of having his body systematically shut down and frozen like some sort of gruesome butcher shop entrée might cause some concern. Yes, that was definitely it!

"My last procedure of the day," Kara Ricci exclaimed, pushing away part of the privacy barrier to enter. Dressed in standard physicians clothing, she wore a confident and assuring expression so typical of any doctor. Michael, however, found this particularly annoying: he hated anything that had to do with hospitals or medicine.

Michael laughed nervously in reply as Kara studied the medical display readouts. Though they had communicated often the previous two years—thus putting aside much of the awkwardness over their indiscretion—this was their first face-to-face conversation since that fateful day his sophomore year. Michael strangely found himself at a complete loss for words.

"Everything looks good," she declared, still examining the readouts before turning to him. "You ready, Michael?"

"I guess."

Despite undergoing such unusual circumstances, Michael found Kara's presence comforting. She had come into her own at NSEA, having become more tempered and focused than the bundle of energy he had met four years earlier; complete professionalism and a wonderful beside manner complemented her nerves of steel nicely.

"Don't worry," she smiled encouragingly, putting her hand on his shoulder. "I've done this hundreds of times—ten times today alone. Most of the process is done after I put you to sleep anyway. Before you know it, you'll be at *First Waking*…. Any questions?"

Michael shrugged.

"Good, let's begin," Kara replied, pulling out a penlight. "Don't be nervous. I had this procedure done just about a year ago. They've made tremendous improvements even since then."

"You didn't have the procedure your first year here, like the rest?" Michael asked quizzically, interrupting her normal exam cadence.

Kara paused, somewhat oddly, before returning to her normal self once more.

"No," she replied casually. "It conflicted with my training schedule when I arrived." She activated the penlight. "Then Cyril sent me away for eight months for some specialized medical training. I did my first cryogenic session when I got back. I was more than happy with the delay: the later the session, the more refined the process."

With an assuring smile, Kara began the exam.

"I'm not *nervous*," Michael added as the light accosted one eye and then the next. Of course, this was a lie. He was more than nervous, and wearing only a sheet didn't seem to help. "This stuff's just really embarrassing."

"Cryogenics is as much surgery as anything else we do here," she stated matter-of-factly while probing an ear canal. Upon completing the examination of both ears, Kara took his jaw firmly in her hands, exploring the soft tissue underneath with her fingers. "And let's face it: The human body is a machine. Sometimes, you just gotta take a look under the hood." That's when she folded the white sheet down halfway, exposing most of his torso. "Besides, I've seen a lot of human anatomy in my day.... But if I see something I haven't seen before—I'll shoot it."

The two went quiet while Kara continued the physical. Michael became visibly self-conscious, his cheeks even blushing a bit. Kara, running a scanner over him, noticed this. Having soon completed the scan, she set the device down and began pressing on various parts of his abdomen. Still noticing his embarrassment—and with a rather peculiar expression coming over her—she added, "Besides, you weren't nervous two years ago, the last time I saw you like this."

"*Ouch!*" Michael recoiled abruptly.

"I'm sorry. Did that hurt?"

Young Gillen watched her warily, noting the slightest, almost indiscernible look of satisfaction creep into her face. The physical was getting rougher too. "I guess you're still made about that, huh?—*ouch!*"

"Not at all. I told you then: I was just as much at fault as you.... Let's do some IVs."

Michael's whole body stiffened as the first needle went into his arm like fire. The young man labored to keep his reaction within, for he would not give her the satisfaction. However, more needles were to come—many more! "Then why did this procedure turn painful all the sudden?—*ouch!*"

"It's just normal discomfort," Kara grimaced. "Don't be such a baby." She paused, appearing deep in thought. Of course, this unnerved Michael when she held up the next IV needle, studying it carefully. "I forgave you then, and I meant it…."—another pause as the needle slid in—"…Still, a girl doesn't easily get over something like that. There's a lot of emotion to work through." When Michael's expression surrendered, she asked, "You never told anyone about what happened, did you?"

"No. I don't plan to either."

"Good," Kara replied with satisfaction. "I don't want anyone else finding out about it—especially Kate." She rebuffed Michael's inquisitive look. "Speaking of which, it looks like you and Kate are pretty close now. Didn't I tell you she'd come around if you just treated her like a friend?"

"Yeah, but a lot of good it's going to do me now," Michael lamented. "According to NSEA rules, all we can be is friends."

Kara laughed, somewhat cynically. "Since when did you ever play by the rules? I wouldn't give up, but be careful."

A very frustrated Kate DeCarreau stood over the navigational field regulator, completely beside herself. Though she had spent the entire evening in a futile attempt to calibrate the infernal device, the calibration readings wouldn't change. Nothing had worked: reprogramming the controller, adjusting the physical settings, or even completely rebuilding it—nothing!

Not even the soft music playing in the background eased her frustration.

The young recruit had come to her wits end. She was exhausted from the late hour—dirty too; her eyes hurt from the dim lighting in the isolated work bay; mechanical grease had worked its way into her hair. The next day was a big day, requiring her to be well rested. Moreover, no one else on the primary or secondary team was struggling as much as she was—they were all probably fast asleep too.

After pulling a loose strand of brown hair behind her ear for the umpteenth time, Kate huffed and angrily struck the regulator with the wrench in her hand. The regulator sat lifeless on the table, unfazed by the beating. However, her hand vibrated painfully.

After wallowing in self-pity for a moment, Kate put the wrench to the device once more, watching the diagnostics display through bleary eyes. However, the device still wouldn't calibrate. *The exercise is pointless, just like my short and fleeting career at NSEA*, she thought. *Just four months, and I'm already washing out!*

"Kate?" came an all too familiar voice from behind her. She turned around as he added, "What are you doing up so late? We've got an early morning."

Michael stood at the open doorway, dressed as if having done so quickly. His cropped, brown hair was a little disheveled. He carried himself as if surprised to have come upon her predicament but ultimately there for her rescue. His blue eyes gazed warmly upon her as if reassuring her that everything—whatever the problem—was going to work out fine, just as he had ensured so many times over their last two years as friends.

Immediately, the young woman regretted not having secured the door.

Not that she was disappointed to see him. No, Michael was a refreshing sight at such a late hour. If anyone could help her, it was he. However, their friendship had grown strained as of late, starting just shortly after coming to NSEA four months earlier. For some unexplainable reason, every conversation with him deteriorated into an argument, and this was not the time to explore why. She didn't need the added tension at such a late hour, not the way she was feeling, not with her nerves on end—and she was a mess at that!

"I'm still working on this regulator," she stated matter-of-factly, continuing to work as though nothing were wrong. "But I'll be fine."

"You don't look fine."

"There you go again ... telling me how I look," she retorted sharply. "Please don't play games with me, Michael. It's too late and I'm *not* in the mood."

"I'm sorry," Michael offered, cautiously stepping into the work bay.

Kate stood back from the regulator, putting one hand on her hip while pointing the wrench at it accusingly with the other. "They assigned calibrating this regulator to me as part of my cross-training." Then she huffed, "But I'm systems, not hardware. I don't know how they expect us to know *everything*.... It's so frustrating!"

Michael cautiously offered while moving closer, "Maybe you should ask Maura for help?"

"Don't you think I've already thought of that?" Kate countered, pointing the wrench at him. She tried not to notice falling into his shadow as he came over her, how his closeness seemed to unsettle her as of late. "I've already asked Maura for help too many times. I think she's getting the impression I don't know what I'm doing...." Gazing at him sharply, Kate turned desperate. "Too many bad reports and they'll kick me off the backup team."

"You're not worried, are you?" he asked, his gaze meeting hers sympathetically.

The young woman sighed and put down the wrench, feeling overwhelmed. Worse, Michael was being more than a friend, taking her rebuffing graciously—she found that completely irritating, of course. She looked down at the regulator, avoiding his gaze. "You wouldn't understand. You're a natural at all this."

"Yes, I *do* understand," Michael replied, a little peeved that she was oblivious to his dealings with Burke. He also recoiled at the thought that she might be giving up. Watching her still avoiding his gaze, he gently took her forearm in his hand. "Kate, this is as much about teamwork as it is expertise. You need to *work* with Maura, just like I'm working with Burke. If you don't, they'll kick you off the team for that too."

Her gaze turned dour once more.

"Are you *trying* to frustrate me?" she replied curtly, breaking his grasp. "It was bad enough when I thought I only had to worry about the regulator."

Michael huffed, "I'm just trying to help, that's all."

"Then say something to make me feel better! Stop making me feel worse!"

Michael regretted ever stepping into the room. "What do you want me to do!?"

"I don't know!" she fumed, staring up at him and shrugging her shoulders. "You're the backup team commander. You should know!"

The two stood almost nose to nose and at odds for quite a long moment.

Both looked at each other accusingly, and Michael fell under her penetrating and reproving gaze once more—just like so many other times in the past several months at NSEA. Yet the more he looked at her, the more he noticed the insecurity haunting her deep, brown eyes. She was nothing but a paper tiger, feigning indignation and protecting herself.

So he kissed her! Not apologetically or timidly. No, he abruptly and forcibly pulled her into his arms and began kissing her with abandon. At first, she met the unexpected advance with sharp indignation and struggled to push away. Michael remained unwavering, keeping her firmly in his grasp and refusing to part from her lips. His gamble began paying off, for each new wonderful moment brought upon him the delights of her increasing reciprocation, the eventual pleasure of her swooning helplessly in his arms.

The couple enjoyed a long moment in the unexpected embrace, clutching each other tightly. Michael, in particular, savored his victory, relishing her acceptance of his advance. Kate was not the type of woman to be cowed by macho impulsiveness or foolish whims. Therefore, some mutual attraction must have already been there.

And as she kissed him back, the young man realized for the first time that she had beckoned him to pursue her all along—and for quite some time. He had missed all her subtle cues that were so glaringly obvious now. And *this kiss*. He had not won her affection; she had won his, and he was okay with that.

The moment soon passed, and the two parted ever so slightly.

With eyes still closed and looking as if completely subdued under his spell, Kate floated in Michael's arms. She stayed mesmerized for another long moment before sighing deeply in surrender, letting her forehead come to rest on his chin. Michael could hear her mumble something under her breath.

"What?" he quietly asked.

Kate lifted her head, gazing at his face nervously. Then she whispered, "I said *what took you so long?*"

She moved in to kiss him once more—

A noise suddenly came from the doorway, startling the two and causing them to jump away from each other awkwardly. Standing in the doorway was Maura Enzler, the primary team's systems engineer—and Kate's mentor too. She was very casually dressed but appearing as if having been awake for a while.

"I'm sorry," Maura apologized, unnerving both Michael and Kate. "I thought I heard something … but I must have been mistaken…. Goodnight."

As quickly as she had appeared, Maura was gone.

"Do you think she saw?" Michael quietly asked, Davidson's warning about dating prohibitions spinning around in his head madly.

"I don't know," Kate replied, her eyes wide and looking back at the doorway a couple of times. The two stood shell-shocked for quite a long moment. Finally, Kate looked at him sardonically. "You have impeccable timing. One word of this and both of us will be off the backup team."

"I'm sorry," young Gillen replied in knee-jerk fashion. But then he abruptly added, "No, I've waited four years to do that. I don't regret it at all." He paused uneasily. "How 'bout you?"

Kate looked at him for a long moment, pondering those four years and all the trouble he had caused her—and all the trouble this incident *could* cause. Finally, she shook her head back and forth and chuckled, "Nothing's ever easy with you, is it?"

CHAPTER EIGHT

Breaking Training

The Centauri backup crew stood huddled together in the hot desert sun: Michael Gillen, Tom Andrews, Kate DeCarreau, David Tashjian, Colleen Abello, and Ale Mertens. The young astronauts-in-training, their heads pointed wantonly toward the sky, watched the NSEA transport ascending rapidly away from them. Soon, the craft shrunk to a mere speck moving against the deep blue canopy, eventually disappearing altogether. The dazed group exchanged uneasy glances at one another. They were completely alone, standing on the edge of a small rise that overlooked nothing but wasteland in all directions.

Now what should they do?

"Does anyone know where we are?" an uncomfortable-looking David Tashjian called out. Already besieged by the scorching sun, the young man took off his brimmed hat and wiped the sweat from his drenched forehead.

"I think they call this *Purgatory*," Tom Andrews replied sarcastically. "I just didn't know Purgatory existed on Earth." He surveyed the immediate area. Brown, straw-like weeds pushed forth from the rough soil, interrupted only by an occasional, irregularly shaped, brownish-green bush—and a whole lot of rocks. He turned back to his comrades. "If they were going to drop us in the middle of nowhere on a survival exercise, shouldn't they have trained us first?"

Michael Gillen appeared less fazed by the unexpected turn of events. While the others looked around aimlessly, the young commander-in-training knelt down and began foraging through the backpack at his feet. "That's not what this exercise is about, and it's not about winning the race back to the relief station either. It's about facing our fears and adapting to the unknown."

"Traipsing one hundred and twenty kilometers across this wasteland ... *I'm afraid*," Kate DeCarreau exclaimed, looking out over the rise. The memories of the exhilarating moments the previous night, when Michael had kissed her, had melted away under the hot sun. Sobered by the realities of the challenge before them, the fetching, young recruit turned to her team in jest. "Someone hit their distress call button. Let Burke and his team win—wherever they may be."

"We're not letting Burke win this one," Michael declared, glancing up briefly from studying the contents of his pack.

Kate watched Michael rifle through his pack, picking up her own pack upon seeing the others assembling for the long journey. She glanced over at Tom and remarked, "I've heard that one before. Right, Tom?"

Tom nodded his head in agreement.

Michael ignored the remark, remaining focused on the work at hand. The outside of his pack housed two full water canteens, while a stash of various supplies lay inside. The items were little to speak of, especially given the harsh desert environment. The pack also contained one distress beacon activator, a homing beacon tracker fixed on the relief station far in the distance, and a medical blanket.

Surveying the horizon, Michael pondered his last statement. Gabriel Burke and the Primaries were out there somewhere, competing for bragging rights over the challenge. If he could only figure out what Burke would do. Nevertheless, he reminded himself to stay focused on the purpose of the exercise, just as he had reminded his team earlier.

"Okay," Colleen Abello began, pointing toward the horizon while studying the homing beacon tracker in her hand. "The locator indicates that the relief station is this way. We may as well get moving."

Upon hearing the comment, the entire team coalesced and started in the intended direction—all but Michael. Instead, the commander-to-be went over beside a rather tall bush, draped his medical blanket over it to make shade, and sat down in the shade by using the frame of his pack as a seat.

"Mike, aren't you coming?" an impatient David Tashjian inquired. The others heard the comment and stopped, turning toward where Michael was settling himself in.

"No," Michael replied deadpan, astonished that the team wanted to set out. "It's the middle of the day. We only have two liters of water each and probably need twice that every day. We'll dehydrate faster if we set out now. Let's wait until evening. Besides, you're going the wrong way."

At this, Abello fastidiously studied the beacon tracker in her hand, using all of her engineering prowess to prove him wrong. "I *know* I'm reading the locator right."

The others looked at him impatiently.

"That's not what I mean," Michael countered while gesturing toward the long, barren plane ahead. "There's nothing out there." Then he pointed a little farther south where a series of large bluffs rolled toward the horizon, lying just a few kilometers away. "But that mountain range … that's the best place to find shelter from the sun, water, and maybe even food." He turned to the larger group. "I say we head toward the base of the range and follow along it. From what I can tell, it won't take us too far out of the way. Regardless, it's our best chance to stay alive."

"We're not going to die," Ale Mertens countered, his remark receiving approval from the rest of the group. "We've got our distress call beacon. Let's just go as far as we can, for as long as we can, and then hit the button."

"Who's been given a distress caller?" Michael asked, standing up. At this, everyone began searching their packs, bringing forth the small devices. "Let me see them."

The small team halfheartedly watched him collect the distress callers. However, when he began deactivating them, their expressions turned to astonishment and indignation.

"Michael, what are you doing?" Kate asked emphatically.

Michael continued disassembling them, keeping most of the device intact but discarding the main power relay. "There's no *I quit* button in real life. Let's train like we really have to survive." When his comment was met with even more grimaces, he declared, "We won't have an *I quit* button four light-years away!"

The team went silent for a long moment, looking at the discarded pieces of the distress callers left on the ground in the center of the circle. Michael remained stalwart, for they had no recourse—outside of mutiny—except to listen to him.

"Okay," he began. "Let's set up camp right here for now. Get yourself out of the sun and off the ground. Settle in and get comfortable about being here. Go through your backpack and figure out how to use everything. Let's brainstorm, but keep talking and activities to a minimum to conserve internal water levels—breathe through your nose." He sat down as they reluctantly began to comply. "Our first priority is to find water. Then we need to figure out how to start a fire and keep it going. These are just the beginning of our challenges, so mentally prepare yourselves for some adversity. But don't worry: I won't let anything bad happen to us."

Reluctantly, the team began making camp as Michael had instructed and demonstrated. During that exercise, Tashjian got up and starting toward a large outcropping of rocks behind the camp.

"David, where are you going?" Michael called.

Tashjian's cheeks blushed just a bit. "You know ... *nature call.*"

"Here," Michael called, rifling through his pack and pulling out an empty, expandable liquid container. He threw the container to him. "But don't fill it up in one shot—and make sure you close the lid tight when you're through."

"What?" Ale Mertens asked in disbelief, noting the others having similarly astonished expressions.

Once again, Michael remained unfazed. "Everyone's going to use it.... You should know better, Doc: A last resort water source is better than none. If we find water, we've just carried a little extra weight. If not, I'm sure your medical and biology training will allow us to recycle and purify it." He looked around at the rest of the team imperatively. "I know it's a little earthy—okay, it's *very* earthy. But this is a survival situation, not a spring social. Let's treat it as such—and recycling our urine might not be the worst thing we have to do. So get your expectations in line with the situation."

At this, everyone looked at each other with the same sour grimace. The discarded pieces of the distress callers lay mockingly before them on the ground.

Tom Andrews was the first to speak. "Mike, have you ever done a desert survival exercise?"

"No, but we'll get through. I promise."

"Any sign of them?" a rather concerned Cyril Davidson called to his subordinate, who was exiting the small transport that had just landed.

"No, sir," the subordinate replied, making his way to the relief station where Davidson, the support crew, and the Primaries were. He joined the rest of the team on the covered terrace, getting out of the blazing sun.

At the news, a rather foreboding silence fell over the entire group.

Today was the twelfth day of the desert survival exercise. The Primaries, having given up over a week earlier, had fully recovered from their ordeal. However, Davidson and the mission support team hadn't heard from Michael Gillen's team since the transport had dropped them off twelve days earlier. Worse, the secret locators hidden in their packs had gone offline two days earlier. Though NSEA had dispatched search crews, the Gillen team remained missing.

The subordinate held out his hand, displaying six small pieces of metal lying in his palm. This drew the attention of the Primaries. "We went back to the drop-off point to retrace their path. Unfortunately, the desert's too malleable. But we found these."

"They disabled their distress callers," Kara exclaimed uneasily.

Burke grimaced. "That has Gillen written all over it."

"There has to be a purpose."

"No," Burke countered smugly. "There's no other explanation. He probably found the locator beacons too—disabled them."

Surveying the parched terrain and realizing just how dire the circumstances had become, Davidson ordered the subordinate to obtain additional search resources. While the assistant left to carry out the directive, the older man caught sight of something out of the corner of his eye. Something was coming over the hill.

The weary band of Secondaries made their way over the top of the hill, their pace slow and deliberate. Laboring toward the relief station at the bottom, they appeared as if coming back from the dead; eyes widened in anticipation of a reprieve; their bodies, withered from the scorching sun, were unable to carry them any faster. They were covered head to toe in dirt, and empty packs hung off their shoulders as if lead weights. Skin not covered in dirt blushed red, while their lips were badly cracked. Tattered clothing hung loosely off their thinned bodies.

Nevertheless, they *had* made it to the relief station on their own resolve.

Michael led his dragging team into the makeshift station, the small band collapsing eagerly onto waiting chairs. Immediately, medics began tending to them.

"Thank God you're safe," Davidson greeted them with a smile. "We've been searching high and low for you."

"And we found pieces of your distress callers at the drop-off sight," Kara added. "You didn't do that on purpose, did you?"

"Yep," a very weary Michael Gillen labored to get out, "and the locator beacons too…. We needed the power supplies."

"But you *had* to run out of supplies a week ago," a defeated Gabriel Burke countered skeptically. "How'd you survive all this time?"

"It was a team effort."

"But how?"

"I think we'd be too embarrassed to tell you," David Tashjian added.

Tom Andrews quickly chimed in. "Let's just say that everyone contributed to the water supply—among other things."

At this point, one of the medics looked up at Davidson. "Everyone's okay, Sir."

Davidson paused for a moment, glancing at Burke before turning back to Michael. "Congratulations, Michael—and the rest of the Secondaries, of course. I call that a job well done."

But Gabriel Burke's expression was foreboding.

"Okay, we're running a little late," the dive instructor began, slowly pacing between the two long rows of Centauri crewmembers assembled in the large bay. "The transport is waiting." Whenever passing a crewmember, the instructor would train a sharp eye on the parachute being packed, carefully looking for any mistakes. However, after several successful jumps, the Centauries (as they would come to be known) seemed to have picked up the tedious process. "But don't let that rush you—don't want anyone falling out of the sky."

At that point, Tom Andrews emitted a rather grim descending whistling sound, receiving a few grimaces from some of the other Centauries, both Primaries and Secondaries.

The instructor continued his pacing and said, "So finish packing your partner's parachute and set them by the door. We'll have the ground crew take them to the transport while we go over the jump formation once more."

Twenty-three-year-old Michael Gillen focused his attention on the parachute container before him, finishing the last step: packing the pilot chute. However, the parachute actually belonged to Gabriel Burke, just as the parachute Gabriel Burke was packing belonged to Michael.

After eight months of being in the astronaut corps, Michael was back on Earth once again.

Davidson had brought the Centauries back to Earth several days earlier, this time to learn how to skydive. Though not essential space exploration training, the exercise was meant to engender team building. Crewmembers, safely packing each other's parachutes, would execute patterns and other multi-member activities while in the air. Having successfully achieved the solo jump milestone, the Centauries were about to execute their first team jump—the first time the parachutes would be packed by another member too.

"Okay, Maura," Tom Andrews called, holding his finished parachute, "You're all set to go." He smiled coyly. "This is the best origami I've ever done ... and the rocks inside don't make it too heavy, either."

Maura Enzler looked at him, winked her eye, and made a gun shooting gesture toward him with her hand. "Right back at 'cha!"

By that time, some of the Centauries had finished, delivering their parachutes to the designated table before exiting into the adjacent briefing room.

Glancing over and seeing Burke asking the instructor to inspect the packed parachute in his hands, Michael decided to perform a third double-check of his own work.

Despite finding no deficiencies, he executed a fourth inspection of the device. After all, Burke had badgered him since losing the desert survival competition two months earlier. Because of Burke's critical attitude, Michael couldn't risk letting anything going wrong. Of course, Burke dropping out of the sky might solve Michael's problem too!

Deciding a fifth inspection was pointless, Michael grabbed the parachute by the harnesses and carried it over to the awaiting table.

Everyone else but Kate had already left the hanger. She had just delivered her parachute—Shay Taggart's parachute really—and was lingering near the table.

Obvious to Michael only, Kate was stealing alone time with him—a tactic used by the young couple since sharing their first kiss, over four months earlier. Though not particularly keen on being so secretive, Michael knew the NSEA dating prohibitions left them no choice. So after he set his parachute down, the two enjoyed the few, precious minutes of small talk while strolling into the briefing room.

The hanger bay lay empty—but only briefly. Through another door, Gabriel Burke came in and over to the table where the parachutes sat.

Stealing a quick glance around to make sure he was alone, Burke hurriedly rummaged through all the parachutes until finding the intended device. The young Primaries leader held it for the briefest moment, as if savoring what he was about to do. Then finally opening the container and pulling a knife from his pocket, Burke proceeded to slice through many of the main parachute's suspension lines. He quickly closed the chute, thereby concealing his work, and left the same way he had come.

With the hanger bay empty once more, the parachutes sat waiting to be loaded onto the transport. The damaged parachute looked as innocuous as the rest, though nothing was further from the truth.

In fact, the damaged parachute was actually in worse shape than what Burke had intended. For in his hurried attempt to disable the main parachute, leaving the reserve chute untouched, the young Centauri hadn't noticed the knife tearing through the back of the parachute compartment, critically damaging the main harness in the process.

Cyril Davidson stood near the center of the landing zone, looking up into the sky with a pair of binoculars. The transport that had taken the Centauries for the drop flew well overhead, moving toward the designated drop zone.

"Sir, the transport has reached altitude and proximity," the aide standing beside the director exclaimed, holding a communicator to his ear. "The pilot's just given the Centauries the order to jump."

The astronauts streamed one-by-one out of the transport far above, appearing as if mere dots to the naked eye. After all twelve had emerged, a singular line formation materialized in the sky. Soon, the pattern bent in upon itself, forming a rather symmetrical circle.

"Mission accomplished," Davidson declared while bringing the binoculars down. "Let's set up the next jump to be a little more complicated—more dangerous too. I don't want these guys afraid of anything."

High in the sky, the Centauries spent a few brief moments enjoying the pleasures of freefall. However, the time quickly came for each member to deploy. One by one, they broke formation and deployed their chutes, until only Maura Enzler, Gabriel Burke, and Michael Gillen were still in freefall.

Having received the signal from Burke to deploy, Enzler pulled away as her parachute began slowing her descent. Surprisingly, Burke then gave Michael the signal to deploy. Though Michael was supposed to deploy last, Burke was nevertheless in charge. So hesitantly, he pulled his ripcord.

Michael felt the tremendous pull of inertia as his chute opened and began slowing him down. The sensation quickly passed, and Michael hung suspended from the parachute, slowly wafting down toward the Earth.

Still in freefall far below, Gabriel Burke took a deep breath before pulling his ripcord. Trepidation over exactly how his vandalized main chute might act filled his thoughts. Would he be tangled in the main chute as it failed? Would he have enough time to deploy his emergency chute? Would he live to fully discredit Michael?

However, time was wasting away, and the earth was getting closer. Therefore, he pulled his ripcord.

Burke felt the initial pull of inertia as the main chute began to deploy, followed by a rather violent jerk; the main chute pulled away and the rest of the attached suspension lines pulled awkwardly on him. That's when the young leader's heart went into his throat! With a violent ripping sound, Burke spun around as if an unwinding yo-yo! His harness had given way, and what was left of the half-deployed main chute pulled the whole parachute compartment—emergency chute and all!—away from him.

Burke was falling to the ground helplessly!

From her vantage point high above, Maura Enzler watched in horror as Burke plummeted toward the Earth. He quickly stopped himself from spinning, positioning his body to slow his descent. Nevertheless, he was still falling. Needing to get to him fast, the young woman cutaway her main chute to freefall.

Nothing! She was still drifting down toward the Earth. Maura had forgotten to disable her cutaway safety.

Not Michael Gillen. No, the second he had spotted Burke in trouble, the inexperienced jumper successfully executed the cutaway procedure. Michael was diving head first with his arms to his side, his body missiling toward a distressed Gabriel Burke.

Michael nervously watched his altimeter indicator speeding toward the red zone, and the device flashed and blared its desperate warnings. He had little time to deploy his emergency chute before endangering himself. Moreover, he still didn't have any way to attach Burke to his chute harness; the jump crew had removed all the training harness mechanisms. With no other recourse, Michael began undoing one of his chest straps and pulling out all the slack.

A few moments later—and it seemed like forever—Michael caught up with a rather petrified-looking Gabriel Burke. Panicking, Burke began gabbing at Gillen's parachute mechanism, only delaying Michael from his intended purpose.

Michael's altitude was narrowly close to red-line, forcing him to disable the automatic emergency chute deploying mechanism—while fighting with Burke too. Using a few wrestling maneuvers, Michael immobilized the panicking free-faller in a chokehold.

"Stop it!" Michael yelled above the rushing sound of the wind. "I'm trying to help you!"

Burke relented, giving Michael enough opportunity to wrap the chest harness slack around him. However, the line didn't go all the way around the man's chest!

The altimeter reading was getting even closer to red-line. The Earth was coming up fast!

Having no time to think, Michael quickly undid one of his leg harnesses and pulled the strap around Burke's chest until it met the chest harness receptacle. With a barely audible click against the rushing wind, the two straps locked, bounding the two men together awkwardly.

Seeing the ground coming up fast, Michael activated his emergency chute. Inertia pulled on the two men as the undersized chute unfurled above them, slowing their descent. Given the awkward and unbalanced position of the two men, both tumbled as they struggled for a landing position.

With an uncomfortable thud—but a safe thud—Gillen and Burke hit the ground.

Davidson and the aide, both of whom were running toward the landing spot, came within a hundred meters of where the two men hit the ground. Continuing to run, the frantic executive director sighed in relief when both men stood up and fumbled out of the parachute harnesses.

Burke quickly put himself in Michael's face. Though still about twenty meters away, Davidson and the aide could hear Burke's indignation.

"What'd you do, Gillen!?" Burke fumed, his chest out and face almost nose to nose with a rather surprised Michael Gillen. "Why didn't you pack my chute correctly!?"

"I did, Burke, honest!"

Finally, Davidson arrived just in time to wedge himself between the two men. "You two okay?"

"No, Cyril," Burke declared while pointing his finger at Michael. "I almost died, thanks to Gillen here! Obviously, he didn't follow the check procedures!"

At this point, Michael became visibly annoyed that Burke was ignoring the fact that he had risked his life to save him. "I followed the procedures to the letter. That chute was packed perfectly. The whole apparatus was fine. Honest!"

"I don't believe you!"

"Gabriel, calm down," Davidson gestured. "You're safe now.... That's the most important thing."

Burke only fumed more. "I can't calm down, Cyril. I'm sorry, but I can't go on with these exercises. I obviously can't trust my backup."

Davidson stood between the two men, mediating the argument. Burke continued with his indignation, while Michael defended himself. The rest of the Centauries began arriving as quickly as they could land and get out of their chutes.

"We found Burke's chute," came a voice over the communicator attached to the aide's belt.

"Any idea why it failed?" the aide asked after bringing the communicator to his mouth.

"...Not exactly sure," the same voice began. "It suffered a lot of damage.... It looks like part of the harness was cut ... hard to tell. It's also a little frayed, so it might be some kind of structural failure."

The entire team of onlookers went silent, but Gabriel Burke was fit to be tied.

"*What'd you do, Gillen!?*" he seethed, pushing Michael hard. "*Cut my harness so you could show us how much of a hero you could be!?*"

Though watching Michael's mouth drop in astonishment, Burke nevertheless took to pounding on him. Everyone quickly dove in, splitting the two apart.

"I didn't do anything!" Michael pleaded, taking in incredulous gazes from Maura Enzler and Shay Taggart. He received supporting looks too: Kate for certain, Tom Andrews, and Kara. The rest were somewhere between those two extremes. "I swear!"

"Don't worry, either of you," Davidson assured. "We'll get to the truth. I promise."

Yet Burke remained inconsolable. "I'm sorry, Cyril, but that's not good enough!" He pointed accusingly once again at Michael. "I can't work with this man! Not after what he pulled. I can't trust him!"

CHAPTER NINE

Building the Team

Twenty-three-year-old Michael Gillen reclined against the heavy log, staring deep into the smoldering embers in the fire before him. Intense, orange-blue heat flared in continuous waves over the surface of the coals. Their dance had become hypnotic, and the young man couldn't help but fall under their spell. Late into the evening in the darkened forest, his troubles seemed so far away—just the thing he needed most.

Almost three months had passed since the skydiving incident. Rather than thanking Michael for saving his life, Burke had instead used the event to justify his distrust. Finding fault with everything Michael did, Burke continually complained to Davidson and the other mission directors. Michael felt as if he were a rook all over again.

Interestingly, the reason for the chute failure had never been discovered—or at least revealed. No, the mission directors remained disturbingly quiet. Burke seemed emboldened by their silence, causing Michael to wonder how long it would take before Burke got him kicked off the backup team altogether. The possibility hung over the young man forebodingly.

So he was glad to be out of NSEA for a while; he was glad to be gone.

A whole group of vacationing Centauries, all of whom Michael had invited to the national park on Earth, sat around the fire with him. Kara sat on the other side of the fire across from him, while Tom Andrews, Ben Morris, David Tashjian, and Phil Marcotte formed the rest of the circle. The small group engaged in frivolous discussion while letting their evening meal digest. Kate stood behind a table in the background, washing dishes in a small tub and listening to music. Every so often, she would shoot Michael an inconspicuous, fleeting glance.

Having rounded out the first year of training, the Centauries received two weeks of leave before the Alpha Centauri fifteen-month launch countdown began. Knowing the work would be quite rigorous, everyone resolved to make the most of his or her time off.

"Do you need any help cleaning up dinner, Kate?" Tom Andrews asked from his chair in front of the fire.

"No, I'm fine. It's my turn on KP, after all. You guys just go do whatever you were going to do."

"She's right," Kara exclaimed, picking up her plate and utensils. "The lake's waiting." After taking her tableware over to Kate for cleaning, Kara walked back across the group, motioning for everyone to start moving.

"Why are we going swimming again?" a reluctant David Tashjian inquired.

Kara stopped at the entrance to the tent she and Kate shared. "Because it's a perfect night, and I don't want to waste my time sitting around a campfire again. Come on." Then the young woman disappeared into the tent to change.

The rest of the group began getting up and dispersing. Tashjian, who was sitting by Michael, stood up with his used dinnerware in hand. He caught sight of Michael's unused plate sitting on the opposite side of him.

"Not hungry, Mike?"

"No."

Tom, having just turned in his dishes to Kate, heard the remark and smiled. "Don't let him fool you, David. Mike's probably got a hankering for desert fare again, just like on the survival test—snakes and bugs beware!"

At this, queasy expressions came over the Centauries, especially those who had participated on Michael's desert team.

"Don't bring that up," Kate grimaced nauseously. "I get the creeps every time I think about it."

"Creeps?" Tom countered comically. "I've still got indigestion from it." He paused for effect. "And don't even *mention* the water."

Again, unsettled jeers rose into the air. Michael, of course, took the banter with the greatest humility, just as he done since returning from the desert exercise.

Over the next several minutes, the campers disappeared into their tents and eventually reemerged, ready for the evening swim. Being the first to appear, Kara waited while the rest of the group assembled. However, Michael remained by the fire and Kate continued washing dishes. Upon seeing everyone set to go, Kara gave the signal, and the small group headed into the forest toward the lake.

"You two coming?" Kara asked, glancing toward Michael and Kate but speaking loud enough for the whole group to hear. She had stopped at the edge of the camp too.

"No," Michael replied, continuing to recline in front of the fire. "You guys go on ahead. I've got some things to do."

Kate shook her no.

"Okay, just don't work too hard," Kara exclaimed. Her pause at the forest's edge had allowed the rest of the swimmers to go on ahead of her. So with a smirk coming over her face, she shot both of them a rather coy wink. Smiling, the young woman disappeared into the forest.

The sounds from the small group moved deeper into the woods until disappearing altogether. Michael remained reclined and staring into the fire, while Kate busily worked behind the table. A moment later, she appeared over him with a fresh plate of food. Sitting down close to him while he wrapped his arm around her to snuggle, Kate began feeding Michael the food.

"I thought they'd never leave," Michael exclaimed, clearly enjoying Kate reclining so close to him. "I'm starving."

"You could have eaten something earlier," she replied. After giving him another fork full of food, Kate took a bite too.

"You kidding? This is the closest we ever get to a real date."

135

"Thanks to Kara. She certainly is creative in getting everyone out of camp."

The young couple relaxed in front of the fire, enjoying their stolen moments together. The ban on dating among astronauts at NSEA had forced the two to become rather creative at finding time alone. So the two shared a quick meal while engaging in small talk.

However, Kate eventually paused, looking pensively at the plate in front of her. "I don't like all this sneaking around. I feel so guilty."

"I think it's kind of exciting—*makes things more interesting,*" Michael smiled amorously at her. Because Kate remained looking down at the plate, the young man took her chin gingerly in his fingers, gently nudging her until she turned and gazed upon him. After a moment of adoring her beautiful features, Michael couldn't help but kiss her. She swooned under his embrace, and the two enjoyed the long moment. Upon parting, Michael added, "And by your reaction, you don't seem to mind."

"No, I certainly don't mind," she replied, surrendering to him for a long moment. However, her pensiveness returned, and she shook her head in frustration. "I just—you know … I don't think we've thought this through. If the mission directors find out, they'll throw us off the backup team." Her expression turned again, this time as if feeling guilty for voicing her concerns. "NSEA's only guaranteeing two launches, so we're taking a big risk." She looked even more intently at him. "And I don't want to get hurt."

"I won't hurt you…. I promise."

When an all too familiar look came over him, she smiled. "I know. You're always protecting me…. Is that why you invited everyone else along on vacation too? Can't trust yourself?"

Though having asked the last question in jest, Kate knew she could have cross-examined herself with the same probing question—making her wonder how she might respond too.

Yet despite the telling look in his eye, Michael didn't waver one bit—just as always. Relishing the contentment his noble efforts afforded her, Kate smiled and kissed him once more before resting her head on his shoulder. "You know, when I first met you, I would have never thought you to be such a gentleman."

Michael sighed. "I don't want to make that mistake again—"

His heart leapt into his throat upon hearing those *stupid* words leave his mouth! The romantic evening in front of the fire with her dissolved before his very eyes, for Kate sat straight up and looked at him intently.

"What do you mean?"

Michael cringed inwardly at his terrible faux pas. Kate's esteeming gaze had disarmed him, letting him say whatever came to mind—the worst part of being in a progressing relationship. The young man was uncertain how to recover.

Honoring his promise to Kara, Michael had kept their indiscretion during his sophomore year a secret; the incident greatly embarrassed him too. Kate—the last person he wanted to tell—would certainly be disappointed in him. In addition, the closer he and Kate became, the more uncomfortable she appeared over his friendship with Kara. Admitting the truth might put doubts about him in her mind. No, Kate just wouldn't understand.

Yet Kate was waiting for an answer.

"It was a *long* time ago…," Michael replied dismissively, looking into the fire. "She developed very strong feelings toward me, and I ended up hurting her…. I didn't mean to, but I guess that doesn't matter in the end."

Of course, a partial truth was still a lie.

"What happened?"

"Can we not talk about it?"

Kate went awkwardly quiet for a long time, remaining drawn away while searching him out with her eyes. Michael could tell that the startling revelation weighed heavily upon her, scaring him fiercely. He felt ashamed too, ashamed at what he had done with Kara so long ago, ashamed at how he had lied just then to Kate.

Finally, and very timidly, Kate asked, "Do you still think about her?"

Michael was at a loss for words again, though knowing the question could not go unanswered. He couldn't bear lying to her again either. No, he needed to answer honestly. "Only when I need to remind myself that I never want to hurt you that same way."

Her searching gaze seemed to acknowledge the response with some satisfaction, though she remained apprehensive over the half-confession and Michael's hesitance to talk about it.

"There's more than one way to hurt someone," Kate finally countered, much to Michael's chagrin. Her expression changed as if wanting to end the discussion. "And I'm afraid our careers are going to get in the way of us dating." Pausing reflectively, she mustered a false pragmatism. "We should go back to just being friends."

"I don't think I can do that," Michael appealed.

"But what if things change?" Kate pleaded. "What if we're forced to go our separate ways?"—looking into the fire—"These missions are for *life*...." She gazed uneasily into the fire for a long moment before turning toward him once again, her eyes betraying her trepidation. "If you had the chance to go to Alpha Centauri and I didn't, can you honestly say you would decline because I couldn't go too?"

Silence fell over the two for another long moment, with Michael's expression becoming telling.

"That's what I thought," Kate conceded soberly, returning her gaze to the fire once more. "And I'm not sure I'd be any different."

"So what do you want to do?"

Silence hung uncomfortably over the young couple. Both watched the flames as if far away. Finally, Kate replied, "I don't know."

The conference room in the NSEA operations complex was tense, to say the least. Everyone attended the mandatory meeting: the primary and secondary launch teams, Cyril Davidson, and the other executive mission directors.

The subject at hand was the *ESS History*, the deep space exploration ship (Gabriel Burke, using his privilege as mission commander, had named it). Having progressed seven months into the Alpha Centauri launch schedule, NSEA had recently discovered significant construction problems with the ship. The problems threatened the scheduled launch, just over eight months away.

Watching Gabriel Burke deliver his latest round of accusations, Michael Gillen couldn't have been more unsettled. Launch preparations were passing gruelingly, with Burke continually voicing dissatisfaction over Michael's performance. He didn't always deliver his complaints so intentionally, as Burke was doing right then. Rather, most times the accusations came across well veiled, with Burke letting the directors and other astronauts come to the intended conclusion. With the list of grievances mounting, the young man feared Burke was within striking distance of having him kicked off the backup team.

This time, the primary team leader was taking a different approach: blaming the entire backup team.

"…So if you look at the problems on *History*," Burke continued, "Many of their origins point to the Secondaries: systems integrity checks, environmental, and navigation."

"Maybe," Cyril Davidson conceded, though shaking his head in disbelief too. "But many problems go back to the original designs, thus requiring modifications. Fortunately, we still have eight months before launch."

"We're not trying to point any fingers," Maura Enzler interjected for Burke, leaning over the large conference room table as if to appeal to the secondary team. "Everyone knows this is a difficult task. We just need more support."

Burke puffed out his chest. "My team has done its job. Now the Secondaries have to step up—treat this launch as if it were their own."

"That's exactly what we're doing," a visibly irritated Michael Gillen countered.

"I'm not seeing it. I'm sorry, but there are too many inconsistencies."

"Burke," Kara Ricci began, "How can you single out a few anomalies from an endless list of problems?"

Maura spoke up again. "What about the navigational field regulators? That's a blaring error."

Kate cringed inconspicuously at the statement.

"Yeah," a rather smug Gabriel Burke looked at Michael. "Navigational fields are supposed to be your specialty. Yet when the engineers double-checked your calibration settings, they found that the regulators were anything but calibrated." He brought the calibration information up on the overhead screen. "Take a look at the findings yourself."

The entire room studied the screen intently, their expressions quickly changing.

"Mike, who calibrated these?" Davidson asked.

"I did, Cyril," a reluctant Kate DeCarreau spoke up. "But I know I followed the procedure to the letter."

Half the expressions turned incredulous.

"Any idea what might have gone wrong?"

Kate just shook her head. "No, Cyril. I was also busy that day loading the computers with simulator code—worked well into the night. I came back late that evening for the final calibrations. Perhaps I was too tired to have done the work."

"At least all the computers check out. That's good."

Michael fumed inwardly, not at Kate, but at Burke. The calibrations were so far off, he reckoned Burke had intentionally changed them to discredit him—yet he had no proof. Kate was about to become collateral damage.

"No, Kate, I'm sure your work was fine," Michael countered, disbelieving what he was about to do. "I didn't log it, but I went back and recalibrated them." He paused, ignoring her quizzical look. "I must have done something wrong—it was late for me too."

The entire room—save Kate, Tom, and Kara—gazed disapprovingly at him. Having falsely admitted to a serious deficiency, Michael had let Burke accomplish his objective: proving Michael wasn't doing his job.

"Okay," Davidson began, visibly tired of the banter. "Let's split the problems list among the teams and start addressing them. We'll convene every day for a status check. Everyone's going to have to work harder if we're going to make up lost time.... This meeting is over."

The team members began dispersing, chief among them a very frustrated Michael Gillen. Wanting desperately to sulk over what had transpired, Michael made a beeline through the labyrinth of corridors to his quarters. He could hear Kate calling from well behind him, getting closer each moment. However, Michael kept going until reaching his room, not in the mood for a confrontation or pep talk. Shortly thereafter, Kate came through the door and closed it behind her.

"You shouldn't be here," Michael exclaimed, still sulking. "Someone will get the wrong impression."

Kate remained undaunted, standing with one hand on her hip and pointing a finger at him accusingly with the other hand. "I don't care. Why did you do that?"

"It doesn't matter."

"Yes, it does," she retorted. "You know you didn't go back afterwards, because you were right there when *I did* the calibrations—one of our late night rendezvous. You know they were done correctly, so why didn't you say that?"

Michael turned away in frustration, staring pensively at the wall. "Because we don't have any proof. You know Burke is out to get me thrown off the backup team. Somehow, he's doing all this."

"It was my work in question. You should have let me take the blame."

"I couldn't let you do that," Michael replied, half-turning around and sheepishly facing her.

"Michael, I don't want to be the reason you get thrown off the backup team!"

"And *I* don't want to be the reason *you* get thrown off the backup team."

The two went silent for a long moment. Kate continued gazing at Michael. Overwhelmed by his sacrifice (for she had struggled more than the other astronauts had), Kate abruptly threw herself upon him and kissed him passionately. Her reaction caught Michael pleasantly off guard. After finally parting, the young couple remained in each other's arms, with Kate nestling herself in the curve of Michael's neck.

Kate remained cradled against Michael, enjoying the comfort of his closeness and the reassuring strength of his embrace. The moment was bittersweet, for Michael had protected her at a tremendous cost to himself. The thought of his sacrifice overwhelmed her, as did the fifteen months since he had first kissed her. With deep emotions welling up within, Kate blurted out in a whisper, "*I love you, Michael.*"

Immediately, the young woman cringed! Her eyes shut hard and her face twisted. She kept her face hidden against the curve of his neck, embarrassed by the gaff. Nevertheless, the words had already left her mouth. The fear of long moments of silence welled up within her. So before Michael could even react, she whispered, "*Whatever you're thinking, don't say or do it.*"

Continuing to hold her in his arms, Michael froze fearfully. Ever since his half-confession during their vacation on Earth, Kate had become fickle. Her demeanor toward him had changed so many times over those seven months, he no longer knew how to respond to her. Perhaps he should tell her what had happened between him and Kara.

141

Perhaps a full confession would heal the schism. Perhaps she would instead give up on him completely. The uncertainty scared him.

Awkwardly and slowly, Kate backed away from Michael, who stared at her like a deer in the headlights—the reason for his anxiousness she could not be certain of. No matter, she fidgeted nervously with her hands. "I should go."

After another uneasy moment and an exchange of expressions the same, Kate left his quarters like a shot. Heading down the short corridor and away from Michael's door, Kate failed to see Gabriel Burke coming from the opposite end of the passage.

Burke watched the fetching, young woman depart quickly, realizing he had noticed Gillen and DeCarreau together more and more.

"This is a beautiful view," Michael Gillen remarked, sitting down at the private table where Cyril Davidson already sat. Descending into the chair, the young explorer couldn't take his eyes off the view out the large observation window next to the table.

The window wasn't the only one. In fact, the circular-shaped restaurant sat atop the highest point on Mid-Earth Station. With the entrance spinning up an elaborate stairway from the lower level and the kitchen and serving areas constructed in the center of the structure, observation windows lined the entire circumference of the restaurant. Each private table had its own view.

However, the table where Davidson sat had the best view of all. Not only did the surface of Mid-Earth Station stretch all the way to the horizon, but also both the Earth and Moon hung low in the black sky.

"There aren't too many views like this on the station," Michael added, finally glancing at his host.

"It's a design flaw—based on old technology," Davidson replied, taking a sip of his water. "All the aesthetics are deep inside. This restaurant was built about ten years ago. I hope more improvements will come. It all depends on whether the station continues as a military base or goes more commercial."

The two men commenced their dinner reservation, engaging in idle chitchat between interactions with the wait staff. Michael remained apprehensive the whole time, a feeling he had carried with him since taking responsibility for the navigational field regulators two weeks earlier. Finding the dinner invitation so uncharacteristic, Michael was sure Davidson had asked him there to kick him off the backup team.

"So not that I don't appreciate the invitation," Michael eventually began, the suspense killing him, "but why am I here?"

Davidson sat back in his chair, comically pleading, "Hey, *I'm* not training for deep space exploration. I need to get out of the NSEA complex every once in a while." He smiled for a moment and took another sip of water. "And I do need to discuss something with you." He paused, looking Michael straight in the eye. "So ... after all my emphatic warnings against it, I see that you took it upon yourself to secretly court Kate anyway, didn't you?"

Michael sat there stunned, subdued under the arresting gaze of his superior. "How'd you find out?"

"It wasn't easy," Davidson replied, still looking him in the eye. "And no one told me—if that's what you mean. I make it my job to know *everything* about my potential crews."

"You don't have me bugged, do you?" Michael nervously laughed.

The older man laughed too, shaking his head. "No, God blessed me with great intuition.... It's the way you two act around each other. There were other indicators too.... So what's going on?"

"Not a lot to tell—nothing immoral or indiscreet."

"Is this something casual or more serious?" Davidson asked. He waited through the long pause. The younger man became reluctant to answer, though his expression was more than telling. "I see," Davidson sighed. "So have you told her about your indiscretion with Kara?"

Michael leaned back in his chair, even more stunned—if that were possible. "No."

"You need to tell her soon."

The two went silent for a long moment. Finally, the older man sighed and shook his head. "You know, you've made this whole thing a mess. It's going to make everything more difficult."

Michael's heart leapt into his throat at his superior's frustration. "Am I in trouble?"

"You should be," the older man declared with steely eyed resolve, "especially after I warned you." However, he let his indignation relent. "No, you're not in trouble. In fact, I made a recommendation to the oversight committee, and they all agree: We want you to command the primary team."

Michael once more was dumbfounded. "I'm not sure I understand. What about Burke?"

"We think you're a better fit for the position," Davidson replied with a rather interesting if not seemingly boastful and omniscient gaze. "We've been watching you, and we like what we see."

"Wow!" Michael mused, realizing his dreams were coming true. That's when the truth of what was going to happen hit him—hit him hard. "I guess I understand your concern about Kate now.... I never thought I'd have to leave her."

"That's why I warned you. Emotions are just as much a part of this mission as fuel cells. But I'll let you in on a secret: I don't want that to happen either." He paused respectfully. "Actually, I made the recommendation to the board to bring both Kate and Tom onto the primary team as well. You three are an excellent team, and I want that synergy on this first mission." His shoulders dropped. "The problem is that I have yet to convince the committee of Kate and Tom." Once again, his expression returned that same interesting look, completely unnerving the young man. "Now, I don't think that will ultimately be a problem, not after you're announced as primary team commander next week. But we'll have to work through it."

"So what's your concern over what happened with Kara?"

At that point, the first of their entrees came, causing the two men to pause until the server left.

"I have to know if Kate can work with Kara—or you, for that matter," Davidson said. "You and Kara are pretty close, and that might be a problem once Kate finds out what happened. That could ruin the team. I can't even let Kate on the primary team until I know how she'll react.... And all this is confidential: You can't tell either Kate or Tom about this discussion."

"You're not going to make it easy on me, are you?"

"No. And until we officially announce the primary team to the press in four months, the oversight committee can change their mind. Once we make the internal announcement, you're going to be swimming upstream trying to get the support of the Primaries. Some have a lot invested in having Burke as their commander. Between that and Kate and Kara, I don't envy you." He lifted his glass. "But congratulations."

"Thanks," Michael said sarcastically.

"I can't believe it!" Gabriel Burke fumed as he came out of his chair in Cyril Davidson's office, located somewhere in the heart of the NSEA complex on Mid-Earth Station. "This is an outrage!"

"Gabriel, calm down," Cyril Davidson pleaded from his side of the desk. The director leaned back in his chair and gestured for the young man to sit back down. "We didn't come to this decision lightly. Also, you still have four months to win back the position before we publicly announce the Centauri mission."

Despite firmly believing Michael was the better choice for primary team leader, Davidson nevertheless loathed having to break the news to Burke. Worse, Burke was appealing for all it was worth.

"We shouldn't even be discussing it!" Burke retorted sharply. "I've done nothing but outperform, while Gillen's performance has been questionable at best. How you can move him into my position and give me the backup slot is beyond me."

At this, the older man decided that he had enough.

Davidson went silent for a long moment, sizing up Burke from across the desk while wearing that all-knowing expression. "You're *lucky* to be on the team at all." He leaned back in his chair and swiveled to one side while putting his hands together finger to finger. "I mean, do you *really* want to discuss what's been going on the last sixteen months? After all, not everything is as it appears—like the skydiving incident, for instance. Do you want *that* to come out?"

"You accusing me of something?"

"You bet I am!" Davidson exclaimed. "And the skydiving incident's just the tip of the iceberg. If I had my way, you'd be out on the streets. However, the other members of the oversight committee don't know as much as I do. I can tell them, if you want me to." He paused for effect for a long moment before relenting. "But I don't want that. I'm giving you the chance to put your resentment of Gillen behind you. You're too talented to throw away."

Burke sat across the table, his face burning with anger. Finally, he declared in as calm of a voice as he could muster, "I play second fiddle to *no one*." He paused. "If you want to throw this program away by putting Gillen in the commander's chair ... then you can have him. I quit!" The young man got up and went toward the door. Right before opening it, he shot one last final look of disgust back toward Davidson. "But I guarantee you one thing: You're going to regret it."

Davidson sat back in his chair, watching Burke leave in a huff. He remained deep in thought for quite a while before closing the file on his desk. "Something tells me Michael isn't going to have it very easy."

CHAPTER TEN

Divisive Announcement

Twenty-four-year-old Kate DeCarreau sat in the back of the large NSEA conference room, patiently waiting for the impromptu meeting to begin. Most of the other usuals had already arrived, while those who weren't present were quickly gathering. Of particular interest, Michael had yet to arrive.

No sooner had her thoughts of him began than Michael appeared. After pausing at the door and taking a quick look around the whole room—stealing a quick but odd glance in her direction, young Gillen took his place a good distance away near the front of the room.

From her more anonymous place farther back, Kate eyed Michael nervously; he was acting strangely around her lately. Not that taking his place far from her was unusual. No, the couple had maintained their distance in public since beginning their secret courtship, just over fifteen months earlier. No, this was different.

Moreover, because his strange behavior had started over three weeks earlier, Kate just knew his aloofness was all her fault.

Staring at him from the back of the room, the young woman regretted *stupidly* confessing her love for him three weeks earlier.

Embarrassed by her moment of weakness and fearing his response, Kate escaped his presence before he could even say a word. The image of his dumbfounded expression lingered heavily in her mind, convincing the young woman that she had made a dreadful mistake.

For the next two weeks, Kate remained aloof from Michael. Fear of his response to what she had said that day made even the briefest moments with him completely awkward. Despite Michael's eagerness to talk about what had happened, Kate kept him at bay.

Shortly after returning from a dinner reservation with Cyril Davidson a week earlier, Michael stopped pursuing her altogether. Perhaps Davidson had found out about their courtship and cowed Michael into reexamining his priorities—and Michael realized she wasn't one of them. Curiosity getting the best of her, she finally mustered the courage to approach him. Michael said nothing, even becoming as aloof toward her as she had treated him the previous two weeks. Every time he looked at her, his face displayed an odd expression.

Right then, Michael appeared as unsettled as ever.

"This won't take too long," Davidson began, stepping to the front of the conference room. Waiting until the noise tapered off, the executive director continued, "We've had some recent changes in the line-up of our teams, and I wanted to bring everyone up to date.

"You may notice that Gabriel Burke is not here today. A personal situation came up, and he has requested an indefinite leave of absence. With much sadness, we reluctantly agreed to honor his request, and we wish him well."

Once more, the director paused as a round of whispers permeated the room. "With that in mind, I am happy to announce that Michael Gillen has been named commander of the primary team. Since Mike has done an excellent job leading the secondary team, we are more than confident he is ready to take the helm of this most critical, upcoming mission. Congratulations, Michael!"

After a round of applause, Davidson continued elucidating details of the announcement, particularly noting how he would announce Michael's backup slot replacement later. Davidson gave Michael a few minutes to express appreciation for the appointment and encourage his new team.

However, Kate heard not a word. No, her heart waxed over, and everything became surreal. Michael was leaving her—forever! In just seven short months, he would be gone. She smarted at her own lack of foresight.

"So if there are no more questions…," Davidson concluded. "You're free to go."

When the meeting began to disperse, Michael quickly found himself mobbed by well-wishing peers and support personnel. Never had the young man shaken hands with so many people. Maura Enzler and Shay Taggart congratulated him as well, appearing more polite than happy for him. This, of course, came as no surprise.

Michael, still surrounded by a mob, caught sight of Kate out of the corner of his eye. Looking rather uncomfortable, she was quickly leaving. He also noticed Davidson catching sight of her abrupt departure too. Breaking through the crowd as politely as he could, Michael pursued Kate out of the room and down the corridors. Each time he called to her, the young woman only seemed to move that much faster.

"Kate," Michael called again, having eventually caught up with her in an isolated hallway overlooking the *ESS History*, "I need to talk with—"

"No, Michael," she pleaded, never missing a step. "Not now."

He grabbed her by the arm, stopping her in mid-stride and causing her to turn around toward him. "I wanted to tell you, but—"

"It doesn't matter who I hear it from," Kate exclaimed, breaking his grip. "You're leaving; that's all I heard." She stood gazing up at him for a very long and awkward moment, a painful expression covering her face. Then she abruptly gathered herself, almost looking proper once more—scaring him something fierce. "Look, I'll be okay…. We discussed this: if I were the one going, I would have done the same thing…. So I understand." She paused hesitantly. "But I think we should stop seeing each other. It's for the best."

Michael shook his head back and forth.

"No, Michael. I told you I didn't want to get hurt."

Though she turned to go, Michael grabbed her by the arm once more. "Kate, we have *seven months*. A lot can happen by then. I promised you I wouldn't hurt you, and I intend to keep that promise. Please trust me."

Kate, giving him a fleeting glance, broke his grip and set off down the corridor.

Twenty-four-year-old Michael Gillen leaned against the railing in the small observation room, surveying the *ESS History* sitting in the NSEA dry dock well below. The time was late in the evening.

History was a dumb name for a ship; that's what the young man thought—and not just because Burke had named it. Rather, the splendid vessel with elaborate and stately lines deserved a name conveying its grandeur. However, renaming the ship, effectively nullifying Gabriel Burke's last contribution, was the last thing the new primary team leader wanted to do.

Thoughts of the Primaries were what consumed Michael—mostly.

That was why he had come to the isolated observation room. Despite the announcement three weeks earlier naming him primary team commander, the opportunity seemed to be slipping away. Davidson's warnings of the difficulties in winning over the crew seemed almost prophetic.

The whole crew wasn't against him, just Shay Taggart and Maura Enzler—Burke's closest friends and staunchest supporters. They resented Michael for replacing Burke, making everything difficult. He also suspected they were purposely undermining his appointment. Regardless, their efforts negatively affected the rest of the Primaries— save Kara—delaying the training schedule too. Davidson had warned him to make peace with the team fast.

In addition, things between him and Kate were worse than ever. Though not completely breaking off their courtship, Kate nevertheless remained aloof. How much worse would things become after he confessed his indiscretion with Kara so long ago? Yet he had no choice; it was a requirement for staying on the primary crew.

Michael knew that telling Kate that Davidson intended to put her on the primary team would heal the discord. That's what he needed most: to heal the discord. However, he couldn't tell her; Davidson had forbidden it. Therefore, the discord would continue. Yet as long as the rift between them existed, Kate remained disqualified for the move to the primary team—a catch-22 if there ever was one!

Somehow, he had to figure a way to work out everything.

"She's a beautiful ship, *Commander*," Kara Ricci said lightheartedly while coming up from behind him. She smiled and sidled up close to him, leaning with her forearms against the railing too.

Michael glanced at her and chuckled cynically, "Commander for *now*. Who knows? They might bust me down to lead janitor soon if I don't turn a corner."

"Don't worry, Michael," Kara replied, still looking out at the ship. "Burke was the primary commander for almost twenty months. That's a long time in this game. You just need to find your stride."

"I'm not sure I'll find my stride with *some* of them—ever. But that's what Davidson is expecting. My position as commander isn't a lock; that's for sure."

"The team is just getting used to working with you," she said, turning toward him. "Ben and Phil aren't hostile, and you know you have my support. You just have to win over Taggart and Enzler. Before you know it, you'll be halfway to Alpha Centauri."

Michael only shook his head. "I wish I could believe that."

Just then—and unnoticed by either Kara or Michael—Maura Enzler walked by the entrance to the observation room. Catching the two of them close together and speaking in hushed voices, the curious, young woman ducked in behind the bulkhead. Though hidden from sight, she could still see and hear what was going on.

Kara, sympathizing with her friend's concerns, wrapped an arm around Michael's and hugged it supportively. Briefly patting his bicep with her other hand, she smiled at him and said, "It'll be all right. I promise."

"You shouldn't do that," the young commander gently warned, though clearly appreciative of her attempts to console him.

"You look like you need it," she replied, continuing with her arm wrapped around his. "Besides, it's taken me a long time to be able to do this and not feel awkward."

Michael just shook his head again. "I don't mean that. The last thing I need is for Kate to walk by and see you clutching my arm; I'm not sure she would understand. I don't want to risk her pulling away any more than she already has."

"Do you blame her? She's trying to come to grips with you leaving forever."

"That's what makes this next part so difficult," Michael added reluctantly. "Cyril ordered me to tell her what happened between you and me."

Kara's jaw dropped, and her arm unwrapped from his while she looked at him in disbelief. "You're kidding, right?"

"No," Michael replied, watching Kara let her head fall. "I don't even know how I'm going to break it to her—but it has to be soon."

Kara's bright blue eyes seemed to dim as they focused far across the dry dock. "That night just won't go away…. I guess it's true: You can't escape your past." She paused, remaining deep in thought before turning toward Michael. "I know it was a long time ago, but Kate's a very traditional girl. She's not going to take you and me sleeping together lightly."

"She already knows that *something* happened with *someone* long ago."

"But she doesn't know it was with *me*…. She'll take that revelation much more personally."

"I know," Michael replied, nodding. "I'm afraid of how she'll react." He went silent for a long moment, his expression churning. Finally, he mustered enough courage and looked at her. "So did you ever get over it? I mean, *really* get over it?"

Kara remained silent for a long time, deep in thought once more. Finally, she sighed. "No, I didn't … and neither will Kate, especially because you took so long to tell her. It doesn't matter that it happened long before you two started dating; monogamy is something everyone wants from his or her partner. I don't know why it's true, but it is…. After all, what was your reaction when Kate told you that *she* had slept with someone else already?"

"*What?*" Michael asked, straightening up and visibly consternated at the news.

Kara laughed. "No, she didn't. I was just seeing how you'd react." Then she smiled sardonically. "Your expression was priceless, by the way—*you hypocrite.*"—her demeanor turning serious once more—"But do you see what I mean?"

Michael nodded in concession, leaning over the railing once more, very discouraged.

Kara continued, "I said that I never really got over it, but I've moved on. I've learned from my mistakes, and it's made me a better person. Coming clean will make you a better person too, and *that* will bring you two closer together."

"If she ever speaks to me again after I tell her."

Kara watched Michael bear the weight of his imminent confession. Supportively, she grabbed his arm tightly once more. "She will." With an assuring smile, Kara kissed him platonically on the cheek.

The two remained in the observation room for some time, watching the exploration ship below and continuing their conversation. However, Maura Enzler, still hidden at the back of the room and realizing the value of what she had just learned, stole away quietly.

"How's everything going?" Cyril Davidson asked while entering the NSEA launch control center on Mid-Earth Station. He took his position behind the main control station where Roel Holt, NSEA's simulations director, sat. About twenty other controllers staffed the other console stations throughout the room.

Before the man could answer, Davidson stole a fleeting glance out the observation windows where *History* sat moored. The ship's bridge, which lay deep inside the large vessel, was where the two Alpha Centauri crews had spent a rather long day. With the ship's construction back on schedule, the two crews were running through various training exercises. The Primaries manned their posts, while the secondary team observed.

"Seven hours of scenario testing," Holt began, staring into the live feed from the bridge, "and the only thing predictable is the infighting."

"It's still early. We've had these problems before, right?"

The subordinate shook his head, saying, "Not like this." Though returning to his monitoring, he saw Davidson gesture for him to elaborate. "Well, eventually the tension reaches a critical mass, with everyone lashing out. But predictably, the tension always starts with either Taggart or Enzler, and it's always directed at Gillen."

Upon hearing the report, Davidson appeared satisfied, even smiling. "Just keep that in mind when you write your reports."

"Always do," Holt mused, looking back at his friend. "But don't think that my reports are going to get the rest of the oversight committee off your back. They're not as sold on Gillen as you are."

"Give it time," Davidson replied confidently. Then he looked at the live feed. "What are they doing now?"

"We were just about to start them on a navigational shield cascade failure—all false readings. We want to see if they can be fooled by a computer readout malfunction."

"Who's on Systems this time?"

"Enzler—all the Primaries are in their principal roles today."

Davidson smiled. "Good. We can test Maura's reaction to the simulation." He paused in thought for a moment. "Loop in some problems with Environmental too. That will put both Enzler and Taggart in the spotlight."

Holt looked at him and chuckled, clearly aware of the man's intention. "Okay. Just give us a few minutes."

Meanwhile, on the bridge of *History*, the two crews were taking a short but much needed break from their simulation exercises.

Michael Gillen looked around from his commander's chair, noticing how cramped the place had become. The thought was less an observation of the bridge's size as it was a frustration over the incredibly tense day. Just as had occurred since Davidson had announced him as primary team commander, Michael was once again the brunt of Enzler and Taggart's attacks.

"Anyone else getting tired of all these simulations?" an exhausted Phil Marcotte asked, breaking the tense silence.

"I'm not even sure why they're running us through traveling simulations," Kara Ricci added. "We're going to be in cryogenic suspension most of the time. It will be up to the computers to get us through."

The bridge went silent, until Ben Morris sat up in his chair while surveying his console. "Here comes another one." He quickly studied the readouts. "The computer is indicating an anomaly in navigational shield A2. It's at ninety-five percent output and dropping two percent per minute."

"At least we have some time to figure it out," Michael observed. "Phil, what's the status?"

Phil Marcotte was already looking at the readouts on his Navigation console. "Generators still indicate full modulation at frequency point-zero-two-five."

"That sounds right. Maura, check the computer systems. Maybe there's a malfunction."

"They all look right," Maura Enzler replied, still looking into her screen. "But I'll check"

The Primaries went about the next few minutes attempting to solve the problem, with the Secondaries standing or sitting near each of their posts and observing. David Tashjian looked onto Ben Morris' propulsion station as the shield output readouts changed once more.

"Shields at ninety-one percent," Morris announced.

Michael soberly nodded, knowing that the mission directors in the control center were closely watching his reactions and decisions. "Okay, we need to work it faster."

The crew diligently worked the simulation for several more minutes. However, Ben Morris eventually said, "Shields at eighty-nine percent."

Young Gillen sat back in his chair, deep in thought. Finally, he turned toward Marcotte and said, "That doesn't make sense. If the shields are degrading that fast, the modulation should be changing. Any sign of modulation?"

Marcotte shrugged his shoulders, indicating that everything was still okay.

Once more, Michael turned to a very busy Maura Enzler and called out, "Maura, run a diagnostic on the computers. It's got to be the computers."

"I did," she partially huffed as if his directions were too obvious to mention. "Nothing."

While the two exchanged irritated stares, Taggart interjected, "We're reading a failure in the atmospheric controller now."

"Great," Tom Andrews comically chimed in, forgetting that his position as a backup prohibited him from talking or interacting while the simulation was running. "We're going to suffocate too."

From the launch control center, Cyril Davidson and Roel Holt remained transfixed on the live feed from the bridge.

"Gillen's getting it," Davidson mused. "That's good."

"Yeah, but he's got to get his team to follow his lead."

From his seat on the bridge, Michael nervously watched his team work the problem. However, Ben Morris eventually announced Shield A2 at eighty-two percent, while Shield A4 had dropped its output by ten percent. In addition, there were still no modulation changes in any of the shield generators.

Had the exercise been real, young Gillen would have begun to worry. The ship would have been traveling at a tremendous speed. Without proper shielding, micro meteors and other space debris would have pelted the vessel mercilessly. At such speeds, more than once around the Earth every second, the ship could not have slowed down in time to prevent catastrophe.

Nevertheless, within the boundaries of a simulation, his crew's reaction to his orders was of most concern. He worried about the mounting tension, particularly at Maura Enzler's post—right where the answer to the shield problem seemed to be.

"Maura, it's got to be the computers," Michael began, keeping his voice as calm as possible. "Perhaps the environmental controllers are shorting out the main computer. Taggart, work with Maura. Do a diagnostics loop on the two systems together."

"That doesn't make sense," Maura huffed. "This is clearly a problem with the shields themselves."

"I've already run a diagnostics," Phil Marcotte said. "Everything's fine."

The young woman's resolve only strengthened. "Everything is fine with my systems too." Then she turned back toward Michael and added, "Why don't we increase power to the shields by ten percent? If we get an increase in output, we'll know it's the generators. Then we can bypass."

"We could risk blowing out the generators that way. Please do the loop diagnostics first."

"I disagree," Enzler declared, folding her arms in front of her defiantly. "You're going about this all wrong."

"Shields down to fifty percent." Ben Morris announced.

"And environmental is still failing," Taggart added, looking with dissatisfaction at Gillen.

Michael pondered the situation for a quick moment, realizing the long day was putting a strain on everyone. So he went over to Maura's console and studied the readouts, avoiding her sharp gaze. Finally, he turned to her to plead. "Maura, look at these readings. The diagnostics don't look right."

"No, I disagree!"

"Shields down to twenty-five percent." Ben Morris announced, becoming the harbinger of doom. "Hull is still intact."

Though finding the news about the hull encouraging, Michael also realized the turn of events might have been just a simulated stroke of luck. He had little time to solve the problem.

"Let's do this together," Michael began as assertively as he could. "Look here at this vector reading. It's got—"

"You're wasting your time!" Enzler retorted, refusing to budge. "We've got to get more power to the shields or drop speed." She paused, training her incriminating gaze on him. "That's what Burke would do."

"Burke's not here," Michael chided. "Do what I ask."

Maura remained where she was, folding her arms in front of her defiantly.

"Shield envelope has collapsed," Morris finally announced. "No reports of hull integrity breaches."

The fact that the computers weren't simulating a complete disintegration of the ship began to prove Michael right. However, Enzler didn't seem to care. In fact, the embittered woman rebuffed the disapproving stares from the rest of the crew and kept eye to eye with Michael. "Yeah ... too bad Burke's *not* here."

Deciding he had had enough, Michael turned to Kate, who was observing Maura's post. "Kate, take over. Figure out the problem with the systems."

While Kate hesitantly began working the console, Maura's expression toward Michael waxed over from indignation to scorn.

"So *she* is what this is all about," Maura exclaimed to Michael with contempt. "This is all about you giving her the chance to show me up, isn't it!? You want her on the primary crew instead of me, don't you?"

Kate, more than astonished at the accusation, paused warily. She looked around the group, not continuing her work until receiving an assuring glance from Michael.

"Mike, you're breaching protocol of the simulation," Shay Taggart added. "Kate's only to observe."

Though an argument of sorts erupted among the crew, everyone went silent when Cyril Davidson eventually came through the entryway to the bridge.

"Here it is," Kate announced. "A malfunction in the environmental interface to the main controllers. It's shorting out the transfer nodes, causing the false shield indicators. I've bypassed the short."

Everyone gathered around the console. Surely enough, all the readings had returned to normal, including shield output levels.

"Maura," Davidson began, "Why didn't you listen to Michael?"

"Commander Gillen might have been right," she huffed, "but only by luck. The readings didn't confirm his concerns."

"Not from what I've seen."

Maura went silent upon realizing that everyone was watching her reaction. Finally, she said, "Okay ... do you *really* want to know what this is all about?" She paused dramatically. "I don't trust him, that's what.... He's not one of us, no matter how much he tries to pretend ... and he's intentionally undermining my performance. He wants me off the team so that Kate can move into my slot." Though Maura looked around the group confidently, their expressions remained mixed. So she blurted out, "Is anyone *else* aware that Gillen and DeCarreau are romantically involved?"

At once, a rather embarrassed Michael Gillen and Kate DeCarreau stood among mixed expressions themselves. No return expression from the couple seemed to defend them against Maura's accusation. Kate's face became particularly blushed.

Enzler continued, "I don't care if they think the rules against dating are for everyone else. But I don't take it lightly when my position on the team is in jeopardy because Gillen is biased."

"That's not true," Michael retorted.

Enzler remained unconvinced—or she was playing it for all it was worth. Michael couldn't tell.

"Why should I believe you?" Maura challenged him. "You're not one of us. We all know it. The rest of us ... we've had to work for what we want; we weren't born into privilege, just broken homes, foster parents … you name it. But not you. So you try to fit in, telling us how hard you've had it. They're just stories."

"That's not true," Kate shot back, with Kara nodding her head in agreement.

Maura looked at Kate for a moment and partially laughed. "I feel sorry for you the most, Kate. Michael's manipulated you more than anyone…. You poor thing…. He's probably taken advantage of you too."

"Maura, don't lie," Kara interjected.

Enzler stood her ground, beaming as if knowing a valuable secret. She traded glances with Michael, and then Kara, and then back to Michael again. Her eyes seemed to relish their bewilderment, and her confidence was disturbing.

Kate watched the silent exchange between the three, still overwhelmed by embarrassment. Watching Maura's smug expression closely, the young woman folded her arms protectively around herself. Warily, she asked, "What do you mean?"

Maura paused, letting the emotion drain from her face. Her voice became deliberate, almost compassionate. "Kate, do you know that Mike and Kara have been sleeping together—just like they've been doing since the academy?"

Though Kate looked to Enzler for some sign of relenting, Maura remained as confident as ever. Both Kara and Michael looked equally indignant and furious at the statement, though neither gave any sign that Maura was lying. The rest of the group appeared more than shocked at the revelation, and all Kate could feel was more embarrassment.

"That's not true!" Kara retorted hesitantly.

A surprised look came over Enzler. "Oh, really? So you deny that you've slept with him?"

At this, Kara went awkwardly silent. She looked at Kate as if to plead and Michael as if searching for support. Her face became equally blushed and her expression more than telling. "No, but—"

"And I suppose you're going to deny being with him late last night … in the upper observation room?"—upon watching how Kara could do nothing but return Kate's searching gaze with a look of abject guilt—"I saw you kissing him last night myself … are you *really* going to try to make *me* out to be the liar?"

Kate began to tremble, if ever so slightly. Her eyes pleaded to Michael for some sort of consolation that none of this was true. Yet she found no comfort, just his dumbfounded and panicky expression; Kara's reaction was the same. At that point, the young woman realized that everyone was staring at her. She had been played the fool! Overwhelmed by humiliation, Kate hurried off the bridge.

After watching Michael anxiously run after Kate, Maura turned to Davidson. "See, I told you he hasn't been truthful."

Kate DeCarreau leaned against the railing in the small observation room, looking out onto the *ESS History* sitting in the dry dock below. She was all alone, except for the many thoughts crowding her mind.

Ironically, the distraught, young woman found herself in the same place Maura Enzler had found Kara and Michael the night before. The place was quite isolated, just as Maura had so viscously implied. Having been humiliated in front of the entire NSEA organization, Kate needed time alone more than anything.

"Kate," Cyril Davidson greeted her, coming up from behind her and barely missing seeing her sigh and roll her eyes. "I've been looking everywhere for you. I was afraid you had already left."

Kate turned her chin side to side while looking far off in the distance. "No, not yet." Then she looked down, pursing her lip. "I'm sorry I left my resignation on your desk without any explanation."

"That's okay," he replied sympathetically. "But I wish you would reconsider. You know, most of what Maura said was untrue."

"*Not everything*," Kate retorted, her eyes narrowing. Finally, she relented. "I know…. Kara already talked to me about it—told me the truth. We're still friends too."

"Have you talked with Michael yet?"

Kate shook her head again, remaining silent for a moment. "No…. I should have listened to you at my entrance interview. You were right when you warned me not to get involved with him. People now know we were seeing each other secretly, and because of what Maura said, they're going to talk. It doesn't matter what the truth is anymore. Either

I'll be the dupe who let him cheat on me, or someone who engaged in the same indiscretions with him. Either way, I've been humiliated—and he hurt me too. So, no, I don't *want* to talk to him."

"You know," Davidson spun around casually. "I've gotten to know you pretty well over these past twenty-one months." He smiled. "Plus, I have your psychological profile."

Kate chuckled halfheartedly but let her head drop away.

So Cyril gently took her by the chin, turned her face toward him, and smiled. "You're like a daughter to me now…. Kate, I see how you look at him—how he looks at you. You're trying to convince yourself it's about all this other stuff. I don't buy it. He's leaving you, and you're afraid of watching him go…. *A lot of people have left you….* So you're looking for an excuse to make it easier on yourself."

She worked her chin out of his hand and gazed at the floor for a long time. Finally looking him in the eye again while her own eyes began welling up a bit, she asked, "Why should I listen to the one who's making him go?"

"I understand," he replied graciously. "But do me this one favor: Don't leave for a while. I'll accept your resignation, if that's what you decide to do in the end. Just give me time to work things out. At least stay around and help your replacement make the transition … *okay?*"

Kate paused pensively for a long moment, feeling the weight of the man's persuasion against her will. Finally, she rolled her eyes and shrugged. "Okay."

CHAPTER ELEVEN

Early Morning Broadcast

A rather groggy Michael Gillen made his way down the long, winding corridor, not exactly ready for the start of a new day. Having quickly gotten up, showered, and dressed, the young man made his way to the common area for a quick breakfast. With each step, he wondered what the new day would hold for him.

Four days had passed since Maura Enzler had spitefully embarrassed him, revealing his most intimate secrets to all of NSEA while embellishing them with many untruths. Becoming the brunt of many disapproving glances, Michael made a futile attempt to set the record straight. Nevertheless, Maura's accusations were already out. Let's face it: Keeping his relationship with Kate a secret made him someone who *had secrets* to keep. His reputation—Kate's too—was in the hands of a very parochial and suspicious group of people. Davidson's warning from so long ago stung terribly.

That's what scared him most. With all the other troubles plaguing him, his position as primary commander was on the line.

The young commander had already been struggling before Maura's announcement. So Enzler and Taggart, Burke's staunchest allies, used the scandal to heighten their complete dissatisfaction with him. Because Kara's support for him was unfairly tainted, a rift had shattered the primary team. Even Ben Morris and Phil Marcotte, though gracious and encouraging, both expressed disappointment over his lack of discretion.

He was losing his credibility, being more than just guilty of disobeying the prohibitions against dating other team members. Worse, some probably considered him some sort of philanderer. Michael thought it only a matter of time before the oversight committee finally overrode Davidson, relegating Michael to the secondary team—or worse.

Then there was Kate. She hadn't spoken to him in four days, save work and general civilities—also being noticeably absent from duty much of the time. She had met his many attempts to reconcile with scorn. He was losing her, just as he had been losing her since becoming the primary commander.

However, he quickly put all these thoughts out of mind, for Michael had made his way into the common area.

"Good morning, everyone," Michael feigned a smile upon entering the room.

His eyes immediately went to the far wall. Being entirely transparent, that wall looked out onto the dry dock where *History* sat. Because the crew living areas were on the lower floors of the complex, a large section of the vessel's underside hull filled the whole field of view. Michael kept his eyes fixed out the observation wall, avoiding any reproving gazes that might be coming from Enzler, Taggart, or anyone else for that matter—perhaps especially Kate. He felt completely out of place.

Quickly, he realized he was the last of the two crews to arrive.

It was a typical morning scene. Everyone lingered around, preparing for the day. Some fixed their breakfast at the kitchenette or ate at the table in the center of the room. Conversations abounded among various people. The television at the front of the kitchenette was on, and Michael could hear some sort of early morning newscast airing.

However, beginning to make his breakfast, young Gillen realized that something was awry. Rather than going about their business, the other crewmembers had frozen in place and gone silent; the voices he was hearing were from the newscast on the television. Though facing away,

Michael could feel their eyes awkwardly fixed on him. He sighed in defeat. *I'm off the primary team*, he thought. *Somehow, they've found out and I'm the last to know.*

That's when the young man turned around. Their expressions were worse than he had anticipated—more awkward too. No one said anything at all. Disturbingly, even Taggart and Enzler's faces were devoid of the satisfaction Michael would have expected to see. No, everyone just kept staring at him. Unable to bear their gawking for too long, he blurted out, "*What?*"

His crewmates didn't answer.

"I'm sorry, Michael," Kate eventually offered.

At this, a whole round of condolences came to him.

"Sorry? Sorry for *what?*"

Everyone remained uneasily silent. That's when he heard the sounds of the newscast in the background. Turning curiously, Michael looked at the screen. The words *Breaking News* scrolled across the bottom of the transmission. This wasn't unusual; the tactic was a typical trick the news agencies employed to get people to watch. Moreover, the ongoing conflict between the Europans and the Mars Federation had frequently made breaking headlines of late.

The scene transpiring behind the reporter was full of commotion and confusion. Wreckage of some sort lay in the background, and smoke billowed into the air. Emergency personnel rushed about the chaos, while an occasional civilian—hurt or otherwise—came randomly in and out of the frame. The words, *Outer Rim: Elara*, displayed in small print as the reporter continued his address:

> "*...Rescue workers are still on the scene, making sure the fire does not spread to anything else in the immediate area. But as you can see, the transport carrying the couple was completely destroyed.*
>
> "*Although not widely covered in the Inner Rim, the two were scheduled to debate Mos Thieren this evening here on Elara. It was a chance to—in their own words—'...set the record straight'. Attendance was expected to be huge.*"

Though still unable to ascertain the exact breaking story, Michael felt the hairs on the back of his neck standing on end. *Elara, Mos Thieren*, and *Debate* were words far too familiar to him and his family.

The reporter continued:

> *"This was to be the first debate of its kind in quite a number of years, as the couple had chosen to remain out of the public eye while raising their children, one of whom died just over four years ago—under mysterious circumstances—in this very settlement."*

Michael didn't want to listen anymore, fearing what he would learn. Nevertheless, the transmission persisted:

> *"Officials are still not releasing any public statements, as they attempt to grapple with understanding many of the details. However, we have heard reports that a militant* Weightless *faction, not yet named, has claimed responsibility for the incident. Mos Thieren has disavowed any involvement in, or foreknowledge of, the plot.*
>
> *"So we only know this: Clifford Gillen, the grandson of the late Jonathan Gillen, the infamous inventor of the gravitational field generator, has been assassinated along with his wife, Marjorie … the victims of a grizzly transport bombing."*

The report continued to spout its insanity—that's how Michael regarded it. He couldn't watch anymore, but neither could he avert his eyes.

"What were they doing on Elara?" he pleaded to no one in particular. Nothing made sense. His parents were on Earth the last time he had talked to them, just over a month earlier. "This is impossible…. They even warned David not to go there."

Cyril Davidson appeared at the door, very much trying to catch his breath from his hurried pace. He saw Michael standing there in shock, watching the grim television broadcast.

"I tried to get here before you saw this, Mike—somebody, turn off the TV!" Davidson shouted, with Phil Marcotte the closet to the device to respond. Davidson put his hand on the younger man's shoulder. "I'm sorry, Mike. I just received a communication from the Earth States embassy on Elara. I just couldn't get here fast enough."

By this time, Michael had sat down, joined by some of the crew. He had placed his hands over his head while staring blankly at the floor. Disbelief and denial buffeted his thoughts. Cliff and Marge Gillen were just simple people—Marge was a housewife! They weren't like those other relatives who had gone looking for a fight.

However, the young man began remembering things: subtle hints here and there, off-handed comments from their close friends about "…*how happy they were to see Cliff and Marge settle down to raise David and him.*" and "…*how his parents had removed themselves out of the spotlight to protect them.*" He lifted his chin. "They didn't even tell me they were going."

"They probably didn't want to worry you," Kara added in a futile attempt to console.

"I can't believe this is happening … *again*."

Nevertheless, it *was* happening again. Dreadful images of how they must have died conjured themselves up in his mind, though he fought them with all the strength he had. They danced among his thoughts mockingly, even conjuring images of David dying too. Michael could not bear up under the assault. He was alone in the universe—the last Gillen alive. The fault clearly lay with Mos Thieren and those despicable *Weightless*.

He desperately desired to leave the room before breaking down completely.

"We'll arrange a transport to take you back home," Cyril remarked as Michael got up to leave. "I'm sure it will take awhile for your parent's remains to be returned to Earth, so you can stay here awhile if you like. Don't worry about the training schedule. Just do what you have to."

Michael paused in thought. In his overwhelming grief, he had forgotten all about the mission. Leaving then might mean surrendering his place on the launch team—maybe a foregone conclusion anyway. After all, the compressed launch schedule could not accommodate such a delay. Of course, his parents were dead; that's all he could think of. So he just shook his head. "Right now I could care less."

With that comment hanging in the air awkwardly, Michael left the room.

Kara turned to Davidson. "Cyril, you have to let him stay on the team."

Mixed reactions followed, with Shay Taggart and Maura Enzler remaining predictably quiet.

"If it were up to me...," Davidson began. "But the oversight committee will make the decision. They're much harder to convince."

The two crews went silent, with everyone looking at each other awkwardly. But not Kate DeCarreau. No, the young woman couldn't take her eyes off watching Michael walk away, his twisted and painful expression of grief lingering heavily in her mind.

Michael Gillen stood over the bed in his NSEA quarters, packing the suitcase lying open before him. After two days of grieving over his parents' assassination, the young man was almost ready to leave for home.

Holding a few items in hand, Michael paused for a moment, eventually letting the things drop onto the bed. Giving out a sigh and letting his shoulders slump, he sat down on the bed. He leaned forward and put his head in his hands for a while, vacantly staring at the floor. Then he looked back up and sighed once more.

Michael Gillen felt numb.

The feeling was self-inflicted, for it seemed to be the only reasonable way to survive his ordeal. No, the senseless loss of his parents, heightened by David's death four years earlier, remained unfathomable. Worse, the tragedies were unfair! They didn't deserve to die that way. Life had dealt them a cruel hand—life had dealt *him* a cruel hand.

He could no longer blame God. No, Michael had expelled Him from existence when David had been killed. If only he could resurrect him once more so as to expel him again. However, someone *was* to blame: Mos Thieren and the *Weightless*. Michael's anger burned against them hotter than ever, and he hated them like no one else he had ever hated—hated the whole Outer Rim too, for that's where most of them resided. The problems in the Outer Rim had fueled the *Weightless'* anger, and his parents were dead as a result.

He caught himself once more, reminding himself to remain numb, to put his grief out of mind, to suppress his disappointment over NSEA continuing without him or losing Kate.

As he resumed packing, a knock at the door caught his attention. Sighing and dreading the unexpected and unwelcome company, Michael reluctantly went over and opened the door. Standing alone in the hallway was Kate—much to his surprise—holding a bunch of her personal items in hand.

"Hi," he hesitantly greeted her, unsure of what to make of her appearance.

"I can't find my suitcase," Kate declared matter-of-factly, making a beeline to where his suitcase lay open. She looked down as if studying the arrangement of his things and then quickly glanced at him. "I'm going to need to pack these in your suitcase, so I hope you don't mind if I move some stuff around."

For a brief moment, everything that had happened seemed to fade into the background.

Young Gillen looked on in astonishment: Kate started putting her things in the suitcase, simultaneously rearranging his stuff. Cautiously, he went over to her.

"What's this about?"

"I told you," she began as if to dismiss his question, choosing instead to focus all her attention on the open suitcase in front of her. Yet she appeared to watch him nervously out of the corner of her eye too. "I can't find my suitcase. I was hoping you could help me." She paused, studying the layout of his things. "Now why don't we—"

Kate felt her forearm suddenly fall into his grasp. Before she could react, Michael gently pulled her around so that she was facing him—she could feel her stomach immediately tying in knots. Michael still had hold of her forearm, and his deep, blue eyes seemed to peer right through her. Part of her wanted to look away, while another part couldn't help but fall under his penetrating gaze. She could feel herself melting before him, and her eyes welled up ever so slightly.

"What's this about?" Michael pleaded. Angst began filling his face, the despairing over his parents' death only aggravating the discord between them. At once, Kate realized she had acted impetuously, choosing the wrong time to extend an olive branch.

"I'm going home with you," her voice cracked nervously. Though her eyes filled with trepidation, the young woman's expression remained hollowly emphatic, as if still holding back.

Impatience quickly came over her suitor. Kate's heart leapt into her throat when Michael abruptly grasped her by the thick of her arms, wrenching her whole body toward him. The fetching, young woman found herself standing as close to him as ever, nervously looking up at his strong features and overpowering eyes—features that betrayed the man's deep anguish.

"Why? What's changed?" he demanded, unable to contain himself.

Kate remained spellbound by his pleading gaze and subdued by his masculine grasp, all the while smarting from the discord of the previous weeks. Helpless—and finding much comfort in that helplessness—she realized she had been lying to herself up to that very moment, fabricating excuses to deny her true intentions for being there.

No, Kate DeCarreau had reached a turning point. For the first time in her life, logic and reason had abandoned her. Perhaps she had caused them to flee, no longer desiring the false protection they afforded. No, looking into his eyes, Kate realized she was being driven by something stronger than mere impulse.

So she threw her arms around his neck, seizing him in a tight embrace, and kissed him desperately.

The young couple lost themselves in the long, euphoric moment. Kate swooned helplessly in Michael's arms, enjoying the security and assurance of his touch. The taste of his lips upon hers captivated her every thought. Yet at the same time, the young woman delighted in a newfound freedom washing over her.

Barely parting from him—trembling and unable to contain the strong emotions spilling out of her—Kate anxiously took his face in her hands and gazed desperately at him.

"I love you, Michael," she said with tears floating in her eyes, still trembling and breathless. Nothing followed: no trace of remorse over saying those words, no fear of his response this time—only affirmation and release.

Michael gazed at her for a long moment, his eyes softening and his touch seeming to assuage the trembling woman's angst. He availed himself the pleasure letting her hold his face in her hands adoringly, reveling in the delicate kisses alighting on his cheeks every now and then. Finally, he smiled. "What took you so long?" The two shared a quaint laugh, and then Michael said, "I love you too...."

Once more, the couple embraced, kissing each other with abandon while trading pleading apologies for the weeks of discord. They doted over each other for several long minutes, letting the intensity of the moment pass while enjoying their reconciliation.

"I'm going with you," Kate exclaimed once more, holding him as close and as tightly as he was holding her. Tears began trailing down her cheeks. "...and I'm going to follow you wherever you go ... for as long as I can."

He recoiled slightly so that he could look into her eyes again. "I don't think time is a problem anymore. I doubt I'm on the primary team now. They're going ahead with the same schedule."

Kate shook her head in defeat. "No, Michael.... That's not the rumor. Cyril is working it out now. They're continuing with the same training schedule, but he's got you locked in as primary commander for when you come back." Once more, she paused while more tears trailed down her face. "That's what makes this so difficult. I'm still going to lose you.... But at least you're here with me now. So let me accompany you home to the funeral."

Michael Gillen and Kate DeCarreau walked arm in arm down the transport-loading ramp, remaining just as close to each other as when they had left the NSEA complex a short while before. Playfully keeping to themselves and speaking in hushed tones amid the other passengers boarding the flight to Earth, the couple found themselves in a world gloriously off to themselves.

Kate, in particular, kept her eyes fixed upon Michael the whole time, occasionally averting her attention just long enough to see where she was going. The young woman was practically giddy, relishing the moment and celebrating the end of the long weeks of discord between them—and seventeen months of fickleness on her part. Despite the dire circumstances of the trip, Kate determined to make the most of every minute with Michael until he finally left for Alpha Centauri. Reveling in her newfound freedom, the young woman considered that day the best day of her entire life.

Upon reaching the bottom of the ramp, Kate noticed Michael's attention turn to something directly ahead. She looked in the same direction, her eyes becoming wide. Standing on the loading platform, holding their own luggage, and waiting to board the flight to Earth were some very familiar faces: Tom Andrews, Kara Ricci, Ben Morris, and Phil Marcotte—even David Tashjian. Cyril Davidson was there too, though clearly not ready for travel.

"What's this?" Michael asked when the couple met the unexpected group.

"It's a mutiny," Davidson quipped, a smile coming to his face. "These guys decided to strong-arm the oversight committee for once. You can't keep to the training schedule if the crew isn't there to train—a pretty bold move."

"But why?"

"We're going to the funeral with you, *Commander*," Tom replied with a typical smirk before turning serious. "Kate isn't the only one who wants to be there for you.... We all do."

"That's what teammates do," Kara added. "They stick together."

"No," Michael began, remaining unconvinced. "That's what a *family* does." Michael and Kate smiled warmly, celebrating the surprising appearance and watching the other Centauries encircle them. The closely knit group exchanged supporting hugs and handshakes all around, causing Michael to pensively remark, "As someone who just lost his biological family ... I can't tell you how much this means to me."

A short moment of silence followed before everything returned to normal. Chitchat crisscrossed the tight circle while the team waited to board the transport. Continuing the discussions, everyone began to realize just how poignant Michael's comment had been: they *were* family. Though the impression went unspoken by the rest of them, the sentiment hung in the air nevertheless.

"Are you going with us too, Cyril?" Kate asked.

The older man shook his head. "No. Someone has to stay back here and keep the oversight committee in line." Then he paused enthusiastically. "No, I wanted to see you off, to tell you how glad I am that you and Michael have finally worked things out.... You've done me a big favor by reconciling, and I didn't want you to leave before I had the chance to tell you the news."

"Tell me what?"

Davidson looked at both Kate and Tom. "I'm moving both of you up to the primary team with Michael." He paused, letting the announcement sink in while relishing their dumbfounded expressions. Another celebration arose within the circle. "That was my intention all along; I just had to work out the details before I could make the move."

"What about Maura and Shay?" Tom asked, not really that concerned.

"Maura doesn't want to be on the team with Michael," Cyril began. "So I'm giving her what she wants. She can go follow Burke, wherever *he* is. And Taggart ... let's just say that it would be better to have you, Kate, and Michael on the same team—the three musketeers, I believe you called yourselves."

"So Michael and I aren't in trouble for breaking the rules prohibiting dating?" Kate asked.

"No, the solidarity of the team nullifies that concern," Davidson replied. "The committee can't do a thing when you people stick together. Besides, who do you think *Maura* was secretly dating?" Then he smiled, watching the surprised reaction from the group. "So everyone, just go do what you have to do. We'll be here. But when you get back, be prepared to work. We have a mission to Alpha Centauri to launch."

Michael Gillen stood in the center of the main exhibition amphitheatre at the Tranquility Base Apollo Museum, waiting for the press conference to begin. Over three long months had passed since his parents' funeral, and the young man had eagerly put the tragedy behind him.

Today, NSEA would publicly announce the Alpha Centauri mission. Michael was nervous over the pending announcement. Yet more than anything, he was enthralled and overwhelmed, for he was standing on hallowed ground.

The young man slowly turned in place while looking around, his eyes wide with wonder. The museum, located on the site of the first lunar landing, lay within the crowded and bustling Tranquility City metropolis. The attraction dedicated itself to those early space explorers. Though other landing sites throughout the Moon had also been converted into historic landmarks, *this* museum had dedicated itself to *all* Apollo missions. The entire antiquity of that era had been gathered at this one, very large complex.

The main amphitheatre sat on the actual landing site, and the Moon's surface lay preserved just a half meter below the transparent floor. Painstakingly, engineers built the structure around the Moon's surface, leaving footprints, equipment, and the Apollo 11 lunar module's descent stage untouched. The only modifications were a faux silver-clad ascent stage to complete the *Eagle* Lander, a full scale replica of the Columbia service module suspended high above from the ceiling, a life-size model of Michael Collins standing in his spacesuit in the open hatch of the service module, and two life-size models of Neil Armstrong and Buzz Aldrin standing in their spacesuits on the surface, saluting an American flag. Controlled walkways wound throughout certain areas of the site, looping back around to the large viewing area in front of the display. Of course, everything was elaborately enclosed, having artificial gravity fields, an atmosphere, and spectacular lighting effects.

Michael was awestruck; Terrae Solaris had come into existence there. The museum was also a fitting place for the Alpha Centauri announcement, just as Cyril Davidson had intended; a place to mark the next generation in space exploration, perhaps even the beginning of a new Terrae Solaris: not just one star, but many—Terrae *Cosmos*?

Michael and the rest of the Centauries (Tom Andrews, Kate DeCarreau, Kara Ricci, Phil Marcotte, and Ben Morris) were taking in the exhibit, while technicians and aides set up the room for the conference.

The Centauries wore their spacesuits, save the helmet. Michael thought wearing spacesuits to be rather corny. After all, rarely would an astronaut wear his spacesuit in contemporary exploration. Nevertheless, the conference was also a photo shoot. Davidson thought paralleling Apollo-era photos would help the public understand the mission's intent.

Glancing across the way to where Kate stood viewing the exhibit, Michael noticed just how eye-catching she looked in her spacesuit. She had a natural innocence about her, being very much unaware of just how alluring she actually was. More than anything, her presence celebrated her participation in the Alpha Centauri mission: She was heading off into the stars with him, making the Alpha Centauri mission a glorious one!

With an announcement from the lead events coordinator, the conference came to order. Michael and his crew took their places at the front of the viewing area, standing just to the right of the podium so that the lunar lander sat prominently in the background. Media lights came up, cameras became active, and reporters spilled into the amphitheatre. When everyone was in his or her places, the events coordinator announced Cyril Davidson.

"Good evening everyone," Davidson greeted the audience after taking his place behind the podium. "Exactly five hundred and thirty-six years ago today—July twentieth, 1969—the Apollo Eleven spacecraft, manned by Neil Armstrong and Edwin "Buzz" Aldrin, touched down *right here* on the Sea of Tranquility.

"It marked the greatest achievement of mankind in that era: the first successful manned exploration of the Moon. However, it also marked the first and most crucial step in our history. Today we, the citizens of Earth States and Terrae Solaris, are the direct beneficiaries of those efforts.

"So in that same spirit of exploration, which has driven mankind since the earliest days of civilization, I am pleased to announce that on Friday, October eighteenth, 2505, the National Space Exploration Administration will launch the first-ever deep space exploration mission in history, just *ninety* short days from now.

"The exploration ship, the *ESS History*, will launch from the NSEA dock on Mid-Earth Station, carrying a crew of six brave explorers.

The ship will spend the next twenty-four years traveling to the Alpha Centauri sun, a triple star system and the closet stars to Terrae Solaris, just over four light-years away.

"Upon arrival, system computers will revive the crew from cryogenic suspension. The crew will then execute a two-year study of the alien stars and any other comets, asteroids, or planets there. If any significant or extraordinary findings are uncovered, the crew has the discretion to extend their stay for as long as they consider safe. Upon completing their assignment, the crew will then reenter cryogenic suspension, remaining that way until arriving back here twenty-four years later.

"This is a significant achievement for Earth States, providing detailed analysis of another star system to help explain the origins of the universe and marking the beginning of a new age in space exploration."

Davidson then introduced the crew, summarizing their qualifications, responsibilities, and biographies. After that, he went into more detail about the mission, noting things predetermined to be of interest: flight details, ship configuration highlights, specifics about why scientists were interested in Alpha Centauri, interesting trivia facts, and the like.

Afterwards, he opened up the floor, and the press overwhelmed him with questions. Upon listening to each reporter in turn, Michael could tell the media largely held a positive view of the mission, wanting to know almost every detail and risk. However, some of the reporters peppered Davidson with challenging questions, such as the questionable timing of such a project, given the costs; the tensions rising in the Outer Rim; whether or not President Mitchell was as supportive of NSEA as former President Turner was. Of course, Davidson handled every probing question with his typical, confident graciousness.

At that point, the reporters' questioning began turning toward the crew. Michael took a deep breath as the first question came his way.

"Michael Gillen," one reporter began, "As commander of the Alpha Centauri mission, please give us your thoughts on what you and your team are about to do."

"Well," young Gillen began sheepishly but also trying to remember his talking points. "We all know this mission holds many risks and challenges—nothing like this has ever been attempted. But NSEA has done a very thorough job of training and preparing us for those challenges." He gestured to the rest of his crew. "Over the last two years, I've come to know each and every member of this crew personally. We've become very close—we're family. I'm convinced of their skills and professionalism, and I can say with complete confidence that NSEA has given me the best crew I could ever hope for. So I'm looking forward to the launch with great enthusiasm.

"On a personal note, this mission is the dream of a lifetime. I get to command mankind's first exploration mission to another star. As I stand here, I feel a deep connection with the past, and I have a newfound appreciation for what the great men who took the first steps here at Tranquility Base accomplished. We have long suspected that Alpha Centauri holds planets. Perhaps I will get the same chance to set my footprints somewhere in that distant star system, just like those brave men who set their footprints here. I can only hope that I will live up to their example."

Michael sighed inconspicuously as the press hung on every word. Davidson turned and gave him an assuring wink.

"Michael Gillen," another reporter called ahead of the mob, "It's been just three months since your parents were killed by *Weightless* assassins, just as they were suspected in your brother's death four years earlier. Do you have anything to say, either to respond to Mos Thieren's statements or about the *Weightless*?—and do you acknowledge any responsibility on the part of the Gillens for the *Weightless'* plight?"

Michael's heart leapt into his chest, his pause allowing a torrent of similarly probing questions from other eager reporters. He had become a lightening rod, just as Davidson had warned him.

He hated the questions. The young man, still grieving, wanted to answer them all too honestly. He wanted to set the record straight once and for all, to tear into that parasite Mos Thieren, to blame the *Weightless* for their own problems, to decry the injustice done to his family.

But this wasn't the time. No, this was the time to take the high road.

"The tragedy that has befallen my family is something I need to deal with personally," Michael pleaded. "So I am sorry, but that is the only statement I will make…. I am more than sad that my father, mother, and brother are not here with me on this historic day. I think they would have been proud of me, and I intend to honor their memory by accomplishing this mission."

Though the political questions aimed at him continued, Cyril eventually managed to turn the meeting off the subject.

At that point, an older woman reporter stood up. Wearing a rather coy grin, she asked, "Michael, you've mentioned how close you've become to your fellow crewmembers ... but *I* understand that you've become rather close with one *particular* member of the crew."

A little bit of fun commotion erupted. Smiling warmly, Cyril Davidson walked over to the Centauries. With a gentle nudge, the older man herded Michael and Kate to one side of the podium.

"Michael has already noted how much of a family this crew of young adults has become," Davidson began, still smiling and standing behind the young couple with his arms around them. "That sort of makes me their surrogate father."

He smiled at the two even more warmly before looking back at the audience. "Michael and Kate have given me the great honor of publicly announcing their engagement to one another. As a surrogate father, I couldn't be more pleased.

"Now, I'd like to invite everyone to the wedding, but we'll all have a little trouble making the ceremony. In a first ever for NSEA—*and them too*"—he laughed—"This young couple will recite their vows to each other after arriving at Proxima Centauri. Ben Morris, who has been sworn in as a justice of the peace, will officiate."

A round of lightheartedness washed over the meeting as the press began having fun with the surprising human-interest story.

"Director Davidson," one reporter interjected comically, "As a surrogate father, aren't you concerned about your *daughter* going off unchaperoned?"

A few chuckles rippled through the audience.

Tom Andrews stepped up, a smirk covering his face. "I can answer that. As Mike said, we're all family here. So that makes me Kate's big brother—Ben and Phil too. So Kate and Mike will have *more* than enough chaperons." Then he put his arm around Davidson. "And *Dad* here has given us all old-fashion rifles loaded with buckshot...." He eyed up Gillen comically as if to warn. "So Mike, you'd *better* be careful."

A round of laugher erupted. The highly educated, well trained, and completely professional astronaut couple found themselves blushing in front of the entire Earth States audience—millions of people who were watching the live feed.

"Can we get some pictures of the couple?" an eager photographer asked amid the uproar. Other press and NSEA photographers were standing by too.

"Sure," Davidson replied, turning to the whole group of them while reporters began getting out of their seats and charging the podium area. "And then let's get a whole round of pictures. This is a big day!"

"I can't believe it!" a horrified Kara Ricci exclaimed, watching with Cyril Davidson and the rest of the Centauries while the devastating pictures continued across the screen.

Today was the Centauries' first day back at NSEA since their big press conference on the Moon. Still basking in the afterglow of the mission announcement, the Centauries had arrived early into the common area for breakfast that morning.

During a rather lively celebratory meal—that's when the television interrupted the celebration, just as it had done three months earlier when Michael's parents had been assassinated. *Breaking News* scrolled once more across the bottom of the screen, and the pictures of mass destruction and chaos looped repeatedly. Reporters would interject every now and then, though the entire broadcast was clearly in mayhem!

All activities at NSEA had come to a sudden stop, and the entire Inner Rim of planets—Mercury, Earth, the Moon, and Mars—had gone on high alert.

"How many did they say were dead?" David Tashjian asked, having just arrived.

"They don't know for sure," Michael replied quietly. "But they estimate thousands—and probably thousands of thousands."

Tashjian stood in shock, watching the terrible pictures with his teammates. "Do they know who did it?"

"No," Cyril Davidson replied. "Not officially. But we all know who it was: the Europans."

A hush came over the small group, while each person pondered the implications.

Michael Gillen, sitting close to Kate, remained silent. The pictures were from Ceres Fleet Base, an Earth States military base located on the borders between the Inner Rim and Outer Rim.

Ceres, the largest asteroid in the solar system and considered a dwarf planet, was located in the Asteroid Belt between Mars and Jupiter. Ceres had been the point of contention that started the first EuroGan war—the Ceres Skirmishes. Upon winning that war, the Allies—Earth States, the Mars Federation, and Mercury—retook possession of the asteroid. Earth States established large fleet and military operations there to prevent any further aggression.

Now, that base lay in ruins! One could only imagine the destructive power the Europans had unleashed upon the unsuspecting base.

Michael, feeling Kate recoil farther into the safety of his arms, held her even more tightly as her eyes remained transfixed on the television.

The young man was at a loss for words. He didn't think about the personal impact the attack would have on him; he didn't remorse over the fact that NSEA canceling the Alpha Centauri mission was a foregone conclusion; he didn't remorse over how close he had come to fulfilling his dream; he didn't remorse over what seemed to be the continual frustration of his aspirations and hopes.

No, all the young man could think about was the destruction he was witnessing: hundreds of battleships destroyed; buildings burning; the tragedy of the dead and the dying—the tragedy and loss imposed upon their families; the tremendous blow to Earth States; the tremendous, looming threat that would avail itself upon the now-vulnerable Earth States; the terrible times that were coming.

Earth States would soon be at war.

CHAPTER TWELVE

Called to Duty

Michael Gillen, the other Primaries, and the backup team filled the science lab aboard the *ESS History*, going through scheduled experiment training for the Primaries' upcoming launch to Alpha Centauri. However, they ran through the training mechanically; the mood aboard the docked vessel was very much subdued—even haunting.

Several days had passed since the Europans had decimated Ceres Fleet Base. Though no more hostilities had erupted, the Europan fleet that had executed the attack had disappeared. Therefore, an uneasy calm had cast itself over the entire Inner Rim. Earth States, half its war fleet destroyed in the first attack, lay vulnerable to another attack. Such an assault could happen anywhere.

Therefore, the Centauries went about business as usual, though nothing was usual anymore. No, Mid-Earth Station could be next. Moreover, though no one on the prestigious team wanted to think about the possibility, the Alpha Centauri mission would probably be the next casualty of the oncoming war—a program that Earth States could no longer afford.

Just as the team was about to move onto the next pointless exercise, Cyril Davidson came into the lab, a sober expression covering his face.

"Hi, Cyril," Michael greeted the director.

The older man paused after coming to the center of the room. "I just got word through the channels. President Mitchell is going to declare war on the Europans tonight."

The lab went silent. The Centauries looked uneasily at each other while pondering the foreboding words.

Davidson continued, "He's going to order a massive realignment of the budget to fund the war effort. All paramilitary organizations will be converted back over to the military." After pausing, he reluctantly added, "The Alpha Centauri mission is canceled. Sorry everyone. I know how hard you've all worked."

The room went silent for another long moment.

"So what happens now?" Michael asked.

"The military is giving me back my commission and rank of admiral. My first orders are to oversee the conversion here at NSEA— quite a challenge, given our eclectic skills and backgrounds. Once that's done, I'll return to Command."

Kate looked around searchingly at the other Centauries before turning back toward Davidson. "So what's going to happen to us?"

"There's a lot of work to do," Davidson replied, looking at the whole team. "I'm going to need everyone's help in the conversion. That should take a couple of months." He gestured around at the lab. "This ship isn't going into mothballs. We need to convert it for military duty, and no one knows this ship better than its crew. After that, we'll see. All of you have academy backgrounds, so you'll have the option to enlist in the military—you'll get officers' commissions, of course. We can talk about it during the conversion."

"Put me down for some sort of medical duty," Kara offered from where she sat.

Some of the other Centauries spoke up, also offering themselves for duty. Kate looked over at Michael. Although saying nothing, he had that same telling expression on his face—and it scared her.

"Good," Davidson declared. I would have expected nothing less. Every one of you will be of great service to the war effort. I can only hope this war ends soon so that we can return here and finish what we've started." He paused thoughtfully. "I wanted to tell you first. Now I have to go and let everyone else know."

Davidson nodded and walked out of the lab. Kate saw Michael making a beeline in pursuit of the older man. Oddly, Tom also followed eagerly after Davidson, even having that same determined expression.

"Michael, what are you going to do?" Kate asked, stepping into his path. Her churning, brown eyes betrayed her deep concern.

Young Gillen paused, watching Tom continue off in the direction that Davidson had disappeared. "I'm going to tell Davidson I want to volunteer."

"But what's going to happen?" she pleaded.

"I don't know," he replied, taking in her trepidation sympathetically. "Things are going to be busy for a while, but we can get married at the next break."

Kate shook her head, her voice hushing upon noticing the others lingering close by. "I'm not talking about that. I'm scared." Her anxious expression pleaded with him. "I don't want to lose you. Wherever you go, I want to go too."

Michael's face changed oddly. Kate searched Michael's blue eyes, desperately wishing he would express the thoughts running through his mind. However, Michael remained unflinching.

"I'll do what I can," he replied. After giving her an assuring kiss, Michael turned in the direction Tom had gone. "Stay here and let me talk with Davidson."

Michael hurried down the narrow corridor, not going too far until finding Davidson and Andrews talking in the middle of the corridor. Tom had beaten Michael to volunteering for the military—being more than eager at that. Michael found this a little surprising, having obviously underestimated Tom's patriotism.

"Why Intelligence?" Davidson asked Tom, continuing their conversation. He smiled, relishing the opportunity to razz him a bit. "You're not bucking for a desk job, are you?"

Tom remained completely serious. "Intelligence had always been my interest, next to space exploration. I took as many classes and training in the subject as I could back at the academy. I think that's where I can help out the most."

"Sounds reasonable," the older man replied after musing over the thought. "But normally they reserve the most critical positions for those who have specialized in it. Would you *really* be willing to start at the bottom?"

"Yes … but I was also hoping you could pull some strings, *Admiral* … maybe get me a level or two."

After looking at him for a moment, Davidson laughed warmly. "Okay. They'll appreciate your enthusiasm. I can't guarantee what level you'll start, but I'll make sure you get in."

"Thanks!"

The two regarded each other one last time. After nodding at Michael, Tom walked away.

"What's on your mind, Mike?" Davidson greeted as if expecting him all along. The older man gestured for Michael to accompany him toward the main operations center. "You here to volunteer for service too?"

"Yep. I'm not sure where I can be of use, but I *do* want to help out."

Davidson smiled while continuing to walk. "That's what I figured, so I already recommended you for a command position. You'll make a great warship captain."

"*What?*" Michael grimaced in astonishment, looking around to make sure no one was listening. Once satisfied, the young man continued, "Cyril, I'm honored, but I think such a position is *way* beyond me."

Davidson remained determined. "Mike, not only did you graduate top in your class at the academy, but your performance in the combat command curriculum was just as stellar…. Commanding a military ship isn't much different than an exploration vessel."

"But I don't have combat experience."

"Neither do most of the other commanders," the older man smiled. "We've been at peace too long. You'll do fine."

The two men continued slowly walking, making their way almost to the main hatch of the ship. Seeing his protégé's deeply concerned expression, Davidson stopped mid-stride, looking the younger man in the eye.

"President Mitchell did everything humanly possible to prepare for the oncoming war," Davidson began. "But until Ceres was attacked, Congress fought him all the way. We lost too many ships in the attack—

we barely have a fleet! We need ships, and we need captains too. Your country needs you." He paused for effect. "Besides, there are a lot of patrolling and support ships needed behind the line. I doubt you'll even see action."

Young Gillen sighed, shaking his head. "I'm not sure that makes me feel any better."

The two went silent for a long moment.

"I just think you need some time to ready yourself mentally," Davidson looked at him empathetically. "That's not a problem. The ship you'll be commanding is still in fabrication. I also need you here now, so you've got a few months to prepare." He paused, letting Michael take in his comments. "You'll be doing me a big favor."

Michael watched Cyril's imploring gaze for the longest time. Though looking back at him as if to plead, the young man felt himself falling victim to his mentor's persuasion. "I want Tom Andrews for a first officer. Tom's good with people and his advice has always been valuable."

"He's dead set on Intelligence. He's not going to like it."

"And I want Kate kept completely safe," Michael pressed. "She wants to go with me, but I can't let that happen. Get her a nice desk job somewhere back here, something that allows her to live back at my family's lake house where she'll be safe.

"Also, Tom and Kate can't know about my request until I ship out. Otherwise, both of them will try to guilt me into changing my mind." Michael, watching his mentor ponder the requests, added assertively, "Those are my terms."

Davidson went silent for a long moment, returning the young man's gaze. Finally, he shrugged his shoulders and said, "You drive a hard bargain, but I accept."

Later that night, the Centauries, Cyril Davidson, and a few of the support personnel had gathered in the crew common area, huddling around the live broadcast of President Mitchell's national address.

The event was taking place in the elaborate congressional chambers on Eratosthenes, the Moon, with Congress and all ranking members of the government present. After preparatory comments by a news media anchor and the ceremonial *Announcing of the President*, President James Mitchell came into the chamber to thunderous applause.

Michael Gillen sat on a couch, snuggling Kate DeCarreau in his arms. They watched the iconic figure walk farther into the legislative chamber, taking his place behind the podium. The man had grown larger than life in such a short time, his predictions of Europan aggression vindicating him. His efforts to prepare the nation amid his opponents' scoffing had become regarded as prophetic.

As the applause died down, Mitchell began to speak:

> *"Three days ago, on July 21ˢᵗ, 2505, the United States of Earth was unexpectedly and intentionally attacked by space faring forces of the Europan Empire. Though Earth States was at peace with that nation at the time, Europa nevertheless chose to inflict upon us hostilities that caused severe damage to Terran peacekeeping forces at Ceres. I regret to tell you that many Terran lives have been lost.*
>
> *"We must also understand that the turmoil defining the entire Outer Rim these past six years continues to press inward toward the peace-loving nations of the Inner Rim. You have seen for yourselves the trouble the Europans, the Ganymedes, the Callistans, and all other nations under Europan control—whether by treaty or by invasion— have inflicted upon the republics of Mars, both eastern and western republics.*
>
> *"It is more than clear that unless we respond to these challenges, the Europans and their sympathizers—this Axis of Aggression—will destroy the peace in Terrae Solaris that our ancestors worked so hard to build.*
>
> *"As President, I have asked Congress, and they have given their unanimous consent: I hereby declare war on the Europan Empire and this Axis of Aggression."*

At once, a thunderous round of applause erupted in the chamber.

Mitchell waited patiently until the long applause died down.

> *"But I assure you that we will not be alone in this effort against tyranny. Today, Earth States has entered into solemn agreement with the Eastern Republic of Mars, the Western Republic of Mars, and the people of Mercury. As an Alliance for Peace, we have covenanted together to put down this hostile aggression."*

Once more, another round of applause rose up from the onlookers.

> *"As Commander-in-Chief of Earth States defenses, I have directed that all measures be taken to our defense, executed in such a way that considers the character of the onslaught against us. No matter how long it may take to overcome this aggression, Earth States and its allies will achieve absolute victory. We will not only win, but we will ensure that this form of sedition shall never again endanger us.*
> *"God bless the United States of Earth!"*

Michael Gillen lay in bed in his quarters, hazy eyes staring up into the darkness. With sleep still pressing in on him formidably, the young man found his mind empty of thought. Oh, he understood that the time was very early—too early to be up. Nevertheless, all other thoughts had fled his mind.

He thought not about the fact that over a month and a half had gone by since the fateful attack on Ceres Fleet Base. Nor was his mind filled with the myriad of activities that had occupied his schedule while NSEA folded itself back into the military. Nor did he think of all the work that still lay ahead. Nor did he think of how Tom and Kate were unaware of the deal he had made with Davidson on their behalf— against their wishes really! Nor did he ponder how he was going to find time to marry Kate, as he had promised. All he knew was that someone was still knocking at his door.

With much effort, Michael clumsily got up and made his way through the darkness. Upon opening the door, the disheveled, young man beheld Cyril Davidson standing there, smartly dressed in his admirals' uniform.

"Cyril, what are you doing here so early?" Michael asked, holding his hand over his eyes so the bright light wouldn't accost him.

"Welcome to the military, soldier," Davidson replied dryly. "Actually, I figured you would want to hear this as soon as possible: Your orders to ship out just came through. You're to report to Lowell Fleet Base immediately to take command of the *ESS Comanche*."

"Lowell Fleet Base?" Michael mused quizzically. The young man pondered the statement, still in a thick fog. "That's Mars Federation. That doesn't make sense." Then the real issue came to him. "—it's only been six weeks. You said I'd have three months before shipping out."

"They did an audible," Davidson replied reluctantly. "Command made a deal with the Mars federation. The western republic is building a limited number of ships for us while our manufacturing industry ramps up production. You have a full Terran crew there waiting for your arrival. Sorry, Mike, things are pretty confused right now. I can only tell you what they tell me. You need to leave at daybreak—Tom too, just like we agreed."

Michael's jaw dropped. "*Daybreak?* I can't leave that quickly. I've got things to do...." He recoiled back, completely overwhelmed while scanning the air in front of him as if searching a list. "I've gotta pack.... I've gotta break the news to Kate that I'm leaving—and she isn't. And if she's still talking to me, I have to ask her to marry me.... *I need time to get married*—I promised her."

"How much time do you need?"

Michael, still flabbergasted, replied, "...ah ... a *few* days—at least."

"I can stall for about two days, maybe a few hours more, but that's all I can do. If you hurry, you might even be able to work in a very short honeymoon. You'd better get moving."

Twenty-six-year-old Kara Ricci stood at the front of a small chapel, somewhere on Mid-Earth Station. As maid of honor, the young woman had garbed herself in her best dress and shoes, and her hairstyle was unusually fancy too—at least as much as such a short notice would allow. Standing to Kate DeCarreau's left, holding a makeshift bouquet of flowers, and watching the young couple exchange their vows in front of the minister, Kara mused at how quickly the plans for her day had changed.

She had barely gotten out of bed before learning that Michael was shipping out to his new assignment. Then came the news that he had asked Kate to marry him—*immediately*. Kate delivered the news herself, proceeding to ask Kara to stand in for her as maid of honor.

Too quickly, Kara stood at the head of the small chapel across from Tom Andrews, the best man. The church was mostly empty. Only the rest of the Centauries—Phil Marcotte, Ben Morris, and David Tashjian from the backup team—Cyril Davidson, and a few of the closer support personnel watched the ceremony from the front pews.

In a whirlwind of excitement, the young couple had announced their nuptials; at that same whirlwind pace, it was all happening—all in the shadows of a terrible war.

Michael and Kate were getting married.

Kara stood to the side, deep emotions washing over her; she had welled-up a bit, and a lump had formed in her throat.

Happiness filled her warmly; her closest friend was marrying the woman he loved. She was jealous for his happiness, reveling in the glorious expression covering his face.

She took in with great fondness the sight of Michael reciting his vows. Handsome as ever, Michael stood over his bride reassuringly, gently holding her right hand in his and gazing into her eyes. Speaking solemn promises, the young man's voice resonated with deep conviction.

Kara hung on every word, as if Michael were speaking to her. In fact, the young woman realized that vicariousness had overcome her: Kate's place became hers; Kate's expressions—she wore them too; when Kate spoke her vows, Kara's lips wanted to mouth them too. This wasn't envy or jealously, just the musings of any aspiring, single, young female.

Perhaps she felt a *little* jealous. Watching the minister officiate the exchange of rings, Kara remembered her days back at the academy: how she had pined over Michael for so long, how she had thrown caution to the wind in order to win his affections—how she had failed miserably.

No, Kate DeCarreau had somehow managed to achieve what Kara couldn't. Yet having become almost as close to her as she was to Michael, Kara understood why Michael desired Kate so much. And so Kara became just as jealous for Kate's happiness too. Watching Kate slip the gold band over Michael's finger, Kara reveled in the sight—but letting the tears and the lump in her throat have their moment as well.

In the blink of an eye, the young couple was married and out the door. Kara stood outside the chapel, shoulder to shoulder with Cyril Davidson and Tom Andrews. The entire group that had witnessed the ceremony stood by, giving best wishes to the newlyweds, throwing rice, and even clapping while the couple made their way to the awaiting transport.

She found herself in a world of her own while watching the young couple leave.

Cyril, who was having a conversation with the preacher about how many impromptu weddings the minister had officiated as of late, noticed Kara's happy but pensive expression. Immediately, the older man understood.

"You okay, Kara?" he asked sympathetically.

She paused for a long moment, a little tearful. "Yeah ... I'm very happy for them."

Tom Andrews, still shoulder to shoulder with her, heard the exchange. Upon seeing her expression, he looked on sympathetically for a long moment, understanding something about her he had never considered. Then a typically comical look came to his face. He looked her in the eye and said, "What do you think, Kara? Maybe you and I should tie the knot before this war gets too crazy."

After gazing at him appreciatively for a long moment, Kara kissed him on the cheek. Then she returned a comical grimace. "I'll have to think about that one for a while."

Tom smiled. "Don't wait too long. Before you know it, we'll both be deployed. I'm only weeks away from flying a desk at Intelligence."

Davidson smiled while listening to the banter. Just at that moment when the transport pulled away and headed down the street with the newlyweds, he interjected, "You're shipping out sooner than you think, Tom."

"What do you mean?"

"Michael didn't want me to tell you before he was gone," Davidson began, smiling once more. "But he requested you to be his first officer on the *Comanche*.... In two days, you ship out with him."

Tom's face immediately went deadpan as he watched the transport disappear down the street.

The modest hotel room, somewhere on Mid-Earth Station, was subdued in shimmering candle light. Two half-eaten plates of food lay abandoned on the small corner table, accompanying two empty wine glasses used in a very personal toast. A bouquet of roses peered out of the shadows from the nightstand, as if watching the young couple slow dance to soft music playing in the background.

Michael Gillen, dressed much more casually than before, held Kate Gillen tightly against him while slowly turning her to the music. An elegant nightgown—one acquired for this particular evening—draped over her form, and she gazed at him in nervous anticipation. They exchanged no talk of the war, no talk of his pending assignment or him shipping out soon, just the pleasure of each other's company and the anticipation of the coming evening.

"I see that look in your eye again," Kate smiled warmly, her deep, brown eyes sparkling. "You don't have to protect me anymore."

Michael mused at the thought while continuing to turn her to the music. A rather coy smile came to his face as he took in her expression. "Maybe I'm just enjoying my newfound appreciation for the term *blushing bride*." When Kate laughed at the comment—her face blushing all the more—he added, "No, I'm just trying to give you a nice, romantic wedding day: a banquet, a toast, and a first dance. You deserve something better than one step above a shotgun wedding."

Kate smiled invitingly, bringing herself even closer. "I woke up this morning, not realizing that by the end of the day I would be *Mrs. Michael Gillen*.... I have a beautiful new ring on my finger"—lifting up her hand to proudly display the jewelry—"and I'm here with you now.... *I couldn't be happier.*"

She brought her cheek to his, closing her eyes and letting the sensation of his skin against hers wash over her. After remaining that way for a long moment, she continued, "But I *am* missing one thing from the tradition: a wedding gift. Michael, give me the promise that you'll come back to me. Promise me you won't let anything happen to you while you're out there."

Michael recoiled a bit. "I thought we weren't going to talk about the war—just live in the moment for now."

"I'm sorry," she offered, shaking her head. "I'm just so worried about you. So much can happen."

"Okay, I promise," Michael replied, less convincing than Kate's expression demanded.

"Michael, I'm serious."

"Kate, I can't control fate."

Kate paused for a moment, looking him desperately in the eye and noting how his expression had changed. "I know you too well.... I know how you get caught up in what you're doing—how you take risks." She turned her chin side to side while keeping her gaze fixed upon him. "I can see the look in your eye, Michael.... I've seen it since the Ceres Fleet Base attack. I know the Outer Rim is where your family was killed, and I know you blame the place for everything that has happened.... You're taking this war personally, and you'll kill yourself trying to win it."

Michael looked at her, flabbergasted but unable to deny the charge. "Kate, I don't know what to say."

"Just give me the promise," she exclaimed, very much determined. "And then apologize for not taking me with you."

Gazing affectionately at her for a long moment, he smiled. "Okay, *I promise....* And I'm sorry." He drew her close again and continued to slow dance. After a moment, he abruptly recoiled away. "Wow!"

"What?"

"Well, I've only been a husband for a couple hours," he began in disbelief. "And I'm already apologizing for something.... I thought those stereotypes were just party jokes."

Kate smiled, wrapping her arms around his neck while bringing her face close to his. Her expression turned more than coy. "*Hmmm* ... this can work out well for you: We've had our first fight, and you've apologized for being wrong.... According to the stereotype, it's time to make up."

With a fleeting but devilish smile, she kissed him passionately. After sharing a long embrace, the young newlyweds parted, if ever so slightly.

"I love you, Michael," she said softly, her face still close to his. She looked at his mouth insatiably, and her fingers delicately caressed the strong line of his jaw. Being so close, Michael could feel her breath—becoming more irregular and strained—being drawing in an out of her lungs.

"I love you too, Katey."

"*Katey...*," she mused, her shimmering, brown eyes stirring with desire. "I like the sound of that."

CHAPTER THIRTEEN

Captain of the Ship

Twenty-four-year-old Michael Gillen walked down the long wharf corridor at Lowell Fleet Station, not being in too much of a hurry. Tom Andrews accompanied him on his right, even less eager to get to the intended destination. Both men, smartly dressed in their Earth States Class-B uniforms, were a minority among the crowd of Martian fleet operations personnel scurrying about the enclosure.

The two officers kept to the right on the passageway, letting forklifts and various other support vehicles pass them by. The whole structure dedicated itself to servicing the warships docked just outside and to the right of the wharf, so keeping to the side kept both men out of the frenzy of activities.

This was no problem; the wharf was over twenty meters wide. The corridor's sidewalls spanned almost as tall, though tapering off at forty-five degree angles about halfway to the ceiling. From about chest high and above, the entire enclosure was completely transparent, giving a nice view of the planet Mars suspended above and to their left. Only the occasional emergency airlock separating each section of the space wharf obscured the view.

That's one reason why young Gillen wasn't in too much of a hurry. The view was spectacular! Because Lowell Fleet Base orbited the planet at only fifteen thousand kilometers, Mars hung in the view prominently. The red-orange northern plains of the planet stretched across the surface, bordered by paler features shaded far darker and sometimes to a very dark greenish hue. Tiny black dots—impact craters and towering volcanoes—speckled the outer regions as if freckles. A bluish-white haze frosted the planet's poles, softening its startling appearance.

"Isn't that amazing, Tom?" Michael exclaimed, still looking at the giant sphere against the blackness of space. "Mars is such a beautiful planet: different from the Earth or the Moon, but nonetheless beautiful." He paused in thought and then added, "Don't you think it's ironic that, despite the fact we were celebrated astronauts, we've never seen much of our own solar system?"

Tom grimaced at him. "Have you forgotten that I'm still not talking to you?"

"How could I forget?" Michael chuckled, knowing his friend was only half-serious. "You've been saying that for two weeks now—almost made me want to jump out the transport's airlock. Besides, I've already apologized for pulling you off Intelligence ... and you should be flattered that I requested you as first officer."

"Yeah, I know," Tom grimaced again. "I'm *good with people and you've always valued my advice*" He shook his head. "I don't need to hear it again."

Michael looked over at him. Tom had a casualness about him that seemed out of place among rigid military etiquette. His brownish-black hair tested the bounds of regulation, even parting to one side under his cap. Though athletic, his somewhat lanky frame was always at ease. His eyes played the jester, and even his most serious expression complemented his singular wit. More than anything, Tom's relaxed sense of humor complemented Michael's seriousness nicely.

Michael remained silent for a few steps and then replied, "You're doing me a great favor. No matter what Cyril thinks, I'm in way over my head here."

Tom nodded, and the two men continued down the long passageway.

With his gaze fixed on the beautiful sphere above, young Gillen couldn't help but allow the inspiration to draw his thoughts to another, even more alluring beauty: *Katey*. The sight above had merely distracted him, for she remained a constant in his thoughts.

The image of her beautiful face lingered before his eyes as if encouraging him on warmly. He could still taste the sweetness of her lips upon his as she kissed him goodbye; memories of those two short days together darted about his mind teasingly. These were merely fleeting shadows, mocking him for the indiscretion of leaving her. Just how much he ached for her—barely two weeks apart—would go unspoken. No, his arms would remain empty far too long and his bed far too cold for the same.

The young newlywed shuddered at the thought of a prolonged war.

Attempting to take his mind off his angst, Michael looked out the transparent wall to his right; a docked warship filled the entire field of view. The ship was just one of many ships similarly docked throughout the vast space station. However, as the two men continued walking, the large engine section of that ship gave way. About sixty meters ahead sat another, more interesting warship.

The vessel sat suspended in space just outside the enclosed wharf, connected to the passage by large docking tunnels ahead that stretched from the wharf to the ship's hull. A network of structural components, much of which wasn't visible from the passageway, stretched around the ship, creating a kind of dry dock.

The ship was very large, even larger than the *ESS History*. However, unlike the *History*, this ship boasted a cache of large gun turrets on every side, and heavy defensive plating composed the hull. Yet the ship had a certain elegance to it too: its lines were sleek as if built for speed. Adorning the bow of the ship were the words *ESS Comanche*.

Gillen and Andrews had made it to their destination.

"It's too small," Tom remarked, looking at the cruiser. "You should have requested a destroyer—something with real teeth."

"If they gave us a destroyer, they'd put us right into the heat of battle," Michael replied. "But with a cruiser, we can get away with a patrol assignment … much safer."

"True … and I'm glad for that," Tom conceded. Then a rather typical smirk came across his face. "But is a cruiser really *fitting* for your esteemed position: the youngest captain in the fleet?"

Michael ignored the intentional jab, watching the ship grow larger as they made their way along. Taking in the daunting sight and pondering his assignment, the young man became rather pensive. "Do you think the crew will take me seriously?"

Tom remained silent for a few steps, noting his friend's sudden lack of confidence. "Why do you think they gave you command of the Alpha Centauri mission?"—pausing for effect—"It's because you *believed* you could do it. You carried yourself as if the position was yours, even if you didn't realize you were doing it…. People take their cues from what they see. This crew will respect you as captain only if you *believe* you're the captain…. Otherwise, don't step foot on the ship."

Tom looked at his friend soberly. Soon, they came to stand at the main gantry to the *Comanche*. Support personnel and crew alike were going about their business, while forklifts moved back and forth between the ship and the wharf. A duty officer stood at a desk to the side, his expression indicating he had noticed Michael's arrival and rank insignias.

Tom looked at Michael, who had stopped at the mouth of the gantry. Reluctance covered his friend's face. Finally, Tom exclaimed, "After you, *Captain*."

"Captain on the bridge!"

The bridge crew of the *ESS Comanche*, caught enjoying a rather casual watch, immediately snapped to the ready and saluted.

Captain Michael Gillen came through the main hatch, quickly followed by Commander Tom Andrews. Looking as formidable as ever, the young captain returned the salutation and surveyed his bridge. Most of the posts remained unmanned, as the ship was still not underway. The officers and subordinates who were there seemed quite taken back at Gillen's sudden appearance. This pleased the aspiring captain;

they obviously didn't know that he had lost his way to the bridge twice already. Tom's advice to look like he knew what he was doing appeared to be working.

"Welcome aboard, Sirs," one of the officers offered, stepping toward them. "*Uh* … I'm Lieutenant Morelli, Operations Officer. I'm also Officer of the Deck—right now, at least." He then turned toward the other men, gesturing at each one while introducing them. "This is Lieutenant Herschel, Engineering Officer; Lieutenant Combs, Combat and Tactical Officer; Jr. Lieutenant Pavia, Supply Officer." After introducing the enlisted men, Morelli turned back toward Michael. "Lieutenant Commanders Sloan, Perez, and Donne are below, overseeing preparations to make the ship ready for launch."

"Thank you," Michael replied, sizing up the men. "I'm Captain Michael Gillen. This is Commander Tom Andrews."

"Your reputations precede you, Sirs. We're all big fans of the space program. Sorry your mission got canceled."

Michael nodded appreciatively. "This is a more important mission, so let's get down to business." The young captain handed a small reader to him. "According to Earth States Military Command Order Two-Four-Alpha-Seven-Epsilon-Bravo, I hereby take command of the *ESS Comanche*. Please note the date and time in the deck log and transmit confirmation of the transfer of duty to Fleet Ops."

"Yes, Sir," Morelli replied, handing the reader to a subordinate to carry out.

"What's the status of the ship?" Michael inquired.

Morelli, a young officer, hesitated for a moment. "It's a piece of space debris, Sir."

"Is that the official report?"

"I had an unedited version, Sir," the young lieutenant began, "but you might bring me up on charges for saying it." He paused respectfully. "This is a brand new ship, but the builders are putting them together *too* fast. Nothing meets spec yet. If we left space dock, I'm afraid we'd fall apart."

Michael raised his eyebrows and replied, "A little surprising, given we're here because the Martians have a fully ramped military industry." He paused, taking in the man's visible dissatisfaction. "What about the crew?"

"Not bad," Morelli replied flippantly, "considering half of them are still being wet-nursed."

Michael sighed and went silent for a moment. "*Great....* So what you're saying is that we've got a ship that is basically a jigsaw puzzle and a crew that's too inexperienced to know how to put it together?"

"That's about it, Sir."

"Okay," the young captain replied, glancing back at a similarly dismayed Tom Andrews. "This isn't the first time I've been given a ship that isn't coming together.... For now, let's keep the command structure as is. Commander Andrews and I are going to go settle in. Assemble the entire executive staff in the ready room in a half hour; we'll go over the problems one-by-one. We have seven days to leave dry dock and thirty days to finish shakedown. So tell the men to prepare for some very hard work."

"Yes, Sir."

Kara Ricci stepped out of the transport, her duffle bag hanging heavily off one shoulder. Dressed neatly in her new military uniform, the twenty-six-year-old major labored down the corridor until coming to the receiving area. After getting directions from one of the attendants staffing the post, the young woman proceeded down a labyrinth of corridors until coming to another station. Upon checking in with the attendant there, Kara plopped down in a chair, dead tired and glad to be off her feet.

What a trip, she thought.

About a week after Michael and Tom had shipped out for the *Comanche*, Kara received orders to report to Randt Medical Base, which was near the front lines, to be a surgical physician. For the next two weeks, Kara had endured every kind of grueling transport known to the military, causing her to question whether she had wisely chosen extended space travel as her previous career choice. Fortunately, she had arrived at the base in one piece, looking forward to settling in quickly—and hopefully being afforded at least a day to recover.

She looked around the small, sterile receiving area, not very impressed. Randt Medical Base was a rather small space station, located somewhere between the orbits of Mars and Jupiter yet still within the boundaries of Inner Rim territory—exactly where, she didn't really know. Its mission was to support front-line war efforts, providing medical treatment to the wounded while staying far enough from the lines to keep out of harms way.

Sitting there waiting, Kara pondered her future. Certainly, the tour of duty would be challenging. That was why she still had a lump in her throat even then.

She also thought of Michael and Tom, who were probably still at Lowell Fleet Base taking command of their ship. Kara wondered if she would ever cross paths with them. Of course, she highly doubted it. The front lines of the war were vast and spread out, far beyond the mind's ability to comprehend such distances. Moreover, given the nature of her work—a surgeon, Kara hoped never to see them until peace finally came.

Her musings ended when she spotted an older man approaching. Though being dressed more casually than was normally appropriate for military duty, the man clearly possessed a sense of authority.

"Colonel Moreau?" the young woman asked, coming to stand and saluting.

"Major Ricci, welcome to Randt Medical Base. I hope your trip was uneventful?"

"Yes, Sir."

The man smiled and said, "Good. We've heard reports about Axis ships attacking our transports, but they've been few…. Come with me. I'll show you to your quarters."

She reached around, picked up her duffle bag from the floor, and swung it over her shoulder. Though her back protested, the young woman continued on, keeping pace with her superior.

"I can't guarantee we're completely safe from Axis aggression here," Moreau explained while leading her down the corridor. "But we're quite a distance from the front lines."

"So how do you effectively treat the wounded?"

"The less serious cases come here simply to finish treatment before being sent back. For our more seriously wounded, the warships have a fairly good team of medics that stabilize those patients until they can get them here."

"No offense, Sir," Kara said, shifting her duffel bag to the other shoulder, "But if I were a critically wounded soldier, I wouldn't be very encouraged at that set up."

Colonel Moreau sighed. "Point well taken—and I agree with you. In fact, our survival rate for critical cases is only sixty-two percent." She followed as he turned down another corridor. "The problem is that this hospital station is far too big and too vulnerable to move any closer to the front. Our redeployment engines are far too small to move our orbit dynamically. Moreover, Earth States doesn't have enough doctors to man every ship."

"Sounds bad."

"Yes," he nodded. "And it won't get any better. After just three months of war, the casualties have been small. However, once the Allies fully ramp the war effort, intensifying the fighting, we clearly expect to see a surge in casualties. You'll have your work cut out for you."

The man's words unnerved the young doctor. Having observed the station's already-strained operations while being led through the complex, Kara didn't know how the place could handle an oncoming surge.

"So what are you expecting from me?" she asked.

"A lot. You're already on the surgery schedule this evening, in fact. Sorry, but we're short-staffed."

The duo came to another corridor, one off the main floors. Kara assumed she was getting closer to her quarters.

"That's no problem, Sir," she replied, her back and feet pleading with her to tell the truth. "I'm eager to get to work."

Moreau smiled at a subordinate who had gestured to him as they passed. When the two were clear, the older man continued, "I was hoping you'd say that. You came highly recommended by Admiral Davidson." He paused. "I want you to get your bearings as quickly as you can—learn the operations just as quick. Command is promoting me to major general soon. When that happens, I want you to be in a position to take over command of the surgical wing."

"That's a little bit of a surprise," Kara exclaimed, hesitating in her stride. But when Moreau continued on like a man possessed, she pursued. "I'm a new recruit."

Moreau shook his head glibly. "This is less military and more medical—though I think you're underestimating your military background from the academy. Your qualifications as a surgeon are exemplary. We'll be getting in many young doctors who are going to need to come up to speed just as quick.... You'll be well ahead of them and can teach them the ropes."

Kara remained silent, thoughtfully considering everything she had heard. Finally, she turned to him and remarked, "I don't know what to say.... I'm a little overwhelmed."

At that point, Moreau stopped in front of a door with Kara's name written on the label. After programming the security system to recognize her, Moreau turned the handle. The door swung open, revealing a rather modest dwelling.

"Get settled in," he said. "Before you know it, everyone will be looking to you to know what to do. See you on the evening shift."

Twenty-four-year-old Kate Gillen—and she had to remind herself that her last name wasn't *DeCarreau* anymore—walked through the entrance to the main floor, following the office manager assigned to get her settled into her new position at Earth States Intelligence.

Kate anxiously followed the older woman to an empty desk, carrying a small box of supplies and personal items. The main floor was a rather large common area crowded with many workstations, an overwhelming majority staffed by women—most of whom had taken notice of her arrival. She stood over the workstation while the office manager gave instructions. Once the quick orientation was finished and the woman gone, Kate looked around, discreetly straightening the navy blue skirt of her new Class-B uniform, and sat down.

The young woman sighed and began setting up her workstation, not sure how she had ever come to the place.

Kate felt all alone. Having been the last Centauri to receive deployment orders, the newlywed was Earthbound and without her new husband—and frightfully worried about him too. Tom had left with Michael three weeks earlier, and Kara had left the next week. Phil

Marcotte had left for the central division of Intelligence at Eratosthenes, the Moon, while Ben Morris and David Tashjian entered top-secret positions in Research. Yet there she sat: in some obscure Intelligence office on Earth, doing some sort of clerk job. The assignment didn't make sense.

Of course, she didn't want to downplay the position either. After all, having had Cyril Davidson personally ask her to take the job, she reckoned he must have considered it an important task. Moreover, the office was close enough to the Gillen lake house that she could live there and set up housekeeping for when Michael returned.

So remaining determined to make the best of things, Kate continued setting up her workstation.

Not too long afterwards, Kate realized that the woman at the adjacent station was eyeing her up. She was close to Kate's age, maybe a little older, and wore her bleached-blonde hair up in a rather conservative style—though nothing else about her appeared conservative.

Before long, Kate spotted the woman coming over to her.

"Hi, I'm Brenda Reid," the woman smiled, standing straight up and extending her hand. "You must be Kate … *Gillen*, right?"

"Yes, nice to meet you, Brenda," Kate smiled politely, shaking her hand.

After looking around quickly, Reid sat down on the corner of the desk. "They told us someone new was starting soon, but I didn't know it would be a celebrity." Upon noticing Kate's quizzical gaze, she added dismissively, "I saw you on television when they announced the Alpha Centauri mission." She paused, searching Gillen's expression; then her eyebrows wrinkled. "Boy, they sure made a big deal of your engagement…. By the way, you're a lucky girl. Your husband's really nice lookin'."

"Thank you," Kate replied, her face blushing just before her quizzical look returned. "How'd you know I actually got married?"

"The ring on your finger was the first hint, dear," Reid exclaimed matter-of-factly. Kate glanced down at the jewelry, bringing her head back up with an *I should have known that* expression. "But I knew the second you walked through the door." Reid held up her left hand, proudly displaying her own wedding ring. "Welcome to the *Kept Wives Club*."

Kate tilted her head, bewildered at the woman's words.

Reid brought her face closer to the newlywed, her voice hushing a little. "Look around…. Notice the inordinate number of women here?" She paused, letting Gillen survey the room. "This is where influential military husbands put their wives to keep them safe from the war." Then she gestured to her ring. "Most of us have one of these. Some don't…. Some are girlfriends." Her voice hushed even more and her eyebrows went up. "We've even got some *mistresses.*"

Kate looked at Brenda, unsure of what to make of her new acquaintance. Reid had a personality that seemed flippant and prone to exaggeration. Yet her gaze remained deadpan. "*Really?*"

"Absolutely!" the woman exclaimed without hesitation. "The military is big and powerful. There's no equality here; they train us equally—they just don't treat us equally. This place isn't for everyone, just those with connections. I mean, do you think Intelligence has branch offices everywhere?"

After pausing for effect, Reid continued, "I'm a tactical officer by trade. Do you know how I got here? My husband's a commander on a Jupiter-Class destroyer—been in the military for a while and has lots of friends." She turned her fingers around, crooking them so as to look at her manicure. Her expression became denying and dismissive. "I don't care…. I didn't really want to get blown up anyway."

All at once, everything made sense to the young newlywed: Michael leaving her behind despite her pleadings otherwise, Davidson *asking* her to take the job. Kate fumed. Had Michael actually been there right then, the couple would have had their first *real* fight.

"How 'bout you?" Brenda asked. "How'd you get here?"

Kate grimaced. "An over-protective husband and a colluding admiral."

"Don't worry about it, dear," Reid replied, noticing the complete look of dissatisfaction on Kate's face. "The nice thing about being here is that we all have someone close to us out there fighting a war. You'll get more than enough moral support. And this is Intelligence—you might even get to keep tabs on what your husband is doing…." Her face sobered. "Of course, there are downsides to knowing too."

"Captain on the bridge!" came the familiar call. The bridge crew of the *ESS Comanche* saluted as Captain Michael Gillen made his appearance, followed by Commander Tom Andrews.

The bridge crew had spent the previous week since Gillen's arrival trying to learn the young man's body language. However, Michael's frustrated expression was more than clear, and today wasn't the first time they had seen it. No, preparing the ship to leave dry dock had come with many complications.

"Captain," Lieutenant Morelli greeted him. "What can we do for you?"

"Commander Andrews and I just got back from an operations meeting with the Martians," Michael replied, shaking his head. "How soon can we get underway?"

The young officer paused in thought, doing some quick mental calculations. His expression also betrayed his surprise at the question. "About an hour. Fuel and provision stores are full, but the fusion engines are cold. It will take awhile to get them to speed. Plus, this will be the first time through the launch procedure—best if we take it a little slow." He paused, watching his superior's reaction. "Should I give the orders?"

"Yes."

Morelli made his way to the unmanned communications console. Picking up the mouthpiece and bringing it to his face, the young man pressed one of the myriad of buttons and said, "This is the acting Command Duty Officer. Captain has given the order to make way. All departments stand ready for launch. Senior officers, report to the bridge for transfer to running command…. CDO out."

"Good," Michael exclaimed before turning to Tom. "Commander Andrews, stay here and oversee preparations for launch. I'm going to my office to get our orders from Command."

Upon seeing Michael making his way off the bridge, Lieutenant Morelli spoke up once more, "Excuse me, Captain. Do the Martians know about the ship's operating deficiencies?"

Michael shook his head, his frustrated look returning. "Yes. Unfortunately, a new cruiser's coming into port from the shipyards to be made ready. We're being evicted to make room."

"I only hope they do a better job with them than they did with us," Tom chimed in, receiving supporting expressions from many on the bridge.

Young Gillen watched the disapproving looks from the other crewmembers, who more than agreed with Tom. Michael agreed too. Nevertheless, the ship had received its orders. "We're just going to have to make up the deficiencies while underway. Regardless, we have no choice. Tom, you and Sloane put together the operations plan for making the ship ready, and I'll review it when you're done." He paused. "I'll be back in twenty minutes."

Then Michael disappeared through the hatch.

An hour later, the *ESS Comanche* got underway. In less than ceremonial fashion, the large docking and servicing tunnels pulled away from the hull. Still moored, the ship waited while the underside of the docking cradle, just a network of large structural beams, split open. The two sides swung down and away, giving the ship a clear path out of the dock. The moorings released, actually pushing the ship down through the gaping outlet. When completely clear, the fusion engines came to life, propelling the vessel steadily forward and away from the station.

Michael Gillen oversaw the launch from his captain's chair on the bridge. The warship continued picking up speed away from the orange-red light of Mars, heading into the blackness of space for its first patrol.

Michael remained emotionless while watching the crew carry out their assignments. His look was only an outward impression, designed to mask his concerns. In reality, the inexperienced captain's stomach was knots and his thoughts racing. His mind could only conjure what fate awaited him—or how terrible the war could actually become.

And the *Comanche* was heading straight into that war.

CHAPTER FOURTEEN

Tour of Duty

Michael Gillen sat rigid in his captain's chair on the bridge of the *ESS Comanche*, which was traveling somewhere in the Asteroid Belt. To say that he was a little unnerved would have been an understatement.

"Lieutenant Combs, where are my port guns?" the young captain pleaded, trying to keep his voice calm and resolute. "We're getting pounded."

The tactical officer shook his head as he stared into his display screen. "Sir, my men are still working the feeds from the power plant. But we'll have them up soon, I promise."

"I'll hold you to that," Michael replied. Of course, by the way the battle was going, the inexperienced commander wasn't sure how much of a delay *Comanche* could afford.

Almost four months had passed since *Comanche* had left the dry docks of Lowell Fleet Base at Mars. Spending over a month getting the cruiser operational, Michael had barely finished the shakedown in time to have *Comanche* begin its first tour of duty: patrolling an obscure patch of Allied territory well off the front lines with the *WMS Lemuria*, a Martian war cruiser identical to the *Comanche* but with a more experienced crew.

With the war raging in other, distant parts of the asteroid belt, *Lemuria* had spent the first three months of patrol taking *Comanche* through combat training exercises—up until that day.

That's when the Allied duo came across its first encounter: a rogue Ganymede cruiser. The intercept point was prominently behind Allied front lines. Armed to the teeth, the vessel seemed determined not to be chased off easily.

Too busy to think about anything but surviving this first conflict, Michael nevertheless found the enemy cruiser's appearance disturbing. After six months of war, the Axis powers were overwhelming the ill-prepared Allies. Three times, Command had ordered *Comanche* to move back its patrol deeper into the Inner Rim due to advancing Axis forces. The Ganymede ship was an omen: the Axis forces were testing the lines, looking for a weakness—a place to stage an invasion. *Comanche* couldn't let the ship get away or get the best of them.

Moreover, Michael found *Comanche's* poor performance in the encounter just as troubling. Though the *Lemuria* was holding its own, Michael was certain he and his bumbling crew were interfering with the more experienced Martian ship. Young Gillen resolved to accomplish a decisive victory. However, an untimely Ganymede artillery round had just silenced *Comanche's* port gunneries—the side facing the conflict—making the ship vulnerable.

"Lieutenant Herschel," he called out to his engineering officer. "Can you give any help to Tactical?"

"We're working it now, Sir."

Michael nodded approvingly. "Let's get those guns up." Then he turned to Tom, whose chair was right beside his. "Commander Andrews, let's *spin* the ship."

Just then, *Comanche* rocked under the power of a forceful concussion. Tactical registered another hit to the ship's weakened port side, causing Herschel to announce that the port defensive shields were dropping.

"I concur," Tom quickly affirmed and then barked out the necessary orders.

Quickly—but not quick enough for Michael—*Comanche* began turning on its forward axis until rotating upside down. Having its starboard turrets ready, the ship sent a torrent of artillery fire into the Ganymede cruiser, rejoining *Lemuria* in the assault.

Finally attacking the intruder from two different directions at once, the *Comanche* and *Lemuria* soon overwhelmed their Axis antagonist.

"Captain," Combs called from his post at Tactical. "The Ganymede cruiser has just gone yellow-line. They're changing course back to Axis territory."

Gillen and Andrews sighed in relief, watching the severely wounded ship make a run for safer territory. Not letting their prey get away, *Comanche* and *Lemuria* pursued, continuing to train all guns on the vessel. Hellcat fighters, Allied one-manned ships, buzzed around it like enraged wasps.

"They're not going to make it back to Axis territory," Tom mused.

The Ganymede cruiser abruptly banked hard to stop; the *Lemuria* had come around its starboard side to intercept. Having its escape route cut off, the Ganymede cruiser had no choice but to suffer under the brutal Allied assault. *Comanche* and *Lemuria* began ripping the Axis cruiser to pieces, and the tactical computer soon changed the ship's status to red-line.

"Sir," the ensign operating the communications console called, "The Ganymede cruiser has surrendered and requests help."

"Lieutenant Combs," Michael called out. "Does Tactical confirm that communication?"

"Yes, Sir. The *Lemuria* concurs as well. The enemy is dead in space."

Michael felt his shoulders relaxing as the tension passed. He had survived his first engagement.

"Okay," he called out, continuing the good work. "Remain at general quarters. Lieutenant Combs, stand down fire, but keep our shields up. Lieutenant Morelli, put us into position to lend aid to the Ganymede cruiser. Lieutenant Sloane, send a rescue and security detachment to pick up survivors. Have Lieutenant Commander Donne head up the medics."

The bridge crew begin carrying out his orders.

Eventually satisfied that the danger had passed, the young captain stood up from his chair and turned toward the tactical officer. "Lieutenant Combs, send a report to Command with the tactical records of the encounter. Request a performance review for training purposes. I hope they'll go gentle on us. Send their feedback to my desk." He started walking off the bridge. "I'm going to conference call with the captain of the *Lemuria*—get some feedback from him too." Just as he made it to the hatch, he turned back toward Tom. "Take charge of the bridge."

Making his way through the hatch and down the narrow corridor toward his office, Michael heard Tom calling from behind.

"I thought I directed you to oversee the bridge?" Michael exclaimed when Tom caught up with him.

"I will, Mike," Tom replied in a hushed voice. "Perez is filling in for me for a minute. I just wanted to make sure you're okay. You seem troubled."

Michael sighed, looking around to make sure they were alone. "Our performance against the Ganymedes was deplorable today; that goes for everyone—including me. I can't let that happen again." He paused pensively. "Once we finish repairs, I'm putting in a request to Command to participate in some minor combat missions in the quadrant."

"You're kidding, right?" a very incredulous Tom Andrews asked. When Michael's expression didn't change, he lowered his voice and moved in closer. "Mike, don't go looking for trouble."

Michael shook his head. "That's the problem, Tom. Trouble *will* eventually find us.... Look how far our patrol routes have been pushed back these three months: over *one hundred and thirty million kilometers*." He paused for effect. "The Allies are losing ships faster than they can produce them—we're losing this war." Then he gestured back toward the bridge. "Today, it's a harmless Ganymede cruiser ... tomorrow, the Europan Republican Armada." He paused once more, looking his friend in the eye. "No, we need to get experience ... and *fast*."

Tom recoiled, and his eyebrows came up as if to plead. "Mike, *don't do this*. Command is just looking for suckers who are naïve enough to volunteer. There's no such thing as a minor combat mission—not in this day." He went silent, hoping Michael would relent. However, upon seeing his friend—now superior—remain stoic, he crossed his arms defiantly. "I *didn't* sign up for this."

Michael remained silent, surprised at his friend's reaction. Finally, he said, "You will support me though, won't you?"

Kate Gillen sat back in the cushioned chair of her personal transport craft, reclining and playing a game on the reader built into the armrest. She had let her long, brown hair down from the constricting bun she had worn all day, while her shoes lay kicked off in the corner. The soft sound of music played in the background, and the cabin remained subdued in dim light. Enjoying the ambiance while unwinding from a very hard day, the fetching, young female looked forward to a very relaxing, long weekend.

She paused briefly to check the craft's AutoNav. Surely enough, the computer remained undeterred, safely navigating the craft through the darkening sky and flying about a hundred meters off the ground. Noting her imminent arrival, Kate deactivated the game and watched the craft begin the landing procedure.

Through tired eyes, Kate peered out the window, watching the familiar landscape. She spied the roadway first, not only because it cut through the forested landscape, but also because the road was the only thing not covered in pristine snow. Then, the all too familiar hillside with the underground residence jutting out from its side appeared. Just over the snowy hillside and stretching deep into the wilderness lay the beginnings of a very large, very flat, frosted-white, twisted oval surrounded by trees: the ice-covered lake.

The sleepy scenery was a remarkable sight. However, she had no one to share the moment with her.

Kate sat back while the AutoNav brought the small craft into the awaiting garage, which was strategically hidden by the rise of the hillside and not visible at ground level. Its roof opened upon receiving the signal from the AutoNav. With little fanfare and a lot of work by the computers, the young woman walked through the garage door and into the kitchen of the Gillen residence.

"Music!" she called just as the lights came up. By the time she had put down her things, the sound of soft music filled the background of the entire house. Satisfied with the improvement, Kate grabbed a cup of coffee from the kitchen, stepped around the utility robot making her dinner, and made her way into the living room.

She stood in front of the couch for a moment, realizing how uncomfortable she was. Too tired to make her way into the bedroom to change, Kate looked around just to make sure she was alone—as if that were even necessary. Satisfied, the young woman loosened the zippered catch on her skirt, letting the heavy, constricting garment fall to the floor and exposing the delicate, white slip she wore underneath it. Undoing a few buttons here and there, the exhausted woman sighed in relief.

After sinking into the plush couch and nestling her bare feet up underneath her, Kate took a sip of coffee, laid her head back, and closed her eyes. She was finally home.

But she really wasn't home.

No, the house was haunted with the images and memories of Michael's family. She *had* no family, at least not until Michael came home. No, everything in the house belonged to someone else, and Kate had neither the strength nor the time to make it her home. Four long months of working in Intelligence during a war made her realize that.

She looked out onto the darkening landscape just outside the large observation windows. Wilderness stretched as far as the eye could see, a soft blanket of white snow draping itself imposingly over the barren land. Many of the trees, their branches laid bare by winter, poked through the cold snow and stretched skyward in spindly fashion, as if grasping at the frigid evening air. The frosted white surface of the frozen lake extended around and behind the far ridge, its lifelessness becoming a melancholy tribute to warmer times.

She was in the middle of nowhere with no one.

Moreover, the frozen lake lay mockingly before her. What opportunity had befallen her: a lake of her own in which to swim, her very favorite activity. She could remember all those years living in the crowded Fra Mauro Highlands residences on the Moon, dreaming of such a place. She could remember chiding Michael so long ago back at the academy for taking the lake for granted. Yet there she sat, unable to avail herself of the occasion.

However, even if summer were in full swing, it wouldn't really matter. In her zeal to share her new life with Michael, Kate had vowed to wait for Michael's return before taking her first plunge into the lake. The vow was just her way of supporting him from afar, something symbolic of many first-time experiences the two of them would eventually share. She would have to wait.

Yes, her life was on hold until Michael came home.

The young newlywed wondered why she had looked forward to arriving or why the long weekend had seemed so appealing. Now that she was home, Kate realized that a long weekend was nothing more than another opportunity to spend even *more* time worrying about Michael, another opportunity to become even more furious over him leaving her behind too. No, this break would be nothing but more sleepless nights and many bad dreams—all accomplished while lying on a tear-soaked pillow.

It was her lot in life, until Michael returned.

The battle cruiser *ESS Comanche* cut through black void of space, keeping in formation with the rest of the large Allied fleet racing toward the potato-shaped asteroid. The colossal rock, well over five hundred kilometers in diameter, loomed ever larger in the view field, quickly filling the whole screen as the ship neared.

Twenty-five-year-old Michael Gillen watched the hurried activity taking place on his bridge. With lighting subdued in standard battle red, the entire ship remained at general quarters. He could feel the occasional buffeting of the ship by Axis artillery, rounds that the defensive shielding easily absorbed at this point. However, the pounding would become more intense as *Comanche* neared its destination. With the crew more than aware of the pending danger, a thick tension hung uneasily in the air.

Michael surveyed the crew, admiring their progress since the first Axis encounter five months earlier. After nine months of being underway, the crew had transformed themselves into competent, professional soldiers. The many dangerous assignments the young captain had volunteered them for were finally paying off. Of course, the crew would need all the help they could get, for this current mission was the riskiest assignment yet.

Comanche was escorting three landing ships full of troops and offensive weaponry to the surface of the asteroid, 4 Vesta. The landing was part of the Allies' boldest move since the war started: the invasion and capture of the Europan-held asteroid, which was the second largest asteroid in the asteroid belt too. If successful, the Allies would finally have a foothold from which to launch more offensives into Axis territory.

The undertaking could be the turning point in the war.

Michael looked over toward Tom Andrews, who was busy overseeing defensive operations. Tom noticed him, respectfully returning the look while letting the tension between them go unspoken in front of the crew. Not that Tom was hostile toward him. In fact, Andrews was more than supportive of him in front of the crew, giving Michael a wide berth concerning the risky decisions he was making. In private, however, Tom was more than vocal about Michael taking on too many missions, endangering the crew unnecessarily, and the like. In particular, he had warned Michael adamantly about volunteering the ship for its current escort mission.

However, all these thoughts had to wait until a less dangerous time.

"Lieutenant Morelli, what's our distance?" Michael asked.

"Seven hundred kilometers and closing," the young officer replied, surveying the navigation console. "Continuing deceleration."

Just then, *Comanche* shuddered under a rather powerful energy blast.

"I guess they know we're here." Tom exclaimed dryly.

Michael turned to Tactical and said, "Lieutenant Combs, trace trajectory of artillery. Feed the data to Lieutenant Morelli's navigation computer." Then he turned to Navigation. "Lieutenant Morelli, keep the *Comanche* between those guns and our landers."

"Yes, Sir. Of course, there are a lot of guns out there."

"Just do your best."

Comanche continued approaching 4 Vesta, keeping protectively ahead of the landing vessels while also trying to dodge the onslaught of energy blasts. The manmade structures on the surface of the asteroid began to become visible.

"Four hundred kilometers from the landing point," Morelli exclaimed.

"Releasing Hellcats," Combs announced.

From the viewpoint of the three large landing vessels traveling behind *Comanche*, one could see dozens of tiny dots erupting from the cruiser's hull. These were Hellcats: small and very agile one-manned fighters. Since battle cruisers did not have an extended fighter bay, the fighters rode directly docked to the hull. Having launched, the squadrons quickly coalesced into formation behind *Comanche's* protective shielding.

The black void directly around and between the fleet vessels lit up when a barrage of Europan artillery met the incoming Allies. Getting closer to 4 Vesta, the fleet became more susceptible to enemy fire. Moreover, small dots—Europan warships seen from a great distance—began to erupt from the asteroid's surface, traveling on an intercept course toward the Allied fleet.

None of this was unanticipated. The Allied invasion fleet of thirty cruisers, ten destroyers, and ninety landers began making the predetermined flight path alterations.

"Two hundred kilometers from the landing site," Morelli announced.

"Okay, Lieutenant Combs," Michael began, sitting up in his chair, "That's targeting range. Start laying down cover fire. Lieutenant Morelli, keep us away from those Axis ships."

Full-blown conflict broke out as Europan forces began engaging the Allied fleet. Energy blasts continued buffeting *Comanche*, the artillery coming much stronger than before. So under Morelli's control, the cruiser veered off and around the brunt of the attack. Nevertheless, the assault was a temporary obstacle; the fleet was moving so fast that *Comanche* streamed quickly passed the first wave of Europan ships.

"Fifty kilometers," Morelli announced.

Michael turned to him and said, "Okay, execute hard stop." Then he turned to the communications officer. "Signal landers and Hellcats."

The small convoy, led by the *Comanche*, quickly decelerated and turned, soaring over the asteroid's surface and toward the settlement. *Comanche's* Hellcats came from behind the ship and dove toward the surface, providing necessary cover fire. After several minutes the *Comanche* slowed, taking up a protective position in front of the convoy's landing site.

Now having a safe window to execute their assignments, the massive landers touched down on the surface. The vessels, having secured themselves to the low-gravity asteroid by landing anchors, opened and began unleashing legions of space-suited soldiers, tanks, and the like.

Suddenly, the entire bridge rocked violently! *Comanche* struggled to maintain its protective position above the surface.

"Damage to K-2 section!" Lieutenant Herschel at Engineering shouted above the din of alarms and chaos. "Stabilizers offline too.... K-2 has suffered a minor hull breach.... Bypassing damaged critical systems should take a few minutes.... We *do* have wounded."

"Isolate that section," Michael calmly replied. "Let's work the containment and get those stabilizers back online." Turning to the rest of the crew, he added, "Everyone hold tight. We can't do anything until the landing crafts safely deploy. Combs, redeploy half the hellcats to cover us."

While Michael watched the frenzied bridge activities, Tom leaned in toward him. "The damage sounds pretty bad. I hope we can hold on long enough."

"K-2 isn't critical to the overall functioning of the ship," Michael replied, thinking more about the assignment. "We should be okay."

Michael looked on as his crew worked both the containment problems and the tactical defense of the landing vessels. The entire landing area turned into a nebulous cloud of dust and laser fire while the Allied armies advanced toward the settlement.

"K-2 isolated," Herschel announced. "And stabilizers are back online."

After about twenty minutes of intense action that had put everyone's nerves on edge, the tactical displays showed the empty landing vehicles lifting off from surface.

"Okay, Lieutenant Morelli," Michael began. "Plot a safe course away from the conflict. Send the coordinates to the landers so they can follow." Then he turned to Tactical. "Recall the Hellcats."

While *Comanche* began pulling away from the dangerous place,

Michael turned back to Morelli. "Once the landers are out of harms way, make sure you plot a course for us to meet up with the second wave of landers."

Captain Michael Gillen sat in his office aboard the *ESS Comanche*, doing various administrative tasks to keep busy. Having successfully led his ship through three separate iterations of escorting landers to the surface of 4 Vesta, the young commander had let his bridge crew continue the required monitoring activities. After all, the ship had stood down from general quarters, and the crew was more than competent to handle things.

While becoming engrossed in the work before him, he heard a quick knock at the door, followed by Tom Andrews popping his head in through the partially opened doorway.

"Hey, Mike," Tom began, "I just wanted you to know that we've completely stood down from all battle conditions. Command has given us approval to revert back to patrol status."

"Good," Michael sighed, leaning back in his chair. "Keep Engineering on the repairs. You never know when we'll run into trouble."

Tom shook his head and replied, "Herschel's on it."

However, Michael was already on to the next subject, beaming with pride. "Did you see how those guys performed back there?" He paused enthusiastically. "They're becoming quite the crew."

"Yeah, well, they've gotten a lot of practice lately," Tom replied, less excited. Coming all the way into the room and shutting the door, he watched Michael go right back to his work, not even paying attention to his concerned expression. "Have you been down to sickbay yet?"

"No, not yet," Michael shook his head. "I'll get there."

Once more Michael's attention went back to his work, much to Tom's dismay. Michael continued, "I'm looking at the operations plan from Command. We have some good opportunities coming up to contribute. Sit down; I want to get your opinions on which opportunities you think we should request before I send back a response."

"How 'bout some shore leave?" Tom asked, astonished at his friend's preoccupation. "*That's* overdue."

Michael shook his head. "I don't think we can do that, and I don't think Command will approve. This is a crucial time: The Allies have just established a good defense against the goons. Command wants to press our opportunity before the Europans readjust." He shook his head once more. "No, we need to keep working—at least for now. But I'll get us on shore leave soon; I promise."

Tom gazed at his friend, partially incredulous and partially indignant. Having heard that promise before, Andrews leaned in toward him. "Mike, we've been out here for *nine* months. You've volunteered us for too many combat missions." He paused for effect. "The crew is tired. Either get us some shore leave or get us back on full-time patrol."

Michael leaned back again, looking at his friend. He didn't speak, being unsure of what to say.

Finally, Tom broke the silence, "So have you thought anymore about my request for a transfer?"

"Yes," Michael reluctantly replied, sighing. "I know you want to go work for Intelligence, but I still need you here."

"Not anymore. The crew is coming along fine. And you can get someone who's regular military, someone whom I sure will be more sympathetic to what you're trying to do." He looked reassuringly at his friend, hoping he would understand. When Michael's expression didn't change, he added, "I don't want to abandon you, but this job isn't for me. I'm an astronaut, not a warrior. I can contribute in a much more positive way at Intelligence."

Michael remained silent, looking at Tom as if to appeal. However, the man remained determined. "I'll pull *every* string I can with Davidson to get you a plumb job…. But I need you *here* right now." He paused encouragingly. "And this challenge is a good opportunity for both of us."

"No, Mike," Tom retorted. "This is *you're* opportunity. All this volunteering you're doing isn't just because of the Allied challenge, and you know it." He was reluctant to continue. "The Outer Rim is where everything happened to your family. In you're mind, you think fighting the Europans is somehow making up for what happened. But you're getting a little reckless. Every combat mission you volunteer us for gets a little closer to destroying the ship and the crew…. You're making this your own personal war."

By this point, Michael was fuming. "Maybe…. But that doesn't mean we shouldn't do it."

Tom got up and went for the door. Just before leaving, he turned back to Michael and said, "Maybe you're right. But before deciding our next assignment, you should go visit sickbay first; go and spend some time with the wounded."

CHAPTER FIFTEEN

Inconveniences of War

Twenty-eight-year-old Kara Ricci stood over her operating table in Surgical Room One at Randt Medical Base, somewhere in the vast expanse known as the Asteroid Belt.

Like the other surgeons working the many other operating tables, Ricci stood garbed head-to-toe in hygienic scrubs, surgical gloves, and a surgical mask; her long, auburn hair remained tucked up under her tightly fitting scull cap. She meticulously worked the medical robot controller in front of her. A badly wounded soldier lay sedated on the table, receiving the benefits of the robot's many and variously configured arms, tubes, processors, and the like.

The young surgeon yawned behind her mask, fending off the heavy fatigue that had become so typical at the medical space station. After eighteen long months of duty, Kara had come to learn just how little sleep she really needed—how much sleep she could really afford.

The nurse working at her side noticed and yawned too. Kara saw the reaction and hoped she wasn't causing a yawning epidemic. After all, the entire surgical staff had worked on wounded soldiers for the last fourteen hours. However, they would soon finish the current wave of patients, much to everyone's relief.

She looked over at Roland Moreau performing surgery at the adjacent table. Moreau, now a major general, was a rare sight in the surgery ward. Having relinquished control of the entire operation to her almost a year earlier, the man only scrubbed in every now and then.

"How's it going over there, Sir?" Kara called to him through her mask while working the patient in front of her.

"Not bad. This patient is almost done. I think that finishes me for today."

"I'm just glad to have you scrub in with us," Kara added. "I'm almost done here myself. Can you stick around? I want to talk with you."

Nodding, the man went back to staring into his surgical robot's display. "I'll catch you outside."

Before long, Kara was walking with Moreau down the center of Surgical's main corridor. Recovering patients in makeshift cots lined the passage, attended by support personnel. So many patients had come through the hospital, the recovery wards were overflowing.

"So how's being Chief of Surgery working out?" the graying-haired man asked, a little coy.

Kara sighed. "After twelve months of doing the job, I'm not sure how you managed."

"You've got far more cases coming through here now," Moreau stated empathetically. "I would say you're doing a great job, given the circumstances."

The two turned into an adjacent break room, where a table of refreshments sat. Moreau poured a cup of coffee and handed it to her.

The young woman took a sip and closed her eyes while savoring the taste. "*Mmmm* ... this is the only thing that keeps me going." Quickly coming back to herself and the subject at hand, she replied, "I'd feel better about the position if our critical case survival rate wasn't dropping. It's down to fifty-one percent."

"That's to be expected. The battles are getting more frequent and more intense."

Kara found no comfort in the explanation. "That's true, but a lot of the wounded are dying on the way here. The medics can't keep up, and some of the more besetting cases don't survive the travel." She paused reluctantly, even cringing a little at what she was about to say. "But I think we can improve."

"What do you suggest?"

The young woman sighed, screwing up her courage. "I want to split the surgical cases into two: non-critical and critical. The non-critical cases would still come back here directly, while we would handle the critically wounded closer to the front lines. I want to put together a surgical vessel—fly it in closer to the fighting."

She waited for a reaction, but the man clearly gestured for her to continue the explanation. "The warships can send us their wounded in either life pods or torpedo tubes modified for medical support. We catch them, bring them into our docking bay, and do the surgery immediately—at least everything necessary to keep them alive." Pausing reluctantly, she finally blurted out, "I think we can not only get the survival rate back up to sixty-two percent, but get it into the seventy or eighty percent range—maybe higher."

Moreau pondered the recommendation. "The problem is finding ships. All the Allied resources are going into building more warships. Even if you could get authorization for a build, it would be months before the test ship arrived—and months before you could modify it for your needs. It would be at least a year before the maiden voyage."

"I know," Kara conceded. "But I've been snooping around. I found a vessel ... the *Windsor*. It's an old civilian transport—pretty antiquated. However, it will meet our needs. And I verified that no other military organization wants it."

"If they don't want it, then why do we?"

"It has a bad propulsion system. However, I struck a deal with some friends in Research. They have some older Class-D fusion drives sitting around from a converted ship. They told me I can have them."

Moreau smiled. "I like your resourcefulness."

"With your permission," Kara began, "I'll write up the order to have the refit done and the ship delivered in three months. We can begin testing in six months."

Moreau once again pondered the idea. Finally, he nodded approvingly. "I like it. If we can get the survival rates up, we can expand the program." He paused in thought. "Go ahead. I'm eager to see what you can do."

Twenty-six-year-old Michael Gillen had sunk deep into the cushions of his office chair, his feet propped up on the desk and the lights down low to soothe tired eyes. His office, which was really just a small room just off his quarters on the *Comanche*, was awash in the soft music playing low in the background. The tune was more than familiar, reminding him of a very special day he had shared with someone just as special, so long ago.

The time was late, not that time really had any meaning in the cold, blackness of space. Nevertheless, that was what the clock said. So he sat subdued in the quiet, not yet ready to turn in for the night.

Nevertheless, the young man was exhausted. His tiredness was not just the result of the late hour, but also from almost twenty-three long months of service aboard the ship, twenty-three months of fighting an incredibly difficult war. Oh, the Allies had made tremendous progress, and *Comanche* could count itself among the most fervent of contributors. However, the war had taken its toll on both captain and crew: many hard-fought battles, too many to count; entire parts of the ship rebuilt repeatedly; the loss of some very good men. Beaten down and wearied by his difficult assignment, Michael Gillen just wanted to go home.

Listening to the soft music, his mind filled with warm thoughts of his bride. The music brought him back to the wonderful evening of his wedding day. Sweet memories played repeatedly in his mind. Yet the song also became a haunting reminder that she wasn't with him. No, Katey was millions of kilometers away, with distance and military wartime protocol preventing any personal communication. Alone in a dangerous war, he wondered if he would ever see her again.

A knock at the door broke the quiet, and Tom Andrews peered in and asked, "You busy, Mike?"

Michael hesitated, pondering Tom's appearance at the door and knowing what had brought him to the office. The reason was the same one that had brought Andrews to the office regularly during the last fourteen months, and the young captain dreaded the impending discussion.

"What's up?"

Tom came in all the way, shutting the door while Michael turned off the music. Tom kind of gulped, "It's been twenty-three months since I came aboard with you...."

"And you want me to finally make good on my promise to let you go to Intelligence?" Michael asked, finishing the sentence.

Tom looked at him for a long moment before continuing. "You don't need me anymore. You've established yourself as captain with the crew *and* Command. You're about as regular military as anyone now ... and it's time for me to move on."

Young Gillen looked at his friend soberly. On and off for fourteen months, Tom had requested the transfer. The request irritated him, for Michael couldn't understand what was driving his friend to be so insistent about leaving, to be so inconsiderate for just how much he needed Tom's friendship and counsel on the ship.

At the same time, Michael wasn't surprised either. Tom had always been somewhat of an enigma. Just like many of the Centauries from NSEA, Andrews kept quiet about much of his personal life, always avoiding discussions about his childhood. What few stories he did recount, Tom told them repeatedly and in exacting detail as if rehearsed. Michael only surmised that Tom had come from a broken home. Even Tom's casual and humorous charm, his defining trait, seemed to be a veneer the man protectively draped over his more vulnerable persona.

Nonetheless, whatever painful memories haunted the man, whatever insecurities he held, none of that had mattered to Michael. No, Michael had benefited from Tom's complete loyalty and friendship for so many years.

So he resolved to let Tom work out his own personal demons.

However, he needed Tom's friendship more than ever. Tom had been right about working the crew too hard and volunteering for too many dangerous assignments. Moreover, the young captain had become wary and unable to shake the haunting feeling that his risky tactics were quickly catching up with him.

"I guess our mission to drop off those coverts on Europa was too much for you," Michael remorsefully replied, remembering the dangerous mission the previous week. The crew had barely made it back to Allied territory alive.

Tom just shook his head and said, "This assignment just isn't for me.... I need to move on to how I think I can contribute to the war effort. I can't explain it.... It's just something I need to do."

"What if I request patrol duty again?"

"Command won't let you," Tom chuckled. "You've proven yourself too well for them to waste you on a simple patrol assignment. Besides, my mind is made up. I'm sorry."

Michael paused once again, becoming very pensive. Then somewhat unexpectedly, he looked at his friend and asked, "Where do you think Kate is now?"

"I don't know," Tom replied. "But I'm sure she's bitten her nails to the nub worrying about you."

Michael laughed nervously. "Before I left, Kate warned me not to go crazy with the war. I didn't know what she meant then.... I guess she was right."

Tom sat quietly, taking in the comment. Finally, he replied, "I don't know why you left her to come out here. You could have served just as effectively back on Earth, or at least closer to where she's staying." He paused respectfully. "She's an attractive woman with a lot of wonderful traits.... If I were you, I would be with her now—not here."

Michael nodded at his friend. He had always suspected Tom held a secret attraction for Kate, just by the way he interacted with her—a little flirty. However, Tom was above all things loyal. So young Gillen took the comments the way Tom had intended.

"Well," Michael began. "I guess we all have our demons to work out." He paused thoughtfully once more. "Fate makes us who we are, and we spend our entire lives trying to figure it all out ... trying to find where we fit in."

"That's why I have to go to Intelligence."

The two went silent for a long time, while Michael looked down toward the desk. Finally, he looked back up. "We're due for refueling and procurement in about thirty days.... I'll contact Davidson immediately—make sure your replacement is transported to the refueling station. We'll make the switch then. You can get a transport from there back to Intelligence."

"Thanks. I won't let you down."

"I'm sure you won't," Michael replied. "I'll let Cyril know about all the good work you've done here. That should get you quite the esteemed position in Intelligence. Whatever your goal, I'm sure you'll have every opportunity to accomplish it."

Gangplank operations on the refueling depot station were in full swing. A newly arrived battle cruiser already sat docked and attached to the small space station by large service tunnels, while support crews and vehicles went about the area in a frenzy to accomplish their assignments. An observation window next to the main docking tunnel looked out onto the nose of cruiser; large letters written prominently on the warship's side spelled out *ESS Comanche.*

Michael Gillen, Tom Andrews, and some of the other bridge officers stepped out of the docking tunnel and into the main service area. Today was the first time in months that any of them had stepped off the vessel.

The docking was a much-needed break from the war, providing respite for the crew and a chance to restock and service the ship. However, the thirty days since Michael had approved Tom's transfer request had passed, and the supply depot was the place where the change of command would occur. Therefore, the arrival at the depot was much too soon for the reluctant captain.

Just as the small band made it to the end of the gangplank, two officers approached them: one a captain and the other a commander.

"Welcome, Captain Gillen," the captain greeted while extending his hand toward him. "I'm Captain Argall, commander of the refueling depot. Welcome aboard."

"Thank you," Michael smiled politely, shaking his hand before giving him a palm-sized reader. "Here's the supply order confirmation we sent you a week ago—mostly standard stuff." His face partially twisted. "Although we have some new *jury-rigged* repairs from a recent encounter that needs properly fixed."

Argall activated the device, quickly perusing the supply requests. "We'll get on it. You're slated to be berthed for five days, so please have your men take advantage of the recreational opportunities. Though we're a small operation, we're not too small that your men can't enjoy themselves."

"We'll certainly do that—including me," Michael smiled.

The other officer, the commander who was standing by, finally found his opportunity. "Captain Gillen, I'm Commander Ivers. I'm your new first officer." He handed him a reader. "Here are my orders."

Never before was Michael Gillen more disappointed to see a fellow serviceman.

"Nice to meet you," Michael said while shaking his hand, letting propriety win the day. Then he gestured to his right where Tom stood. "This is Commander Andrews. You'll be replacing him." After pausing to let the two commanders greet one another, Michael continued, "So do you have any combat experience?"

"A little," Ivers replied. "I was just recently promoted from lieutenant commander. The *Welles*, my previous assignment, had taken part in a few transport convoys. Several times, we encountered Europan FW-190 squadrons."

Michael was appalled, for Command had sent him a rookie. Of course, that sentiment would go unspoken and unexpressed in any way—though he sensed that Tom understood his dissatisfaction. "You'll find it a little more intense on the *Comanche*. I hope you're up to the challenge."

"Yes, Sir. I look forward to the opportunity."

"Good," Michael nodded. "I want you to shadow Commander Andrews for the next five days. He'll get you up to speed before he leaves."

Kara Ricci stood in the center of the chaos at the Randt Medical Base docking terminal, completely frazzled.

The docking tunnel ahead of her led to the *ESS Windsor*, Kara's front-line medical relief ship. After six months of propulsion retrofits, reconfigurations, and the like, the ship was ready for its maiden voyage. By the end of that voyage, Kara would know whether her big recommendation to improve the critical case survival rate would work. The undertaking had become a big gamble.

And a lot of work needed to be done just to launch.

She stood among a mass of subordinates preparing the ship to get underway. Though Kara had planned every detail of the vessel and its operation, execution of the first launch left a lot to be desired; getting underway had become quite tedious. However, she was about to receive good news.

"Major Ricci," one of the aides called, coming up to her. "All personnel are accounted for. We're ready to depart."

"Good," Kara sighed. "Notify the captain that he's clear to leave in ten minutes."

Another aide standing close and wearing a communicator interjected, "We're still having a little trouble with the pod retrieval system. It's a calibration issue."

"We'll just have to calibrate it en route."

The aide acknowledged with a nod and turned to relay the message.

"Major Ricci, do you mind a stowaway?" an unfamiliar voice came from behind her.

Kara, not really interested in whoever was trying to be humorous, turned around. Her jaw dropped. "General Rier? This is a surprise."

Indeed, the man's appearance *was* a surprise. General Rier oversaw all Earth States military field hospitals. Though having never met the older man, Kara recognized him from pictures and other communications.

"It shouldn't be," he replied. "I sent a communication saying I was coming to observe your surgical ship operations."

Kara sighed, still taken back and more than embarrassed. "I'm sorry. I wasn't informed—we've been pretty busy around here." However, upon realizing what the man had said—his explanation striking her with fear—she looked at him quizzically. "*Coming to observe my surgical ship operations?* But Sir, this is our maiden voyage. We haven't even performed a shakedown. We haven't worked out the kinks yet—we don't even know what they are at this point."

"That's not a problem," Rier waved dismissively and put down his travel bag. "This isn't an inspection, either. No, I had a similar program in mind a long time ago, but I couldn't seem to make the idea work. I'm eager to see how you've improved on my model."

Kara looked at her superior, taken back even more. However, the young woman couldn't think of one credible excuse to prevent him from boarding. "You're welcome to come along. We're heading off to Sector Eight. There's supposed to be a lot of intense fighting there."

"I'm up for the challenge. I'll even scrub in."

"Then let's get aboard. We're leaving in ten minutes."

Kara Ricci and her sizeable crew of surgeons, nurses, and support personnel gathered at the front of the triage bay of the *ESS Windsor*. The crowd of medical professionals spoke very few words, for all of them suffered under varying degrees of trepidation. After traveling over a day's journey, the vessel had arrived near the front lines, waiting for the first wave of injured soldiers to arrive. Worse, they could only imagine what fate awaited them so close to the fighting.

Kara, though outwardly calm and collect as ever, was a complete bundle of nerves inside. Her eyes surveyed the docking and transfer bay directly in front of her, anxiously searching for anything she might have missed in its design.

The bay was the most complex of its kind ever constructed in the fleet. Multiple small channels ran parallel to one another in the center of the bay, designed to deliver medical torpedoes captured in flight. The left side of the bay had a revolving life pod docking vestibule. To the right were multiple docking tunnels designed to accommodate larger ships. The whole premise of the operation allowed the delivery of wounded on a mass scale while making sure the delivery vehicles were promptly redeployed for use in the next wave.

Upon receiving arriving medical torpedoes, the channels would carry the torpedoes directly into the triage area, while corpsman would deliver wounded from life pods and transports into the same area.

After a team of nurses and doctors had triaged the wounded, corpsmen would deliver them in priority into the awaiting surgical wards adjacent to the triage area.

Kara drew her attention to the large tactical display prominently positioned high overhead. The display, a representational hologram of the region, showed a myriad of medical torpedoes, life pods, and medic transports racing toward the *Windsor*—and who could ignore the faint traces of the intense battle being waged in the distance?

"Show time," General Rier quipped, glancing at her quickly before turning back to the display. The man stood garbed in sterile scrubs, just like almost everyone else in the bay.

She nodded in acknowledgement, turning back to the display as well. Though welcoming an additional surgeon to the team, Kara found the man's presence unnerving. She couldn't help but feel as if his visit was more of an inspection, despite what the man said to the contrary.

Whatever trepidation and anxiety plagued her, Kara would have to suppress it for the moment.

The first medical torpedo appeared from the service tunnel, rolling down the long channel toward triage. Upon coming to rest at the end of the channel, the tube was lifted waist-high by supports underneath. The top of the metal tube opened with a *hiss*, and the complex medic robot just inside the shell moved up and away, giving a clear view to the inside. Within the shell lay a very dirty, blood-soaked man with several gaping wounds. He was visibly distraught and in a tremendous amount of pain.

"Okay people!" Kara shouted, moving toward the torpedo. "Let's look alive!"

While Kara made her way toward the wounded man to begin triage, medical torpedoes began arriving one after the other. The life pod vestibule became active, and the transport docking tunnels indicated arrivals.

Watching Triage quickly fill with wounded and hearing the sounds of chaos rise into the air, Kara wondered whether her team could keep up.

Michael Gillen walked into the command center of the refueling depot station, located somewhere in the remote parts of the asteroid belt. Right behind him walked Tom Andrews; behind Tom followed Commander Ivers, Andrews' replacement. *Comanche* had sat docked at the depot about four days. Their vessel being the only ship docked at the station, Michael and the entire crew had unhindered access to the basic but nonetheless enjoyable amenities the space station provided.

Michael, in particular, had spent his entire free time with Tom. Enjoying a respite from duty, the two could finally relate to each other as friends again. Michael found the rest an opportune time to mend fences with him. Though things had gone well, Michael realized he had only one day left before Tom shipped out for good, a fact the young captain found to be rather discouraging.

Despite whatever frivolities he had engaged in, the young man found them temporarily interrupted; Captain Argall, commanding officer of the small space station, had summoned Michael to the command center.

Upon entering the center, the three men received fleeting glances from Argall and a few of his subordinates. Instead, the small depot command team remained focused on the tactical display unit in the center of the room.

"You wanted to see me, Captain Argall?" Michael asked, coming all the way into the room.

"Yes, take a look at this," Argall replied, not taking his eyes off the holographic display. Instead, he gestured for the three men to join him. "We've received an encrypted distress call."

Gathering around the large device, Michael, Tom, and Ivers saw in the three-dimensional display the representation of some sort of battle. A small Axis fleet, comprised of one large destroyer and four battle cruisers, was engaging an equally small Allied convoy of seven battle cruisers escorting a single transport. One-manned fighters from both sides, just tiny dots on the display, buzzed around the larger vessels like swarming bees.

The scene drew quizzical looks from both Michael and Tom, who had seen more than their share of wartime conflicts. They looked at each other, not sure why the convoy was sending a distress call—especially an encrypted distress call. Though executing a rather conservative tactic, the Allied ships were more than capable of defending themselves against the Axis onslaught.

Argall saw their inquisitive gazes and pointed to the small transport traveling in the middle of the Allied convoy. His face went sober. "That ship is the *Executive One*."

Michael and Tom looked at each other in complete astonishment.

"…And that's why it's an encrypted distress call," Argall continued. "Apparently, no one without the need to know is to be made aware of its presence in the Asteroid Belt—or the dire circumstances it faces."

"What's President Mitchell doing so close to the front lines?" Tom asked, his face still twisted in bewilderment.

"No one knows," Argall replied. "The only reason we've been given access to the signal is because *Comanche* is in range of lending aid." He paused. "It doesn't really matter; the President is in desperate trouble— and he needs your help. I hate to be the one to tell you this, but your ship is the only other warship in the area right now. We're extending the distress call, but it will be awhile before reinforcements arrive."

Michael studied the display, the grim circumstances sinking into him quickly. The Allied fleet would protect the President's transport at all costs. That made the Axis fleet, its massive destroyer playing the trump card, a very dangerous threat. That's why the Allies were in such a defensive posture, thus making the convoy so vulnerable. They could only fight back when their duty to protect the transport afforded them. Certain doom awaited the small convoy—and any other ship that might come to the President's aid.

Michael realized what a dire cup fate was handing him. Yet duty called him nonetheless.

"Signal my ship," a very serious-looking Michael Gillen exclaimed, continuing to peer into the display. "Tell the OOD to order an emergency departure."

"I already did," Argall replied. "Your ship is powering up now, and they're going to general quarters too. Your navigator already has the coordinates. I've also changed the security status of your ship. As far as Command is concerned, you're off the grid."

"How far away is the convoy?"

"About forty-five minutes from here," Argall replied. "At *Comanche*'s top speed, that is."

Michael sighed, turning to Tom's replacement. "Commander Ivers, get to the bridge and oversee the power-up. I'll be there in a minute."

Ivers acknowledged with a nod and quickly left the command center, looking more than a little nervous.

"I hate to leave you like this, Mike," Tom said apologetically, watching Ivers walk away. Not that Tom's concern was over Ivers, but rather the impossible odds *Comanche* faced. Using words like *slaughter* and *don't stand a chance* would have been unseemly for someone leaving the ship—as he was about to do. Nevertheless, the two men knew what the *Comanche* was walking into, so neither chose to verbalize such thoughts.

"Don't worry," Michael assured him with a rather optimistic, albeit false expression. He smiled. "Just do the type of work at Intelligence you did on the *Comanche*, and I'm sure the war will be over in no time."

"I hope so."

The two men went pensively silent for a very long, awkward moment. Finally, Michael said, "I hate to leave so quickly, but duty calls…. Goodbye, Tom."

Michael extended his hand and smiled warmly once more. Tom reciprocated and the two men shook hands awkwardly, with Tom barely able to say anything. Before he knew it, Tom stood alone, watching Michael walk away.

Before Michael walked out of earshot, Tom called, "Hey, Mike!"

Michael stopped and turned around, gazing at him. Once more, Tom remained dumbfounded over what to say, prolonging another awkward moment. So Michael just nodded his head and smiled one last time. "I know." Michael paused for another long moment and then added as he turned, "Take care of Kate for me."

"I will."

With one last esteeming glance, Michael Gillen turned around and disappeared, leaving Tom Andrews wondering whether he had seen his best friend alive for the last time.

When Michael Gillen arrived onto the bridge of the *ESS Comanche*, he received no salutations. Neither did the seasoned, young captain expect any. Rather, the bridge was in chaos, as the crew was preparing for their unexpected departure. The sounds of the engines coming to speed could be heard in the background, while various orders and commands from loudspeakers resonated throughout the ship. Michael dove right into the mayhem, barking out orders to the crew and taking his captain's chair.

The tactical display to his side was already patched into the distress call feed from the President's convoy, still over forty-five minutes away. The status of the conflict was still dire, requiring *Comanche* to get there quickly.

"Captain, fusion engines to speed," Herschel barked out over the din. "We can depart at any time now."

Michael turned toward Navigation and said, "Okay, Lieutenant Morelli, you've got control of Moorings and Docking. Take us out of here."

"Can someone give me a ride to the party?" an all too familiar voice came from behind Michael.

Immediately, Michael's eyes lit up as he turned around. "Tom, what are you doing here?"

The whole bridge crew turned, pleasantly surprised to see Tom Andrews standing at the entrance to the bridge.

"I don't want you to have all the fun," he quipped in comical tone. "I'm coming along too." He paused and went serious. "Permission to retake my post."

"You sure?" Michael asked, stealing a fleeting glance at Ivers. "It might be the last thing you ever do."

"I'm sure," Tom nodded. "Do you mind, Commander Ivers?"

Ivers stood at his post, a little taken back. After a long moment, he replied. "No, I guess not." He paused, turning toward Michael. "I hope you don't take this as any disrespect for your situation, Sir, but with no post of my own, I'm a little out of place here. If you don't mind, I'm going to return to the station."

"Not at all," Michael replied. "I understand. Just hurry, because we need to get out of here."

Ivers nodded and quickly headed off the bridge.

With a few minute's pause to let Ivers off the ship, *Comanche* released itself from the station. Without hesitation, the large fusion engines came to full power, propelling the battle cruiser swiftly into the darkness.

CHAPTER SIXTEEN

Distress Call

Captain Michael Gillen stood command on the bridge of the battle cruiser *ESS Comanche*, carefully surveying the flurry of activities taking place. Circumstances forced him to subdue the fears and doubts racing through him. Urgently, he searched for potential trouble, unconsidered options, and any other variable that might mean the difference between life and death. Though his anxiety increased as *Comanche* raced toward its destiny, Michael remained determined to radiate an assuring confidence to his crew.

To his subordinates, he was cool and unwavering, exhibiting the marks of a shrewd and well-seasoned military commander. Yet his stomach was in knots, and his mind was replete with second-guessing.

With his ship traversing the cold, black void of space, Michael thought about his two years aboard the *Comanche*. His tenure as commanding officer had been fraught with danger, and the fierceness of the war had hardened him beyond his years. Having faced death many more times than he could count, the young man had learned to live with the grim realities of combat. However, the stakes this time were high, and the pleadings of the distress call from President Mitchell's convoy haunted his mind.

Michael was more than eager to respond. Patriotism aside, he personally revered the noble leader. The man's warnings so long ago of a rising Axis threat had been prophetic. Though his words had fallen on deaf ears at the time, never did the man shrink back from his convictions. Fighting the laissez-faire politics of the day, he had toiled to ready the country for impending war, and history had exonerated him. Through the dark days of the first attacks, Mitchell had kept a steady hand on the pulse of the nation. He came into office as if destiny had personally chosen him to lead the Allies out of the turmoil.

And now, destiny was calling upon Michael Gillen.

Unfortunately, *Comanche* would add little relief to the beleaguered convoy far ahead. No, the convoy needed at least two, maybe three or more cruisers just to even the odds. Overwhelmed by the impending conflict, Michael's mind swam in the ceaseless array of options. Never before had he been called to such an important mission.

Uncharacteristically, Michael even failed to admire the beauty of the small asteroid they were passing. The sun's light reflected off crystalline mineral deposits embedded in the asteroid's rocky surface, bathing it in a hazy, colorful glow. The spectacular sight was a rare one in the void of space. However, the moment quickly passed. The tumbling asteroid panned to the edge of the huge display screen and disappeared, leaving only the coldness and emptiness of space.

The atmosphere on *Comanche's* bridge was not much warmer. Military engagement protocols concentrated power to shielding and weaponry, causing lighting and environmental controls to operate at minimum levels. Officers and soldiers alike worked by the illumination of display screens set before them. Proximity indicator lights and tactical analysis displays cast an eerie red glow throughout the bridge.

"Lieutenant Combs," Michael barked, "How much time until we intercept?"

"We will be within targeting range in ten minutes, Sir," Combs replied. He paused to clear his throat and added, "However, I'm sure you're aware that the Europan Jupiter-Class destroyer has a thirty second targeting advantage over us, assuming they choose to engage."

Michael did not relish the thought of provoking the enemy destroyer. The vessel was three times the size of a battle cruiser and armed to the teeth. Nevertheless, duty called.

"What's the status of the President's ship?"

Combs carefully studied the data in front on him. "*Executive One* is in excellent shape. Shield outputs are strong … only negligible damage to the outer hull…. Engines are at one hundred percent and reactor outputs are stable."

Unfortunately, Michael knew what the man would say next.

The officer continued, "Of course, Allied escorts have taken significant damage. Only a few Hellcats are left. The *Eris* has no weaponry and is on the verge of environmental collapse. The *Dorn* has some weaponry but is close to the same condition as the *Eris*. The *Trafalgar* and the *Pyroscaphe* have taken on marginal damage. Three other cruisers I can't identify have been destroyed."

"What's the report on the Axis fleet?"

"Markings indicate they are part of the Europan Standard Fleet. They have a healthy advantage over us. Ten one-manned fighters are left. Three remaining cruisers have taken on damage, though not life threatening. The third cruiser is yellow-line, while the Jupiter-Class destroyer is stable. Even with our added fire power, the tactical computer predicts the President's capture or defeat in thirty minutes."

Michael stepped over to the full three-dimensional display console table in front of the officer. The battle appeared in holographic miniature, suspended above the backlit surface of the large table. The computer duplicated each ship's size, position, and movements. Colors indicated their status: green-line, yellow-line, or red-line. Various pointer icons flashed on and off throughout the model, indicating tactical weaknesses, movements, and opportunities. Artillery exchanges appeared as tiny white dots. When they hit their intended target, the computer enhanced to demonstrate damage.

Michael watched the ongoing conflict, amazed that the convoy had lasted so long. Normally, four Allied battle cruisers could stand their own against the Axis antagonists. However, the need to protect the *Executive One* kept them in a tightly sealed formation around the vessel. The result was foreboding. The Axis ships had encircled the fleet, cutting off their escape route and pounding them at will.

Putting aside for the moment the probable outcome, the young captain directed his subordinate. He pointed to the tiny, one-manned Axis fighters, called FW-190s, buzzing around the larger ships and said, "As soon as we're in range, have the gunners target the fighters. They are the most immediate threat to the President. After that, give Lieutenant Morelli the coordinates to run a sweeping pattern on their cruisers. Hopefully, we can take one of them out."

"What about navigating a blocking pattern for the President's ship?"

Michael appeared polite but dismissive. "No, our cruisers will continue blocking until the very end. We need to go on the offensive."

Tom Andrews swaggered up beside him, still as casual and out of place as ever among the rigid military etiquette, still having his brownish-black hair testing the boundaries of regulation, and still looking as if playing the jester. And never before was Michael so thankful to have him at his side.

"What do you think?" Tom asked, looking up at his slightly taller friend.

Remaining focused on the display, Michael lifted off his cap and ran a hand through his brown, cropped hair. "I don't know...." He looked toward his companion. "You may regret leaving the fueling depot."

Tom wasn't shocked at the statement. Instead, he looked down at the display, hoping to find some evidence to the contrary. Finding none, he decided that humor was the only appropriate response. "How exciting could Intelligence have been anyway? And if I die, I'll just never speak to you again."

The moment of small talk quickly passed. Silently, Gillen stood over the tactical post, watching the battle unfold.

The Europan ships continued outflanking the convoy to prevent its escape. Otherwise, the Allied cruisers could more easily protect the *Executive One* from behind as it fled. Instead, the battle cruisers kept a close, parallel course to the transport, shielding it from Axis guns. The Europan ships rewarded them with heavy artillery fire, which showed up as red blotches on the tactical model. With each hit, the cruisers' statuses degraded.

Far off the immediate battlefront loomed the Europan Jupiter-Class destroyer. The mammoth vessel lingered in the shadows, deliberately waiting out the eventual demise of the Allied convoy. Once its smaller companions had exhausted the convoy's defenses, the destroyer would sweep in for the kill.

However, the immediate threat to the President was the swarming Europan FW-190s. Their small size and speed allowed them to bolt through the Allied blockade and deliver less destructive but nonetheless stinging fire to *Executive One*. Upon delivering artillery rounds, they would quickly retreat to safety and then set themselves up for another run.

Becoming more enraged as he watched, Michael realized he could do nothing about engaging the one-manned fighters one on one; the squadrons of Hellcats normally docked to *Comanche's* hull were still being serviced back at the refueling depot—a complication of having to leave so abruptly.

Soon Tactical broke the silence.

"Sir," Combs began, "We are now in targeting range of the Jupiter-Class destroyer."

Michael nodded in acknowledgement, while he and Tom quickly secured themselves into their command chairs.

"Is it too late for my transfer?" Tom comically quipped.

"Okay everyone," Michael called out to the bridge, "Let's keep alert. The President deserves our best efforts."

Moments later, turbulence buffeted the *Comanche*, whose shields absorbed the first wave of energy blasts. The impacts were relatively light, and the battle cruiser continued on undeterred. Tactical readouts showed what Michael had anticipated: These blasts were from the destroyer's secondary guns, for *Comanche* was not yet the primary target. Of course, the young captain clearly understood that the impacts would become more severe as they neared the main battle area.

"Sir," Combs called from Tactical, "I'm receiving running coordinates for *Comanche* from the *Executive One*. They want us to sidle up into a defensive position within the convoy."

Pondering the news for some time, Michael flippantly asked. "Did the coordinates come in as an order?"

"The computers don't transmit that information, Sir," Combs answered, more than perplexed at the question. "But *Executive One* is in charge of the defensive."

Michael went silent, exchanging glances with Tom Andrews while pondering his next move. Finally, he shook his head. "We've lost too many cruisers already using only defensive tactics. No, let's stay on the offensive for now." Upon receiving stunned expressions from the rest of the bridge officers—Andrews excluded—he turned back to Combs. "But keep the coordinates, just in case."

Comanche was approaching the conflict from behind the Europan offensive. Most of the Europan FW-190s were lurking in the protective shadow of the battle cruisers. Michael knew the fighters would soon start another pass for the presidential transport.

"Weapons, begin targeting the fighters," Michael commanded. "If you can't hit them yet, at least force them into the open."

The weapons officer quickly relayed the orders. Seconds later, the observation display filled with a barrage of outgoing artillery fire. Many of the lethal rounds dissipated before or strayed from the intended targets, though some of the artillery found success. Four of the Europan FW-190s took impacts. One fighter burst into flames, leaving a plume of smoke as the wreckage fell through space. Three other fighters registered critical damage on the tactical display.

The tactic had accomplished its goal. No longer safe behind the Europan cruiser, the fighters scrambled into the general battle zone, quickly engaged by the Allied fighters.

At least we're making a difference, Michael thought.

The Jupiter-Class destroyer responded with a blast that rocked *Comanche*; *Comanche* had entered the dangerous conflict.

Kara Ricci stood over the operating table in the surgical bay of the *ESS Windsor*, staring down at the badly wounded soldier lying there anesthetized and ready for surgery. The medical robot hovered over the primary wound—a gaping, bleeding hole in the man's stomach—ready to execute her commands. If she didn't start surgery soon, the man would die.

However, Kara suddenly was at a loss over what to do next.

The sensation suddenly overwhelming her had lurked in the recesses of her conscience for some time, starting as a simple, fleeting thought and then slowly building with the mounting chaos that was quickly engulfing the entire medical ship.

She surveyed the mayhem inhabiting the surgical bay. Every operating table in the large chamber was stacked up with patients waiting their turn for a chance to live. Doctors, haggard from long hours of work, desperately wished to stop up their ears from the blood-curdling pleas coming from the wounded soldiers begging them for mercy. Corpsmen went about in a frenzy, trying to keep up with all the activities. Arguments and disagreements were quickly becoming the norm.

And the wounded just kept coming.

From her table, Kara could see Triage in the distance. The area was replete with wounded and dying soldiers, seemingly heaped almost as indiscriminately as the dead; more medical torpedoes, life pods, and transports were arriving every minute. The doctors and nurses overseeing Triage were quickly becoming overwhelmed, just like those in the surgical bay.

The ship rocked once more, just as it had done occasionally the last several hours; the power grid phased in and out before compensating. Stray artillery from the front lines had obviously hit the ship once more.

How long will this battle go on? she thought desperately. However, she didn't really want to ponder the question. Though realizing the ongoing conflict was just another day for those on the front lines, Kara nevertheless found the circumstances completely nightmarish. No, Kara realized just how much Randt Medical Base, so far from the front, had insulated her from the true ravages of war. She was finally seeing first hand what the medics aboard Earth States warships had seen all along—and it scared her.

The young woman looked down at the soldier lying on her table, not sure whether to begin operating, go help the besieged Triage bay, or supervise the surgical staff to keep them moving. Attending to one patient quickly became imminent death for another—chaos and the overwhelming challenges began destabilizing the team's efforts! Too many wounded were dying, and the mortality rates were increasing fast.

And from the corner of her eye, she could see General Rier watching her from the adjacent operating table.

Kara looked at the medical robot awaiting her instructions. The robot was a glorious device: state of the art technology loaded with algorithms the human brain could never contain all at once, having more arms and protruding devices than could be easily counted; excruciatingly precise and thorough. Under the directions of a skilled physician, the robot would methodically fix almost any problem with the human anatomy.

That's when Kara realized just how out of place the pristine technology was among the brutality of war.

"Okay, surgeons," she called out in a loud voice above the din, having temporarily removed her sterile mask. "Scrap the medical robots. Operate directly."

The young woman had never seen so many incredulous and disapproving looks gawking back at her from the staff. Rier looked on curiously too. However, Kara remained unfazed. "The robots are too slow; we're losing too many wounded before they ever get a chance to get on the table. Fix the major problems and get them stabilized. We can go back later if they need additional surgery.... Let's move!"

Out of the corner of her eye, Kara watched the surgical staff reluctantly begin to comply. Setting an example, the young woman quickly pushed her own robot to the side and nervously hovered over the patient with a scalpel in hand. Putting the sharp metal instrument to the patient's flesh, Kara became thankful that the medical profession had never completely abandoned traditional surgical training.

"Engage sweeping pattern on battle cruisers one and two," Michael Gillen ordered from his captain's chair on the *ESS Comanche*, looking into his tactical display. "Fortify aft and starboard shields."

The young captain held his breath, just as he did at the beginning of every offensive. Having arrived at the President's convoy to lend aid (coming within targeting range of the menacing Europan Jupiter-Class destroyer and achieving marginal success against the Axis one-manned fighters), *Comanche* was about to join the brawl.

"Last hit caused only marginal damage," Herschel, the engineering officer, noted.

Barreling down into the epicenter of the conflict, *Comanche* dove headlong into the battle. Artillery from the ship's guns rained down onto the two Axis cruisers as it passed. Though receiving some pain of its own, *Comanche* avoided much of the retaliation through old-fashion bobbing and weaving. Despite finding satisfaction in the ship's initial performance, Michael knew he would eventually lose his advantage.

With the *Comanche* fully engaged in the dogfight, the dynamics of the struggle slowly began shifting more favorably to the Allies. Not that they were winning—far from it. Nevertheless, the convoy had at least managed to slow down its own demise.

The Europan FW-190 fighters quickly succumbed when *Comanche* had forced them into the open and engaged them at point-blank range. The Allied Hellcats would easily handle those FW-190s not eliminated by *Comanche*.

With the fighters neutralized, Michael shifted his focus to the first two Axis cruisers. *Comanche*'s tactical computers linked to the convoy, allowing the Allies to coordinate their efforts. With *Comanche* being somewhat of a new factor in the conflict, the Allies managed to inflict significant damage to the Europan cruisers, forcing them to withdraw temporarily behind the destroyer.

Michael enthusiastically observed the two Axis cruisers change from green-line to yellow-line on the main tactical. All three enemy cruisers were yellow-line. However, his heart sank when the computer rewarded his efforts with a meager five minutes of additional survival time for the President. Worse, the computer began counting down *Comanche*'s demise: three minutes earlier than the President's projected demise.

The destroyer bit back viciously, violently rocking *Comanche* with a hailstorm of energy blasts. Michael clutched his command chair, anxiously waiting for the stabilizers to engage. Once stable, the young officer had to remind himself to let go of the chair.

The bridge crew responded to the emergency with a flurry of containment activities.

"Damage to Section-D and Section-F," Herschel declared from Engineering. "The hull is still intact. One auxiliary power transfer coupling was hit, causing a fire in Section-F.... Containment crews responding.... Minor injuries reported.... Shields and artillery still active in those areas."

Michael sighed in relief at the relatively good news, even though the thought of injuries always unnerved him a bit.

Tom looked up from his tactical display. "All the FW-190s and Hellcats are gone. At least we're even on that."

Michael, pleasantly surprised, drew his attention back to his tactical display. With all his attention focused on the larger ships, he had missed this fact. Yet before Michael could respond, the tactical officer begged his attention.

"Sir," Combs began hesitantly, "The *Eris* is breaking up."

The entire bridge crew turned their attention to the main view screen. The image shifted to the convoy. The Allied cruisers flanked the *Executive One* on all sides, effectively blocking incoming firepower. The *Eris* had set up position on the transport's front starboard side, heroically taking the brunt of the attack. Pockmarks, the charred remains of laser blasts, covered the ship's hull. Gases vented into space from several gaping blast holes.

Michael and the entire bridge crew watched sympathetically as the cruiser fought to continue. The vessel moved as if a mortally wounded animal refusing to yield to its fate. For a couple of moments, *Eris* stayed its course, bearing the whip of energy blasts that painfully sank deep into its hull.

Finally, the ship's resolve to exist evaporated. Laboring to protect the convoy from its own demise, *Eris* veered away. A few moments later, the injured vessel's starboard side burst open under the force of a reactor detonation, spilling its insides into space. Seconds later, another explosion ripped the ship in two; then another, and another, until the debris of the dead ship finally drifted off in all directions. *Eris*, its captain, and its crew took their place in history.

The loss of the *Eris* left a big hole in the convoy's defenses. No longer would the *Executive One* be shielded on all flanks, unless *Comanche* filled the gap. Neither scenario came without risk. The latter would eliminate the Allies' offensive capabilities, while the former would increase the transport's exposure risks. Either way, the Axis forces still held the trump card: the Jupiter-Class destroyer.

Which choice was the lesser evil?

"Sir," Combs from Tactical predictably called. "I'm receiving running coordinates for the *Comanche* from the *Executive One* again. Its captain wants us to replace the Eris in the convoy."

Michael thought for a moment, sizing up his predicament. Fighting his own instincts and sense of duty, the young captain looked at the three Europan cruisers, two of which were newly yellow-line. The Allies had accomplished much, having shifted to the offensive. None of the small successes would have been possible otherwise. No, he reasoned, the conflict would end terribly unless someone stayed on the offensive.

"Lieutenant Combs," Michael called, "Send back a counterproposal to have the *Pyroscaphe* and *Trafalgar* repositioned to replace the *Eris*." Then he turned to the communications officer. "Send a message to the *Executive One*, explaining that redeployment will take too long, leaving the ship's starboard side exposed—we're too far away and going in the opposite direction." He looked at Andrews. "We'll let them figure out that our tactical proposal is the most prudent action now."

"A great excuse for disobeying an order," Andrews smiled. "Or at least a great stall tactic."

Michael watched the subordinates carry out his orders. Quickly enough, the *Pyroscaphe* and *Trafalgar* repositioned themselves to fill the hole left by the *Eris*. Tom smiled at Michael.

"Message conveyed, Sir," the communications officers called. "But they don't sound too happy over there."

Nevertheless, Michael's recommendation had won the day. However, now that the fleet had sanctioned his recommendation, Michael needed to act.

"Contact the *Trafalgar* and the *Pyroscaphe*," Michael commanded his communications and tactical officers. "Advise them to concentrate artillery on the two yellow-line cruisers. Our only chance is to take them out. *Comanche* will draw the cruisers into their firing range, giving them a clear targeting path. Tell the *Dorn* to do what it can too."

Michael punched his strategy into the tactical computer at his side. "Transmit this to the convoy and prepare to execute."

Combs obliged. Upon receiving the detailed instructions into his computer, Morelli executed the command. *Comanche* immediately changed course and picked up speed.

Executing a wide, sweeping arc around the main area of the battle, *Comanche* swung into position on the opposite side of the destroyer. This maneuver tipped Michael's hand to the Axis captains, diverting a significant amount of artillery fire away from the presidential transport and toward the *Comanche*. Though shuddering at the blasts, the ship held its position.

Comanche positioned itself so that an Europan cruiser traveled between it and the destroyer, shielding *Comanche* from the destroyer's wrath. Michael reasoned that the Europan cruisers would suffer from overconfidence in the destroyer's ability to protect them. Michael also reasoned that the third cruiser on the opposite side of the convoy would continue to engage the *Dorn* and *Pyroscaphe*, though he could do nothing about that at the moment.

Comanche began its approach toward the enemy's established fortification. The Europan ships, in turn, began moving into position for the showdown. Michael noticed one of the cruisers stop short of a full flanking position, careful not to stray into the firestorm of energy blasts from the *Trafalgar* and the *Pyroscaphe*.

"Yes!" Michael shouted, knowing that the enemy captain had just tipped his hand. Gillen quickly adjusted his attack plan. "Make the following modifications to Tactical."

"He must be more damaged than we know," Tom added. "*Or*, he's just unlucky."

"It's *not* bad luck," Michael exclaimed confidently. "Now we must take advantage of it."

The three enemy ships loomed larger on the view screen as *Comanche* neared. So as not to reveal his true intentions, Michael ordered an intercept path to the second cruiser, virtually ignoring the more injured one.

The buffeting from Axis laser cannons increased so that *Comanche* shook recurrently; the sound of straining metal echoed throughout the ship with each blast. Michael knew he would not come out of the maneuver unscathed. Even then, he could see the containment activities increasing.

Comanche picked up speed right up to the intercept point, defiantly engaging its adversaries. Upon coming into close proximity, the battleship quickly veered in the direction of the injured Europan cruiser and targeted all guns the same. Upon completing the maneuver, *Comanche* had slightly overshot its prey and was once again using it as a shield from the destroyer. This time, though, Michael managed to avoid some of the second cruiser's artillery fire.

Comanche held its position, raining artillery fire down on its victim. Though retaliating against the assault, the wounded Europan cruiser's defenses clearly began giving way. The grim fact that *Comanche* could outlast the vessel became readily apparent, eventually being confirmed when Tactical changed the Europan cruiser's status to red-line. Michael looked over to Tom, grinning smugly.

Michael had clearly taken the enemy captain off guard. The injured cruiser was traveling passed and away from the destroyer, so reversing course back into the protection of his fleet would take too much time. Instead, the vessel picked up speed, turning in a wide arc to flee to the other side of the destroyer.

Comanche pursued. That is when the second enemy cruiser began pursuing *Comanche* from behind.

Coming around the destroyer, the red-line Axis cruiser fell directly into weapons fire from the *Trafalgar* and *Pyroscaphe*. Michael welcomed the duo's efforts because the *Comanche* began losing some targeting ability while struggling to stay out of the destroyer's gun sights.

Even better, the destroyer silenced its guns as the red-line cruiser crossed the targeting path to the convoy—a stroke of luck that would not last long. Keeping a close eye on the pursuing second cruiser, Michael decided to wait for the injured cruiser's demise.

Again, Combs begged Michael's attention. "Sir, the *Dorn* has just gone red-line."

Michael, preoccupied with his current situation, had forgotten about the *Dorn*.

As the view screen switched, Michael could see that the ship had taken on significant damage since he had last checked. A split second later, a round of energy blasts erupted on the *Dorn's* hull, at once breaching it in several key places and causing explosive decompression.

As with the *Eris*, the insides of the ship—equipment, structure, and crew—spilled out into the void. The *Dorn* went dead, and inertia carried the ship off into space.

The third Europan cruiser had kept itself on the *Executive One*'s port and fore sides, staying on the periphery of the Allies' targeting range. With the *Dorn* eliminated, the *Executive One*'s port side became exposed. The Axis cruiser moved in for the kill. Michael reluctantly ordered his navigator to replace the *Dorn*, though belaying the order when his saw *Trafalgar* sidle into that position.

With both the *Eris* and the *Dorn* eradicated, the Axis fleet matched the Allies, battle cruiser for battle cruiser. Yet the Allies still needed to provide protection to *Executive One*—a significant disadvantage. The massive Axis Jupiter-Class destroyer continued to contain from a distance, waiting for its moment to strike. The battle once again began turning in favor of the Europans.

Michael began second-guessing himself. Should he abandon the offensive and order the *Comanche* into defensive formation? Certainly, the loss of the *Dorn* increased the transport's risk of injury that much more. Yet the offensive had caused the Europan cruisers to scramble, spreading them out and away from the transport. The offensive seemed to be keeping the Europans at bay. In addition, now was the time to finish off the Axis red-line cruiser. Therefore, he resolved to embolden his offensive tactics that much more.

"Abandon efforts to avoid the destroyer's guns and target the red-line cruiser."

Comanche came out into the open, buffeted once more by deadly artillery rounds. Nevertheless, the cruiser continued with the *Pyroscaphe* to beat away at the crippled enemy cruiser.

Moments later, proximity warnings sounded throughout the *Comanche* bridge. The sound heralded the fate of its prey. Instinctively, Morelli steered the ship away from the dying cruiser. As *Comanche* reached safety, the Axis cruiser erupted into a massive explosion, practically disintegrating into dust particles.

"Direct hit on the ammunitions stores!" Tom cheered. "You don't see many of those."

Studying his tactical readout, Michael's tension began to subside. His gamble to stay on the offensive had paid off. True, Tactical was still the oracle of doom, and the Allies were still outgunned. Yet the tiny convoy had outlasted the original thirty-minute defeat prediction. With the Europans down to only two yellow-line cruisers, the Allies could mount an offensive and still keep the transport protected—as long as the destroyer stayed back.

The destroyer was still staying back.

Michael pondered this odd fact. Why wasn't the destroyer moving in? Was it hurt? No, tactical scans indicated only minimal damage. Then what? He could only hypothesize that the Europans planned to capture the President, not eliminate him. Under that scenario, the destroyer would lay back and let the Europan cruisers finish off the escorts. Then the destroyer would force the *Executive One* to surrender.

Without warning, *Comanche* shuddered under a tremendous concussion, almost throwing Michael from his chair! *Comanche* shook violently and began helplessly turning on its axis!

CHAPTER SEVENTEEN

Impossible Rescue

Brenda Reid sat at her desk at Earth States Intelligence on Earth, mostly watching the clock make its slow progression toward the lunch hour. Not that the thin, bleach-blonde woman was adverse to work—on the contrary. However, today just seemed like *one of those days.* So she sat there, prim and proper in her Class-B military uniform, performing busy work to pass the time and to keep her mind at ease.

While the young woman kept busy looking busy, she spotted out of the corner of her eye Kate Gillen working at the adjacent desk. Like all the other women in the office, Gillen sat garbed in her nicely fitting white blouse and grey skirt combination regs. Having perfect posture and long, brown hair pulled back in a typical bun style, the young woman seemed to set the standard of professionalism. Kate had become a familiar sight in the office, having just achieved her two-year anniversary at the agency. Kate was a good friend too, providing hours of enjoyable conversation, mutual support, and the occasional friendly smile across the way.

Brenda always thought Kate to be a bit out of place at the office: certainly far less catty than most of the women and a pleasure to have around. Kate also appeared impervious to the advances of certain notorious gentleman officers in the agency. Brenda had seen Kate rebuff these mashers many times, for her stunning good looks made her a worthwhile target. Reid wished that the other women working in the office had such resolve, including herself.

Continuing her busywork, Brenda noticed that Kate's expression had turned. Gillen, having abruptly stopped her clerical work, stared desperately into the reader screen hovering over the desk before her. With one hand, Kate nervously stroked the thick hair on one side of her head, while the sparkle in her eyes faded as she welled up a bit. Brenda had witnessed the expression many times before—far more than from any other woman in the office.

"You okay?" Reid called to her quietly.

Kate just kept staring at the screen and shaking her head. "He's *off the grid* again."

Reid sighed sympathetically, clearly understanding the comment.

Part of the advantage of working in Intelligence and having limited security clearance was the ability to inquire on the whereabouts of ships, personnel and the like. This gave many of the women in the office the ability to learn limited information about their loved ones fighting the war. Though technically a security violation, most of these inquiries were considered harmless—though heavily monitored. And so internal security turned a blind eye to the practice, unless the activity became suspicious.

However, even knowing limited information could become a curse to the interested party. Kate was no exception—probably the poster child. Reid was more than aware of just how much time Gillen had spent worrying about her husband, who had spent most of the last two years throwing himself into harms way. Moreover, being *off the grid* meant he was doing something so secretive, most of Command was completely unaware of it.

"You gotta stop looking at that stuff, dear," Reid pleaded, tilting her head. "You'll worry yourself sick."

The young woman, still a newlywed in her own mind, just kept staring helplessly into the screen, her eyes welling up a little more. "He's going to get himself killed."

Reid got up and went over to her. She half-sat on the edge of Kate's desk and put a hand on the distraught woman's shoulder. "That's what you've said *every* time. Michael obviously knows what he's doing. He's been *off the grid* more times than you can count, and each time he eventually shows up again. That's not luck—that's skill. I'm sure he's all right."

"I wish I could find out more," Kate lamented, partially conceding. "These inquiries never tell you enough."

"Don't go looking for more details," Reid interjected. "That'll get you in trouble and kicked out of here quick." She paused and patted Kate on the shoulder. "*He'll be fine.*" Brenda briefly looked over to her desk and then turned back, smiling. "Hey, it's almost time for lunch. Why we don't get out of here and go to a restaurant. You can tell me all about what you're planning for his upcoming leave."

Twenty-six-year-old Michael Gillen went numb as the tremendous shock wave passed through him, and his eyes caught sight of the navigation computer showing *Comanche* still reeling uncontrollably.

Comanche had taken a terrible hit!

The strike had come at an inopportune time. Both the *Eris* and *Dorn* were gone, leaving the *Trafalgar*, *Pyroscaphe*, and *Comanche* little ability to mount a defense against the three Europan warships—one of them being a menacing Jupiter-Class destroyer. Michael wondered how much longer the *Executive One*, the President's transport ship, could remain safe.

However, the young captain had not the luxury of thinking about his strategy. No, he was too preoccupied with just surviving the artillery strike. Michael could feel the tension rising in the pit of his stomach, not even needing the damage report to know what had happened.

Morelli, his navigator, labored over his console to gain control of *Comanche*. Though the instruments were merely computer interfaces, Morelli strained as if he were personally trying to wrench the ship back on course.

"Damage!" Michael called out to Engineering, feeling the ship quake again under another artillery round.

Lieutenant Herschel struggled to his feet, having been knocked to the deck. Quickly analyzing the incoming data, he replied, "Auxiliary power generator in Section-D has been hit, cascading into the"—again the ship rocked violently under the power of several smaller explosions— "cascading into the navigation controls. Hull has experienced some damage but is contained. Three crewmen are dead and one has been wounded. Section-D can't take another direct hit. Nor can its auxiliary shields be activated if the mains are lost."

Michael winced as if having personally taken the hit himself. The Europan destroyer captain had skillfully attacked *Comanche*'s weakness caused by the previous strike to Section-D. The cost of Michael's lack of foresight was several lives and a wound to the ship that the Europans could exploit. Nevertheless, the offensive must continue.

"Bypass navigation controls away from Section-D. Send containment crews. Let's not let this get out of hand!"

"Crews already on their way," Herschel replied. "Navigation is in the process of bypassing. We should be okay soon."

"Mike, I'll go see what I can do," a very serious Tom Andrews exclaimed while leaving the safety of his chair to go help the containment activities below. Like a shot, the man was gone from the bridge.

Michael, encouraged and satisfied by the responsiveness of his crew, continued the fight.

"Lieutenant Morelli, lay in a course to expose the second yellow-line cruiser to the *Pyroscaphe*'s guns." Then he turned to Combs at Tactical. "Have all rear guns target the yellow-line."

The young captain watched his subordinates begin executing his orders.

Comanche quickly stabilized course as the navigation bypass finished. Without pause, the vessel then shifted directions, leading the Europan cruiser chasing *Comanche* right into the trap. *Comanche* came into proximity of the *Pyroscaphe*, keeping a parallel course as it passed.

Michael watched in satisfaction when the tactical display showed what he had hoped to see: the Europan cruiser continued to follow him, receiving a torrent of artillery from the *Pyroscaphe* as its reward. *Comanche* rained plasma torpedoes onto the Europan's fore, while the

Pyroscaphe pockmarked the cruiser's facing side with its huge energy cannons. With even more satisfaction, he noted that the destroyer became helpless to defend its smaller companion; the behemoth could lend aid to the beleaguered cruiser only at the risk of hitting it.

From his smaller tactical display, Michael watched the Europan cruiser taking tremendous hits. Repeated detonations splattered from its hull, sending bits and pieces of the ship in all outward directions. With each passing moment, the vessel became even more crippled.

Moments later, the Europan cruiser's status turned to red-line.

The Axis battle cruiser found itself at a severe disadvantage, its red-line status portending certain doom. Michael reckoned that panic was quickly setting in on its crew, having to defend themselves in two different directions at once. Regardless, the *Pyroscaphe* became the Axis cruiser's target of choice due to its parallel course to the ship. The Europan cruiser inflicted significant damage while passing its broad side. As a result, *Pyroscaphe's* status turned to yellow-line.

The Europan red-line cruiser, thoroughly abused in the exchange, relented. Breaking off pursuit of the *Comanche*, the ship began heading back to the protection of the destroyer.

The time to finish it off had come.

On Michael's orders, *Comanche* quickly swung around and fired upon the helpless vessel. The red-line cruiser, laboring arduously under the assault, turned itself away from *Comanche's* guns. Morelli, the navigator, quickly countered. With a few cannon blasts to the already pummeled engines, the Europan cruiser became adrift in space. However, the vessel's guns were still active.

Comanche loomed over its helpless prey. As if taunting, the predator darted around its victim, delivering piercing blows as it went along. Though receiving some ire from the destroyer, *Comanche* overwhelmed the injured cruiser with artillery rounds; debris surrounded the dying ship in a nebulous haze. Succumbing to the assault, the ship's power plant erupted from within. Hull plating splintered, spilling the ship's innards into the void so that only the skeleton remained—blackened and lifeless.

The entire *Comanche* bridge erupted into ovation! No, the Allies weren't winning, nor had they forgotten their circumstance. Nevertheless, a glimmer of hope had appeared amidst the turmoil.

No longer did the Axis forces completely outgun the Allies. No, the Europans were down to a single, wounded battle cruiser. Though knowing the circumstances would force the destroyer out of waiting, the Allies could continue defending the President with its three remaining cruisers.

While inertia carried the lifeless metal hull of the Europan cruiser into open space, *Comanche* executed an arching pattern to reverse directions and proceed back to the main battle. Morelli skillfully accomplished the move while using the dead hull as a shield from the destroyer's main guns.

Though making the most of the dead hull, *Comanche* came into the open just as it finished its arc. Michael braced himself, knowing that his vessel was the complete focus of the destroyer's attention.

"Target the destroyer—all guns"

Concussions rocked the cruiser as artillery rounds exploded against *Comanche's* shielding. Michael held his breath, rapidly scanning the tactical display for any sign of indirect damage. He knew that even full protection would not insulate the ship from minor damages, damages that could cascade into larger problems. He consoled himself with the knowledge that sections D and H, still suffering from the last encounter, were not on the side of the ship facing the destroyer.

The two ships exchanged blows for several minutes while *Comanche* hurried back to the *Executive One*. Upon arriving, *Comanche* would tag-team with the *Trafalgar* on the third enemy cruiser.

Amid the buffeting by many artillery strikes, *Comanche* shuddered oddly under the force of three recurrent hits to its starboard side, right over the gunneries. The strikes weren't particularly violent, just detonating as if counting out the beats on a metronome. The ship itself remained unaffected, its shielding easily absorbing the energy blasts.

However, Michael suddenly felt his heart begin to race! Though hearing no alarms, the man's years of combat experience told him something was wrong. Was the gunnery shielding wobbling under the stress while still reading strong?

Before he could bark out a warning to his crew, tactical showed another incoming round on the same destructive heading. The tiny white dot slammed into the model of his ship. *Comanche* quaked violently!

Alarms wailed! The whole crew futilely attempted to brace themselves from the blast, while power faded in and out. Only after a few terrifying moments did the bridge seem to stabilize.

"Morelli," Michael began, not waiting for the damage report, "Execute a ten degree turn to port!"

Michael cringed, bracing for another blast. Seconds seemed to turn to hours while the ship turned. Doubts clouded his mind: would the direction change be enough to prevent another hit to the damaged area?

Herschel, the engineering officer, quickly analyzed his console and turned toward his captain. "Direct hit to starboard guns in Section-J. Guns completely disabled; artillery hit just prior to a reload from the arsenal. Section-J's hull has been completely breached; twenty-one crewmen lost…. Fire in Section-I's environmental controls due to a power overload from the gunnery blast. Containment crews responding and systems have automatically restored environmental via a bypass. No wounded reported in Section-I."

Michael mourned for his lost crewmembers, though paradoxically relieved at the same time. He mused over how much worse the damage could have been. Had the blast occurred while the guns were interfacing the main arsenal, the exposure of the arsenal might have annihilated the ship into space dust. At the same time, *Comanche* was keeping the destroyer's focus away from the *Executive One*. From those perspectives, the action was successful.

The young captain sighed in relief when *Comanche* entered back into relative safety behind the allied convoy. Once again, the *Pyroscaphe*, continuing to protect the transport and being closest to the Europan fortification, would become the focus of the destroyer.

Just then, Tom Andrews appeared back on the bridge, taking his seat once more.

"I almost bought it on that last explosion," Tom quipped, still catching his breath. "I came up the starboard side, thinking it was the safe side of the ship. Didn't know we had turned."

"Everything okay down there?" Michael asked, not to ignore Tom's statement.

Tom nodded and replied, "Yeah. Let's just hope we don't have too many hits like the last one."

With that sober thought, the two men returned their attention to the conflict.

"Sir," Combs from Tactical beckoned. "*Executive One* is sending us running coordinates again, requiring *Comanche* to take up a defensive position within the convoy."

"And I'm receiving a communication from its captain," the communications officer added, watching Michael hesitate. "He wants to speak with you personally."

While motioning for the communications officer to transfer the communication to his post, Michael said to Combs and Morelli, "Don't punch in those coordinates just yet."

Right then, Michael's communications display just to his right came to life, showing the image of an older fleet captain. The insignias decorating the man's uniform clearly conveyed his formidable seniority over the younger captain. Tom Andrews sidled up to Michael's chair to hear the conversation.

"Greetings, Captain Gillen," the man said. "I'm Captain Vaughn of the *Executive One*."

Michael nodded respectfully, hoping the man hadn't heard his order to belay executing the mandated coordinates. Before Michael could exchange pleasantries, the older man continued.

"We need the *Comanche* to fall into formation with the convoy. You've made a great contribution to our efforts by staying on the offensive, which is why I indulged you earlier when you ignored my last two directives. However, with all our losses, we can no longer adequately protect the President from all sides without the *Comanche*."

"With all due respect, Sir," Michael hesitated, daunted by the man's esteemed position and authority, "*Comanche* moving into formation will only focus all combat efforts on the convoy. It would be better if the *Comanche* stayed on the offensive, thus diluting Axis efforts—keeping them on the run."

Vaughn shook his head. "We have reinforcements on their way. We need to keep the President protected until their arrival. It might mean sacrificing your ship as well as the others, but we have no other choice."

Michael thought for a moment, once again sizing up his predicament. Looking at the remaining Europan yellow-line cruiser, the young captain relished the thought of taking it out, thus leaving the Axis forces with a single, lumbering destroyer against three nimble cruisers. The opportunity was too enticing to pass up.

"I'm sorry, Sir," Michael replied nervously, looking to Tom for support. "But we'll be sitting ducks if we do that. No, *Comanche* needs to remain on the offensive."

"This isn't a recommendation, Captain. I'm *ordering* you to fall into formation."

Michael briefly glanced at Tom, who looked just as nervous as Michael felt. "I'm sorry Sir, but *Comanche* is remaining on the offensive. It's the only way to save the President."

"Gillen," the irritated superior began, "I looked at your records when you joined the battle—even your academy records. You have an exhaustive history of impulsiveness, most of which hasn't served you well. Disobeying a direct order intended to protect the President isn't just the end of your career: it's mutiny—possibly treason! Fall into formation!"

Michael muted the transmission, feeling pulled in many different directions while fighting his own instincts and sense of duty. The man's words stung him terribly, and Michael knew he had based his offensive strategy on nothing more than gut instinct—he could be dead wrong. Memories of past disappointments, other times where he thought he was doing the right thing, filled his mind. Moreover, he was a Gillen, a family unfairly renowned for letting Terrae Solaris down. Did he really want to become the man who let down the President of Earth States in his time of need? Should he play it safe? At a loss, the young man looked to Tom Andrews. "What do you think?"

Tom hesitated, the most serious expression coming over him. "If you were trying to glory-hound a science project, the man might be right. But this is life and death."

"What would you do?"

Once again, Tom hesitated. "Mike, I can't tell you what I would do. I'm a chicken by nature and would take the safest route. You have to do what you think is right." Upon seeing Michael's mortified expression, he added. "I'm no philosopher, but I see a whole fleet at the President's disposal, commanded by officers whose only job is to *protect* the man—men who fall inline and know how to take orders. So the convoy will stay on the defensive until the end.

"But that's not you, Mike. You *are* impulsive. You take more risk than anyone I know." He paused in thought. "But perhaps that's why destiny has called you here today.... Perhaps the President needs someone *reckless* enough to do the right thing."

Michael pondered his friend's words for a long moment. Finally, he unmuted the communication. "Sorry, Captain Vaughn, *Comanche* is staying on the offensive. I'll surrender myself tomorrow for court-martial."

Then he cut the transmission while an enraged Captain Vaughn was still yelling at him. With the confrontation over, the two men returned their attention once again to the battle.

Michael watched the tactical display as his ship moved into position against the third Europan cruiser. He had precious few minutes to ponder the chess game unfolding before him. Something quickly caught his eye, something he had failed to notice during the heat of battle and the ensuing artillery blast. Something was wrong—or in this case very right.

He motioned to his first officer. "Tom, have you noticed that the destroyer continues to do nothing but prevent the convoy from escaping the area?"

Tom fought back the urge to respond, *do you mean other than trying to blow us to smithereens?* "Now that you mention it ... yes. What do you think?"

"It *has* to move. It *should* have done so when we destroyed the second Europan cruiser. Otherwise, we get the chance to take out the third."

"Even though *Pyroscaphe* won't last long," Tom began, picking up the logic, "We can still double-team the destroyer and perhaps break through its containment."

"There is only one reason for him to be cautious," Michael replied. "He's more wounded than our tactical displays indicate. This wouldn't be the first time the computer's been wrong about the status of an enemy ship ... and every good captain hides his weaknesses."

"When will we know for sure?" Tom inquired.

"When the destroyer waits to move until the very last second before the third cruiser is destroyed." The two pondered the scenario silently for several moments, affirming their hypothesis with an eventual and mutual head nod. "We may get out of this yet." With renewed vigor and hope, Michael readied himself in his captain's chair.

The third Europan cruiser was quickly coming into range. Michael surmised that the vessel should fall easily; it had operated at yellow-line status since the time *Comanche* had joined the battle. Though avoiding significant damage by staying on the battle's periphery, the Europan cruiser had nevertheless received considerable artillery fire from the *Trafalgar*.

Navigation adjusted trajectory as *Comanche* approached its target. With damage to both the starboard and port sides of the ship, the crew would have to be mindful of these weaknesses and adjust accordingly. Somehow, they needed to find a balance between caution and cavalier.

The Europan cruiser fired the first shot in defiance of its newfound antagonist. *Comanche* responded in kind, not to be outdone. Artillery from both the *Comanche* and the *Trafalgar* pummeled the vessel. Realizing its disadvantage, the Axis cruiser began shifting course away from the duo.

"He's moving!" Michael shouted. "Keep him at the President's port side and in range of both our guns." Michael concluded that the enemy captain would retreat to the other side of the transport. Once there, the cruiser would team up with the destroyer against the *Pyroscaphe*. That would also bring *Trafalgar* and *Comanche* into the path of the destroyer's guns—an unattractive scenario.

Morelli responded, increasing speed to intercept the fleeing vessel. Simultaneously, forward gunneries concentrated their assault on the cruiser's main engines.

Michael looked in satisfaction when several small explosions erupted on the enemy's engine manifold. Though not significant enough to disable the vessel completely, the damage caused the cruiser to slow. *Comanche* shot passed the ship, veering into its path and cutting off its escape route. With no ability to run, the Europan cruiser turned to protect itself.

"Yes!" Michael exclaimed triumphantly when tactical showed the cruiser turning to red-line status. Though being in desperate trouble and needing to flee, the wounded cruiser found itself trapped and at the mercy of the two Allied ships. Obliteration became just a matter of time.

Comanche and *Trafalgar* seized the moment. Every gun focused on the dying Europan cruiser, causing it to disappear in a cloud of brilliant artillery fire and burnt debris. Each blast ripped into the cruiser's hull, tearing the ship apart piece by piece.

Michael found his attention diverted from the action. His tactical display showed him what he had anticipated: the destroyer began making its move toward the epicenter of the skirmish. Though still a little while before posing an immediate threat, the destroyer would soon give the convoy its most dangerous challenge yet.

Michael recoiled as the *Pyroscaphe's* status turned from yellow-line to red-line.

Comanche and *Trafalgar* continued their assault on the Europan cruiser. Though responding with artillery fire of its own, the Axis cruiser failed to inflict any serious damage on its assailants.

Not so for the Allies. Explosions on the Europan cruiser's hull breached the protective shell, causing sections to spill their contents into space. Guns went dead. The cruiser continued breaking apart piece by piece, its death becoming imminent. In an act of desperation, the beleaguered cruiser jettisoned its power plant and arsenal reserves into space—fundamentally surrendering.

Both *Comanche* and *Trafalgar* redirected their guns to the jettisoned equipment. Having no shielding whatsoever to protect them, the targets succumbed to the first artillery blasts and detonated into a brilliant display of light and dust. The Europan cruiser was no longer a threat.

Comanche safely maneuvered passed and away from the lifeless Europan cruiser.

Michael redirected his attention back to the tactical displays. The Europan destroyer was lumbering around the front of the convoy, traveling on an untimely intercept course with the *Comanche* and *Trafalgar*. Though arriving too late to help its smaller companion, the mammoth vessel battered the convoy in a furious rage.

The beast was loose!

Pyroscaphe continued to pace the destroyer, keeping itself as a constant obstruction between the destroyer and the *Executive One*. The destroyer rewarded the ship's heroism with artillery fire, tearing it apart piece by piece. Nevertheless, *Pyroscaphe* defiantly shot back at its larger antagonist, refusing to concede.

At the same time, *Trafalgar* closed in on the *Executive One*'s starboard side, creating a protective wedge in front of the transport. *Comanche* traveled on an intercept course with the destroyer, speeding just behind and to the port side of the *Trafalgar*. With this formation, the Allied cruisers would have an open season on the destroyer as it swept in front of the convoy. Michael nodded in satisfaction, knowing that a three-to-one dogfight turned the advantage back to the Allies—at least on this run.

The destroyer continued to sweep across the front of the convoy, spewing forth venomous energy blasts. Yet the severity of the effect lessened as the rounds spread out in three different directions. Nevertheless, *Trafalgar*'s status turned to yellow-line, an unavoidable consequence of its close proximity to the destroyer.

The three Allied cruisers responded concurrently and fiercely from each of their positions, pounding the massive metal hull of the destroyer while the vessel sped by. Though maintaining its shields, the destroyer's hull became pockmarked and blackened, yielding evidence of wear. The Allies could bring down the hurting giant with the right tactic.

Just as the destroyer passed directly in front of the convoy, Michael noticed the *Pyroscaphe* veering away from the *Executive One*. His spirits fell, realizing the maneuver signaled the *Pyroscaphe*'s demise; its captain was moving the ship away to avoid damaging the transport.

Michael watched—*mourned!*—as the cruiser fought to continue. The vessel labored under the artillery assault to stay its course away from the transport. *Pyroscaphe* heroically cleared the convoy. Moments later, several successive explosions blew the ship into oblivion, scattering debris into space in all directions. The place where the ship had been was once more empty, as if the *Pyroscaphe* had never existed.

Michael Gillen felt a newfound hole in his spirit; his strength of mind waned. The tensions of the battle, the constant shifting of strategies, and the uncertainty of each incoming artillery round was slowly eating away at his stamina. The Allies had lost many ships and thousands of crewmembers. Worse, *Comanche* was following the same fatal path as the *Dorn*, the *Eris*, and the *Pyroscaphe*.

He looked around the bridge, noticing the same exhaustion in the eyes of his crew. Realizing that demoralization could bring only failure, he straightened up in his chair and put his emotions in check. The President needed protected, and the *Comanche* would protect him at all costs.

"Okay, everyone," Michael began, "Let's focus. The destroyer can't contain us here by itself. Communications, send a recommendation to the *Executive One* and the *Trafalgar* to break away behind her aft and accelerate to full speed. We'll keep the destroyer at bay and try to prevent it from pursuing."

"Yes, Sir," the communications officer replied.

Shortly after Communications relayed the proposal to the convoy, the *Trafalgar* and *Executive One* began to edge out and around the stern of the passing destroyer.

Though not completely unexpected, the maneuver put the destroyer at a significant disadvantage, having taken advantage of the destroyer's perpendicular trajectory and its far less formidable aft guns. Also, the vessel's lack of agility prevented it from quickly turning to contain the convoy, exposing itself to the guns of the *Comanche* at the same time.

The Allied duo cautiously made their way around the destroyer as if trying not to provoke it. However, the destroyer retaliated with its smaller guns, pockmarking the *Trafalgar's* hull with energy blasts as it passed. Michael winced, knowing that any hit at such close range could be troublesome to the wounded vessel. Nevertheless, the President's transport remained untouched and in the protection of its escort.

Upon making their way out from under the destroyer's shadow, the two vessels quickly came to full speed. The *Executive One* promptly took the lead, while the *Trafalgar* followed behind the transport to protect. The direction to Allied territory would take them dangerously close to the destroyer's starboard gunneries. Rather than tempt fate, they instead turned in a wide, sweeping arc pattern, keeping on the periphery of the destroyer's firing range.

The destroyer turned to pursue—right in front of the *Comanche*. The chase was on!

"Fire!" Michael commanded.

Comanche's guns showered energy rounds upon the hull of the turning destroyer, having caught its adversary in a moment of weakness. Still firing upon the destroyer, *Comanche* shifted course and accelerated to catch up with its companions. Though firing back some volleys of its own, the destroyer found itself at a disadvantage until completely turned and in pursuit. *Comanche* rocked from artillery but held its own in the exchange. The quick moment passed and the cruiser left the destroyer behind.

Comanche labored at full throttle to catch up to its companions. Though slower than a cruiser, the *Executive One* had gained considerable distance. While the vessel chased the convoy, detonations buffeted its aft shields. The destroyer had shifted course and was in pursuit. Finally, *Comanche* pulled into protective position behind the transport and the *Trafalgar*.

With all three Allied ships reunited, the small fleet sped toward safety. The destroyer was on an angled intercept path. The two cruisers fanned out in a slanted formation behind the transport to protect. If they could only hold the line for a short while, the convoy would eventually outrun the destroyer.

Comanche thrashed violently under a terrifying concussion, and Michael flailed in his chair like a rag doll! Once again, alarms wailed in protest! Once again, the bridge crew rushed about frantically! Tactical readouts grimly changed the vessel's status from green-line to yellow-line. Michael cringed, waiting for the bad news.

"Critical damage to Section-D!" Herschel shouted above the din of alarms. "Indirect damage is causing interference with main engine power feeds! Shields—"

"Bypass power!" Michael angrily shot back. "Don't let those engines skip a beat!"

"But we'll have to take the arsenals off-line to do it."

"Do it!"

However, the ship fell behind the speeding convoy. Quickly losing ground, *Comanche* began exposing the *Trafalgar* to the destroyer's weapons. Given its condition, the *Trafalgar* would not last long.

Watching his ship continue to fall out of formation for such a long time, Michael could be patient no longer. "Where are those engine repairs!?"

"We should have restored power in a couple minutes," Herschel nervously replied.

"By that time, we'll be completely out of formation.... Keep on those engines.... Communications, give me the rest of the damage report."

The communications officer fumbled a bit as he reprogrammed his display for engineering. "Section-D shields are gone. Stable otherwise. Complete hull breach and environmental failure in that section. I'm detecting structural damage as well. No casualties because of the previous evacuation.... I'm also detecting indirect damage to sections E-1 and C-3. However, they are still stable."

"Okay," Michael acknowledged. "Reset the alarms and ensure auxiliary shields are engaged from Section-E and extended over Section-D. Bypass all critical functions in E-1 and C-3, if possible. Evacuate all non-essential personnel. Log activities and results and then send to the Engineer's reader for review after the engines are restored."

Michael studied his readouts, desperately scanning for signs of hope. However, the more he searched, the more he became convinced that *Comanche* was in desperate trouble. The crew struggled to keep the ship whole. However, damage was mounting, and the destroyer was a formidable adversary. *Executive One* might get away only at the cost of the *Comanche*. Though his sense of duty told him he was doing the right thing, the thought sat uneasily in his stomach nonetheless.

With *Comanche* trailing well behind the convoy, the destroyer focused its guns on the *Trafalgar*. The Axis ship would continue to do so until having a clear shot at the President's ship. Michael watched the two ships engaged each other. *Comanche*, with its guns offline, could do nothing to help its companion.

Though being slowly outrun, the destroyer brutally assailed the wounded *Trafalgar* from behind. Just like the *Pyroscaphe*, *Trafalgar* was torn apart mercilessly. Concussion after concussion exposed the vessels innards to the cold void of space. Debris littered its wake. Michael's tactical readout quickly changed the ship's status to red-line.

Michael, purposely calming himself, turned back to his trusted engineer. "Herschel, *Trafalgar* won't last long. Let's be prepared to take its place."

The subordinate quickly acknowledged with a nod while coordinating the containment efforts.

Comanche continued falling behind the convoy, though still keeping ahead of the pursuing destroyer. However, the cruiser was almost completely out of play. The destroyer, on the other hand, was no longer at an intercept angle. Instead, the vessel was traveling almost directly behind the convoy and to its port side, forcing the *Trafalgar* to move in closer to the *Executive One* to protect it from the destroyer.

Trafalgar continued to take strikes from the destroyer, though the blasts were concentrated at its stern. The debris trail continued to increase, practically obscuring a direct view.

Herschel energetically looked up from his display. "Engines stabilized! Weapons back online."

"Good job!" Michael replied. "Lieutenant Morelli, put us back in formation. Lieutenant Combs, reengage the destroyer."

Comanche quickly accelerated to catch up to the convoy. Guns sent volleys of artillery at the destroyer. However, its new efforts were too late. The entire bridge crew watched in horror as the *Trafalgar* erupted into oblivion. Large chunks of debris flew in all directions, and the presidential transport was left exposed.

A new sense of urgency came over Michael and the *Comanche* crew. The ship stood alone in its defense of the President.

"Close formation!" Michael shouted, knowing the ship was already at maximum speed. Morelli responded as if pushing the ship even further to the limit.

The destroyer took advantage of the opportunity, directing its guns at the presidential transport. Immediately, artillery blasts erupted on the transport's hull. Though fortified, the transport would quickly succumb against the leviathan.

Yet at the same time, Michael could see that the destroyer was surgically targeting the blasts. This confirmed his theory that the destroyer's interests were in detaining the Allied leader rather than eliminating him. As demoralizing as an assassination could be, the President's capture could be worse. Regardless, Michael had to prevent both outcomes.

Comanche was quickly closing in on the *Executive One* and moving to shield. Debris began spilling from the transport as laser blasts drilled into it. Suddenly, one of the transport's five main engines—the largest of the five—burst into a blinding sphere of fire. When the brightness dissipated, nothing remained but a gaping, blackened hole where the engine was supposed to be.

Immediately, Michael's tactical display changed the transport's status to yellow-line. *Executive One* slowed, forcing *Comanche* to hard-slow to avoid a collision. Quickly, the two ships adjusted formation and continued on—but at a much slower pace.

Michael Gillen's shoulders slumped in imminent defeat. His bridge crew responded in kind as the destroyer began closing in on them. Soon, the leviathan's guns would be upon them at point-blank range. *Comanche* would faithfully stay by its wounded companion, bearing the brunt of the attack until meeting it own demise.

The tactical computer began its gruesome countdown. *Comanche* had less than nine minutes of life, with the checkmate of *Executive One* occurring a minute later. Michael had ignored the harbinger most of the battle; it had been wrong too often. However, its projections took on a dreadful credibility.

"Sir," Combs beckoned, "I am detecting Allied reinforcements on long-range scanners: two destroyers and seven cruisers at full speed. They'll intercept in thirty minutes."

Michael acknowledged and laughed, painfully aware of the irony. "Great, they'll arrive twenty minutes too late."

CHAPTER EIGHTEEN

Dancing with Giants

Kara Ricci stood over her operating table in the surgical bay of the *ESS Windsor*, overwhelmed by an incredible sense of despair. Outwardly, the young surgeon was calm and resolute, performing tasks with the utmost efficiency and directing the mission with a commanding demeanor. Yet inwardly, she was beside herself.

She found little consolation that her team had treated all critically wounded soldiers, their survival rates rebounding after the surgical team abandoned the use of medical robots. She also gained little consolation that hostilities in Sector Eight had finally ceased, or that the *Windsor* was racing back to Randt Medical Base. Nor did she really find consolation that the marathon surgery session would soon end. And certainly, Kara could have cared less about the approving expressions coming from General Rier of late.

No, the memories of that day filled her with dread, and the young woman was certain she would never forget it.

Taking a quick pause from operating on the patient in front of her, Kara stole a quick glance around the surgical bay. The whole area seemed to be drenched in blood. Corpsmen were finally making progress at cleaning up the gruesome sight, having been overwhelmed during the intense session. Yet with the entire surgical staff still working, the bay looked like something out of a horror movie.

Blood covered her too. The crimson substance saturated the front of her scrubs all the way down her legs, while her surgical mask displayed a gruesome polka dot pattern. Somehow, blood had worked its way underneath her cap and into her auburn hair. She could even feel blood squishing in her shoes. The feeling was completely dreadful, and the young surgeon's skin crawled as she thought about it.

However, the grisly sight was simply a fading shadow of the nightmare that had permeated every part of the bay for so many hours before. She could still see the gruesome memories in her mind's eye as if they were still happening.

She could still see herself swimming in wounded soldiers, men—sometimes women—with such ghastly injuries: bodies burnt beyond recognition, their uniforms vaporized off charcoal covered flesh; flesh that had melted under such intense heat it could no longer be recognized as human; soldiers having only a gaping, bloody hole where the rest of their torso should be; people with their faces blown off; soldiers with organs shredded beyond recognition; severed limbs lying abandoned, becoming heaped into huge piles.

Worse than the gruesome sight were the haunting cries of agony that had filled the entire ship. Kara wondered if hell itself had shuddered at the constant wailing and moaning offered up by those suffering.

They had looked at her desperately. Their haunting gazes had transfixed her as they were dying. Many of them did die—*she had seen so many die that day*. Their faces, twisted from the agony, still haunted her mind.

And she knew the images would never leave her—ever.

Comanche quaked under the ever-increasing torrent of artillery. However, the assault was only a taste of things to come.

Michael Gillen sat in his captain's chair, suffering through the onslaught and at a loss. With all the other Allied vessels gone, *Comanche* found itself all alone defending the President's transport (a ship slowed down by the hit to one of its five engines). Though wounded, the massive, Europan destroyer remained a formidable opponent, causing the young captain to consider that he and his crew were in their last minutes.

The destroyer was fast approaching, coming up on the duo's port side. Morelli at Navigation adjusted course to keep the presidential transport shielded. The destroyer quickly closed in, assuming a parallel course to the convoy. *Comanche's* entire port side faced the destroyer, and the assailant wasted no time training its large guns on the smaller cruiser.

Within seconds, the destroyer began pounding *Comanche's* hull! Bulkheads ripped open under the blasts. Debris hurled into space. Though firing back and inflicting its own damage, *Comanche* was clearly outgunned.

Michael's tactical display grimly updated *Comanche's* status to redline.

The bridge turned into chaos, symbolic to a lesser degree of the devastation pervading the entire ship. Piercing alarms declared shield collapses, hull breaches, environmental failures, and the like. However, the alarms went unnoticed amid more important matters. The bridge crew frantically went about, not trying to protect the ship, but rather to keep it a target.

Hope of survival vanished, replaced by desperation. They were desperate, ironically, to suffer under the wrath of the destroyer as long as fate would allow. Yet could they last until the reinforcements on long-range scanners arrived? The thought became a fleeting dream.

Tom looked over to his captain. "Mike,"—formality getting lost in the confusion—"We won't last long if we continue flying along side that thing."

"You're right," Michael replied, looking into his tactical. "But we may not have to."

Acting on his friend's cue, Tom redirected his attention back to his tactical display. The destroyer was executing an intercept course to cut off the convoy and drive it back toward Axis territory.

Should the mammoth vessel beat *Comanche* there, the destroyer might be able to squeeze itself between the two Allied ships—checkmate!

"What do you think?" Tom asked.

Michael paused and looked up coyly. "I think it's time for a game of chicken."

The bridge crew's attention immediately turned toward the exchange.

Tom shrugged in disbelief, though quickly realizing that his friend was serious. Relenting, he turned to the crew. "You heard him."

Immediately, Morelli began trajectory and speed calculations. The rest of the bridge crew began preparations as well. The flurry of work masked a rush of nervousness and fear that hung thick in the air. Yet duty called for such peril.

"Let's force him to the port side," Michael began, shrugging off the tension, "but let him think it was his idea. Lieutenant Combs, prepare for close-range targeting; we won't get a better chance to hit him. Lieutenant Herschel, prepare for accelerating back to formation, should we survive the tactic; we don't want to leave the transport open long."

A quick moment later, *Comanche* accelerated on to an extended intercept course to the destroyer. Having eventually traveled slightly ahead of the behemoth, *Comanche* suddenly veered into the destroyer's path. Proximity alarms wailed as the two vessels closed in on one another. Both ships continued to exchange weapons fire while moving dangerously close.

"Steady…," Michael directed. "He'll move."

Anxiety mounted on the bridge while the two ships traveled their perilous courses. Fear pervaded *Comanche* as the ship passed into the shadow of the destroyer.

At the last second, the destroyer relented, veering away and slowing as it turned.

The dance began. Though the destroyer had flinched, *Comanche* needed to convince the vessel to change its direction one hundred and eighty degrees. Navigation carefully steered the cruiser, accelerating just ahead of the destroyer's new direction and repeating the same game of chicken. Morelli broke into a sweat while attempting to balance posturing with caution. Executing a great effort over several minutes,

Comanche forced the destroyer to reverse its original course. Then *Comanche* relented, though continuing on the destroyer's starboard side and forcing it to execute a complete circle. Upon seeing the destroyer predictably begin to respond, Michael gave the order to break off and head back to the *Executive One*.

With his ship speeding back to the transport, Michael studied his tactical display in satisfaction. The lumbering destroyer struggled to reverse course quickly to intercept. *Executive One* traveled quite far ahead, giving the destroyer a run for its money. Despite having a wounded engine and unable to outrun the beast, the transport had nevertheless gained some valuable time.

Despite having taken on damage during the challenge, *Comanche* had managed to stay out of the path of the destroyer's main guns. The destroyer, on the other hand, had not been as lucky. *Comanche* had maneuvered close to the destroyer's softer underside, allowing the cruiser to deliver significant firepower. As a result, the destroyer's status had turned to yellow-line. Michael remained uncertain whether the small success was skill or luck; there was too much confusion during the game of chicken to know. Either way, he was certain that the opportunity would not repeat itself.

Interestingly enough, the Allies had gained four additional minutes according to the clock of doom. However, the young captain sadly realized how impossible it would be to stretch out another sixteen minutes, the time needed for the Allied reinforcements to arrive. *Comanche* was still doomed.

Comanche continued closing in on the *Executive One* at full speed. However, the ship would not be in position to protect the transport for another minute. Meanwhile, the destroyer had successfully completed its circle and was heading back on an intercept course.

From its disadvantaged position still far behind the Allied ships, the destroyer shot continuous artillery rounds at the transport. Though many missed because of the distance, a few hit their intended and stung the transport viciously.

Michael watched in dismay as the *Executive One* suffered under the assault. The vessel's shields were weakening, and each successive concussion splattered hot metal bits from its hull into space. Soon, the blasts would begin to penetrate the ship's innards.

"Lieutenant Combs," Michael called out, "See what you can do to improve our offensive."

Combs acknowledged with a nod, though Michael realized his orders were a fleeting wish; *Comanche* was already on full offensive with the destroyer.

Moments passed, and the destroyer narrowed the distance between it and Allied convoy. Artillery exchanges became more frequent, increasing damage to all three ships. Because of its more vulnerable design, the transport's condition was rapidly deteriorating.

Forebodingly, the *Executive One*'s status turned red-line on the tactical display.

Michael and Tom looked at each other in silence, realizing they had reached a turning point in the skirmish. The President's fate lay in *Comanche*'s hands. Whatever happened from there on out would result in either life or death—and the weight rested on Michael Gillen's shoulders.

The Allies found themselves in their most desperate hour.

Comanche finally pulled into protective formation to the starboard side and just behind the transport, allowing the entire bridge crew to breathe a collective sigh of relief. The *Executive One* was safe—for the moment.

Immediately, minor tremors reverberated throughout the battle cruiser as it absorbed artillery meant for the transport. The smaller blasts portended the vessel's imminent demise. In its current condition, the Allied ship would not last long under the destroyer's larger guns. *Comanche* had entered into its last minutes of existence.

"Sir," the communications officer beckoned to Michael, "Captain Vaughn of the *Executive One* wants to speak to you again."

Though hesitating, Michael motioned for him to patch the communication through. Once more, the communications display at the young captain's right lit up with the image of Captain Vaughn.

"Captain Gillen," Vaughn greeted him again. "I'm sure you're aware that we're in bad shape over here."

"Yes, Captain," Michael responded supportively. "Is the President okay?"

"For now," Vaughn replied. A long pause ensued. "Captain Gillen, I know you've taken on a lot of damage over there—and I'm sure this goes without saying—but we need you to do whatever you can to prevent the President's capture."

Michael paused in silence for a moment. "Yes, Sir, I understand. The problem is that we won't last long enough."

"Unfortunately, I agree with you," Vaughn exclaimed. "I don't have any suggestions, but please just do what you can."

"You have my assurance that we will do everything humanly possible."

"I know you will," Vaughn replied soberly. The older man hesitated for a long moment. "I also wanted you to know you were right about staying on the offensive earlier. We wouldn't have made it this far without you disobeying my orders."

Michael nodded appreciatively.

"And I made the President aware of your contributions today," Vaughn continued. "—how you put me in my place and got him this far. He asked me to pass along his eternal gratitude for everything you've done."

"Thank you very much," Michael acknowledged. He ran the words through his head several times in disbelief. *The President is thanking us?*

"Good luck," Vaughn exclaimed just before the transmission ended.

The tremors rippling through *Comanche* increased in intensity as if the ship were being subdued under the power of a coming storm. The destroyer traveled on an intercept path to the convoy, moving up on its starboard side. The vessel would once again come along side *Comanche* and begin ripping into it, accomplishing *Comanche's* destruction shortly thereafter.

"What do you think?" Tom asked, sidling up to Michael.

Michael stared into his display vacantly. "I don't know.... We could force the destroyer into another—"

Comanche shook violently and its starboard side burst open under a terrible detonation. Debris scattered outward in all directions, and the vessel began wobbling on its course. When the brightness of the blast dissipated, a large gaping hole remained.

The conclusion would have been apparent to any onlookers: *Comanche* was dying.

The explosion had caught the bridge crew off guard. The destroyer had found and exploited a weakness—or it was just dumb luck.

Either way, the tactical harbinger of doom decreased *Comanche's* demise projection from five minutes to one.

Michael had only seconds to react. Yet, what more could he do? The blast had knocked out most of his weapons, and Morelli could barely keep the vessel on course. Surrendering remained unthinkable. He could only think of one other hand to play.

"Morelli, prepare to ram."

The bridge crew went silent and looked at him, waiting—*hoping*—that he would rescind the order. However, the hope was to no avail, for no reprieve would be given. Therefore, realizing their demise was inevitable, the crew began pondering their mortality.

"You heard him," Tom exclaimed, confirming the grim order.

The crew resigned themselves to their fate. For one the last time, Morelli began calculating speeds and trajectories. Herschel scanned for stress points and other weaknesses that might affect the outcome. The entire bridge went about their duties in stunned silence, grappling with the irony that they were carrying out their own death sentence.

Michael Gillen empathetically watched his crew going about the gruesome task. The sight was a morbid one to behold—and sad too. Some frantically busied themselves with unimportant tasks as if hoping to deny their fate; others already appeared as if shrouded in death. However, most of the crew existed somewhere between those two extremes, wrestling with the uncertainty of their own mortality.

Moreover, many were whispering prayers under their breath as they worked. This came as no surprise to Michael. After all, much of the population was religious to some extent. Some of them, driven to complete sincerity and desperation from the dire circumstances, reminded him of his long gone brother, David. The memories of David and his conviction to his beliefs began flooding the young man's mind.

Of course, Michael had done away with any religious notions so long ago.

However, the crew was looking at him too—watching *his* response to imminent death. He could only wonder what expression covered his face.

"I'm sorry people, but let's get this right," Michael said, attempting to focus his crew—almost apologetically. "We need to disable that thing."

Combs at Tactical acknowledged, though he was already in the process of feeding Morelli the data on the destroyer's weak points.

"He'll think we're playing chicken again," Tom remarked with a seriousness that Michael had never seen.

Michael regretfully relished the thought. "And he won't flinch as quickly as the last time. It will be his weakness."

Comanche labored to execute the required maneuvers. The dying vessel began to turn, the whole ship whining in protest. The creaking of structural members, weakened from the continual pounding, echoed eerily throughout the ship.

The destroyer continued on its course, unabated and unconvinced of the cruiser's intention. The two ships neared each other once more, the destroyer spewing forth artillery rounds at its challenger. The cruiser's hull was coming apart, and *Comanche* swam in a sea of its own debris.

Not until the destroyer realized that the smaller vessel was speeding directly toward its mid-section did it begin to hard-break and turn sharply. The leviathan slowed and abruptly shifted course, demonstrating more agility than its wounded challenger. *Comanche* helplessly began overshooting its target; its trajectory would cause the cruiser to pass harmlessly in front of the destroyer. *Comanche*, severely damaged from its injuries, would not have another chance.

"Adjust!" Michael yelled.

"Sir, reactor breach in ten seconds!" Herschel forebodingly announced.

Morelli wrestled the controls, though they responded faintly. Left, right, up or down—the ship wouldn't budge from its course! *Comanche* began to pass harmlessly in front of the destroyer, and the navigator could not shift course to ram. He quickly looked to his captain, who seemed to be reading his mind. In kind, Michael glanced back, as if giving him his final order. Bracing himself for the inevitable, Morelli executed a hard-stop—right in the path of the speeding destroyer.

Comanche, less than a half of a kilometer off the nose of the beast, came to a dead stop. The destroyer was moving fast—too fast to slow or change course. The ship's large size and immense mass became its downfall, forcing inertia to carry the behemoth directly into the mid-section of the *Comanche*.

The cruiser's mid-section crumpled under the bludgeoning weight of the beast as if made of paper. The destroyer continued by inertia through the ship as though the cruiser wasn't even there. *Comanche*'s giant metal structural beams bent away under the brutal collision, snapping like twigs. Internal bulkheads gave way, causing the environments behind them to spill out into space.

When run all the way through by the destroyer, *Comanche* split in two. Its fore section tumbled slowly and away into space. The aft section, with power plants and arsenals, fell away in the opposite direction.

Not going very far, *Comanche*'s aft section bounced several times off the destroyer's hull, appearing as if a stone being kicked along by a child. Each collision inflicted increasingly more damage to the aft section remnant until the power plants inside gave way, causing the pummeled section to erupt into a blinding explosion.

The mighty Jupiter-Class destroyer, far too close for such a blast, quickly became engulfed in the violent explosion. Bulkheads melted under the intense heat, while section after section shattered away. Fuel and ammunition reserves, once protected deep inside, became exposed and erupted violently. The chain reaction continued until the whole destroyer's fore section, including the command and control centers, became nothing but charred remains.

The beast was dead.

CHAPTER NINETEEN

Casualties of War

Twenty-six-year-old Michael Gillen found himself lying in a pile of rubble that was once his bridge. He couldn't remember how he had gotten there, nor could he remember the collision with the destroyer. It was as if one second he was bracing for the crash, and then the next he was caught up in the tangle of smashed consoles and electrical cabling. The thought also occurred to him that he did not know how long he had been there.

He looked around the bridge, finding the place barely recognizable. Streams of dim red light cut through the darkness, obscured by thick smoke. Equipment, smashed to pieces, lay in the shadows. An occasional bloodied limb protruded from the rubble, marking the dead and those waiting to die. Sounds of moaning and wailing rose up from the darkness, each one instilling into him more fear than the former. His uniform was torn to pieces, and he could feel the blood of another crewman covering him.

So this is what it's like to be forsaken, Michael Gillen thought, mourning the feeling.

Among the devastation, only one sign of hope remained: the large tactical console table. Though lying smashed on the floor, the device's holographic image amazingly continued to display, flickering randomly. The image, not always discernable, rotated end over end because of the fore section's tumbling motion.

The display showed inertia carrying the fore section deeper into Axis territory. The remains of the destroyer floated away on a perpendicular course. A new blip appeared on long-range, approaching from Axis territory. This was probably Axis reinforcements. However, thousands of kilometers away and speeding in the opposite direction, *Executive One* continued undeterred toward Allied territory.

The President was finally safe.

Exhausted, Michael laid his head back down on the rubble. Though knowing he should try to attend to his crew, the young man couldn't find the resolve within him. With the consolation that *Comanche's* sacrifice was not in vain, he could finally rest.

Nevertheless, he had rescue work to do.

Why can't I get up? Michael eventually thought. He needed to help the surviving crew before the fore section destabilized. So straining every muscle, he pushed against the deck to lift himself to a sitting position. However, after a hard-fought couple of inches, his strength dissipated, causing him to painfully crash back down onto the pile of debris.

Pausing to gather his strength, Michael spotted a small searchlight coming toward him in the darkness; it was Tom Andrews. The man was bleeding from a gash in his forehead and was favoring his left leg.

Tom knelt down and began tending to him, trying to keep the flashlight steady.

Michael noticed a look of grave concern on his face, though he didn't understand why—and the uncertainty scared him. Though Tom was talking to him, Michael couldn't understand—the words seemed unintelligible.

Young Gillen quickly realized that he felt out of sync with reality. Time was moving in slow motion as if he were detached from his senses. A thick fog clouded his mind like the thick smoke hanging in the air. He knew he was feeling pain, though the sensation registered as if merely an unimportant notion.

He found himself in the midst of the surreal.

Michael looked down, noticing Tom's left hand pressing firmly on his side; blood seeped out from underneath his palm. Though seeing Tom pushing hard on the wound, Michael realized that he could barely feel it. Then the truth hit him: *he was hurt.* The blood covering him was *his*—not another crewman!

All the strangeness of the last moments coalesced into a cold, grim reality. Grief overwhelmed him, and his reaction to it caught him off guard. During the entire battle, the young captain had prepared himself for the end. But now that death was upon him, Michael filled with the sensation of incredible loss. Despite having his friend at his side, he was completely alone.

Michael soon labored to breathe. An invisible shadow hung over him, and a sense of apathy to the external began encompassing him. Even the exhortations from his friend faded into the indifference.

Feeling his strength leaving him, Michael's mind filled with warm thoughts of his family, especially his brother, David. Lying there in the rubble and dying, young Gillen wondered if David would have been proud of whom he had become or the sacrifice he had made. He wondered if David would have approved of his life, even though Michael had shunned the one thing David valued most: his "belief in God and faith in Christ", to use his brother's words.

None of these thoughts really mattered to him—yet they consumed him too. He still labored to breathe. A cold darkness was quickly enveloping him; death was beckoning. *Death comes to everyone, no matter what they believe*, he thought. Of course, young Gillen found no consolation in that thought.

With his last moments upon him, Michael struggled to bring his hand to his chest. With great effort, he reached into his pocket and pulled out a tattered photograph.

In the picture was Katey, as radiant and as beautiful as ever. Long, brown hair draped her sculpted shoulders, and her facial features were warm and inviting. Her eyes searched deep, and her smile engaged.

Michael gazed into her eyes as his strength withered, smiling as if far away. The warmth of her smile staved off the oncoming coldness—at least a little. He moved his finger across the picture as if stroking her hair, savoring the memories filling his mind.

However, with each passing moment, Michael felt those memories being torn from him mercilessly, and he frantically grasped at them as they faded. Though fighting the oncoming certainty, the young man could not fend it off.

Finally, darkness enveloped him.

Twenty-eight-year-old Kara Ricci appeared from the hatchway of the physicians' locker room on the *ESS Windsor*, following General Rier down the main corridor. Another surgeon followed them out of the locker room, veering off in another direction. Just as her superior, Kara barely managed to put one foot in front of the other while walking down the hall. Never before had the young woman been so tired unless actually being asleep. Having finished the long, grueling session of surgery, both officers had cleaned up and changed into new scrubs. Despite her exhaustion, she still managed to convey a professional demeanor, for she was still in charge of the ship. Kara could not rest until the *Windsor* docked at Randt Medical Base and the wounded— the dead too—were transferred from the ship.

The young woman still found her mind swimming in all the horrible images of the day. She only hoped that a long rest would expunge them from her thoughts, for the dreadfulness of what she saw had turned her insides to jelly.

However, wallowing in her despair was for another time; General Rier was more than excited to debrief the mission.

"I haven't worked so hard in years," the graying man remarked as he walked, sighing for effect. "What did you think, Major Ricci?"

Kara kept pace with the man. With her expression somewhat vacant, she shook her head. "I was very disappointed in our performance. The critical case survival rate was only fifty-three percent—only two points higher than the overall average."

"You're being too hard on yourself, Major," Rier replied, acknowledging some personnel who stood off to the side of the corridor and watched them pass. "This is the first mission. Many things go wrong on a first mission. The rate was down to forty percent before you figured out to scrap the robots. Few surgeons would have made such a bold call. But if you had done that sooner, you would have gotten the survival rate up to fifty-five, maybe even sixty percent—just like you predicted." He paused while continuing to walk. "With more missions, I'm sure you'll get the survival rate into the seventies or higher."

Kara winced at the words *go wrong*. The expression seemed a trite way to gloss over her lack of foresight—mistakes that had cost people their lives. "I should have made that decision earlier, Sir. It was a terrible mistake."

Rier only shook his head. "Nonsense. That's part of learning." He remained silent for several long moments as the two turned down an adjoining corridor. "This was your first time to the front. Half the battle is just surviving that first experience."

"I'll make sure we get it right the next time, Sir."

The two continued walking until Rier came to stand in front of his quarters.

Holding the door open from the outside, he added, "Your program worked great. It's proven we need more physicians closer to the front, and it's given us a way to do it." He paused. "Get used to running a tight ship, Major, because I want you to be able to show other medical bases how to do it."

The tired, old man began through the doorway but then abruptly turned back toward her. "Your upgrade to the rank of colonel will be processed when we get back…. Good job!"

With a parting smile, General Rier disappeared into his quarters.

Kara paused reflectively at the closed door for a short moment before continuing down the corridor and hooking on to another passage. The whole way, her downcast expression failed to change, despite the man's encouraging remarks. Making it to just outside her quarters and eager to be alone for a while, Kara opened the door to enter. That's when an aide approached.

"Sir," he began, "The captain would like to debrief the mission with you right now."

Kara held out her hand in a stopping motion while holding the door open with the other. Her expression turned emphatic. "Give me fifteen or twenty minutes."

The aide reluctantly nodded and went off.

Once again alone, young Ricci entered the darkened room, shutting and locking the door behind her. At once, the lights came up. Still looking as determined as ever, Kara made a beeline straight into the adjoining lavatory. The lavatory lights came on as she shut and locked that door too, revealing just how small the tiny room was. She had reached the end of her journey, coming to lean against the sink with both hands propping her up.

Finally alone with her tortured thoughts, Kara stared at herself in the mirror for a long moment. The terrible images from that day began unloading on the young woman, who found herself unable to stop the swell of emotions coming over her. The faces of those she had let die—mostly by her own decision—haunted her.

Her face twisted painfully, and she brought her hand up over her mouth as if to muffle a scream. Churning eyes welled up uncontrollably. In desperation, young Ricci fell back helplessly against the door just behind her, becoming increasingly inconsolable as her body slithered down the dull surface in surrender. Finally falling into a heap on the floor, Kara wept loudly and bitterly.

As the young woman fell completely to pieces, in a place where no one could see her cry, in a place where no one could hear her desperation—and foreseeing many similar missions to the front—Kara realized just how familiar the tiny room would become.

Tom Andrews knelt down in the rubble that used to be the bridge of the *ESS Comanche*, pointing the small searchlight down to where Michael Gillen lay.

With blood still trickling down Tom's face from the gash in his forehead, the injured commander felt light-headed while keeping his vigil. The phasing in and out of the artificial gravitational field, damaged from the collision, did nothing to help his disorientation. Acrid smoke hanging thick in the air choked him something fierce, and his whole body hurt terribly.

None of that concerned him.

It didn't matter to the young man that he needed medical attention, or that some of the crew were still alive under the rubble and needed help too. It didn't matter to him that the fore section of the *Comanche*—or what was left of it—was on the verge of collapse. It didn't matter to him that the ship remnant, tumbling through space since the collision, had been righted. He didn't even care that Europan soldiers had boarded the ship and were rushing the bridge.

No, even as two Europan soldiers came over him, pointing their rifles squarely at his head and telling him not to move, Tom Andrews paid them no mind, at least not right then.

No, all he could do is look down at the lifeless body of his best friend.

Brenda Reid casually sat on the edge of the reception desk at Earth States Intelligence on Earth, leaning back slightly while swinging one leg back and forth and laughing like a schoolgirl. The gentleman standing in front of her, a lower ranking officer who worked in the building, couldn't help but notice the eye-catching appendage moving back and forth, or how the conservative, navy blue skirt had ridden up on her legs just a little.

Reid considered him a masher, one of those men that preyed on the vulnerability of the women whose husbands were far from them. She made no bones about it, even telling him as much to his face; he agreed. However, the man's habit was why she regularly kept his company at the office. The intent was nothing serious on her part, just a little flirting to pass the war.

At least that's what she told herself.

The two had carried on their conversation alone in the reception area for a little while, passing their time on a coffee break while the receptionist was away. That's when two ranking officers, obviously visitors, appeared at the doorway across the room.

Reid's face immediately went pale, and her leg stopped swinging.

"Here we go again," the man Reid was talking to exclaimed. "This is becoming too much of a habit."

"At least you don't have anything to worry about," Reid replied sharply. Turning her head back toward the door, she stared at the two visiting officers with such trepidation.

Finally, the receptionist, who was in eyeshot of the door from the other direction, saw the visitors and came over to them.

Watching the three talk, Reid found herself short of breath. However, when the receptionist went away in the other direction, Reid sighed in tremendous relief, even putting her hand over her heart.

"I wonder who they're here to see this time?" Reid's coffee break companion asked.

"I don't know. Too many women work here. But we can't be standing out here like this."

Almost on cue, as if they had witnessed the imminent scene far too many times—and they had—the two moved to a more inconspicuous place; not to hide, but to make themselves less noticeable.

"When she comes out," the man began flippantly, "Do you think she'll have that blank expression on her face, as if she doesn't know what's going on?"

Reid looked at him crossly but then turned back to watch the two visitors. After several long moments, she got a very quizzical look on her face. "The admiral looks familiar. I know I've seen him before. I just don't know where."

"Must be someone important this time. We don't normally see admirals for this."

That's when Brenda's jaw dropped. "*Oh no....*"

Just then, Kate Gillen appeared with the receptionist, smiling brightly and shaking hands with the two visitors—but also having a very puzzled expression on her face.

"See," the man-friend mused. "There's that blank expression."

"Shut up, you idiot!"

The two watched the older visitor with the admirals' stripes gesture, leading Kate Gillen into the conference room right there. The walls were mostly transparent glass, providing Reid and the male officer a rather unobstructed view.

"It always starts the same way," the male officer told her remorsefully, watching Kate and the two men exchange pleasantries.

Brenda began tearing up when Kate fell silent at the Admiral's words. Though unable to hear the exchange through the glass, Reid had witnessed far too many similar encounters not to know what was happening. The longer Kate listened, the more her expression changed. Simple concern changed to disbelief; disbelief deteriorated into Kate defiantly shaking her head in denial.

Reid welled up even more upon watching Kate resist imbibing the bitter truth. Despite appearing overly sympathetic, the admiral's words continued as if piercing the young woman mercilessly. Overwhelmed, Kate's defiance melted. Her head shook back and forth once again, this time marking the woman's descent into deep despair. Her face twisting painfully, Kate fell into the admiral's arms and wept bitterly.

The two continued watching the dreadful scene from a distance, unable to avert their eyes. Finally, the man turned to Reid and said, "And it always ends the same way."